A bit of a Nomad herself, **K.A. Finn**
and the UK for decades before settl
husband and kids (two and four legged).

Visit K.A. Finn online:

www.kafinn.com
(trailers, excerpts, artwork, playlists etc)

Facebook: kafinnauthor

Instagram: kafinnauthor

Twitter @K_A_Finn

Also by K.A. Finn

Nomad Series (Space Opera)

Ares

Nemesis

Perses

Chaos

Mania

Cronus

Blackjacks Series (Paranormal Romance)

Breaking Phoenix

Reviving Davyn (2022)

Defying Shep (2023)

Broken Chords (Rockstar Romance)

Fractured Rock (Gregg – 2022)

Split Rock (Tate – 2023)

Shattered Rock (Dillon – TBA)

Crushed Rock (Luke – TBA)

Broken Chords #1

BROKEN Rock

K.A. FINN

Cover design by Deranged Doctor Design

www.derangeddoctordesign.com

Photographer: Wander Aguiar

www.wanderbookclub.com

Model: Jonny James

Published by Cooper Publishing

www.cooperbookservices.com

Edited by Desert Mystic Literary Editing

www.desertmysticliteraryediting.com

ISBN: 978-1-914177-08-8

Coming soon

Broken Chords #2

Broken Rock Extras

Although I haven't mentioned any song lyrics or real bands in this book, that doesn't mean music didn't play a MASSIVE part in its creation.

If you want to check out the playlist that I had blaring in the background on continuous replay while I was writing, you can find it on my website, by scanning the QR code below, or by searching the following songs:

Change – Poets of the Fall
If I Die – Maybe The Last
Hurt – Eclipse
What If I Was Nothing – All That Remains
Broken Bones – Rev Theory
The First The Last – Tremonti
The Verdict – Dear Agony
Unshatter Me – Saliva
Song for the Broken – Take The Day
Catch Me If You Can – Walking On Cars
I Refuse – Five Finger Death Punch
All For Nothing – Kensington
Streets – Kensington
Part Of Me – Kensington
A Little Bit Off – Five Finger Death Punch
Echoes – Ignite the Fire
Roses – Poets of the Fall
Atlas Falls – Shinedown
Fading Star – Weaving The Fate
Price of Fame – Submerged
Best I Can – Art Of Dying
All the Way / 4U – Poets of the Fall

This playlist was on every time I wrote, edited, or just read through the book.

The bands, the songs, or the lyrics remind me of Tate and his story in some way. It's still a playlist I listen to at least once a day and it always brings me back to Tate and the rest of the band.

I also had fun writing this series because it's all local to me. *Broken Rock* is set in Co. Wicklow, Ireland and every location mentioned in it is a real place. I grew up in Wicklow and still have family there so the area is so special to me, and I absolutely love it. I've been to all the places Tate goes to. I've eaten from the same take-aways, sat on the same beaches, and visited the same breath-taking scenic spots.

I've put together a map with each of the locations mentioned in the book marked on it so you can visit and see for yourself.

If you want to check out the playlist or the aerial views of the locations, go to:

www.kafinn.com/brokenrock

Well, enough from me. I'll leave you in Tate's more than capable hands – have fun!

To Jennifer.
Without your virtual ass-kicking and woo woo editing powers,
the 'real' Tate wouldn't have broken free.
Thank you x

Tate Archer turns off the main road and heads down the track to his parents' farm. He opens the window, letting the sea air in to help to blow away some of his tiredness. He looks longingly at the track heading down to the beach, sorely tempted to veer off and go there instead. It would make him seriously unpopular with his family though, so he keeps driving towards the house.

The headlights on his pickup cut a path through the absolute darkness on the country lane until he turns the corner and faces his parents' old farmhouse.

He stops the truck and leans on the steering wheel as he looks at the brightly lit house. Seems his dad went to town on the Christmas lights this year. In addition to the lights on the house, every tree lining the yard to the front is decorated. He's even got lights hanging off the animal sheds.

Tate parks around the side of the house and shuts off the engine.

He'd give anything and everything not to go in there. Even from inside the truck he can hear the Christmas party is in full swing.

God, he hates these family shindigs. The family gathering had started a few hours ago and would continue well into the early hours. It was a tradition he hated but still attended every year. It wasn't worth upsetting his mother by refusing. He was already late which was bound to go down like a ton of bricks.

The thought of spending a few hours forcing himself to engage in polite conversation with people he has no interest talking to is as appealing as a visit to the dentist. No wonder he's still skulking in his truck. Fuck it. The sooner he gets in there, the sooner he can disappear again.

Tate glares at his reflection in the rear-view mirror. He looks exactly how he feels. Wrecked. As well as two impressive black rings under his dark blue eyes, his short brown hair is more dishevelled than usual. A few hours with his family then he's heading to bed.

He jumps when someone taps on his window. 'Jesus Bria. You scared the hell out of me.'

His sister laughs and throws her arms around him before he's fully stepped out of the truck. 'Where the hell have you been? Mum is going nuts. You said you'd be here by seven. You're over an hour late.'

'I know.'

'If you think coming late will lessen the pain for you, you've wasted your time. Doesn't work that way. You're late and everyone has noticed you're not here. Sandy has already commented four times that you probably wouldn't show. You're too important or something like that.'

'Yeah, and that's why I don't want to be here. It's like a fucking backstabbing contest.'

Bria pushes her long strawberry-blonde hair back from her shoulders and takes his hand. 'I'll protect you, don't worry.'

'Great. Now I feel so much better.' He grunts as she whacks him in the stomach then pulls her into his arms again. 'I missed you. How's work going?'

Bria smiles widely. 'It's so good. I really love it, Tate. I can't tell you how amazing it is to be bringing in a regular salary. Working as an intern was great but having money is so much better. You know, I could use my expertise to whip your wardrobe into shape.'

Tate looks down at his boots, jeans, and shirt. 'What's wrong with my wardrobe?'

'I didn't say there's anything wrong with it. The designer I work for has some amazing pieces. You could revamp your look with a little help from yours truly of course.'

Tate snorts as he turns away from her and walks over to the house. 'Nice try but there's no fucking way you or your boss are revamping anything.'

'Can't blame a girl for trying.'

He opens the door to the house and puts on his game face when he hears someone announcing his arrival, instantly putting up obstacles between himself and his target of the kitchen. Relatives swarm towards him and for the next few minutes he's pulled into too many embraces to count.

Questions are fired at him from so many angles he doesn't get a chance to answer any of them. He nearly groans aloud when his mum appears in the kitchen door. She hurries towards him and gently makes her way through her family.

'Excuse me! Back away from my son. It's my turn for a hug.' She pulls him down into a bear hug and squeezes him tightly. 'Welcome back. You must be starving.' She grabs his hand and leads him to the kitchen, politely dissuading anyone from following them.

His mother, Becca, stands back and examines him. 'Have you been eating? You look like you've lost weight.'

'We really going to have this conversation every time I'm away for a few weeks? I promise I eat, Mum.'

She grunts then pulls out a chair at the wooden kitchen table and directs him to sit down. 'How was your flight?'

'Fine.'

'You look tired. You're not pushing yourself too hard, are you?'

'It's just been a long few months. I'm looking forward to a few weeks off.'

She places a plate of lasagne in front of him. 'I do appreciate you getting back in time for tonight. It wouldn't be Christmas without everyone here.'

The door bursts open and he is pulled off his chair backwards, nearly sending the food in front of him flying.

'Oh for goodness sake, Shane. Let him eat first.'

His older brother slaps him on the back and takes a couple of beers from the fridge. He passes one to Tate then sits down opposite him. 'I'd take your time eating that. The hordes are desperate to get a piece of our superstar.'

'Please say you're kidding.'

Shane shakes his head. 'Afraid not. Emma and Stacey have already picked out a few songs you're going to sing.'

'Who?'

Bria pokes him in the back as she walks past on her way to the fridge. 'You haven't been away that long. Cousins, Tate.'

He smiles and nods at her. 'Ah. Right. Great.'

His mum squeezes his arm. 'Just say no. I'll find your father.'

'I think he's hiding in the shed.' Shane laughs as his mum glares at him before shutting the door behind her. 'You look wrecked.'

'Thanks. I've already got that from Mum.'

Bria sits down beside Shane and leans against his arm. No way you could miss the fact the pair are related. Both have the exact same strawberry-blond hair and brown eyes. If not for the ten-year age gap you'd think they were twins.

Shane holds up his beer and taps it against Tate's. 'Congratulations by the way. Christmas number one for the second year running. Well done.'

'Cheers.' He can't quite believe it himself. Getting to number one at Christmas last year had been completely unexpected. Getting it for a second year was taking time to sink in.

Tate stifles a yawn. He only arrived back in Ireland yesterday after touring around Europe for the last month with Broken Chords. Gregg, Dillon, and Luke had the day off, but he wasn't so lucky. Being frontman for the band means he has the added job of going to more interviews than the others. He didn't mind it in the least. The more publicity the band gets the better. He'd just prefer he didn't have to get in front of a camera a few hours after getting home.

The door opens and his father, Rick, steps in. He pulls Tate into a rib-crushing hug before releasing him and dropping into a chair. 'Welcome back. What do you think of your welcome home party?'

'I'm trying to avoid it.'

Rick laughs. 'You and me both. I was just ambushed by your mother. So much for hiding in the shed. I think I'm in trouble later. By the way, avoid your aunt Sandy. Half an hour about the ins and outs of her appendix operation. I can tell you the entire surgery in detail.' He shudders and makes a face. 'I know things about your mum's sister I never wanted to know. And now can never forget. Oh, by the way, Bria. Your friend just arrived.'

She jumps to her feet and disappears from the room.

'You back for long?'

Tate swallows the last forkful of dinner and nods. 'A few weeks. I've got to head over to Germany mid-February.'

Rick leans back in his chair and smiles. 'My two boys. International travellers. Couldn't you have picked jobs that keep you closer to home? Give your mother two less things to stress about. And make my life easier,' he adds under his breath.

Shane grins at him. 'Canada is my home.'

'And I live less than an hour down the road,' Tate adds.

'When you're here. Don't get me wrong. I am absolutely not complaining. You just need to have a chat with your mother about the whole worrying thing.'

'You're on your own with that one. I've tried.'

'Tried what?' Becca asks as she joins them again.

'I was just telling these two that you worry when they're away.'

'Of course I do. Especially about this one,' she says, gesturing to Tate. 'I don't know where he is from one day to the next.'

'You've got my schedule so don't even go there.'

'I know. Anyway. I'm afraid we've hidden you away in here long enough. My dear family would like to see the celebrity. Don't look at me that way. Better to get it over and done with. Like pulling off a plaster. Nice and quick.'

An hour later, Tate makes a much-needed break for the kitchen. His fucking jaw aches from all the smiling. He doesn't want to sound like an ungrateful git, but he's had constant celebrity stuff for the last month and he seriously needs a break from it.

He leans against the sink and smiles as he watches his mum weaving through the room with two plates of nibbles. She loves this kind of thing. Loves fussing and looking after people.

Shane joins him and nods towards a slightly unstable man who appears to be talking to the Christmas tree. 'Gary's enjoying the red wine as usual. Having a great old chat with the tree.'

'As long as it doesn't answer back, we're good.' Tate nudges Shane. 'Who the hell is that with Bria?'

'Looks like we're about to find out.'

They stop talking as Bria approaches with a guy who looks like he's about to piss himself. 'Tate. Shane. This is Robbie. He's my boyfriend.'

As if well-rehearsed, they cross their arms and stare down at Robbie. His eyes dart from Tate to Shane before settling back on Tate again. The guy swallows deeply as his eyes move over the two men.

As Bria's brothers, it's their job - and absolute right - to make sure the poor fucker knows exactly what would happen if he stepped out of line. The thing is, neither of them actually have to say anything to get their point across.

At six-one and six-three, the brothers look intimidating. They both work out and it shows, but it's Tate that is getting most of the attention. Partly because, as the taller of the two, he stands out. But mostly the attention is thanks to his tattoos. The ink covered his entire upper torso, neck, and hands. It was those very tattoos that had Robbie transfixed.

Bria wraps her arm around Robbie and glares at her brothers. 'Would you both knock it off. The intimidating stares aren't going to work. Ignore them Robbie. They're being asses.'

Robbie finally finds his voice. He holds out his hand but withdraws it when it isn't taken by either of them. 'I saw you on TV,' he says to Tate. 'You were on a chat show with the rest of the band.'

Tate nods. 'What one?'

'I don't know. You sang a song on it.'

'We did that on three shows recently. You'll have to narrow it down.'

'I can't remember.'

'Bit pointless mentioning it then, wasn't it?'

Bria thumps Tate in the stomach. 'Stop it!'

They laugh and Tate slaps Robbie on the shoulder nearly sending him flying. 'Sorry. We're just fucking with you. Nice to meet you.'

Robbie grins. 'Yeah. You too. I really like your music.'

'Cheers, Robbie. Appreciate that.'

Bria leads him away, mouthing *dicks* at them as she walks away.

'I don't like him,' Shayne mutters as Bria and Robbie disappear into the crowd.

'Nope. Me either.'

Shane grabs another bottle of beer from the fridge and passes one to Tate. They clink bottles. 'Happy Christmas.'

'Yeah. Happy Christmas.'

His best mate Gregg stops in the doorway and holds up a bottle. 'There you are. Heard you decided to grace us with your presence. How'd the interview go? Did it drag on or did you make sure it dragged on so you could avoid all this festive fun?'

'It dragged on without any help from me.'

Gregg sits on the edge of the counter and takes a swig from his beer. They'd been friends for over two decades, but Gregg had only joined the band about a year ago as their drummer. He'd been an instant hit with the fans. No surprise there. Gregg was one of those people it was impossible not to like. He was always smiling, rarely got stressed about anything, and he's an incredible musician.

Tate examines his friend as he takes another mouthful of beer. Gregg's usually tousled dark-blond hair is combed back from his face and it looks like he's trimmed his beard instead of letting it go where it wants.

'Who the fuck are you trying to impress?'

Gregg sits up tall and pushes his shoulders back. 'It's Christmas. Nothing wrong with making an effort. Maybe you should try it. Let Bria show you there's more in the world of fashion than just jeans and t-shirts.'

Tate narrows his eyes as he glares at his friend. 'She's got to you.'

'She may have mentioned something in passing. And there's nothing to say a little added sparkle will do the band any harm. It'll make us stand out from the other rock bands, that's for sure.'

Shane joins in as Gregg laughs at the look on Tate's face.

'I should get a photo of that. Your face is priceless. You're too easy, mate.'

'Just for that I'm dragging the rest of you along with me next time I'm being interviewed.'

'Ah now that's not how it works, buddy. Your job description is song writer, lead guitarist, lead vocalist, and the person who has to show their face in front of our adoring public as much as possible. That means you get all the tedious interviews to handle alone. Part of the deal.'

'Thanks,' Tate replies sarcastically while failing to stifle a yawn. 'How the hell do you have so much energy? I'm seriously struggling.'

Gregg holds up a bag of sweets. 'Sugar rush, my friend. Who needs sleep when you've got gummy bears? I'm not looking forward to landing after these babies.'

'Are Dillon and Luke still here?'

'Went home about an hour ago. Too many all-nighters finally caught up with them. So, you give out many autographs yet?' Gregg asks as he pops another few bears into his mouth.

'What? No. I haven't. They're my family. Hang on, have you?'

He nods. 'Four. You know, I could get used to this celebrity thing. Had a few requests for tickets to our next gig too.'

'Fuck sake. I'm sorry, man. That's not on.'

Gregg shrugs. 'Whatever. Let them ooh and ah over us. It's Christmas.'

Shane nudges Tate on the arm and raises his bottle towards the door. Their uncle Eric is pushing through the crowd, waving frantically in their direction. Gregg looks over his shoulder then turns back to Tate. 'You didn't tell me you have a groupie in your family?'

'If either of you leave me alone with him, I will kill you,' Tate mutters under his breath before smiling widely. 'Happy Christmas, Uncle Eric!'

'Nice to see you, Tate. I hear congratulations are in order. Christmas number one for the fourth year.'

Tate glares at Gregg as he waves and makes his escape into the living room. 'Thanks, but it's only the second year.'

'Are you sure? Ah. Never mind. Are you back for long?'

'A few weeks. We've got the second leg of our tour starting in February.'

'It must be so exciting travelling all over the world. I was only telling Dara the other day that he should have kept up the guitar lessons. He could have been part of your band. Imagine that. Two cousins playing guitar together in the same band.'

Tate takes another drink from his beer as that image plays out in his head. There's no fucking way he'd ever have his cousin in the band. First, he's family, so that's a big no. Second, Dara had been a pain in his ass for as long as he can remember. Tate had grown up being compared to him and even to this day he still fell short. Dara's a happily married successful lawyer. He's a successful rock star with a string of very public, failed relationships. Apparently, being thirty-six and still unattached is a major life fail.

Tate swallows his beer without choking and smiles at Eric. 'Yeah. Shame about that. That would have been great. How is Dara?'

'He's good. Made partner in his firm finally. Baby on the way too so it's all very exciting.'

He ignores Shane sticking a finger in his ribs. 'That's great. Tell him I said hi.'

'Wait one minute. I should show you a picture of the baby.' Eric rummages in his pocket and pulls out his phone.

'I didn't think it was due yet?'

'The scan picture,' Eric replies. Tate's acting skills come in a treat as he makes all the right noises when Eric shows him a black and white image of what looks like a kidney bean.

Tate breathes a loud and obvious sigh of relief when his dad joins them at the sink and Eric disappears into the living room.

'Picture of the bean?'

Tate smirks. 'You got it too?'

His father nods. 'I was always terrible at figuring out what's what in those scan photos. I remember with Bria and Shane I couldn't tell if I was looking at the top or the bottom.' He ruffles Tate's hair like he's done ever since he was a kid, ignoring Tate when he swipes his hand away. Rick grins as he grabs a bottle of wine and joins the others in the living room.

There aren't any scans or baby photos of Tate. Well, not with this family anyway. The Archers adopted him when he was seven.

He always felt like he didn't fit with the ideal image some of the extended family had in their minds. He hadn't been the best academically and found himself in trouble more times than he would have liked. Part of it was acting up, trying to find his place in his new family. Part was genuine struggle.

When he joined their family, he was so far behind all the other kids. He caught up eventually. Hell, he'd more than caught up, but those initial years of suspensions and visits to the principal's office had remained at the front of some of his relative's memories.

So he took to the role of black sheep with enthusiasm.

His choice of career, his tattoos and piercings, his lifestyle... it was all commented on. They'd never said it to his face, but his parents had told him some of the remarks. At least he won't have to see any of them until this time next year. Something to look forward to.

He grunts as his two nieces barrel into his legs, each one clinging onto him and squeezing tightly. He bends down and picks one up in each arm. 'Should you two still be up?'

'No,' Shane replies. 'It's way past their bedtime.'

'We can't sleep until Uncle Tate sings.'

'Ah now, we talked to you about this. He's been singing for the last few weeks. He probably wants a break.'

'Ignore your Dad. Of course I'll sing. There should be a guitar in the annex. Can you grab it and bring it to the living room? I'll be there in a few minutes.'

Both girls cheer and squirm to be released. 'Do not drop the guitar!' Shane shouts after them, but they've already disappeared into the crowd. 'Please say it's not an expensive one.'

Tate shakes his head. 'It's just a cheap one I keep here for entertaining the masses.'

'You don't have to do this.'

'Are you kidding? Those girls are my biggest fans. The least I can do is sing a few songs for them.'

After singing quite a few songs accompanied by Gregg, Shane, Bria, and other random family members, Tate escapes outside to get some fresh air. He closes the door behind him and blows out a long breath as he checks his watch. Just past eleven. Most of the family had left for the night, but there were a few stragglers not willing to bid goodnight to the free food and drink just yet.

He zips up his jacket and sits on the tailgate of his Ford Raptor. He lies back in the load bed and rests his head on his hands as he listens to the waves crashing on the beach in front of the house. He missed the sound of the sea when he was away. Missed the comfort it gave him. His life was brilliant, and he wouldn't change a thing, but it did take over.

He's not proud of it but he'd fallen prey to the lifestyle over the last few years. Drink and drugs had helped keep him going through the long hours on the road followed by performing, then countless interviews and photo shoots. It wasn't something that controlled him in any way, but, at times like this, with his whole fucking family in the house, he wishes he had something other than beer to take the edge off.

The rhythmic comforting sounds of the waves mixes with his exhaustion and he dozes off for a moment, only to be rudely awoken by someone coughing loudly beside his car.

'No bed to go to?'

Tate opens his eyes and looks up at his cousin, Dara. 'Must have nodded off.'

'Doesn't look too comfortable.'

Tate groans and pulls himself up. 'It's not.'

Dara hands him a pile of post. 'Your mum asked me to give this to you in case she forgets. You not updated your address?'

'Only for the important stuff. This is junk. Congrats on the baby, by the way.'

'Cheers. I presume Dad showed you the scan picture.'

'He did. He seems pretty excited.'

Dara nods. 'You could say that. First grandchild and all that. So, I hear congratulations are in order for you too. Another number one single. Sell out tours. Screaming fans wherever you go. God you make me sick.' He grins at Tate and they both laugh. Dara climbs onto the tailgate and sits beside him. 'I remember when we took guitar lessons together for a few months. Did you ever think you'd end up here?'

'No way. Any regrets giving up music?'

Dara shakes his head. 'Dad keeps going on about it. Like if I stuck with it I could have been as good as you are. I didn't have the patience for it though. It's something you either have or you don't. Sort of like the ability to listen in Mr. Donnelly's maths class.'

'I don't know what it was about that man. He walked into the classroom and my brain switched off.'

'Might have been easier if he put you on a permanent detention. Would have saved him a few minutes every day.'

'Don't remind me. Mum and Dad must have spent nearly as much time with the principle as I did in detention.'

'It was quite the family scandal at the time.'

Tate snorts. 'Yeah, I'll bet.'

'You've shut them all up now though. You've got to be worth more than all of us combined. Bet that feels good to prove them all wrong, huh?'

'I didn't do all this to prove anything.'

'I didn't mean it that way.'

'I know. We all worry a little too much about what everyone else thinks.'

Dara nods. 'Couldn't agree more. But that's the fun of family, right? Anyway, I suppose we better head back in and help clear up. Gary should be finished talking to the tree by now.'

'I'll be there in a minute.'

Dara smiles at him and jumps down from the back of the truck. Tate watches him walk back into the house then lies back and looks up at the sky. He didn't dislike Dara, but he had little to nothing in common with him anymore.

He holds up the bundle of post and shuffles through the letters. Most of it is junk but one letter in the middle stands out. The envelope has his name and parents' address printed on it but there's no stamp.

He sits up and shines his phone torch on the print. It looks like whoever sent it used a typewriter.

He tears it opens and pulls out the sheet of paper. At the top of the page in the same typewriter print is a line of writing above a printout of a photo showing a woman with her arms around a young boy.

Is it your fault she's dead?

He turns the page over but there's nothing else. He directs his phone torch on the photo and his heart hammers loudly in his chest. What the fuck? That's him in the photo. He's a bit younger than he is in the first photos the Archers took when they adopted him. Maybe a year before so he'd be around six, but it's definitely him. Did that mean the woman in the photo is his mother? He doesn't remember his biological parents. He was told they died.

'Is it your fault she's dead?'

Saying the words out loud doesn't produce an answer. If it is his mother, is it his fault she died? But he was only a kid, how could it be down to him?

He reads the words again. Who the fuck would send him something like that?

'Hey! You too much of a celebrity to help? Tate? Hello!'

He looks up at his mum waving at him from the door. 'What?'

'Gregg is attempting to polish off the tray of leftover sausage rolls without you. If you don't come in now, he'll devour the lot, and then he'll be sick. I'm not having a replay of last year. I've only just got the stains out of the rug.'

'Yeah. I'll be there in a sec.'

Tate wipes a hand over his face and folds the sheet of paper. He climbs down from the truck and stuffs it into his back pocket. Whatever the fuck is going on there is no way he's going to mention this to her. The Archers gave him a family when no one else wanted him. Thanks to them he's had an amazing life for nearly thirty years. That's all that matters to him.

Tate stares at the phone on the couch and wills it to stop ringing. He closes his eyes and drops his head against the back of the couch when it does just that. But then it starts again. He curses and grabs it off the seat. 'What?'

'Where the fuck have you been? I've been ringing you for ages.'

Tate winces at Gregg's shrill voice in his ear. 'I was asleep until you woke me up.'

'Are you drunk?'

He looks at the empty twelve pack of beer on the coffee table in front of him. 'No. Just tired.'

Gregg snorts. 'Is that so? Cause it sounds like you're fucked. It's only ten in the morning.'

'I'm not drunk. Did you just call to get on my case or do you want something?'

'Charming. I was calling to see if you want to grab a burger later.'

He rests his feet on the table, wincing as he accidentally knocks over a bottle which takes out all the others like dominos. 'Fuck.'

'What's wrong?'

'Nothing. Just dropped a glass. Listen, I'm just going to crash. I'll catch you another time.'

Gregg snorts. 'Yeah right. That's the third time you've blown me off this week. What's going on? You were a grumpy bastard over Christmas then just upped and left. Shane's kids barely got to spend any time with you. They haven't seen you for six months. Do you not think you could have maybe spent more than a pathetic two days with them?'

Tate peers into the bottle in his hand and tosses it on the couch beside him. 'You done?'

'Don't be a dick, Tate. What's crawled up your ass?'

'I've been with you every single fucking minute of the day for weeks. I need space.'

'Fine. I hear you loud and clear.' Gregg ends the call. Tate stares at the phone then dumps it on the couch beside him.

Everything Gregg said adds to the impressive load of guilt he's already buried under. He decided to leave his parents place and come home when he'd shouted at his four-year-old niece. It wasn't her fault. She was excited to spend time with him after so long and hadn't given him a moment to himself the whole day. When she asked him to read her a story, refusing to take no for an answer, he'd snapped. She'd run off in tears to Shane and he'd felt like a complete bastard.

He'd apologised to her and she'd quickly forgiven him... well, as much as a four-year-old can, but he didn't want a repeat. If either of his nieces were nervous around him or didn't trust him, he'd never forgive himself.

He doesn't even remember what excuse he used to explain why he needed to leave. Work was his usual go-to excuse. Whatever he'd said had done the trick and less than an hour after shouting at Tilly, he'd packed his bags and left.

16

Since that fucking photo arrived, he's seeing things he knows must be memories, but they're so unfamiliar he doesn't know how to deal with them. The nightmares started the next day and with them came the end of any sleep. Every time he closes his eyes he sees the woman from the photo. He can't make sense of the nightmares. They're just flashes of images like snippets from a horror film – complete with lots of screaming and lots of blood.

He knows he should talk to his adopted parents about this, but he can't. He's given them enough headaches over the years without adding this to it. They've always been cautious about the attention his career choice brings with it. If they thought a fucked-up fan had not only sent him something like that, but hand delivered it to their house, they'd freak out. It's not the first time he's got something less than complimentary sent to him and it wouldn't be the last. It is the first time it's contained personal shit though.

He closes his eyes again but this time the intercom on the gate disturbs him. Tate take a ridiculously long time to stumble through the living room to the intercom.

'What?'

'It's Eddie.'

He opens the gate and waits for Eddie to pull his car into the driveway. The tall, dark-haired man gets out of his shiny new BMW and saunters over to the front door. Eddie pushes past him and whistles as he walks around Tate's kitchen.

'Very nice indeed. I like it.' He wanders into the sitting room and stares at the bottles on the coffee table and the floor. He probably should have picked those up before he let Eddie in. 'I see you've been having a good time. I have to say, the life of the rich and famous isn't overwhelming me at the moment. I was expecting... less drunken lout and more pampered rock star.'

Tate flops back into the leather armchair and rubs his forehead. 'Sorry to disappoint.'

'I wouldn't call it a disappointment, more of an eye-opener if anything. You look like you're in a bit of a hole.'

'I just got back from a few weeks away. I'm unwinding.'

'Looks to me like you're getting well and truly smashed.'

Tate doesn't bother answering. If he says anything, he'll just drag this conversation on for longer. He wants Eddie out of his house asap.

'Not sure all this fame stuff is worth it. I've got a delightful afternoon planned with a stunning blonde I met last night. What are your plans for the day? Hiding in the dark and getting off your head on whatever you can find? Can't say I'm jealous of your life, Tate.'

'You've got to work on your sales technique. It's shite.'

Eddie laughs and settles into the other armchair. 'I don't need a sales technique. The fact you called me means I'm walking away with your money in my pocket. Just not sure how much yet. To be honest, I thought you were done and dusted with all this. Haven't seen you for what? Must be heading on three, maybe four months now.'

'I'm just wound up after the tour. My body clock is fucked. I'm awake when I should be asleep and vice versa. Just need something to help.'

'That I can do.' He places a bag of pills on the table in front of him. 'Try those for starters. If they don't work give me a shout and I'll bring round something stronger.'

Tate rubs his jaw and looks down at the bag. Fuck it. If they help him get a few hours without the nightmares hitting, he'll give anything a try.

'Fine.'

Tate shouts and bolts upright in bed, gasping for breath. He scrambles to the bathroom and empties his stomach. Once his pitiful last meal is dealt with, he pulls himself to his feet and leans heavily on the sink. He closes his eyes but the woman from his nightmare reaches out to him. But he can't help her. It doesn't matter how many times she pleads, how often she begs, he can't save her. He may not remember much about what happened, but he does know that much. Whoever the woman in the photo is, she's dead.

He's seen her lifeless eyes staring over at him enough times to know that much. Tate holds up his shaking hands and sees her blood covering his palms. He turns on the hot tap and scrubs with the nailbrush until they're red and raw. It doesn't matter how many times he washes his hands, he can't get rid of her blood. It's always there. When the pain becomes unbearable, he turns off the tap and stares down at his hands.

The last two weeks have been hell. It's like someone has torn him from the life he knew and dumped him into a fucked-up reality he has no control over. He's being dragged from hour to miserable hour and nothing is helping to break the cycle.

He wanders back into his bedroom, grabs his duvet and drags it down the stairs behind him then dumps it on the couch. He switches on the TV and turns the volume up loud. Anything to drown out the constant screaming in his head.

He pulls a beer from the fridge and drops onto the couch. As he's downing half the bottle, he glares at the sheet of paper on the table in front of him. The fucking autopsy report arrived in the post yesterday and brought with it a whole new level of hell. Just like with the photo, the text was short and to the point.

'It is your fault she's dead.'

No longer a question. Just a statement.

According to the few sentences on the report the sender didn't black out, the woman had been beaten to death.

He rubs his eyes, but his vision won't clear. It feels like his eyeballs are full of sand. His last full night of sleep was while he was still on tour. He's so far beyond exhausted at this stage. The new pills Eddie gave him are doing fuck all. If anything, the dreams got so much worse since he started taking them. He's going to bring over

19

something stronger in the morning. He just needs to hang on another few hours. Then he might get some peace.

Tate pulls the duvet around himself and hits the remote on the fire. He can't get warm. Can't stop the shakes no matter how high he turns up the heat. He must doze off for a few minutes because instead of being in his living room, he's on the floor of a cold, sparsely furnished room. Tate jolts himself awake just as the dark figure looms over him. He beats his fists against the side of his head over and over again. 'Fuck off! Please.'

He shoves the duvet off and goes into the kitchen. He opens the fridge then slams it closed again. He's not hungry. Maybe working out will tire him enough to knock him out for a few hours? That idea falls flat after a pathetic ten minutes. He worked hard to keep himself in shape. All that was going to go to the dogs unless he can get himself together.

He wanders back to the couch and wraps the duvet around himself again. He just needs to hang on another few hours.

Tate opens the door and is shoved to the side as Gregg forces his way into the house. He groans to himself and shuts the door then follows Gregg into the living room. His friend comes to a stop and looks around the open plan space. He slowly steps around the dozens of people sitting on the floor and on the expensive couches. He stops under the mezzanine level, grimacing when he sees yet more bodies upstairs. He turns around, grabs Tate by the arm, and leads him back outside.

'Who the fuck are all those people?'

Tate shrugs. 'Not sure.'

'Excuse me? What the hell do you mean you're not sure? Your house is full of drunk strangers.'

'It's a party.'

Gregg pulls the bottle from Tate's hand and gestures towards the house. 'It's Tuesday. Who the fuck has a party on a Tuesday? And while we're at it, what the fuck is Eddie doing here?'

Tate takes the beer back from Gregg. 'What do you want?'

Gregg turns to face him and crosses his arms. 'You've been ghosting everyone for nearly a month. I know we all need space after touring but you've never been off the radar like this before. And no offence mate, but this drunken, rock star, hobo look isn't doing anything for me. When was the last time you slept? Or ate? Or had a shower? Or did anything except drink? You look shite.'

'You want a drink?'

'No I don't want a fucking drink, Tate.' He peers in the window and gestures at the crowd inside. 'They're destroying your house. I'm surprised your neighbours haven't called the Garda on you. I can barely hear myself think.'

'You going to call your old mates in to break up the fun?'

'You really think I want them to see what I stepped away from a fucking good career for?'

'No one's forcing you to work with me. You can go back to fighting crime and putting the fucking world to rights.'

Gregg laughs and takes a few steps back. 'At this moment in time I'm sorely tempted. What the fuck is going on with you, Tate? We're friends. Talk to me. Has something happened?'

Tate finishes his drink and drops the empty bottle in the flowerbed. 'Nope.'

Gregg points to Eddie's BMW parked beside Tate's pickup. 'I thought you were easing off on contact with Eddie? We all agreed we'd knock that on the head.'

'I changed my mind. What the fuck is the problem? We have the month off. I'm relaxing.'

'You know we're due to fly to Germany in two weeks, right? You seriously telling me you're ready for that? Cause right now if you walk on stage looking like that, people will be asking for their money back.'

21

'Give it a rest, Gregg.'

He turns back to the house, but Gregg grabs his shoulder and spins him around. 'What are you taking?'

Tate shrugs out of Gregg's grip and pokes him in the chest with his finger. 'How about you mind your own fucking business.'

He turns away again, but Gregg steps in front of him, blocking his escape. 'What are you taking?'

'Get out of the way.'

'Not until you tell me. In all the years I've known you you've never been this far gone. I just want to help.'

Tate tries to sidestep around Gregg but he's not backing down. 'I don't need help. Move!'

'No.'

'You're seriously pissing me off, Gregg. Get the fuck out of my way or—'

'Or what?'

Tate punches Gregg in the jaw. He may have been letting himself go to shit lately but he's still strong enough to send his friend stumbling back against the wall. Any regret or shame is overshadowed by the desperate need to get Gregg away from here. He doesn't want Gregg to witness this sorry fucking show. He's falling apart. He can see it happening, but there's nothing he can do about it. He just hit his best mate but the only thing he can think about is getting back inside so he can wallow in his own fucking misery.

Gregg stares across at him as he wipes the blood from his lip. 'You really think clobbering me will convince me you're okay?'

'I couldn't give a damn if you're convinced or not. Keep your nose out of my business, Gregg. I mean it.'

Tate smiles as a scantily clad blonde steps outside and takes his hand. 'You're missing the party, Tate.'

Gregg curses under his breath. 'Can you give us a minute... whoever you are.' She hangs off Tate's arm and makes no move to disengage.

'Get out of here, Gregg. We're done.'

Tate lets the woman lead him back inside and locks the front door behind him so Gregg can't come in. He slumps back on the couch before the blonde stranger straddles him. She pulls off his t-shirt and he closes his eyes as she runs her hands over his chest. He doesn't care what she does to him as long as she distracts him. So far, she's doing a pretty good job.

He slips his hand around the back of her head and pulls her towards him. She attacks his mouth like her life depended on it. Her hips gyrate as she kisses him, her short mini skirt riding up her legs as she moves against him.

She pushes back from him and runs a long bright orange fingernail down his arm. 'Time for more?'

'Yeah. Time for more.'

Tate rests his head against the back of the couch and closes his eyes. The woman lifts his arm and rests in on her lap. He barely feels the needle going into his vein anymore.

As soon as the drug hits, time ceases to have any meaning for him. People come and go. Different faces appear in front of him, but he doesn't think he knows any of them. Every time he comes back to his senses, there is always another fix ready to help him slip away from all the mental shit that's torn his life apart the last few weeks.

Whether it's been days or weeks, his mind has been blissfully silent since that first hit and that's all he cares about.

He keeps telling himself the next fix will be the last one. It sounds convincing when he says it to himself, but his body isn't on board with that plan. It needs him to keep going. It needs something to silence the tremors and cravings that own him now. Maybe he'll try to stop after the next one.

Chloe Quinn closes her book as the plane lands at Dublin Airport. She slips her book into her bag and pulls her headphones out of her ears. It's only been a year, but she feels like she's been away from Ireland for forever. She follows the crowds through the terminal and collects her bag from the carousel. Her gran is easy to spot when she steps through the glass doors into the arrivals lounge. She waves frantically and rushes over to Chloe, throwing her arms around her.

'It's so good to see you.'

Chloe smiles and squeezes her back. 'I missed you.'

Her gran, Dorothy, links arms with her and leads her out of the airport into the multistorey car park across the road. 'How was your trip?'

'It was fine. I'm glad to be back on the ground. So, have you made a decision about going away?'

Dorothy smirks at her. 'Eager to get rid of me?'

'Of course not.'

'I'm not having a go at you. I'd imagine after spending all that time living under your uncle's roof you could do with some time to yourself. You'll have to endure my company for a few months then I'll have no choice but to leave you for a bit.'

Chloe laughs at the sour expression on her gran's face. 'It's a holiday.'

Dorothy makes a face and waves her hand dismissively. 'Some holiday. Your aunt is the most irritatingly organised, scheduled, perfectionist I had the pleasure of giving birth to. How that woman shares DNA with me I'll never know. I'm in for a month of being fussed over and told what to do and when I can do it. Why would I be looking forward to that?'

Chloe climbs into the driver's seat of her gran's battered pickup and smiles across at her. 'You'll have a blast. You did last time.'

'Yes. For a few days. Anyway, I will endeavour to be on my best behaviour and not disrupt her household too much.'

Chloe pulls out of the parking spot and glances sideways at her. 'Oh Gran. Please behave.'

Dorothy smirks and settles back in the seat. 'My dear, I am always on my best behaviour. How could you suggest otherwise?'

Chloe smiles but doesn't bother responding. Her gran has the mentality of a mischievous child at times, but that's what makes her amazing and so much fun to be around.

It takes an hour to get through the busy Dublin traffic to Newcastle where her gran lives. She pulls into the driveway of her gran's cottage and hops out of the car. The sea breeze whips her long dark hair around her shoulders. She closes her eyes as she takes a lungful of the fresh, salty air.

'Oh my God, that smells—'

'Fishy,' her gran finishes.

'No. I was going to say it smells... actually it does smelly really fishy. What is that?'

Dorothy points a finger at the hedge separating her house from the neighbour. 'Jim next door. Daft man took his boat up to repair. Smells like a rotten fish. He promises it'll be back in the water and stop offending the neighbours by tomorrow. Come on, dear. Let's get you settled in,' she says as she unlocks the bright red door.

Chloe brings her bags upstairs and sits on the bottom of the creaky double bed. The spare room is stuck in time – just like her gran most of the time. The floral wallpaper matches the floral duvet which matches the floral lampshade and the floral curtains. The old floorboards are worn and creak with every footstep. She flops back on the bed and smiles up at the beams in the ceiling as she yawns. The flight was long and her body clock is completely off.

A few days of relaxing by the sea will sort her out. She's not due to start her new job until late August so there's no rush to do anything. She can't remember the last time she had absolutely nothing planned.

Looking after her cantankerous uncle for the last year after he took a nasty fall was different but also hard work. It didn't help that he lived off-grid in the arse end of Alaska. No power. No running water. No flushing toilet. She shudders when she thinks back to that part. It was a once in a lifetime experience but getting back on the flight to Dublin had been such a relief.

Time to spoil herself. She laughs as she looks over at the door to the bathroom. Having a flushing toilet is heaven.

She closes her eyes as the hours of travel finally catch up with her. Maybe she'll have a quick nap to refresh herself. This summer is going to be a good one. Plenty of sea air and drawing. What could be better than that?

Three months later...

Tate rolls over and stares at the clock on the bedside table. Five am. He rubs his eyes and flops onto his back. A few more hours of sleep would be nice but he's done tossing and turning in bed. With a long sigh he turns and looks at the calendar hanging on the wall beside him. He slides the pen from the holder and draws a large line though the date.

Eighty-two days. Eighty-two lousy days clean. No alcohol. No drugs. And in a few hours, no more rehab.

Time to face the world again.

Not something he's looking forward to. In truth, he's fucking dreading it. At least in here everyone had fucked up in one way or another. Out there he's going to be another failed rock star who took things too far.

He dresses quickly and walks through the corridors to the gym and breathes a sigh of relief when he finds he's got the place to himself. The last thing he wants to do is have another forced polite conversation. He's had his fill of them since he checked himself into the facility. It's part of the deal, but he came here to sort out his problems, not make friends.

After an hour, another resident appears so he makes his escape back to his room to pack his things. Three hours later, with the reams of paperwork completed and follow up appointments booked, he slips on his sunglasses and steps into the early May sunshine. He walks through the lush gardens towards the visitor's car park beyond.

He wipes his hand on the leg of his jeans. It's strange being back in his own clothes. The facility preferred them to wear these god awful pale grey tracksuits and matching t-shirts. Something about no one standing out. Everyone being on an equal footing. It was a battle they wouldn't win. With the price tag for the place far beyond most people's reach, it was clear exactly what footing everyone was on.

In his scuffed biker boots, jeans, and t-shirt, you'd be hard pressed to see how he could afford to check himself into this place. But that's the thing with being a celebrity. It didn't matter what you wore or where you grew up or how you looked. It only matters how many people know who you are.

In his case it's quite a few. Which doesn't make checking himself into a rehab facility something he could keep quiet for long. It was only a matter of time before the world knew how much he'd screwed up. Hell, they probably already knew. Then his career would take a nosedive. Something to look forward to.

He pulls himself out of his thoughts as he nears the car park and spots Gregg sitting on the bonnet of his beat-up Defender. Gregg wolf-whistles and waves.

'Hey gorgeous.'

Tate can't help but laugh. He's never known how Gregg manages it, but he could always be counted on to cheer him up. Which is something he desperately needs right now. He honestly doesn't know how he would have survived the last few months if not for his friend.

He fully expected never to see Gregg again after he hit him, but he wasn't so easily pushed away. And that's something Tate is unbelievably grateful for. His friend had been with him every step of his recovery, visiting regularly and going to as many family counselling sessions as he could.

Gregg pulls him into a bear hug and slaps him on the back a few times.

'Fuck me, mate. You've bulked up a little.'

'Not much else to do in there.'

He squeezes Tate's bicep. 'You're just making me look bad now. You ready to get out of here?'

'More than ready.' He throws his bag on the back seat and climbs in beside Gregg. 'Thanks for coming to get me.'

'Not a problem. Right, so before we head off, I may have a slight confession.'

Tate raises his eyebrow as he looks sideways at his friend. 'What?'

'I may not be taking you back to your place.'

'Gregg—'

'No, hear me out for a sec. Your folks are worried about you. They want you to stay with them for a few weeks. Just until you're ready to set off by yourself again.'

'I'm a big boy, Gregg. I don't need a babysitter. I need to get back to normal. How the fuck am I going to do that if I'm living with my parents?'

'Don't be like that. They're all worried about you. And I got to say I agree. I don't think you should be by yourself just yet.'

'Do I have a choice?'

'Nope. Afraid not. I've already taken some of your stuff over. They're putting you in the annex, so you'll have your own space. They want to make sure you're okay.'

'Fine. Can we just get out of here? I'm done with this place.'

'As you wish. Let's get you home.'

A feeling of dread settles on him again. It wasn't a surprise his parents wanted him where they could keep an eye on him. He could put his foot down and go home, but he's put them through hell recently. The least he can do is give them what they want.

If he's really being honest, deep down he doesn't want to go back to his place. That's where he'd made the fucked-up decision that brought him to the facility. That's probably why his folks don't want him to go back.

They were the lucky ones who had found him. His house was trashed, and he was lying unconscious on his couch with a fucking needle sticking out of his arm.

The overdose wasn't intentional. That wasn't what he was doing. He doesn't know how many times he said that to Gregg, to his parents, to the endless hospital staff who wouldn't give him a second to himself after he eventually woke up after six days in a coma. No one believed him and who can blame them. He hadn't given them any reason to.

'Hey? You with me?'

'What?'

'You zoned out on me. You good?'

'Yeah. Sorry.'

Gregg nods towards his arm. 'You going to lay off that?'

Confused, Tate looks down at his hand scratching away at the inside of his left arm like crazy. He stops and rests his arm on the door. 'Sorry.'

'Can you stop doing that too?'

'What?'

'Apologising. You've apologised enough.'

'I've got a load to apologise for. I've fucked everything up.'

'You made a mistake and you dealt with it. You've got to move on.'

'It's gone public, hasn't it?'

Gregg makes a face which is all the answer Tate needs.

He scrubs his hand over his face. 'Fuck. How the hell did that happen? I thought the plan was to keep it under wraps?'

'Hey, don't you go looking at me that way. We didn't say anything. The story just got out a few days ago. Ellen and her team haven't got a clue where it came from, but it's...'

'It's what?'

'Well, it's accurate.'

'How much is out?'

'All of it. I know it's not ideal, but—'

'Not fucking ideal. Are you serious? We're done. You know that, right?'

'The most important thing is getting you sorted. We can figure out the band stuff later. Tate seriously don't stress about it. Nothing's been officially confirmed from our side. It's all speculation at the moment. All you need to do is concentrate on getting through this. You can make a statement in a few weeks. There's no rush.'

'You got my phone?'

'Tat—'

'Just give me my phone.'

Gregg sighs and pulls it out of his pocket. Tate powers it up and types his name into the search engine. He scrolls down the screen and his stomach drops. 'Fuck. Oh this is just perfect.'

'Ignore the headlines. Most of it's crap anyway.'

'Junkie rock star sent to rehab. Broken Chords frontman, Tate Archer, destroyed his two million Euro Blackrock house when he held a three day party which ended with the singer overdosing on heroine.' He scrolls further down the screen. 'Friends of Mr. Archer reported that he'd been struggling with both drugs and alcohol for years. Perfect. Oh and apparently said friends had tried to get me help but I denied I had a problem.' He looks over at Gregg. 'Friends?'

Gregg shakes his head. 'You know how these things grow arms and legs. Friends could be someone you met at a bar ten years ago and had a drink with. Who the fuck knows? Stop reading that stuff. It

31

won't do any good.'

Tate grunts and frowns at the screen. He laughs harshly and curses again. 'Fucking Astrid.'

'What? Your ex-Astrid?'

'Should have guessed she'd jump on the bandwagon. Listen to this. 'I caught Tate using drugs a few times while we were together. I tried to convince him to get help, but he wouldn't stop. I hated that he could only go on stage if he'd had a drink or took something beforehand'. Bullshit. I was always stone cold sober when I went on stage. Every fucking time. And I never used while I was with her.'

'Kinda hoped you were using. Might have explained why you were with her in the first place.'

Tate glares up at Gregg, but his friend just grins at him.

'What? You know full well she was absolutely not the right person to be with. You were thinking with your dick when you got with Astrid.'

'Cheers. And don't mention my dick in the same sentence as Astrid.' He slumps back in the seat and looks out the window. Gregg is right though. Astrid had been another of his mistakes. They'd used each other. He got sex and she moved up the social ladder she desperately wanted to climb.

He took her to all the star-studded exclusive parties she wanted to go to. Paid for anything she wanted. She wasn't happy when he ended things after a month. Hell of a way to get back at him. 'Has any of this come back on you, Dillon, or Luke? Me using I mean.' It's one thing him being called a junkie. He didn't want the rest of the band being tarred with the same brush.

'Ellen's been contacted about us, but she's doing her manager thing and shutting them down. It's all good.'

'Yeah, well I don't think she's going to be able to shut all this down,' he says, holding up his phone. 'I'm sorry, Gregg.'

'Don't even go there, Tate.'

'I've fucked things up for you guys too.'

'Hey, we're all okay. It's not like the three of us are going to end up on the street if you take some time to get sorted – and all this will be sorted. People will forget and move on to the next celebrity scandal. It'll pass. To be honest, a bit of time off isn't going to do any of use any harm.'

He nods but doesn't feel put at ease. The band may not be on the breadline but that didn't mean he could take his time getting back to work. And it wasn't just the guys he had to think about. A lot of livelihoods depended on him getting his shit together.

Tate just about manages to restrain his groan as they pull into his parents' driveway. His welcoming committee is out in force. 'Is it too late to go back?'

Gregg snorts and slaps him on the shoulder. 'Stop being a wuss and get your ass out of my car.'

Keeping his head down and eyes away from his parents' faces he climbs out and walks around the front of the car. He stuffs his hands into the back pockets of his jeans to stop himself from scratching his arm again. It's a fucking irritating habit he picked up and it's refusing to let up.

Even when his mum hugs him, he keeps his eyes away from hers. 'I'm so glad you agreed to stay with us.'

Like he had a choice. 'Thanks for letting me stay.'

'Don't be silly. I've got lunch ready. I hope you're hungry.'

The thought of sitting through an awkward family meal kills whatever appetite he may have had, but he's not going to rock the boat so soon by refusing. 'Thanks.' He follows his mum back to the house and accepts the hug and pat on the back from his father.

Tate faces his sister and knows she won't be welcoming him back with open arms. She barely looks up from her phone. He's surprised she's even here. The three painful counselling sessions she attended in the centre with him had been a complete disaster. He'd killed their relationship and hasn't got a fucking clue how to fix it. His mother must have pulled an emotional blackmail card from her supply. There's no way Bria would be here otherwise.

'Hey Bria.'

'Hi Tate,' She glances up from her phone to look at their mother instead of at him. 'I've said hi to him. I've gotta go now.'

'Bria—'

'Mum, I told you I've got some designs I need to get finished for tomorrow. I really can't stay.'

'Just stay for lunch, please.'

Tate puts a stop to this before it gets more uncomfortable. 'It's fine, Mum.' The last thing he wants is what's already going to be an awkward lunch made so much worse by forcing Bria to stay. It's glaringly obvious she'd prefer to be anywhere else but here.

Their mum smiles and nods at Bria. 'Drive carefully. I'll call you later.'

Bria glances over at him before getting into her car and driving away. Becca links arms with Tate and guides him towards the house. 'She's really busy at work.'

Tate nods but isn't fooled for a second. Bria is pissed off with him, or angry at him, or disappointed in him, or embarrassed by him. She can take her pick, there's enough to choose from.

Gregg grabs his bag from his hand before he can stop him and disappears into the annex while Tate is directed to sit on the couch. He parents sit opposite him and look about as uncomfortable as he feels. If this is the shape of things to come, he'll last till the morning before he does a runner.

'Do you want anything to drink?'

'Mum, I'm grand really.'

She smiles and clasps her hands together. 'I'll check on lunch.'

His dad waits until she's out of earshot before he speaks. 'Thanks for agreeing to stay here for a bit. I'm sure it's not what you want.'

'It's grand.'

Rick snorts and shakes his head. 'Of course it is. Your mum is just worried about you. Give her a week or two to see you're doing okay, then you can make your escape.'

'Right. How is she?'

Rick pauses and blows out a long breath. 'She's better than she was. Having you here will help.'

'She can't keep an eye on me forever.'

'Just give her a few weeks, Tate. That's all I'm asking.'

He nods but isn't fully on board with staying here for a few weeks. 'How's Jove?'

His dad laughs loudly. 'That horse and you are too similar. He's a stubborn git too.'

Tate has to laugh at that. Jove was definitely temperamental at the best of times. 'I might take him out later.'

'He'd appreciate that. Dara's been riding him once or twice a week, but he could do with a good run.'

'Dara?'

'Yeah. Himself and Eric have been spending a fair bit of time here. Helped to distract your mum from worrying about you. Dara offered to take Jove around the paddock. He wouldn't risk setting him lose on the beach but at least he got some exercise. He helped out a little around the farm too when he was free. I was missing those muscles of yours around the place, but don't worry. There's still plenty of jobs for you to get stuck into when you're up to it.'

Tate nods, but isn't overly thrilled to know his cousin had been anywhere near his horse. Then again, it's not like he was in a position to do anything about it. Why should Jove suffer because of his stupidity?

With the growing pressure of his fuck-up weighing down on him he stands up and points to the annex door. 'I'll go unpack before lunch.' He makes his escape and closes the door behind him.

Gregg steps out of the bathroom and wipes his wet hands on his jeans. 'Hey. You needed to escape already?'

Tate shrugs out of his leather jacket and flops onto the bed. 'I feel like I'm under a fucking spotlight.'

Gregg lies down beside him and crosses his arms. 'Give it a few hours and everything will be back to normal.'

'Our albums are gone.'

'What?'

Tate turns his head to glare at Gregg. 'Don't what me. The collage thing Mum made of our album covers is gone. It was on the living room wall.'

'Oh, right. Well maybe your folks thought seeing that would... I don't know... stress you out?'

'Acting like they don't know me is stressing me out. Why the hell would seeing our albums— Oh I get it. Seeing what I've fucked up would push me over the edge again and I'd relapse.' He looks back at the ceiling and scrubs his hands over his face. 'Fuck!' He drops his hands to his sides as he continues to glare at the ceiling. 'For the last fucking time, it had nothing to do with singing or touring or working non-stop.'

'What was it then? We've been mates for going on two decades. I'm not going to pretend we're a bunch of fucking saints by any means, but you took it to a whole new level this time.'

Tate clenches his jaw to stop himself from telling Gregg to drop it and move on. He knows by now it won't work.

'So you've got to understand why the people who know you the most have a hard time accepting you went from an occasional user to a heroin overdose in a few weeks for no reason.'

'We went through all this in counselling. You want another apology?'

'This isn't about an apology, Tate. This is about why.'

'I made a mistake.'

Gregg snorts. 'You made a mistake? We know you made a mistake. That doesn't explain why you made the mistake. You've had a hell of a lot thrown at you over the last few years and you've always picked yourself up and got back to it. What the fuck happened this time?'

'It was just a stupid spur of the moment mistake.'

'Fuck off.'

'What?'

'I said fuck off. This was so much more than a spur of the moment decision.'

'I just want to forget about it and get on with my life. And that includes getting back in the studio in a few weeks.'

'Are you sure that's such a good idea?'

Tate just looks at him.

'Fine. Whatever. You're the boss. We'll be there when you're ready.'

'Cheers.'

'So what are you going to say?'

'To who?'

'Your adoring public of course.'

'About what?'

'Where you've been? You can't just pop back like nothing's happened. The truth is already out. You need to get on top of it. What did Ellen say about it?'

'I haven't spoken to her yet.'

Gregg shoves him in the shoulder. 'Why the hell not? It's her job to figure out these sorts of things for you.'

'I'd prefer not to say anything about it.'

'Ah come on, mate. You know that's not going to work. Surely, it's best to bite the bullet and get it over with in your words. Knock all these exaggerated headlines on the head, including Astrid and her nonsense. Just think about it, okay?'

'Will do.'

'So you want to do something this afternoon?'

'I was thinking of taking Jove out. He probably thinks I've abandoned him. You can borrow Mum's horse if you fancy joining me.'

Gregg snorts. 'No thank you. There is not chance in hell you'll get me on the back of one of those things. They're lethal.'

'But a motorbike is fine?'

'A motorbike can't think for itself. Big difference, buddy.'

'You're a strange one, you know that?' Tate looks over at the door as his mum shouts that lunch is ready. 'Presume you're staying?'

'When have you ever known me to turn down your mother's cooking? And don't go thinking for one second this is over. You know me, Tate. I will get the truth out of you sooner or later.'

Chloe pulls into the driveway and smiles as she looks at the bright red door on the cottage. Her gran should be boarding her flight by now and Chloe's got the place to herself for a month at least. If she knows her gran, she'll be convinced to stay longer, but a month is a good start. After living with her uncle for the last year, a month to herself is heaven.

She climbs out of the car and strolls up the gravel path to the door. She stands in the hall and smiles when only silence greets her. After making a cup of tea she wanders outside. At least the overpowering smell is fish is gone. Her gran's neighbour had finally moved the boat back to the harbour after too many fights. In the end he gave up for the sake of peace.

She leans on the railing and takes a long inhale of the fresh sea air. With absolutely no plans for the month she intends on doing a lot of drawing, a lot of sleeping, and a lot of nothing else. As soon as school starts she'll be busy so she has no qualms being as lazy as humanly possible until then.

She frowns as she spots something moving along the beach towards her so goes back inside to get the binoculars from the kitchen. She focuses on the far end of the beach and sees a stunning black horse galloping along the water's edge. It's difficult to make out details from here, but the rider is male. As the horse approaches he comes into focus and she smiles to herself.

'Well, hello there.'

Even from this distance he's one good-looking guy. As the horse and rider near the end of the beach just below her gran's house, he says something to the horse and straightens his legs so he's standing tall in the saddle. The horse slows then comes to a stop, snorting loudly as it catches its breath. The rider pats it on the side of the neck then swings his leg over the saddle and drops to the sand.

Chloe climbs onto the bottom railing and leans over to get a better view. He's even better up close... well, closer. His dark hair is cut short at the back and slightly longer at the front, so it trails over his forehead. He runs a hand over his short beard, and she frowns.

'Oh dear. Really?' she mutters to herself. Both hands are tattooed. That probably means he has more. She doubts he'd start with his hands.

Ignoring his hands she moves back to his face. Yet more tattoos cover the side of his neck and the ear she can see is pierced. Not necessarily a bad thing but not something she'd usually be attracted to.

He takes off his boots and socks and Chloe utters a silent prayer of thanks as he pulls his shirt off. He drops it on the sand and places his phone on top. The black tank top follows next giving her a more than adequate view of his heavily tattooed impressive chest. Chloe's mouth drops open as he unfastens his belt and pushes his jeans down his toned legs. He leaves his black boxers on, much to her disappointment, then walks into the sea and dives under a wave.

'Dear God, what are you doing to me?'

He surfaces further out and flicks his wet hair off his face. The horse patiently follows along the shore as he spends the next ten minutes swimming back and forth in front of her.

When he's done with his swim, he stands up and pushes through the water back to the shore. Watching his body emerge from the sea a little at a time leaves her mouth dry and her cheeks flushed. Chloe has no doubts that image will be the highlight of her summer holiday. After getting dressed again, he takes hold of the reins and pulls himself into the saddle. He says something to the horse and it takes off up the beach at an impressive speed.

Chloe sighs and lowers the binoculars then climbs back to the ground. She toys with asking her gran about the man. She knows everyone in the area but thinks better of it. As with the rest of her family, the second they get the slightest whiff of a love interest for her they pounce. If she asked her gran, she knows Dorothy would try to find him so she could set them up. That's one way to scare away any potential men.

She'll just have to try to bump into him herself. Chloe nearly laughs at that idea. The mere notion she'd be able to saunter up to a stranger and ask them out is ridiculous. Her sister is the confident one. Steph would have no problem asking anyone out. Chloe preferred to hang in the side-lines and watch as every suitable single guy was snapped up while she tried to motivate herself to act. And she's also assuming the guy on the horse is single, which she very much doubts.

She looks back up the beach, but the horse and rider are a dot in the distance.

Tate opens his eyes and stares up at the dark figure looming over him. He curls into a ball as the blows come, hard and fast, bruising his skin and breaking his bones. He pleads for the man to stop, but he doesn't. The more he begs, the harder the man hits him. Tate turns his head and sees the woman crying in the corner, screaming at the man.

The man grabs his shoulders and starts shaking him. Tate buries his head under his arms and begs the man to let him go.

'Relax, Tate. It's me. It's me.'

The bedside light turns on and Tate scrambles up the bed, slamming his back against the headboard. He wipes his sweat-soaked hair off his forehead and takes a few deep shaky breaths. His dad is sitting on the edge of the bed looking seriously worried. 'You okay? You were shouting in your sleep.'

'I'm good. Thanks. Just a bad dream. You go back to bed.'

'What was the nightmare about?'

'I can't remember.'

His dad quietly looks at him and Tate has no doubt he doesn't believe him for one second. 'You fancy watching some TV for a bit?'

'I'm grand. You go back to bed.'

'Tate-'

'I said I'm grand!' He curses himself and takes a few breaths to calm down. 'I'm sorry. I'm just tired.' His father nods then gets to his feet and closes the door behind him.

Tate climbs out of bed and goes into the en-suite. He splashes water on his face, trying to clear the remnants of the nightmare away with little effect. In frustration, he slams his hand against the sink.

'Fuck!'

Four months and the nightmares are getting more vivid by the day. Who's he kidding? It's not a nightmare. It's a memory coming back to him. Something from his past that he had locked deep in the back of his mind. Now it's been set free, he can't shake it. Can't shake the feelings it brings back. Can't get rid of the helplessness, the absolute terror, the crippling guilt that the woman is dead because of him.

He'd pushed too far. He'd wound up the man who was maybe his father, maybe not. He doesn't know for sure. What he does know is that she was trying to protect Tate from him and now she's dead.

Tate makes the mistake of glancing down at his hands and sees her blood smeared all over them. He closes his eyes and takes a slow, deep breath before looking down again. The blood is gone.

He pushes off the sink and shuffles back into the bedroom. There's no way he's going to risk sleeping again tonight so instead he slumps back on the bed and turns on the TV. The choice is limited at four in the morning, so he flicks through looking for anything half decent to take his mind off the dream.

Instead he finds a music channel playing one of their songs. He'd usually change the channel, but not today. Nothing like reminding himself what he's lost to cheer himself up. Seems he's in luck today. It's a whole hour of their songs. The next song comes on but he can't remember the words. He doubts he'd remember the chords either.

Fuck this. Staring at the TV until morning isn't going to improve his mood. After throwing on an old pair of jeans and hoody, he creeps outside, wincing as every footstep seems to find a creaking floorboard in the old house.

Once he makes it outside without waking everyone, he locks the door behind him, and breathes in the cool morning air. He loves this place. Not just his parents' house, but this stretch of coastline. He'd grown up here and, no matter how long or short his breaks from work were, he made it his business to come back here every single time.

There was something about the rugged, unspoilt beauty of the place that calmed him. His life was... had, been crazy. When he was working, he could be going for twenty-two hours straight for days at a time. His schedule was gruelling, but he would never complain. He loved what he did but needed a break from time to time. Needed to be with his family and not worry about his celebrity status. Here he's just Tate. Now he's not so sure who he is anymore.

Tate's mood lifts when he nears the stables around the back of the hay shed. His black Irish Draft, Jove sticks his head over the door and snorts loudly at him. He rests his forehead against the horse's head and rubs the side of his face.

'Morning, buddy. Fancy blowing off some steam?' He saddles his horse and leads him out of the stable and across the yard towards the welcoming sound of the waves crashing on the beach.

He waits until he's out the small gate to the path that leads to the beach before he climbs up and adjusts the stirrups. Since his career took off, he hadn't had as much time for things like this. His grandfather got the orphaned foal from a friend years ago and Tate had instantly clicked with the animal. Two lost souls who had been given a second chance.

Gran and Pops had always joked they were made for each other. Something his mother didn't quite agree with. She thought the Draft was far too big for Tate, but then Tate didn't stop growing for quite a bit. When he finally stopped he was a shade over six-foot-three, and more than a match for the impressive horse.

He guides Jove along the path and down to the vast beach. The smell of salt and seaweed instantly soothes him. Jove knows exactly where he's going so Tate sits back and tries to turn his brain off. The gentle waves lap around Jove's legs as he wades into the sea, stopping just as the water hits Tate's boots. He couldn't care less if he's getting wet. Being on Jove like this with no one else around is the only thing that calms him. Who needs expensive therapists when you've got a horse and a beach?

Jove gets a little impatient, so he guides him nearer to the shore, turns him towards the far headland and adjusts his grip on the reins.

'Time to blow away the cobwebs. Ready buddy?'

Jove stamps his feet, desperate to stretch his legs. He taps Jove's side and he picks up pace, faster and faster until the crashing of hooves in the sea drowns out all the screaming in his head.

Chloe sits in the grass with her notebook on her lap, watching the man on his horse. He had more than piqued her interest when she saw him from her gran's garden high on the cliff, but from the same level it's a whole other story.

She'd visited the beach around six am for the last three days and for each of those days he'd made an appearance. So much for sketching the wildlife. Since the minute he appeared, nothing else around her had been able to hold her attention as much as he does. She's still working on the same drawing she'd started when she arrived.

Chloe ducks down in the grass careful not to be seen. It looks like he beat her down here today. He's already been for a swim and is walking at the water's edge, followed by the enormous black horse. Not much of a horse expert, Chloe had been amazed how the horse followed the man along the beach like an overgrown dog. The man stopped, so did the horse. He walked and the horse fell into step beside him.

He comes out from behind the horse and faces the animal. Chloe smiles as he rests his forehead against the horse's head and talks to it. Something about him is familiar but she can't figure out what. She seriously doubts they've met before. There's little chance she would forget an event like that.

Whoever he is, he's breaking her heart. She's seen him kick at the sand, watched as he rocked himself, his hands buried in his hair. Something is tearing him apart. Something happened or is happening that he can't deal with. Something he can't get through.

She feels terrible spying on him, but she doesn't want to leave him alone. He's suffering. She'd never forgive herself if something happened to him when he was alone down here.

He mounts the horse and it wades into the sea until the water is half way up the man's legs. As the horse pushes through the sea, the man reaches over and runs his hand through the water. Chloe can't take her eyes off him. Her heart is doing a crazy dance in her chest at the sight. She can't think why. It's just a gorgeous guy in the sea on his horse. Nothing to get excited about.

A slightly larger wave hits, soaking him, but all he does is laugh and brush his wet hair off his face. Nothing at all sexy about the image in the slightest. Just like there was nothing sexy about him emerging from the sea, waves crashing around him, the water droplets clinging to his toned chest and stomach that first day she saw him. Nope, not sexy at all.

All too soon, he guides the horse to the edge and gallops back down the beach and around the corner. 'See you tomorrow.'

She gathers her pencils, stuffing them into her rucksack and walks back along the beach and down the path to where she parked the truck. She stops by her gran's battered pickup and rummages in the bottom of her bag for the keys. As usual, they prove to be illusive, hiding among the pencils and pieces of paper.

'Damn it.'

Chloe freezes when she hears a loud snort behind her. She grimaces and slowly looks over her shoulder. The black horse is standing on the path opposite the one she came from. The man is on its back and he's even more breath-taking close up. A lot taller than she initially thought too. His dark blue eyes are serious as he looks down at her from the back of his equally large horse.

Instead of staring into his eyes, or at his face, or his broad chest, she looks down at his legs. His jeans are wet and covered in sand as are his boots. She can feel his dark eyes boring into her as she dumbly stares at his legs. She has to say something before this goes from just plain awkward to seriously awkward.

'Hi.' She looks up at his face but instead of responding he continues to silently look at her. 'Sorry. I'm just looking for my keys.'

'They're on the ground at your feet.'

His deep husky voice is a perfect match for him, but does nothing to steady her school girl nerves. 'Thanks.' Chloe picks her keys off the ground and shakes the dirt off. 'I know this beach is private, but it's stunning. The beach I mean. Anyway, I am sorry for trespassing, but

I couldn't resist the scenery.' She feels her cheeks burning. 'The scenery around here it's pretty special. Is it yours? I mean, is the beach yours?'

He frowns and slowly shakes his head. 'No.'

Chloe blows out a breath. 'Phew. So we're both trespassing. That's a relief. I won't tell if you don't.' Oh dear god would you please shut up. She hears the words pouring out of her mouth but doesn't appear to have any control over the embarrassing uncontrollable babbling.

'I've got permission from the owners.'

She nods. 'Ah. Right. Well that's different. Can you please forget you saw me? I won't come back. I promise.'

'You're not local.'

'No. I'm here for a few months. My grandmother lives a few miles up the road. I presume you're from around here. Unless you have a horse trailer hidden somewhere.'

He pauses and his frown deepens. 'Yeah. I'm from around here.'

'It's a beautiful area. The wildlife is spectacular.' She pats her rucksack. 'I draw in my spare time. Well, I try to.'

He nods but doesn't say anything. Instead of listening to common sense. She lets her mouth take control. 'I mainly like to draw landscapes and wildlife, hence coming down here.'

'Right.'

'Great. Okay, so I better go before the actual owner finds me here.'

He nods again and guides the horse away, up the path and around the corner. She waits until he's gone before she closes her eyes and bumps her head against the car window.

'What the hell was all that?' Maybe if she'd been prepared she could have come out with something a little more intellectual than mentioning the fact she's trespassing then rambling on like a nervous teenager. Great way to leave an impression for all the wrong reasons.

She pulls open the door and climbs inside. Probably best she avoids this place for a few days. Maybe given enough time he might just forget the entire conversation. Not that it could really be called a conversation. More like an embarrassing interaction.

Still cursing herself, Chloe turns the key but the engine whines and dies. She glares at the centre of the steering wheel and tries again. Same whine then nothing. She slams her hand against the wheel, jumping when the horn blares out.

'Oh come on!' She tries again and again, cursing the vehicle and anything else she can think off.

Finally giving up, she rests her head against the steering wheel and closes her eyes. She screams as a knock sounds on the window. Chloe frowns at the figure beside the car but her brain takes a ridiculously long time to make the connection. The man tilts his head down to look in the window as his horse watches from just behind him.

She rolls down the window and smiles apologetically. 'Sorry. I hope I didn't startle your horse.'

'He's fine. You okay?'

'Yeah. Well, no actually. The damn thing won't start.'

'Open the bonnet.'

She bends down and locates the lever, watching out the window as he disappears under the front of the pickup. 'Is it serious?'

The man grunts from under the bonnet. 'Try it again.' The same irritating whine then silence. 'Just the battery. It'll need a jump.' He slams the bonnet closed and wipes his hands on his jeans. 'You got someone you can call?'

Chloe checks her watch and makes a face. 'It's seven in the morning. I'll ring a garage later and get it sorted.'

He nods and scratches his jaw. 'You live nearby?'

Chloe points up the track. 'Top of the hill. Cove View Cottage.'

He leans against the load bed and crosses his arms as he scrutinises her. Chloe can feel her cheeks burn as he looks over at her, but she can't turn away. His eyes are the most incredible shade of dark blue she's seen. And it not like she's being rude by staring. He's doing a pretty good job of that himself.

'So you must be Dorothy's granddaughter.'

Chloe nods, releasing the breath she was holding when he finally looks away from her to his horse. He whistles and the horse stops sniffing whatever had caught its attention and walks back over to him.

'Yeah. You know my gran?'

'Everyone around here does. She mentioned you'd be coming to stay for a bit.'

'I'm Chloe. Nice to meet you.' She smiles awkwardly as he frowns again but doesn't offer his name. 'Do you have a name?'

'You want to know my name?'

'Well, only if you want to tell me.'

He mulls over that for longer than necessary. It's just his name. It's not like she's asking for his phone number. Not that she wouldn't mind if he gave it to her. After her disastrous initial meeting, the odds of getting his number aren't worth mentioning.

Chloe smiles and points over her shoulder to the track back to the road. 'Well, I better get back. Thanks for your help.'

'Tate.'

'I'm sorry?'

'My name is Tate.'

'Oh. Right. That's a lovely name.'

His frown deepens. 'What?'

Chloe grimaces. That last sentence was absolutely meant to stay in her head. 'Nothing. I better let you go. Thanks for your help, Tate.'

Tate pulls himself back on the horse, then shakes his head and turns around to face her again. 'You better let me take you home. It looks like it's about to lash.' As if waiting for him to utter the words, the heaven's open, quickly soaking into her sweatshirt. 'Can you ride?'

'Well, I sat on a horse once when I was a kid. I really don't think you'd classify that as riding.' She looks up at his horse and isn't so sure she even wants to attempt trying to climb up on its back.

He points to the back of the pickup. 'Get into the load bed.' She climbs up and Tate brings the horse closer to the truck then holds out his hand. Chloe hesitates for a second then places her hand in his.

'Stand on the back of my leg and I'll pull you up'. He bends his leg back and Chloe climbs up while he helps by lifting her. She's suitably impressed and unbelievably relieved when she gets her leg over the horse's wide back without flying off the other side or landing against Tate.

'Put your arms around my waist and don't let go.'

Tate looks down at Chloe's small hands resting against his stomach. This day is certainly heading in a different direction than the way it started. He wanted a few hours to himself before going back to the house and putting on a performance for his parents for the rest of the day. Bumping into an attractive trespasser wasn't on his to-do-list.

The land that runs the length of the beach belongs to his parents. He'd bought it for them when he paid off the house a few years ago.

They have no issue with people using the beach whenever they want, but for some reason finding her there had completely thrown him. He's used to occasionally meeting locals walking their dogs but no one like her before.

The rain picks up, soaking through his navy hoodie, but he doesn't care. Chloe presses tighter to his back as Jove steps down onto the sand.

'What's his name?' Chloe asks.

'Who?'

'The horse.'

He glances over his shoulder at her. 'Jove.'

'Roman God of the sky and thunder. You like mythology?'

'I was really into it when I was a kid. The name just seemed to suit him. You said you're not local. Where are you from?'

'I'm actually from the area years ago but have been moving all over the country my whole life. I spent the last year in Alaska. My uncle got a crazy idea to live off-grid in the wilderness a few years ago. He had a nasty fall and refused to stay in hospital while he recovered. I decided what the hell. I had nothing else planned, so I moved in with him for a few months. I ended up staying just short of a year.

'I came back to Wicklow to spend some time with my gran before I settle into my new career in a few months. She's visiting my aunt so I've got the place to myself for a bit. Absolute bliss. I can't tell you how amazing it was to have a shower with hot running water I didn't have to pull from a well and heat over the stove. And don't get me started on the toilet situation.' It feels like she hits her head against his back. 'Sorry TMI.'

He smiles as he tries to keep Jove to a walk. He's used to going a little faster on this stretch of the beach. 'Already forgotten. Did you like it? Alaska, not the toilet situation.'

'I thought you said you'd forgotten?'

'I will in a few minutes. I promise.'

'I'd appreciate that. Alaska was amazing. Don't get me wrong, it's a hard life he's chosen, but so nice. I'm thinking of heading back next year for a few months. So Tate, what do you do?' She must notice his body tensing at her question. 'Sorry, it's none of my business.'

'No, it's grand. I guess I'm just used to everyone around here knowing everyone else's business.'

'You can safely assume I know nothing about anyone.'

'I'm a musician.'

'Wow! That's amazing. Are you any good?'

He brings Jove to a stop and looks over his shoulder. She honestly doesn't have a clue who he is. He examines her face but can't see anything off. In fact, everything is pretty damn perfect. Her green eyes narrow as she looks at him.

'Are you okay? What did I say?'

'Did you seriously just ask me that? The part about me being any good.'

Chloe shrugs. 'It's what people ask, isn't it? Then again, I guess it's a loaded question. It's not like you're going to say you're crap.'

He turns more in the saddle and rubs a hand over his jaw as he frowns at her.

'Why do you keep frowning at me like that?'

'Sorry. I guess I'm good at it... music not frowning.'

'I wouldn't be too hard on yourself. You're not too bad at frowning.'

Tate laughs and shakes his head as he nudges Jove forward again. He hasn't had a normal conversation like this in a long time. Lately it's been all about how he's feeling, or other deep and meaningful questions meant to get into his head so he could be fixed. This feels strange but in a good way.

Chloe adjusts her hands around his waist, holding onto him a little tighter. 'So do you make a living out of music?'

'Yeah. I make an okay living out of it.'

'Congratulations. It must be great to be paid for doing something you enjoy.'

'Yeah. I guess it is. You make a living from drawing?'

She snorts. 'Not even close. It's a hobby. I'm a teacher. Well, will be in August. Primary school. I couldn't take all those teenagers. Too much hassle.'

He brings Jove onto the steep single lane track leading to the road. If he could turn around and head back in the other direction he'd happily do it. He's not ready to say goodbye to Chloe yet. When they get to the gate of Dorothy's house, Tate brings Jove over to the low wall so Chloe can dismount easier.

'Thank you for bringing me home. I wouldn't have fancied that walk up the hill. It's a killer.'

'The garage opens at half-eight. They'll sort the car for you and drop it back to the house. They're good like that.'

'Thank you both.'

She rubs Jove's neck and he nuzzles against her. Not a bad sign when he likes someone. He's usually a little temperamental with new people. 'No problem. I'll leave you to it.'

'Em, do you want to come in?' Chloe asks. 'I mean you could have a cup of tea. Do you drink tea? I know some people don't. I just thought I'd ask.'

'Can't stand the stuff.' The automatic response pops out before he can stop it. He'll drink a gallon of fucking tea if he can talk to her a little longer.

'Oh, okay.'

'I'll have a coffee though.'

She smiles widely and nods. 'Great. What about Jove?'

'I've brought him here before. I'll tie him up on the patio.'

She unlocks the front door as Tate brings Jove around to the back. He ties him up and peers around Jove's neck into the kitchen window. He smiles when he sees Chloe frantically tidying away dishes off the table and stuffing them into the cupboard over the fridge. She takes the basin of dirty dishes out of the sink and desperately looks around the kitchen before settling on hiding it in the cupboard under the sink. After brushing the stray crumbs from the table, she fills the kettle and examines a handful of mugs, dismissing half a dozen before settling on two.

He'd heard so many stories about Chloe from Dorothy over the years but doesn't remember meeting her before. He's sure he'd remember that. She's so different to women he's dated recently. They'd been in the limelight like him. Always performing in front of the camera. Every hair in place. Make-up perfect. None of the relationships, if you could even call them that, lasted longer than a few weeks before he got bored and called it quits. There had been a lot of sex but not a lot of anything else.

He never got to see the 'real' them, just the 'on camera' version. It's nearly impossible to have anything remotely meaningful with someone like that. Then again, it's not like he let them see the real him either. No one he's dated has seen that side of him. The version of himself the public saw was the one they usually got.

The woman stuffing dirty dishes into the cupboard is as real as they come. Her long dark, curly hair is windswept. He's sure there's some grass sticking out of it but he doesn't want to risk embarrassing her by pointing it out. She didn't have any make-up on or if she did it was minimal, but she didn't need it. Her jeans and shirt were nothing special but put it all together and she got and held his attention in a way no one has for a long time. Maybe the fact she doesn't have a clue who he is was adding to the attraction.

Since he found fame, he'd lost a lot of his privacy. It was rare to meet someone around here who didn't know him. Most of the locals had known him since he was a kid. They didn't see him as a celebrity and that was part of the reason he loved it here so much - especially after his recent spectacular disaster.

When he'd come across Chloe, he assumed she'd recognise him. It wasn't him being a self-important prick. It just happened more often than not. When he realised she didn't have a clue who he was it completely threw him. For even a few minutes, speaking to someone who didn't know him, didn't know what he'd done, it was... freeing is the only word he can think of. They had a normal chat too, which was something he's missed the last few months.

He doesn't consider what he did lying. He told her his name but she didn't react. It's not like he was going to introduce himself and hand her a list of his albums and awards. She didn't know him and maybe, right now, that's a fucking god-send. It might just keep things uncomplicated, and that's exactly what he wants.

It's absolutely the wrong time to be thinking about introducing someone to his disastrous life. Bringing someone into his current situation would be unfair. It would absolutely be a really bad decision to even think about seeing her again.

He smiles as she tries to straighten her hair in the reflection on the microwave door, completely missing the grass poking from the top.

Then again, he's not exactly renowned for always making the right decision. Recent events have proved that if nothing else.

Chloe looks around as Tate appears at the back door. The room seems to shrink when he steps inside. It wasn't built with someone his height in mind. He washes his hands in the sink and opens the fridge to grab the milk. Clearly he's been here quite a few times. Then again, knowing her gran, most of the town would have been up here at some stage. 'I've only got instant.'

Tate leans over her and reaches into the back of the top shelf. Whatever cologne he's wearing is seriously intoxicating. He steps away from her and hands her a packet of real coffee. 'She hides the good stuff. Don't worry, she lets me have a cup every now and again.'

'Milk and sugar?'

'Yes and one.'

Chloe prepares the drink and turns around to place the cups on the table. How she avoids pouring both drinks over her hands she has no idea. Tate has removed his sodden hoody and is sitting at the far end of the table. His black long-sleeved t-shirt is nothing spectacular. It's what's underneath, and clearly visible under the material, that causes the issues. What she felt through his sweatshirt while she was hanging on to him is just the tip of the iceberg. His arms and upper chest are pretty damn impressive. She places the coffee in front of him and sits at the far end of the table.

He wraps his hand around the mug and stares into the drink as she stares at him again. His soaking hair is hiding his eyes so she extends her staring longer than is polite. He's got multiple piercings up both ears along with quite a few tattoos up his neck, across his shoulder peeking out from under his t-shirt and on the back of the hand gripping his cup. There's a narrow silver chain around his neck, again hidden under the top she has a building desire to remove. The hand gripping the cup has two thick silver rings - one on his thumb and one on his middle finger. No wedding band. As if that matters. They're hardly on a date. More's the pity.

Up close she would absolutely peg him as a musician. She could easily see him on a stage playing a guitar. He has that look about him. A kind of rugged edge that calls to her which makes no sense. Yes, he's gorgeous, but she usually goes for uncomplicated and clean-cut. Tate is firmly in the dark and brooding category.

'What do you play?'

He blinks and looks up at her, like he was in a world of his own. 'Sorry?'

'You said you're a musician. What do you play?'

He brushes his hair back from his forehead then holds on to the cup again. 'Guitar mainly, but I can play the piano and violin too.'

'Wow. That's impressive.' The guitar was a given, but the other two take her by surprise. 'Don't take this the wrong way, but you don't look much like the violin type.'

He laughs at that.' Yeah, probably not. Reckon that's why my mate dared me to learn how to play it.'

'I'm taking it you won that bet?'

'Oh I won. He's still more than a little bitter about it.'

'Have you been playing for long?'

'As long as I can remember. I started guitar lessons when I was about ten I think. Piano was something I learnt in school and picked up again recently. The violin was a few years ago too. My family are like one of those clichéd Irish families you see on TV. Music is a big part of our gatherings.'

'So you have a big family?'

Tate nods. 'Well, big extended family. I've got one brother and one sister. Too many cousins to count. You?'

'Younger sister. She's living in London and works at some fancy law firm. She's PA to one of the partners but you'd swear she ran the place single handed. What do your brother and sister do?' She knows she's prying into his life, but she wants to keep him here as long as possible.

He takes a drink of his coffee before he answers. 'My older brother is a lawyer in Canada. He has his own firm.'

'How did he end up in Canada?'

'He went there with a few mates after college and fell in love with a girl and the country. He was only meant to be there for three months. He ended up getting a visa and moved there about a year later. He married Annabelle a few years later and they have two girls. My younger sister is working for a fashion designer in Dublin.'

'Wow. So does she try to style you?'

He snorts and just about manages to keep his coffee from spilling over the table. 'She tried numerous times but I think she's given up at this stage. I'm sticking to jeans and t-shirts. End of story. So, how long are you staying with Dorothy for?'

The question is entirely innocent but that doesn't stop the spark of excitement when she hears it. 'School doesn't start until late August so I'm free as a bird until then. I plan to look for an apartment nearer the school, but I can commute from here if need be. To be honest, I'm not in any hurry to leave the area. It has a lot going for it.' Did she seriously just say that? Hopefully he thinks she's talking about the scenery outside the window not the scenery inside. 'What type of music do you play? I'm guessing it's not classical.'

He laughs again and scratches his jaw. 'No. I guess the easiest description would be rock, but we mix it up a little.'

'Do you do covers or your own songs?'

'I write everything we play. I'm a bit of a control freak like that.'

'So you sing too?'

He nods. 'Like I said, bit of a control freak.'

'That's impressive. You'll have to let me know when you're performing next. I'd love to come and see you.'

He frowns briefly then smiles. Why does she get the feeling she just said something stupid, but has no idea what.

'Do you have your own place here?'

He shakes his head. 'I've been staying with my folks for a few weeks.' He pushes the chair back and gets to his feet. 'Thanks for the coffee. I better leave you to it.'

Before she can utter a word, he's out the door. A few seconds later, she hears the side gate open and Jove passes by the front window.

'Great to see you haven't lost your touch,' she mutters to herself as the sound of hooves fades away. She wanders into the hall and frowns at her reflection in the mirror. She looks a right state. She leans closer and curses under her breath. There's actually some grass in her hair. Well that's just perfect. Not only did she say something to scare him off but she also sat through the whole conversation with grass sticking out of her hair. If she sees him again it will be a bloody miracle.

Tate allows Jove to set the pace on the way back to his parents' house. He didn't want to leave Chloe, but he had no choice. As soon as she asked where he lived he had to get out of there. The next question was bound to be why he was back with his folks. It was only natural. He wasn't ready to open that can of worms with her. Maybe not ever.

He curses as his phone rings in his pocket. He pulls it out and checks the display. It's his dad. He's probably wondering where he is. He's been gone longer than usual. Tate shivers as the rain continues to soak into his clothes. In such a rush to get out of Dorothy's he'd left his hoody on the back of the chair.

That's not entirely a bad thing. Until he freaked out, he'd been enjoying Chloe's company. He'd like to see her again, but that means he'd have to tell her exactly who he is. She'd probably figure it out herself by then anyway. All she needs to do is mention him to her gran and the gaps will be filled in for her.

He guides Jove through the gate and grimaces when he sees his dad under the shelter outside the stable area. Looks like he's not entirely happy. Tate leads Jove into his stall and unbuckles the saddle.

'Everything okay?'

Tate rests the saddle over top of the door and glances at Rick. 'You timing me now? How long can I be gone for before you send out the search parties?'

'Don't bite my head off. We're bound to worry about you.'

'Oh give me a fucking break. What the hell am I going to do to myself on the beach with a horse. I took him for a longer run. Nothing to worry about.'

'Drop the attitude, Tate.' He looks at Tate's wet clothes and shakes his head. 'You go swimming again or is that just down to the rain?'

'I went for a swim.'

'In your clothes? You do realise they've invented these things called swimming trunks.'

'I didn't plan to go for a swim.'

'You should get changed before you catch a cold. I'll finish sorting Jove out for you.'

'For fuck's sake. I can manage!' He takes a deep breath and turns back to Jove. Tate secures the lightweight rug over Jove and shuts the stable door a little harder than necessary.

'Are you done or do you fancy going for a full-blown tantrum? You could always give the stable door a kick if you're looking for a big finish.'

Tate turns and faces his father. The two men stare each other down until Tate finally breaks. He laughs and scrubs his hand through his wet hair. 'I'm sorry.'

'I get it, okay. I get you're frustrated and the last thing you want is us looking over your shoulder but cut us a little slack. You scared the hell out of us, Tate. Don't get your nose out of joint when we show a little concern.'

'I know and I'm really not trying to be ungrateful, but... I feel like none of us are comfortable with me being here. You're all walking on eggshells around me and I'm—'

'Thirty-six and back living with your parents,' his dad interrupts. 'Like I said, I get it. All this being fussed over isn't doing much for your image.'

'Oh you mean the failed rock star, junkie, alcoholic image. Think I could do with losing that one.'

Rick leans against the stable door and looks out at the beach beyond the hedge. 'Sounds like it's time you give them something new to talk about. Gregg mentioned you want to record the new album you were working on before you went on tour.'

Tate nods but feels less enthusiastic about that than he does about staying with his parents for another few weeks. 'Yeah. I'm thinking about it.'

'Well, maybe it's time you stop thinking and actually pick up your guitar.' He nudges him in the side and nods towards the house. 'C'mon. I'll make you something to eat while you get changed. If you get a cold your mother will wrap you in a blanket on the couch and force-feed you chicken soup for the next week.'

Tate follows him into the house, kicking off his wet boots at the door. Rick opens the fridge and pulls out a packet of bacon. 'Bacon butty?'

Tate shakes his head. 'I'm not really hungry.'

His dad peers at him around the side of the fridge. 'Try again.'

He's going to have to force it down whether he wants it or not. 'Sounds great. Thanks.'

'Better. You've got ten minutes.'

He leaves his dad to the breakfast and shuts the door to his room. He hurries through the bedroom conscious that his jeans are leaving a trail of wet sand on the carpet. After turning on the shower, he peels off his wet clothes and dumps them in the hamper in the corner of the bathroom. He steps into the shower, the steaming water washing the salt and sand off his skin. His arm stings as the jets beat against the open scratches, but he ignores the pain.

He knows his dad is right about getting back to work. It's what he loves and he's damn good at it. It's been nearly five months since he picked up a guitar and he desperately misses it. He may have told Gregg he wants to get back in the studio but he's not so sure he's ready. He can't even face their manager, Ellen.

The shame of what he did is eating him up. He's not sure if it's the fact he accidentally overdosed or that it's gone public that's giving him the most issues. It's probably a bit of both.

Each day things were supposed to get better for him. He knew he wouldn't get over what he did quickly, but this is getting fucking ridiculous. He's terrified of the memories that have suddenly come to life and won't leave him, even when he's awake. Terrified of someone finding out how messed up he really is. Terrified he'll never pick up a guitar again. Never sing again. Never perform again. He's terrified this is his life now.

He scratches his arm again and winces as the water hits the raw scratch marks. The scratching is nearly worse than the addiction was.

It's becoming a habit he can't shake, especially when he's lost in thought.

He's been told there's nothing the doctors can do about the scratching. The itch isn't actually there. It's in his head not on his skin. His shrink was trying to help him with it, but Tate switches off more and more during the sessions. He knows he's not doing himself any favours, but he can't talk about it. He'd prefer just to forget about it. Apparently that's not the way it works, or so his doctor keeps telling him.

He didn't realise he'd zoned out until his dad shouts through the closed door, calling him for breakfast. Tate grabs a clean pair of jeans and long-sleeved t-shirt from his cupboard and makes sure the scratch marks are covered before he goes back into the main house. His mum is at the table with Rick, and, as usual, the conversation stops when he steps into the room.

'How was your ride?' his mum asks as he pours himself a cup of coffee.

'Good.'

'You've got your appointment at ten. You haven't forgotten have you?'

He slams the cup onto the counter with more force than he intended. Of course he'd forgotten. 'Right.'

The silence continues behind him. Slamming the cup down would have caused a few raised eyebrows and knowing looks. 'I have a few things to do in town so I'll drive you.'

He takes a calming breath before he turns to look at his mother. 'It's fine, Mum. I'll drive myself.'

'Your car and bike are at your house. It's really no trouble. I'll drive you.'

'Fine. Can you drop me at my place instead? I'll pick up my car. I'd prefer to have it here anyway.'

And there's the look again. His father takes the lead in the negotiation. 'Okay, how about you take my car and Becca can drop me at your place and I'll pick up your car for you. It'll be here for you when you get back later.'

Guilt and shame are bastards to live with. Any other time, he'd have laughed at them and done his own thing. Scrap that. Any other time, there wouldn't be an issue with him going back to his own fucking house to get his car. But after what happened, they don't want him to go back there. Or they don't want him alone there. Or maybe they don't want him to have a car he can escape in. Whatever the reason, he's all out of fight. Admitting defeat, he nods and slumps down in the chair.

'You should still have a spare set of keys to the truck in the drawer in the hall.'

His breakfast arrives and he forces it down, not tasting any of it. In the background, conversation continues between his mum and dad, with him giving a nod every now and again when the silence tells him they were expecting something from him.

'Whoa, fellow.' Tate brings Jove to a stop and looks over at the grass along the edge of the sand further up the beach. He smiles when he spots Chloe at the far end, sketchpad on her knee. Jove takes a step towards her but Tate holds him back. Is he really ready to make an ass of himself again? Then again, it's not like he has anything to lose. She probably already thinks he's a little odd. It can't get worse than that.

He leans over and rests his head against Jove's neck. 'If it looks like I'm about to say or do anything stupid I fully expect you to stop me.'

Jove snorts.

'Yeah. Cheers for that. C'mon then. Let's see if I can do this without making a complete eejit of myself... again.'

He brings Jove closer to Chloe and climbs off. He pulls the stirrups up and leaves Jove at the bottom of the grass bank as he climbs up the path to the top. He peers over Chloe's shoulder at the drawing she's working on.

'That's good.'

Chloe screeches and drops her pencil in the sand. She blows out a long breath when she sees Tate standing behind her.

'You scared the hell out of me.'

'Sorry.'

She looks around and makes a face. 'Guess you caught me again. I know I'm trespassing, but I just had to finish this drawing.'

'I'll put in a good word for you with the owners when I see them. Your drawing is really good.'

She looks back at the unfinished landscape and makes a face. 'It's taking me too long to get it right. I think I'm falling out of love with it.'

He crouches down beside her and points to the side of the drawing. 'You've that bit bang on. The way the waves are hitting the headland… it's damn perfect. Give it time. The rest will come.'

'Is that the inner artist speaking?'

He smirks a little. 'Guess so. Creating doesn't always come first go round. Got to give it time to work its way out.'

'You're probably right. Oh, you left your sweatshirt at the house. I've got it in my bag.'

'Thanks.' He pauses and looks down at the sand. 'Speaking of that, I'm sorry for leaving like I did. It was rude. It had nothing to do with you, I promise.'

'It's fine, Tate. Really.'

He glances across at her and smiles. 'It's really not. Dorothy will kill me if she hears I wasted a cup of her expensive coffee.'

Chloe laughs at that and brushes her hair behind her ear. 'I won't tell her. So, where's Jove today?' He whistles and Jove appears at the bottom of the hill. 'He's like an overgrown dog. You trust him not to run off on you?'

'He's not going to go far. Do you mind if I watch you for a bit?'

'Sure. I wouldn't expect anything exciting to happen. Well, unless

I decide to fling the whole sketchpad into the ocean.'

'Bit of an overreaction if you ask me.' He stretches his legs out in front of him and takes the pad from her hands. 'Forget about this for now. Just look out there. Don't think about drawing it. Take a deep breath and look at the view.'

She does as he suggests and spends a few minutes silently taking in their surroundings.

'Now close your eyes.'

When she does that he places the pad back on her knee and lies back on the sand to give her some privacy. 'Now open your eyes and draw.'

He rests his head on his hands and closes his eyes, peeking over at her after a few minutes. The pencil is rapidly moving across the paper. She pauses and chews on the tip of her pencil for a moment then continues drawing. Before she catches him staring, he closes his eyes. That only lasts a few seconds before he has to look at her again.

A long lock of hair has escaped her ponytail so she tucks it behind her ear then slips the pencil between her lips again. Fuck, if she keeps doing that he's going to be in serious trouble. His body is already telling him to make a move, but he's not even going there. The problem is his body isn't on board with that and if he doesn't get it under control he'll have to make a rapid exit before she notices.

He hasn't been with anyone for over three months. Not since whoever that woman was that Gregg saw him with at his house. He's disgusted to admit he doesn't even remember being with her. He woke up beside her in bed and all he does remember with any certainty is the relief when he saw a condom wrapper on the bedside table. Not that it makes the entire situation any better. It was one of the low points for him. And there are plenty to choose from.

There's no way he's ready or willing to add Chloe to that particular list. He's attracted to her and that's why he's not going to fall into his usual routine with her. For once, he'd actually like to get to know her more.

'How's this?'

He sits up and pulls one leg up to hide the growing bulge in his jeans. His dick has no intention of abiding by his new rules. 'You got it.'

Chloe looks back at the page and smiles widely. 'How did you do that? Get me to focus like that?'

'You were stopping yourself. I do the same sometimes. You just need to step away and see what you're trying to achieve. Then go back with a clear mind. I've written some bloody awful songs which turned out pretty good once I stepped away for a bit.'

'Thanks, Tate. That's really helped. Are you busy for the next while?'

'No, why?'

'Well I was wondering if you'd like to hang around. You can give me a nudge if I get stuck again. Only if you want to.'

'Yeah, I'll stick around for a bit.'

Her stunning smile sends a shiver through his body and undoes all his efforts to calm his dick down. Luckily she turns back to her work leaving him to discretely adjust himself without her noticing.

Normally Chloe would keep trying to prise conversation out, but she's on a roll with her drawing and Tate seems content enough to just be here with her. At least if he's keeping her company he's not down on the beach, alone, falling apart. Tate stretches out again and lies back on the grass with his hands behind his head as she works on her drawing.

What he had said to her had done wonders for her drawing. She's done more on it in the last twenty minutes than she has for the last few weeks. It's probably not doing any harm having him lying beside her, although if she keeps stealing sneaky looks at him, she won't get much more done.

His irritatingly addictive face is on full view today thanks to the baseball cap keeping his hair out of the way. It's hard to place an age on him but Chloe thinks he's a little older than her, perhaps mid-thirties. She doesn't know what it is about him that stops her asking questions she'd usually ask. After the way he left the house yesterday, she realised she has to take things slower with him. Whatever happened to cause him to suffer so much on those few times she saw him, it's still there, still inside him. The last thing she wants to do is potentially make it worse.

She's also being a little selfish. She likes him. Really likes him. He has to be one of the most confusing people she's ever met. The way he looks and his choice of career matched. She's a little embarrassed to admit she thought that was all there was to him. But then he mentioned the violin and piano which completely threw her.

The more she spoke to him, the more her initial impressions of him altered. The way he talked her through her block just now only added to her confusion... and her attraction. She barely knows him but she feels completely comfortable around him. If he's content to keep her company, she's going to take it.

About twenty minutes later she glances across at him and knows something is wrong. She was so wrapped up in her drawing she hadn't noticed he fell asleep at some stage. But now, it looks like he's having a nightmare. His brows are scrunched and his eyes are squeezed shut. He groans in his sleep and the whimper of pain hits her like a blow to the gut.

Chloe dumps her notepad on the ground and leans over him, gently shaking his shoulder.

'Tate? Tate, wake up.'

He curls onto his side. 'Please, don't...'

Chloe's pulls her hand away. 'Tate!' He buries his head under his arms. 'Tate? Wake up!' She shakes him gently again and he suddenly opens his eyes. 'It's me. It's Chloe. I'm sorry if I startled you. You fell asleep.'

He pushes away from her and scrubs his hands over his face. 'Shit. Sorry.'

'It's fine, really. Are you okay?'

He stands up and brushes sand off his jeans. 'Yeah. Sorry. I gotta—'

'Please don't go,' she says before he can disappear. 'We don't have to mention it again. Just stay. Help me with this blasted drawing. Please.'

He whistles and Jove joins him on the grass. 'I better go. Good luck with the drawing.'

He pulls himself into the saddle and takes off down the beach. Chloe stares after him and resists the urge to scream. Either she's losing her touch, which was never incredibly effective to begin with, or Tate is dealing with something that's so far beyond her.

'Blood hell, mate. You look shite.'

Tate glares over at Gregg as he leads Jove into the stable. 'Cheers. Appreciate that.'

'You okay?'

Tate ignores Gregg while he sorts out Jove then leans against the closed stable door. 'I dozed off on the beach.'

'Okay. We've all done that at some stage. What's the problem?'

'I wasn't...'

'You weren't what?'

'There was someone else there, with me, okay. I fell asleep, which was bad enough, then I had a nightmare.'

'Nightmare about what?'

Getting my mum killed. 'Don't remember. I feel like such a fucking idiot, Gregg.'

'I'm presuming this was a female someone.'

'Why'd you say that?'

'Lucky guess. Who is she?'

'Dorothy's granddaughter, Chloe. She's staying for a few months. Her car broke down yesterday and I brought her home. Then I met her again on the beach, but... well... I fucked that up by falling asleep. I mean, who the fuck does that?' He bangs his fist against the door, startling Jove.

'Okay, first, relax. Next, you're coming with me. We're getting out of here for a bit.'

'I'm not in the mood.'

'You're never in the mood, but I'm done listening. Now, get your fucking arse in the car or I'll do my best to drag you there. I know, good luck to me, but I'm willing to give it a damn good try.'

Tate attempts to glare his friend into backing off but it doesn't do any good. It never does. 'Fine.'

He follows Gregg around the front of the house and over to his dark blue Defender. Gregg disappears into the house for a minute. Probably telling Tate's parents he's taking him out for a bit.

Gregg reappears and shakes a set of keys in his hand as he skips over to Tate's truck. 'No fucking way, Gregg. Get the hell away from my truck.'

Gregg unlocks the Ranger and jumps in before Tate can get to the driver's side. Tate tries to open the door but Gregg locks it and starts the engine. He smiles out the window and points to his ear, pretending he can't hear anything.

Tate flicks him the bird then walks around the front of the truck. He's seriously going to regret putting Gregg on the insurance. The passenger door unlocks and he climbs in. 'One fucking scratch and I will kill you. You get that, right?'

Gregg grins. 'Have no fear my friend. I'll treat her like she's mine.'

As they roar out of the driveway, Tate can't help but look at the battered blue Defender. 'Is that a new dent on the side?'

Gregg waves his hand. 'I will swear until the day I die that the tree moved.'

He lets the silence remain while they leave the coast and head to the mountains. After a few minutes, Gregg gets the hang of the gears and the truck stops screaming in protest.

Tate looks out the window, not really seeing the scenery as it flies by. That's twice he's messed up with Chloe. He doubts he'll get another chance. Running hot and cold is a fucking understatement. He's acting like he's crazy. Unpredictable. Messed up. Clearly he's far from ready to have anyone in his life. Hell, he may never be ready again. His mobile rings and he pulls it out to check the screen, before silencing it and stuffing it back in his jeans.

'Problem?'

'Keep your eyes on the road. It was Ellen. She's been trying to get a hold of me for a few days.'

'Right, so why are you ignoring her? She's our manager, Tate. It's her job to talk to you.'

'I'm not ready to talk to her.'

'Oh so you're going to keep ignoring her and hope she gives up. Great plan. Problem is, she's kind of important if you want to do your fucking job. And my job too. Just saying.'

'I know that. I just don't know what to say to her.'

'How about you start with hi. She's your friend too. Jesus, Tate, she's one of the good ones, you know that right? What if she's got some amazing gig lined up?'

Tate knows exactly where this is going. He's well aware the longer he takes to get his shit sorted the longer the guys are out of work. They can't exactly do their jobs if he wasn't doing his. Without a lead singer they're not much of a band. It's an extra pressure that's always weighing on him.

He scratches his arm. The fucking thing is driving him crazy. How the hell can he think about performing when he can't even stop scratching?

'You picked up your guitar yet?'

Tate sighs and looks out the window.

'Yeah, thought not. How about the bike?'

'How about you mind your own damn business and concentrate on not crashing my truck?'

Gregg glares across at him but keeps any further questions to himself until he pulls into the car park overlooking Lough Tay in the Wicklow Mountains. He kills the engine and turns to face Tate. 'See. No scratches.' He runs his hand over the steering wheel. 'I like this.'

'Yeah, so do I. Get out.'

'Ah nuts. Seriously?'

'Seriously.'

Gregg curses as he climbs out of the truck, then glares at Tate as he passes him on the way to the passenger side. He slumps back in the passenger seat and slams the door. 'Spoil sport.' He pulls a bag out of his pocket and offers it to Tate. 'Gummy bear?'

Tate grabs a handful and they eat in silence for a few minutes until Gregg speaks.

'You know, I've been thinking.'

'What have I told you about doing that?'

'Ha ha. So glad to know your sense of humour comes back when taking the piss out of me.'

Tate smirks at him as he chews on a gummy bear. 'I've got to have some fun.'

Gregg flicks him the bird then sits back in the seat again. 'What I was trying to say is that I realised something about you this morning when I was in the shower.'

Tate looks sideways at him. 'You were thinking about me when you were in the shower?'

'Of course. I do a lot of thinking in the shower.'

'Is that right?' Tate leans back against the car door and frowns over at his friend. 'Am I the only one you think about in the shower?'

Gregg looks over at him and grimaces when Tate smirks. 'Oh God. Not like that, you ass. Yeah. Fine. Go on, laugh it up.'

'Sorry, Gregg. You walked into that one.'

'Fair enough.' Gregg chews on another sweet as Tate laughs. 'You know, I missed that.'

Tate opens the window, letting the fresh mountain air into the truck. 'Missed what?'

'You laughing. Felt like I got my old mate back again just now. Glad to know he's still in there under all the glaring and brooding.' Gregg smiles to soften his words.

He knows Gregg wasn't having a go, but his words still hit home. He has been a moody, awkward, irritable fucker lately. It's not something he's consciously doing. Since he woke up in hospital, going on the defensive and snapping at people has been his default setting. 'I know. I'm sorry. I just...' he sighs and scrubs a hand over his face. 'I don't feel like me anymore. That doesn't make sense.'

'Of course it makes sense, you eejit. You're all over the place and that's what I'm saying. For as long as I can remember— Okay, for the last few years at least, there's been two things you've been attached to - your guitar and your bike. They're as much a part of you as your arm is. Now, correct me if I'm wrong, but I've not seen you in the company of either since you got out of rehab. What the fuck are you waiting for?'

'You bring me up here to give me a lecture?'

'You going to answer the question or keep dodging. What are you waiting for?'

'Nothing.'

'Right, so do something about it. You told me you want to get back

74

to performing but you haven't done a damn thing about it. You realise in order to perform you need to touch a guitar, right? That's kind of your thing.'

'Yes, Gregg. I know that, but it's not that easy. You really think anyone will want to come and see me now?'

'You won't know unless you speak to Ellen.' Gregg searches in the bag for another sweet and pops it into his mouth. 'You've got to stop doing this to yourself, mate.'

'Doing what?'

'Whatever the hell you're doing to yourself. You seem intent on beating yourself up. You got to get out of the pile of crap you're buried under.'

Tate laughs harshly. 'Right. Grand. Will do.' Tate yelps when Gregg punches him in the arm. 'What the fuck was that for?'

'You're being a dick again. I know you think you messed up and it's the end of the world as you know it. But it's not. You need to get your life back. I'm not just talking about singing. I'm talking about bringing you out up here.' He taps the side of his head. 'You're free to get back to your life.'

'What life?'

'And that there is exactly what I'm talking about. You've given up. Thrown the towel in before you've even tried to sort things out. Let us help you. Your family, your friends - we're all here for you. Stop pushing us away.'

He scratches at his arm again, stopping when Gregg slaps him on the chest. 'Hit me again and I'm seriously going to flatten you.'

'Stop scratching your fucking arm. Let's see the damage.'

'Leave it.'

'Pull up your sleeve, Tate. C'mon.'

He gives in just because he doesn't have the energy left to argue. He pulls off his hoody and shoves his t-shirt sleeve up. Gregg whistles slowly. 'You've made a right pig's ear of that, haven't you?'

Tate looks down at the inside of his left arm. Raw scratch marks spread out a few inches above and below his elbow. He's even managed to tear at the griffin tattoo on his left arm, adding a deep gouge to its back leg.

Gregg leans closer to get a better look. 'You got some skin thing I don't want to know about?'

'What? No, it's in my head. I don't even know I'm doing it half the time.'

'You need to leave it alone or it'll never heal.'

'Oh well, cheers for those words of wisdom. Where would I be without you?' Tate slumps back in the seat and looks at the patch of red, raw skin. If he keeps this up he'll need to get some of his tattoos redone.

'So you want to tell me about this lady you dozed off on?'

'Near not on. There's nothing much to tell. I was out on Jove and bumped into her on the way home. Her car was dead so I brought her back to Dorothy's and she made me a coffee. We got to chatting and she asked where I was living so I cleared out before she could ask why I was back living with my parents. I saw her on the beach again today and thought I'd give being normal another shot.'

'Losing battle, mate.'

'Yeah, thanks. We talked for a bit then she got back to her drawing. I laid down on the grass beside her then normal went to shit. I haven't been sleeping well. I guess I dozed off and had a nightmare.' He moves to scratch his arm but stops himself in time and goes for his jaw instead. 'I ran like a fucking idiot. I didn't even try to explain or apologise. Just jumped on Jove and fucked off.'

'Yeah. That's monumentally embarrassing. So, is she cute?'

He nods. 'More than just cute. She's gorgeous, Gregg.'

'Are you attracted to her or do you just fancy having your way with her and moving on like usual?'

Tate bites back his harsh reply. A few months ago that's probably what he would have done. 'I'm attracted to her, Gregg.'

'Interesting. Are you hoping to move from sleeping near her to sleeping with her at some stage? Unless you've already slept with her of course.'

'That supposed to be funny?'

Gregg grins. 'I thought it was. So?'

'No I haven't sept with her. I've only met her twice on the beach.'

'And? Never stopped you before.'

Tate looks across at Gregg. 'You're really not helping.'

'Sorry, I'm just surprised to hear you talk like this. Don't get me wrong, that's absolutely not a criticism. Nice to know your dick doesn't fully control you.'

'Have you been stockpiling these comments to use when I need a motivational speech or are you just on a roll today?'

'A little of both. I'm trying to lighten the mood.'

'Yeah, well thanks. I feel so much better. It doesn't matter anyway. I'm not in the right place for this. I should leave her alone and... I don't know...'

'Wallow in self-pity for the rest of your life?'

'You think that's what I'm doing?'

Gregg shrugs. 'A little. Not saying I blame you, but you're letting what happened get to you. Hear me out before you do that eye roll thing of yours. You don't wallow. Never have. You wouldn't be an international fucking superstar if you did. You get knocked back, pick yourself up and plough on regardless. Always have. Face it like you would any other knock you've had. Fight it. You're letting it win and it's killing me.'

Tate slowly looks across at his friend and frowns at the devastation on his face. Gregg didn't do serious. Through the months of slow recovery, Gregg kept every situation light-hearted. It was Gregg's positivity that helped drag him out of his depression. 'Gregg, I don't want—'

'I'm not blaming you for how I feel so don't even go there. It just gets to me when you're letting that dick destroy your life.'

'What do you suggest?' Gregg doesn't reply so Tate looks up and frowns at him. 'What's that look for?'

'Who was it?'

'What?'

'I said it gets to me when you let that dick destroy your life. You didn't correct me. What you should have said is 'Who are you talking about, Gregg?' but you didn't. So, who pushed you too far?'

Fuck. That wasn't supposed to happen. 'I've told you I don't want to talk about it.'

'And I've told you that you will. Who pushed you?'

Tate starts the engine, but Gregg leans over and pulls the key out. 'No. You're not running from this.'

'Fuck you.' Not the best response but it's all he's got. Needing to get away from the look Gregg is throwing at him, he climbs out of the truck and slams the door. He kicks at a rock that's looking at him the wrong way, sending it flying over the edge of the track and down the side of the valley.

Gregg isn't going to let this go now. He's well and truly screwed himself. He's too tired to keep things straight in his head. Tate squeezes his eyes shut and she's there again. Staring accusingly back as him. Blaming him for her death. He beats his fist against his forehead hoping to force the images from his head.

Gravel crunches behind him as Gregg walks over.

'Why do I get the feeling you were imagining my head in place of that rock you just sent over the edge?' He looks down as Gregg crouches in front of him and places another rock near his boot. He can't help but laugh when he sees a smiley face drawn on it in marker. 'Don't get me wrong, it was an impressive kick. Let's see how far you can get this one.'

He sends rock Gregg number two a good few feet further than its predecessor.

'Not bad. Now that you've kicked the shit out of me, fancy talking?'

Tate sits on the bench overlooking the lake trying to get his story straight in his head as Gregg sits down beside him. 'I got a letter when I was home at Christmas.'

'Love or not so much?'

'Not so much. It was about my childhood. You know before I was put in foster care. I don't remember anything before then. Well, I didn't until that fucking letter arrived. But all these memories came back over the next few days. I think I was hit as a child. A lot. I couldn't sleep because the nightmares kept coming. I got stuck in them. It was like the memories were on fucking replay. I was reliving everything that happened.'

He looks down at the lake and shrugs. 'Then another letter came. And another. Each one hinted at more shit that went on. My biological dad sounds like a prize asshole. Anyway, I tried so many different things to distract myself, but nothing worked. I couldn't stop thinking about it. I just wanted to... forget everything for a while.'

'And that's where Eddie comes in.'

He nods. 'This is going to sound unbelievably stupid, but I don't think it even registered with me that I was taking heroin. And I didn't get the first letter then go straight to that. Nothing else I tried had worked. Fuck, some of the stuff Eddie gave me made the dreams worse. When the letters kept coming I... I guess I didn't care what he was giving me. Once I tried it though I couldn't stop. Probably didn't help that there was a near constant supply.'

Gregg snorts loudly. 'Yeah, I'll bet. Eddie's good like that. All part of his excellent customer service.'

'Yeah. I don't know what I did while I was using. It's a blur of...' He looks down at the gravel between his boots. 'Well, stuff I'd like to forget.'

'Like that woman I saw you with. She seemed overly friendly.'

79

Tate grimaces and nods at the ground.

'Forgive my bluntness but you did get checked... you know... down there?'

Tate frowns at him then catches on. 'Oh Jesus, Gregg. Yes.'

'What? It was a perfectly reasonable question.'

'Cheers for the concern but that was all part of the series of humiliating tests I had to take. Anyway, I didn't plan to overdose. Not that anyone does, but I wasn't trying to kill myself. It was an accident. I mean that.'

'I believe you.'

Tate turns to look at Gregg. 'You do?'

'Of course. I knew that all along. About the accident part. Thanks for telling me though.'

'You were going to piss me off until I did.'

'Too right. So, what now?'

'What do you mean?'

'What are you going to about these letters?'

Tate shrugs. 'Fuck all I can do. You know that as well as anyone.'

'Are they still coming?'

'They've stopped. Last one I got was just before I put myself in hospital.'

'You think it could be someone close to you?'

'I honestly haven't got a clue who it could be but they've seriously fucked with my head.'

'Enough for you to be tempted to use again?'

Tate shakes his head as he looks at Gregg. 'No. I just dealt with it badly the last time. The letters have stopped, and I can deal with the dreams. There's no way I'm going back to that, Gregg. Well, I'm not planning on going there again.'

'Do you have any of the letters?'

Tate knows exactly what his friend is hinting at. Gregg spent a little over a decade as a Garda before he joined the band. That was part of the reason they all tried to cut down on their drug use when he signed up. 'No, Gregg. You're not taking this further. I told my mate about this, not an ex-Guard. Drop it.'

'Sorry, but this is an ex-Guard matter. C'mon, Tate. This is fucking serious.'

'It's probably just some fucked up fan getting carried away.'

Gregg snorts. 'If we have fans like that, I'm picking a new career.'

'I've had hate mail before.'

'This is a teeny bit more than some jealous boyfriend whose nose is out of joint because his girl has you plastered over her wall. You need to take this seriously, Tate. It's private stuff about a kid. It's fucking serious. I have contacts who could look into it for you without the press getting wind of it.'

'There's nothing they can do. They'll end up in a file with all the other 'I hate Tate' letters. There isn't enough to go on.'

'I'm not saying there's anything they can do about it but let me at least check for you. And even if they can't find out who sent them, at least the letters will be on file. Please mate. Let me get someone to look into it.'

Tate turns the ring on his thumb as he thinks about what Gregg said. 'There's... it's not something I want out there.'

'Hey, I get it. We all have private shit we'd prefer stayed that way. And you're right, it'll probably come to nothing, but at least if they check it out you'll know for sure. Can't hurt, mate.'

A part of him wants to agree, but he'd just be opening up a Pandora's Box of shit he's not sure he wants to deal with. There's nothing on the letters to hint at where they came from. The only thing that will happen by handing them over is more spotlight on him. Whatever happened is in the past and he'd give anything for it to stay there. If they go digging and find out his nightmares are based on fact, find out he's actually responsible for his mother's death...

'No.'

'Tate—'

'I said no. It's done. Leave it. And I don't want my parents to know, I don't want my family to know, and I don't want Ellen to know. Keep your fucking mouth shut, Gregg. I mean it.'

'Fine! Jeez, drop the death glare. I won't say a word. If you change your mind just let me know. It won't get out there.'

'My stint in rehab got out. Things always find a way out, Gregg. Drop it, please.'

Gregg blows out a long and exaggerated breath then nods. 'Whatever you say. You've got an appointment in the morning with your sponsor from the clinic, right?'

'Amazing way to change the subject. Thanks.'

'What I meant was that I'll drop you to your appointment, take your truck back to yours and load up your bike, then race back to pick you up.'

'First, no racing in my truck. Second, I don't need a babysitter to make sure I go to my meetings. Third, why get my bike?'

'First, I wasn't going to actually race. Figure of speech. Okay stop looking at me like that. I really wasn't... well not anymore. Moving on. Second, I wasn't insinuating for one second that you needed a babysitter, but now I'm thinking maybe you do.'

'Gregg...'

'Joking. What number are we on now? Oh yeah. Third, I'm getting your bike because it's about time you get back to yourself. That fucker who sent the letters is not going to do this to you. And you're not going to let him or her - whoever they are. And because I'm your oldest, dearest, and wisest friend I am going to insist you take this girl of yours out tomorrow afternoon on aforementioned bike. Show her a bit of the real you. It's still there underneath. You just need to give it a chance to come out. This whole feeling sorry for yourself look... it's not doing it for me.'

'No offence, but I don't want to do it for you.'

'Valid point.' He pops another sweet into his mouth. 'Listen, buddy. You've sang in front of thousands of screaming fans all over the world. You need to get a bit of that Tate Archer confidence back starting by asking her out. The last two times you met her you didn't exactly show your best side.' He snorts to himself. 'Fucking understatement. Falling asleep beside her doesn't exactly scream I'm interested in you. Don't worry about that now though. Think of it this way - it can only get better from here.'

'Seriously? That was the worst pep talk I've ever heard.'

'It wasn't my best I'll admit. You play guitar, you ride a bike, and you sing well enough I suppose. It's what you're known for. Has this girl seen any of that yet?'

'Ah. There's one problem with that.'

'It's you. Of course there's a fucking problem. Do tell.'

'Chloe doesn't know who I am.'

'What do you mean? You haven't told her your name?'

'No, I did. Well, just my first name. I told her my name and said I was a musician.'

Gregg raises his eyebrows. 'And?'

'And she didn't recognise me.'

'Are you serious?'

Tate nods. 'I thought she was just pretending not to know me at first, but she's been off-grid for the last year. What the hell was I supposed to say? Hi my name's Tate and I'm famous. I'd sound like a right fucking dick.'

Gregg sits back and rubs a hand over his face. 'Damn, buddy. You finally found an eligible female who doesn't watch TV. Wow, didn't think they existed anymore.'

Tate makes a face and sighs. 'Tell me about it. With her, I'm just me. We have normal conversations. The last few months don't come up at all. It's kind of a nice relief.'

'You need to figure out a way to tell her, you know that right?'

He rubs a hand over his face and looks across at the mountains in the distance. 'I'm not trying to deceive her, Gregg. I just... damn it, I just want to be with someone who wants to be with me. The real me. No celebrity stuff. No cameras. No thinking they already know me because my fucking bio is on a website they read.'

'I get that, but look at it from her side. When, and it is a when, she finds out, it'll go down one of two ways. One, she'll be super thrilled to be up close and personal with the legendary Tate—'

'If you say Tate Archer I'll deck you.'

'Sorry. Or two, she'll feel utterly humiliated, betrayed, and foolish because she was with the legendary... well, you, and you lied to her about it.'

'So it's a win-win for me.'

His sarcasm isn't lost on Gregg. 'Yes. It'll be terminal. You have to tell her the truth, Tate. Ideally before you're surrounded by a horde of screaming fans when you're out with an unsuspecting Chloe. Just come clean with her.' Gregg winces when he realises what he said. 'Sorry. Bad choice of words.'

Tate grimaces as he looks back to his friend. 'Then there's all that. Why the fuck would she want anything to do with me after all that?'

'Oh come on, man. You got yourself sorted. You should be proud of that.'

'I'd be more proud if I hadn't used in the first place, but that doesn't change anything. Chloe deserves someone with a few dozen less issues than I'll be throwing at her.'

'Fair enough. So you'll walk away then?'

He doesn't realise he's scratching his arm until Gregg sends another thump his way.

'Find another way of getting rid of your frustration and leave your fucking arm alone.'

'I'm not frustrated.' Gregg looks sideways at him, one eyebrow raised. 'What?'

'Yeah well you'll be frustrated and some if you don't get yourself together. You messed up. You sorted yourself out. No big deal. Time to move on. We're all human and we all fuck up from time to time. You can't let one mistake define who you are. Learn from your mistakes, not sit around and wallow in them.'

'It's not done though. It's always going to be there, lurking in the background.'

'Oh for the love of God. Since when have you been such a drama queen? How can you possibly expect anyone else to accept what happened if you can't? Call her. Make a date. Or so help me I'll do it for you and that would seriously mess with your tough guy image.'

Tate stands at the door to Dorothy's house and looks over his shoulder. Gregg waves at him from his truck parked a little way down the hill. Nothing like an audience, but Gregg refused to go until Tate had asked Chloe out. Gregg waves to him and points to the door. Tate clenches his jaw and looks at the brightly painted red door. If he can get on stage in front of thousands of people and sing, he can ask Chloe out. It's not a big deal.

Except it really is.

A part of him is worried she's going to say no. He wouldn't blame her. He hasn't exactly been painting himself in a good light. If anything, he's firmly wedged himself in the slightly odd stranger category. Not once has he been so hesitant about asking someone out. He'd see someone he likes and that would be it. Nerves had never played a part before. He doesn't know if it's so different with her because, for once, he actually gives a damn about her, or if he's knocked his confidence to a seriously pathetic level after what he did.

Gregg flashes the truck lights at him and Tate counters with a glare that does nothing to dampen Gregg's irritating mood. He straightens his shoulders and takes a deep breath before pressing the doorbell.

Maybe she's not in. That might not be a bad thing. Then the door opens. Chloe smiles when she sees him which isn't a bad start. Her hair is tied in a loose bun and she's wearing tattered jeans and a paint splattered t-shirt.

'Hey. This is a surprise.' She looks down at her clothes and blushes. 'I'm doing some watercolour painting. I'm not the neatest so I plan for a paint explosion. Better safe than sorry.'

Tate thinks she looks beautiful, but he keeps it to himself. Nothing like complimenting someone just before they tell you to get lost.

She steps back and gestures to the hall. 'Do you want to come in?'

'I can't. I've got to be somewhere.'

Her face drops a little, but maybe that's wishful thinking. 'Okay. So did you want me for something?'

He stuffs his hands into the pockets of his jeans to stop himself from fidgeting. 'Yeah. I want to apologise for what happened on the beach. I'm trying to deal with some stuff and I'm not sleeping great because of it. It wasn't anything to do with you— er, me falling asleep I mean. I don't want you to think I was bored by your company or anything like that.'

She smiles widely at him. 'Yeah, I have to admit that was the first time I've driven someone to sleep before. It's fine, really. I was just worried about you when you ran off like that.'

'Yeah. Classic actions of a mortified man.'

'There's nothing to be mortified about. It's not a big deal. Forget about it.'

He forces himself to smile, hoping it doesn't come across as a grimace. Hurdle one safely negotiated over. 'I actually wanted to ask you something. Do you have any plans for lunch tomorrow?'

Chloe frowns at him but doesn't say anything for longer than he would have liked. 'Me? No... why?'

'I was thinking of taking my motorbike up the coast for a spin. I thought you might like to come... with me... on my bike. We could have a picnic. If you want... or not. We could do something else if you'd prefer. I'm not fussed about where we go, I mean. Not about you coming...' For fuck's sake Tate shut up! If he could punch himself in the jaw without scaring her away once and for all he'd do it. He throws her another uneasy smile and prays for the ground to open and save him from whatever the hell is going on.

'I'd love that. A picnic sounds lovely.'

'What? Really?'

'Why do you sound so surprised?'

'I don't know. I just thought... Nothing. Okay, so I'll pick you up about noon tomorrow. I'll sort out the food.'

'Are you sure?'

'Yeah. Anything you don't fancy?'

He could swear she looks him up and down before she shakes her head. 'No, nothing I can think of.'

'Great. So I'll see you tomorrow. Oh and make sure you wear jeans for the bike.'

Her smile nearly knocks him on his ass. 'I can't wait.'

He nods and leaves the doorway before he makes a complete tit of himself. He climbs in beside Gregg and slowly turns his head to face his friend. 'If you don't wipe that fucking smile off your face, I'll make you walk home.'

'I take it the delightful Chloe accepted your proposal?'

'You really want me to say it, don't you?'

Gregg continues grinning.

'Okay. You were right. Thank you for sharing your infinite wisdom with us mere mortals.'

Gregg nods and points down the road. 'That wasn't too hard to say, was it? Now, home please. You've got a picnic to plan.'

Chloe tightens her grip around Tate's waist and smiles widely under the helmet. When he called around yesterday and suggested they take a spin up the coast on his bike, she had said yes without thinking about it. Then the realisation of what she'd agreed to settled in and most of the evening was spent mentally kicking herself and trying to talk herself into it.

It had nothing to do with the picnic with Tate. It was entirely down to the motorbike part. It was one thing sitting behind him on Jove. It was quite another to be on the back of a motorbike when she could go flying off at any second and die in so many horrible ways. Her fear had diminished a little when she finally saw the bike in question. In all her scenarios, it had been a small, dirt-bike style thing that didn't give much protection from the road. What he arrived on was an entirely different machine. The black and red Kawasaki was enormous and looked like something from a science fiction film.

After a few minutes she found herself enjoying the experience. Tate handled the bike like a pro, not once doing anything to make her feel uneasy. It also wasn't overly unpleasant having to tightly wrap her arms around his stomach to stop herself from falling off.

He pulls in at a metal barrier at the side of the road and stands the bike up as he dismounts and unlocks the padlocks. He drives through and locks the gate again. The path weaves around the headland to a small clearing at the top. He stops the bike and kills the engine. Chloe takes off the helmet and accepts his help to dismount. She rearranges her hair as much as she can and glances up at him. When she sees his face she smiles widely. He looks so much happier than she's seen him before.

'You loved every second of that, didn't you?'

He smiles down at her, sending Chloe's heart on a free fall. 'I missed it. It's been a long time since I've had it out.'

He holds out his hand to help her step onto the path that runs down the side of the cliff and doesn't let go. And Chloe doesn't want him to. She could get used to this Tate. She knows whatever is hurting him is still there, but if he can get some true happiness from moments like this, it's bound to help him.

She's never been like this around anyone before. Something about Tate knocks her off balance and she's scared, but not of Tate himself. Even with whatever is bothering him deep down, she feels safe with him. It's everything else she knows about him that's scaring her. He's so opposite to her in so many ways. Maybe in too many ways.

He's a gorgeous, tattooed, and pierced musician who rides a motorbike. What could he possibly see in her? She's not putting herself down, just being realistic. Surely she can't be his type. Then again, maybe he doesn't see her like that. Maybe she's just someone to talk to... or not to talk to. He's not exactly overly chatty. Whatever his reasons for wanting to spend time with her, she knows he could so easily hurt her and not even know it. That's the part that's scaring her. She likes him more than she should and certainly more than the sensible side of herself thinks she should.

They get to the cliff edge and Chloe covers her mouth with her hands. On the ground in front of the brightly painted summer house is a picnic blanket with an impressive array of nibbles laid out.

'Did you do this?'

'My mum's friend lives further along the track. I asked if I could bring you here for a picnic and she insisted I let her arrange the food. She wasn't bowled over when I mentioned I was planning a few sandwiches and a packet of crisps.'

'What's wrong with that? Sounds like every picnic I've ever had.'

He smiles widely at her. 'Thank you. That's exactly what I said to her. Anyway, she didn't agree so she sorted all this out.'

'It looks amazing.'

'Probably best we get stuck in.'

They sit down and Tate takes the covers off the various containers and plates. He hands her a glass and fills it with lemonade. 'Cheers.'

She taps her glass against his and sips her drink. She seriously doubts he'd go to this much trouble unless he at least liked her.

Tate looks out at the sea and smiles to himself. This went better than he thought. He'd never done anything like this before. Romance and him didn't quite gel, but he wasn't going to back down from the challenge. He'd made a right tit of himself every other time he'd seen her. The fact she even agreed to this after his disaster of an invitation was a miracle. One he wasn't going to waste. It was time for her to meet the real him. Well, the real non-celebrity him.

He glances over at her and a knot forms in his stomach. Her long dark curly hair is tied back in a low ponytail with shorter strands framing her face. Her long neck is exposed and begging to be kissed. Through the unassuming t-shirt and jeans, he can make out every curve of her body and he loves what he sees. Having her sitting tight against him on the way up here was torture. The feel of her hands on his stomach, of her body against his made it damn difficult to concentrate. Everything about her makes it difficult to concentrate.

She stretches her legs out in front of her. 'It's beautiful up here. Do you come here often?'

He nods. 'Grace lets us use it whenever we want. First time for something like this though.'

'Really?'

'Really. I usually come here alone to write or get away for a bit. It's a great thinking spot.'

'I can see why. I could get lost up her for hours. Just me and my sketchpad.'

'That my cue to go?'

'You can stay a little longer. If you go I'll have to eat the rest of this food. If you stay, I'll be polite and limit myself.'

Tate laughs at that. 'Forget being polite, go for it.'

'So,' Chloe asks as she piles salad onto her plate, 'I know you said you're staying with your parents for a bit but where do you live when you're on your own?'

'Blackrock. I'm hoping to move back soon. I got used to living by myself. Going back to living by their rules under their roof is wearing a little thin.'

'I know what you mean. I'm in between places right now. I'm just glad Gran is away for a few weeks. She can be a little eccentric.'

'Dorothy? Hell, she's more than a little eccentric. I mean that in a nice way, believe it or not. She's crazy but in all the best ways.'

Chloe laughs at that. 'I don't think I could have described her better myself. How long have you been staying with your parents?'

Tate takes another bite of a carrot stick before answering. He kind of opened the door to this conversation. That doesn't mean he wants to step through. 'A few weeks.'

'Do you mind me asking why?'

And there she goes, showing him through the door. 'I wasn't well for a bit. I'm better now, but I guess they're still worrying. I could have gone home but it was easier to come back here for a few weeks.'

He watches her face as she takes in what he said. The natural thing would be to ask what was wrong with him, but surprisingly she doesn't go there.

'I'm glad you're feeling better now. I'm sure your parents appreciate having you close. I would imagine Jove likes having you around too.'

He smiles and a little of the weight lifts from his shoulders. He knows if things continue to go well between them, he'll have to tell her the details, but not today. 'Yeah. It wasn't easy for them so I guess letting Mum fuss over me for a bit isn't too much to ask. I've got to admit, being this close to Jove is a bonus for me too. I miss not being able to take him out every day when I'm back in town.'

'Do your parent's ride him when you're not here?'

'No. Mum has her own horse and Dad doesn't ride. Don't get me wrong, they look after him, but he can be a bit of a handful. Their neighbour takes him out for me. I shoot him a text when I know I won't be around and he'll exercise him for me.'

'That's a great arrangement for both of you.'

'I know. Ideally I'd like to get somewhere in the country or on the coast. Somewhere with room for him, but I need to be based a little closer to civilisation right now.'

'You're not a city guy then?'

Tate shakes his head. 'No. I'm a fan of wide open spaces and not a lot of people. You?'

Chloe leans back on her elbows and looks out at the sea. 'After being with my cantankerous uncle for nearly a year in the middle of nowhere, I'm appreciating having people around. Long term though, I'd probably prefer space to a crowded city. For now having somewhere of my own is the priority. I really couldn't care where it is.'

'You looking at places?'

She shakes her head. 'Not yet. I need to stay with Gran for a few months and build up a bit of a bank balance. She's letting me live there rent free so I'm going to take advantage and save like crazy. It works well for both of us. My parents moved to Cork last year so I couldn't stay with them. It was a win-win situation.'

She smiles at him then looks back at the sea. Tate can't take his eyes off her. He can't remember ever wanting to kiss someone as much as he wants to kiss her. He genuinely likes her and that's what's causing him problems. The last thing he wants to do is blow it by moving too fast. But not moving at all isn't working for him either. He wants to taste her. He needs to taste her before he goes crazy. She takes a sip of her drink and licks her lips.

Fuck it.

Chloe swallows and focuses on the view in front of her instead of getting lost in the view beside her. She knows it's her imagination playing tricks on her, but she could swear she's caught Tate looking at her more than once over lunch.

She risks a quick glance to her left. He's propped up on one elbow, his long legs stretched out in front of him. His head is down, his attention on his hands, staring intently as he turns the ring on his thumb. Then he lifts his eyes to look at her.

If he's surprised to see her looking at him too, he doesn't let it show. If anything, catching her staring has the opposite effect. He doesn't turn away and neither does she. Tate's gaze moves from her eyes to her lips and Chloe swallows again.

This time she knows she's not misreading or imagining the signals. There's no misreading the way he's looking at her. She has no idea what possesses her but she glances from his face to his groin. Yeah, she's not imagining how aroused he is either.

Before she can stop eying up his package Tate reaches out and takes the glass from her hand.

Tate's fingers touch her chin and he tilts her head towards him. Chloe swallows again trying to dislodge the lump in her throat but her mouth decided to rid itself of any moisture the second he touched her. The heavy ring he wears on his thumb brushes against her chin as he slowly traces her lips. Oh God she wants him to kiss her. Please.

Then he does just that. Tate's hand slips around the back of her neck and pulls her to him. His lips are soft and he tastes amazing. The kiss starts off slow but doesn't stay in that category for long.

She has no idea what comes over her but she finds it impossible to keep her hands off him. She cups his face, running her hands over his tight beard before moving into his thick hair. Everywhere she touches she finds something else she wants to keep touching. Everything about him is new. Everything feels amazing. His hand moves along her waist sending sparks up her spine when he touches her skin.

Tate lifts himself over the unfinished picnic and covers her with his body, one hand resting on the ground to keep him from crushing her.

Chloe groans as his fingers trace up her side under her t-shirt, leaving a trail of goosebumps in their wake. He nudges her legs apart with his knee and his solid chest presses against her. Tate moves from her mouth to her neck as she tilts her head to the side to allow him easier access.

Her hand slips under his t-shirt and explores his stomach, tracing further up his smooth chest. He hisses as her fingers brush off something hard in his right nipple. 'Piercing,' he mutters quickly as he works his way around the other side of her neck.

For some unknown reason, the fact his nipple is pierced does nothing to calm the situation. If anything, it's something she didn't expect to be so turned on by. Chloe runs her fingers over the bar again and Tate responds by pushing his leg against her crotch, driving her crazy.

She should stop whatever is happening between them before it goes any further. But she doesn't want to. If anything she wants so much more. More of Tate and more of what he's doing to her. Before the sensible part of her brain can talk herself out of it, Chloe takes hold of his hand, guiding it down her body to where she wants it.

Tate stops kissing her and looks around them. 'Summer house?'

'Summer house.'

He pulls her to her feet and uses the key over the door to unlock and re-lock it once they're inside. Tate looks at her and Chloe can feel every nerve ending in her body tingle in anticipation. She squeals as he picks her up and lies her down on the couch against the side wall of the summer house.

He takes the bottom of her t-shirt in his hands and Chloe lifts her arms above her head. She wants to feel his hands on her skin and clothes aren't going to help that. When he pulls off his t-shirt, Chloe groans out loud. She knew he had an impressive body but seeing it up close is a different story. Every inch of his upper chest, neck and both arms are covered in intricate Celtic tattoos. She runs her hands over the hard muscles tracing the ink that extends up each arm and across his wide chest. 'Wow.'

He smiles and pulls her nipple into his mouth through her lace bra. 'What do you want, Chloe?'

He nips at her other nipple as she tries to string together something that sounds coherent. 'I want you to touch me.'

She kicks off her shoes while Tate opens her jeans and pulls them down her legs, followed by her panties. He kneels on the floor beside the couch and moves down her abdomen, sucking, kissing, and biting every inch of skin. He stops and looks up at her. Chloe reaches down and tugs at his hair, directing him where she wants him to go. He smirks and she gasps as he buries his tongue inside her. Chloe's head rolls back and her grip on his hair increases. What the hell is she doing? She doesn't do stuff like this. She barely knows him, but all she can think about is getting so much more of what he's doing.

'You taste fucking amazing.'

She makes the mistake of looking down at Tate and groans. He's looking at her, his dark blue eyes refusing to let her out of their spell as he licks and sucks on her. Chloe drops her head back against the couch and buries her hands in his hair. He grips her waist in his hands, the ink on his skin curling around her as he pulls her towards him.

'Oh God, Tate.'

He rests one hand on her stomach, holding her in place as he

96

moves his other hand lower. Her back arches off the couch when he slides a finger deep inside, but he holds her steady, keeping her body where he wants it. His tongue flicks over her clit, teasing her with a mind-blowing combination of sucking and massaging. She gasps as his finger presses deep, finding that perfect spot inside, sending shudders through her body. He keeps up a steady pressure, rubbing back and forth as his tongue slowly drives her insane.

Tate sucks her hard as he plunges his finger deep sending her flying. Chloe tries her hardest not to scream but fails miserably. The tremors work from her toes through her body in waves but Tate doesn't stop. He keeps working her until she has nothing left. When Chloe eventually opens her eyes, Tate is looking down at her, one arm to each side of her body, putting his chest right in front of her.

'That was... Wow.'

Tate smiles down at her. 'That's two 'wows' in the space of a few minutes. I'm on a roll.'

'Believe me, that deserves so much more than a wow. I'm just struggling to think straight.'

'Glad to hear it. I've been wanting to do that for a while.'

Chloe frowns up at him, trying to keep her eyes from travelling down his body. 'You have?'

He lowers towards her and kisses up the side of her neck. 'Too fucking right.' His hand runs over her body again and she sucks in a breath. 'You've been driving me crazy.'

'Me? How?'

Tate straightens his arms and licks his lips as he looks at her. 'By chewing the tip of your pencil when you're thinking about what to draw. By using that coconut shampoo or whatever you use on your hair. By having that maddeningly addictive dimple on your right cheek. By tucking your hair behind your ear when you're nervous or embarrassed.' He runs his thumb over her lips and tilts his head to the side. 'And by being fucking gorgeous of course.'

As hard as she tries not to, Chloe blushes. She's never had anyone say things like that to her before. Especially not someone like Tate. 'Really?'

'Yes, Chloe. Really. Even soaking wet with grass sticking out of your hair I'm attracted to you.'

'Oh God. I was hoping you didn't notice that.'

'Didn't want to embarrass you by pointing it out after only knowing you a few minutes. And like I said, you still looked gorgeous.'

When he hits her with one of his smiles, the heat rises in her body again. Tate brings something out in her she didn't know existed. She wants to do things to him. Things that required him to be naked, but she's not sure about taking that step with him just yet.

She wasn't exactly shy when it came to sex, but she was very much in the vanilla category. It was always nice, but she'd never been with someone who distracted her as much as Tate does. Even looking at him has her mind heading off on an unfamiliar tangent. It's not helping that his chest is right in front of her, begging to be touched.

She traces her fingers along his chest, loving how his muscles shift under her touch. His body is incredible and even though she had never been a fan of tattoos, they emphasise every curve and dip of his toned chest and arms. Tate straightens his arms, giving her an unobstructed view of him. Her fingers move down his chest to the waist of his jeans, but Tate takes hold of her wrist and moves her hand away.

'Hang on. I'm sorry, Chloe. I can't.'

Tate regrets the words as soon as he says them. Chloe instantly turns red and tries to cover herself. 'I didn't mean it that way. I want to, believe me.'

She slides out from under him and pulls her t-shirt on. 'It's fine, Tate. I'm sorry I made you feel uncomfortable.'

'Can you sit down for one second, please. Jesus Chloe, I want to be with you, I really do. I've got to tell you something first though.'

That gets her attention. She fastens her jeans and turns to face him. 'What's wrong?'

He pulls on his t-shirt too. Being half naked isn't going to help the situation. 'Sit down, please.'

She lowers onto the couch and he sits beside her. He absolutely does not want to have this conversation with her, but after being with her, he knows he has to tell her the truth.

He's disgusted with himself, but a part of him thought if he just had her once, he'd get her out of his system and he could move on.

That plan went to shit as soon as he tasted her. Being with her only made him want her so much more. As desperate as he is to let her continue whatever she was planning when he stopped her, he can't without her knowing who he is. Fact is there's a strong chance he's already put the nail in his coffin by not telling her before he touched her.

'Are you okay?'

Tate leans forward and clasps his hands together. 'I need to tell you who I really am before this goes any further. I should have told you when we were in your gran's house, but I chickened out.'

'Okay, now you're worrying me. What do you mean who you really are? Is your name not Tate?'

'No, it is. It's more about my full name. Fuck it.' He takes a deep breath and looks over at her. 'My name is Tate Archer.'

He pauses as she frowns sightly. His name is familiar to her.

'The band I'm in...it's called Broken Chords. We've had a few number one songs and albums that hit the same spot. I'm... I fucking hate the term, but I'm a celebrity, famous... whatever way you want to put it. Have been for about five years or so. I thought... I really thought you knew who I was when we met. When I realised you didn't I—'

'Oh my god!' Chloe stares over at him like a switch has been flicked as everything he said registers with her. She pulls out her phone and Tate keeps quiet as she confirms what he's saying. Chloe checks the images on her screen then looks at him again. Usually when someone recognises him he's met with a very different expression to the one Chloe has on her face. She's hurt and confused and it's all his fault. She holds the phone up to him and points to the photo. 'That's you?'

'Yeah.'

'You're a famous rock star, Tate. I mean really famous.'

'Yeah, I am.'

She looks from her phone to Tate then back again. 'You didn't tell me. Why didn't you tell me? Why did you lie to me?'

'Hang on. I've never lied to you, Chloe.'

'Not telling me is the same thing, Tate.' She gets up and unlocks the door then bursts out of the summer house. Tate follows her but gives her some space to get things straight in her head. She walks over to the railing surrounding the headland and laughs to herself.

'I am such an idiot. I can't believe I didn't know.' She closes her eyes and takes a few deep breaths then looks down at the phone again.

He leans on the railing beside her making sure not to crowd her. 'Not recognising me absolutely does not make you an idiot. I know I should have said something sooner but... Do you have any idea how many times I meet someone who doesn't know who I am? I can count the times on one hand. When I met you... When I realised you didn't know me, I liked it. I could just be me with you, you know? For the first time in a hell of a long time, I could actually be myself.'

'Well, I'm glad my stupidity helped you, but do you really think that is going to make me feel any less mortified? Why didn't you tell me before? Why wait until after you got to do what you apparently wanted to do for ages? Do you have any idea how that makes me feel? Do you even care?'

'Of course I care, Chloe. I meant every single word I've said to you. Okay, I omitted some information, but I never lied to you. I know I should have told you before, but I couldn't figure out how to.'

'You sit me down and tell me. Like you just did, only before you laid a finger on me. I knew this would happen. I mean how could it not?'

'Knew what would happen?'

'I knew you'd hurt me.'

'What?'

She glances down at her phone again and her frown deepens. He knows she's reading, and he has a fair idea what it is.

'Is this true? What they're saying about you?'

'Depends on what you're reading.'

'That you're a heroin addict and you overdosed?'

Nausea twists his stomach as she says the words. For some reason hearing it back from her makes it sound so much more unbearable. With that statement he sees whatever might have been between them die. He nods and her eyes leave his.

'I'm clean now.' Tate hates how desperate his statement sounds. 'But, yeah, it's true.'

'Tell Grace thank you for the amazing food.' She turns away from him, grabs her jacket off the picnic blanket then heads down the track.

'I'll give you a lift back.'

She spins around and laughs harshly. 'You've done enough. Just leave me alone. Please.'

'I'm not going to let you walk home from here.'

She turns away and storms up the path towards the road. She can be mad at him all she wants but he is going to make sure she gets back safely. Even if that means dragging her kicking and screaming onto the back of his bike. He quickly packs the remains of the ruined picnic away and puts the basket back in the summer house.

He finds Chloe a little way down the road and pulls in just ahead of her and climbs off. 'Get on the bike, Chloe.'

'I'm fine.'

'We're miles from your gran's. I get you're angry at me and I completely understand. Let me take you home and then I'll leave you alone. I promise. You'll never hear from me again if that's what you want. I just want to bring you home. Please.'

Chloe looks at the bike and her shoulders drop. 'Fine.' She takes his spare helmet and fastens it as she climbs on behind him. In stark contrast to the ride up here, he can barely feel her hands on him as he drives her home. He has to keep looking down to make sure she's still holding on.

He's barely come to a stop outside her gran's house before she gets off and hands him the helmet. The bright red door closes behind her and cuts off anything he was planning to say to her.

Chloe drops down in front of her laptop and types in the two words that have confused the hell out of her since she heard them an hour ago and hits enter.

And there he is. Tate Archer. Lead singer, lead guitarist, and songwriter for Broken Chords. How did she not recognise him? Now that she sees him she doesn't know how she missed it.

Then again, she wasn't expecting to find a celebrity on a small beach near her grandmother's house.

As soon as he said his full name it was like a veil had been lifted. Even without checking on her phone she recognised him. It's not even like Tate is a common name. But is it really that naïve of her not to make the connection?

She clicks on the images tab and slowly scrolls down. Lines and lines of photos of him with the band, by himself, fully dressed, with no shirt on, there are so many of them, and in each one he looks like the guy she was with an hour ago. There's no fancy camera tricks, it's just him. She feels like such an idiot for not seeing what was right in front of her.

She moves away from the photos and goes back to the search results. Apart from lists of their songs and albums, there are a lot of pages detailing what happened to him recently. The fact he's a celebrity is hard enough to assimilate, but it's his time in rehab that she's struggling with the most. Telling her he wasn't well for a while is a bit of an understatement.

According to one news website, he got back from a few months on the road with the band, spent Christmas with his family then disappeared. The second leg of their tour due to start in February was cancelled and that was it until he was reportedly released from rehab in May.

From what she can see he hasn't made a statement about what happened to him so the speculation is rife. There are reports of the pressure of touring getting to him. Other reports blame excessive partying. You name it, someone has mentioned it as a reason he found himself in rehab.

Chloe stares at the words on the screen. They're talking about Tate. She can't get it straight in her head.

Her focus drifts to a photo of Tate with a stunning blonde woman by his side. Just another one of his many ex-girlfriends. This one in particular had taken the break-up badly. She skims through the latest article and can't help but take an instant dislike to her.

Astrid had dated him briefly until he broke things off citing 'personality clashes' as the reason for the split. Astrid remained silent on the break-up until just before Tate was released from rehab. Then, from what Chloe can see, she had been quite vocal about his issues. Her view was that Tate had been so deep into drink and drugs she could no longer be with him. He refused to admit he had a problem, so she had no choice but to call it a day on their relationship even though he begged her to stay with him.

How helpful of her to throw dirt at someone trying to deal with what he was dealing with.

She collapses back in the chair and stares at the screen. Is that why he gets so upset on the beach every morning? Is it to do with what happened with his overdose? Was it these hurtful comments from people who were quick to walk over his name if it meant gaining a little of the spotlight for themselves? Was it something else that was getting to him? Having his career and his life put under the spotlight was no doubt extremely hard to deal with. Especially if he is just out of rehab.

She glances back at the news article and struggles to match that person with the Tate she thought she had gotten to know a little over the last week. Why didn't he tell her the truth? She wouldn't have expected him to tell her about his ordeal, but who he really is would have been a start. Especially before what happened in the summer house.

Why did she even let that happen? She got carried away in the moment and, as incredible as it had been, the memory is tainted by what happened after. As soon as he kissed her she knew she wanted him. It was impossible not to. The way he looked at her. They way her touched her. She couldn't get enough.

Before she can stop her finger, it moves the curser over to the video tab and clicks on it. She shakes her head as she reads the names of the songs over each video. She knows most of them which just makes not recognising him even more embarrassing. In her defence, she can't remember ever looking at the videos. She knows she's seen him on TV a few times, and she knows she's heard their songs, but didn't link the two. If she did, she probably would have known who he was that first day. She cringes when she thinks about how that first conversation would have played out if she knew who she was actually talking to.

She randomly picks one of his music videos and hits the play icon. The music begins and she slowly pulls the laptop closer to her as Tate appears and sings. His voice is incredible, and she quickly gets drawn into the song and the visuals.

Seeing the performer version of Tate is so strange. Like with the photos, he looks and moves like the Tate she knows, but there's something so different about seeing him like this. In the next shot he's with the rest of the band playing a guitar. Chloe squirms in her seat as the image hits her where it has no right to hit.

She exits that video and tries the next one. This one's even worse but for very different reasons. There's a half-naked woman all over a half-naked Tate. No thank you.

Chloe curses and leaves her imagination to come up with all sorts of unhelpful images of how that plays out in the video.

In the next one he's fully dressed and it's just him and the band. No dressed, half-naked, or fully naked women to be seen. As Chloe watches him singing, a sadness comes over her. She had spent hours with Tate and never heard him sing or play like that. He had told her he's a musician but what she's watching is so much more than that and she deeply regrets not seeing that part of him while she still could.

Chloe pauses the video and stares at the image on the screen. Ending things with him was the right thing to do. He'd lied to her. He'd made a fool out of her. So why does she get a sinking feeling she's just made a rash and foolish decision?

She looks back at the image of him at the top of the screen. She paused the video at a moment when Tate's looking directly at the camera. Almost like he's looking at her.

Chloe shuts the laptop and walks over to the sink. The only thing she can do is try to salvage a little of her dignity and move on. She seriously doubts she'll see Tate again. Well, unless it's on the TV, which she is going to have to avoid for a few months at the very least.

She looks down the beach but there's no sign of Jove. Why is she even looking? If he was there would she race down and apologise? Chloe goes upstairs and pulls her art supplies out of the box at the end of the bed but has second thoughts when she sees the drawing she was working on with Tate's help. So much for distracting herself.

Chloe goes back downstairs and grabs her bag off the hook in the hall. If she stays in the house she's going to replay every single second of the time in the summer house with Tate. She can still feel his hands on her, still feel his tongue running across her skin.

'Oh would you knock it off,' she scolds herself. 'It wasn't that amazing.' Now who's telling lies?

With one last look down the beach Chloe turns in the opposite direction and walks up the road. Maybe a walk far away from anywhere she might bump into Tate will help. Then again, maybe it'll just give her more time alone to think about the whole sorry situation over and over again.

Tate pulls the bike into the garage and kills the engine, but doesn't move to get off. He's just fucked things up with Chloe for good this time. There's no coming back from this. For the first time in as long as he can remember, he found someone he genuinely likes. Not only that, but he was also attracted to her. So much so he found it difficult to keep his hands off her. Why the hell didn't he tell her who he was from the beginning? He was being a selfish prick and it backfired on him. Big time.

He slides off the bike and stares at the workbench opposite him. The pressure builds in his chest as he glares at the line of tools neatly laid out on the top. He kicks the leg of the bench and watches as the tools slide on the wooden surface. Tate shouts and kicks out again and again. He attacks the table like it's the source of all the evil and pain in his life. The leg collapses under the assault, sending the tools clattering to the floor.

Strong arms wrap around him, but he's not backing down so easily. He breaks free and slams his foot against the wood, cracking the plank before he is pulled away again. Gregg slams him against the wall and presses his arm to Tate's neck.

'Stop it!'

But he has no intention of stopping. He's bigger and stronger than Gregg and frustration has him firmly in its grip. He pushes his friend away and lunges for him. Gregg ducks and tries to grab Tate's arms but Tate barrels into him, throwing them both onto the gravel outside the garage. Gregg holds Tate's arms back but is struggling. Tate momentarily gets distracted when someone shouts his name and Gregg takes advantage. He flips Tate over and straddles him, using his full weight to pin his arms to his lower back.

'Jesus Tate. Calm the fuck down.'

'Get off me.'

'Oh yeah, sure. Like that wasn't filled with the promise of another beating. I'm not moving until you calm down.'

'I'm calm, all right!'

Gregg snorts which doesn't help ease any of the tension running through him. 'Of course you are. What the fuck crawled up your ass?'

Tate bucks against Gregg but without his arms he's not going anywhere. 'Seriously, Gregg. Move.'

'Oh seriously? Still no. I'm going to use my Spidey senses and guess she didn't take to your celebrity status well.'

'Going in for the I told you so already?'

'Of course not, you idiot. You want to talk about it?'

'I want you to get off me. It fucking hurts.'

Gregg leans over and frowns at Tate. 'You still want to hit me?'

'I'm thinking about it.'

His dad appears above him and taps Gregg on the shoulder. 'I got this, Gregg. He's not going to hit anyone or I might just be tempted to return the favour. Tate, sit on the wall and do not move a fucking muscle. Do you hear me?'

Gregg glares at Tate then slowly gets off him. Rick points to the house. 'Gregg, get yourself inside. We'll be in once we've had a chat.'

'You sure?'

'We're good, thanks.' Tate ignores his father's hand to help him up and drops onto the low wall running along the side of the driveway. He rests his head in his hands as he tries to get his temper under control.

Rick sits beside him and looks sideways at him. 'Well? I'm waiting.'

'For what?'

'For you to get your fucking head out of your ass, Tate. You realise you just fought with Gregg?'

Tate glares over at his dad.

'You can drop that look too. He's on your side. He didn't deserve that.'

His father's right. First Chloe and now Gregg. He's on a roll today. He angrily scrubs his hand though his hair then covers his face.

'I'm not going anywhere until you tell me what's wrong. And don't even consider saying nothing because I'm not buying it.'

'It's just woman problems, okay.'

Rick smiles at that response. 'Kind of glad to hear it's not something more serious. I saw the comments Astrid made about you.'

'Please don't even go there. It's got nothing to do with her. It's nothing, really. Just some silly... it wasn't even anything.' He needs to stop talking. Needs to end this topic before he pours his heart and soul out. 'I'm grand, okay.'

'You need to talk, Tate. Are you opening up to your counsellor?'

'I have an appointment every week.'

'I know you do. That's not what I'm asking. When you were in the centre did you talk or did you just sit there giving everyone dirty looks?' Rick grins as Tate lifts his head to look at him. 'Yeah. That's the one.'

'I'm—'

'Don't you dare say you're grand again. You just kicked the crap out of an inanimate object then rugby tackled Gregg. C'mon mate. I'm your dad. You can talk to me.'

The snort comes out before Tate can stop it. The total dick mood is in force today.

'What the hell was that for?'

'You can drop the concerned father bullshit, okay.'

Yeah, he's a total fucking dick. He knows what he just said will have hit Rick as if he punched him. None of this is Rick's fault. Just like it's not Chloe's fault. Or Gregg's fault. The complete lack of response from Rick is nearly worse than if he yelled at him, which he absolutely deserves.

'I didn't mean that. Ignore me.'

'Not happening. I can't believe you just threw that at me.'

He can't believe it himself. With no response to offer up, he rubs his hand over his jaw and looks anywhere but at Rick.

'Since the day we adopted you, you've been part of this family. You are my son so don't even go there just because you're pissed off. Do you honestly think we'd be putting up with your shit if we didn't think of you as family? You're not that amazing, mate. Quite the opposite at the moment actually.'

That at least earns a small laugh, but he still feels unbelievably shit for even going there.

'I'm sorry. I'm being an ungrateful moody ass.'

'Too right you are. What the hell is going on with you?'

'I don't know, okay! I'm—' he pauses and digs his fingers into his hair. 'I don't know. Ignore me.'

'No. Talk to me.'

'Just drop it, Dad. I don't want to talk. I just want to forget about it.'

'Don't think that's working for you or my poor workbench. You really think we're all going around with our heads in the clouds? Do you really think we don't see what's going on with you?

'I know you have nightmares every night. I know you take Jove to the beach and break down. I know you come back to the house and force breakfast down then work out until you're exhausted. Hoping you'll be so tired you won't have the nightmares? I don't know. I do know that you're not getting better.

'Your mother may think the sun shines out of your arse, but I'm not so naïve. I know full well you were using long before the incident in January. That's a whole other discussion. What I want to know is what happened in January to escalate that?'

Tate pushes to his feet, wincing as his foot protests after ploughing into the bench. 'Just leave it, okay.'

Rick stares at him for a long time without saying anything. He finally sighs and shakes his head. 'Don't worry. I know I'm fighting a losing battle. I'm here when you're ready, okay. Oh and by the way, Ellen rang again. She really wants to speak to you. Maybe you should do her the courtesy of phoning her back. She deserves that at the least.'

Rick dusts off his jeans and heads the same way Gregg did. Well, that's a pretty fucking spectacular afternoons work. He's driven away three people. Maybe he shouldn't ring Ellen back. She could be number four.

'I want my workbench fixed today or I'll be storing my tools on that bike of yours,' Rick calls back to him.

Keen to avoid the house for as long as possible, Tate goes back into the garage and admires his handiwork. The workbench is fucked. There isn't a hope in a hell he's going to be able to repair it. Looks like he's going to have to fork out for a new one.

An hour later he comes back from the hardware store and attaches the metal legs back onto the new sheet of wood and stands back to check out his work. Not too bad. Should get his dad off his back for a bit. He lines the tools back up on the top and wheels his motorbike out of the garage before locking the door again.

He's outstayed his welcome here. What happened today is all the confirmation he needs. If he's to have any chance of getting his head straight, he needs to go home. If he stays here much longer, he's going to end up doing something to completely alienate himself from his entire family for good.

The thought of going back to where he'd fallen apart isn't filling him with a hell of a lot of good vibes, but he needs to do it sooner or later. He needs space. They all do.

He pulls the ramps out from under his pickup and pushes the Kawasaki on to the load bed. He throws a tarp over it and secures it to the truck, then goes back into the house and packs his things.

His mum steps out of the kitchen as he's walking out of the annex with his bag. 'Tate? What's going on?'

'It's time I go home.'

'Don't be silly.'

'Mum, I'm going. I need to go.'

'If this is about what happened with Gregg, you can sort it out. He's gone back to his place. All you need to do is apologise to him. I'm sure you can work it out.'

'This isn't just about that. I need space, Mum. I've been living in other people's pockets for months. I need to be by myself for a bit.'

'I don't want you going back there alone.'

He drops onto the arm of the couch and rubs a hand over his face. 'Mum, it's grand, really. It's my home. I want to go back.'

'But it's too soon. What if...'

'What if what?'

'I'm just worried about you, Tate.'

'You really think I'm going to go straight to Eddie and stick a fucking needle in my arm again, don't you.'

'Tate, please—'

113

'I'll see you soon, okay.'

He grabs his bag and walks out to his truck. He doesn't even get to the door before his dad calls him from the house. In keeping with the foul mood he's in, he ignores him and opens the back door to load his stuff in. He climbs in and starts the engine, driving away before his dad can get near the truck.

Half an hour later he pulls up at the gate to his house and pushes the button on the remote. The gate retracts and he looks at the vast property. From the outside you wouldn't know what had gone on here a few months ago. He doubts the upper class residents he shares the street with will ever forgive him. He must have devalued every single house when he had his out of control party.

With a feeling of dread firmly in his gut he unlocks the door and turns off the alarm. When he finally convinces himself to walk into the living room he smiles. The place looks completely different. New furniture, new colour on the walls, new flooring, new blinds. Feeling a little better about being here, he goes upstairs to his bedroom. Like downstairs, everything is new and looks completely different to what was there before. He sits on the end of his bed and rubs his hands over his face.

When he went into rehab, he asked his parents to give all the furniture to charity and get someone in to clean the house for him. His unknown guests had trashed the place, turning the two-million Euro house into a squat.

He wasn't expecting them to redo the whole house while he was away. He'll have to find some way of thanking them after he figures out how to apologise for storming off like he did.

Tate goes up to the second floor and unlocks the door to his studio. He's just grateful he'd kept that locked when his guests were here. It would cost a small fortune to replace the kit. He pulls the blackout blinds open and looks out at the view of the sea.

Coming home was absolutely the right thing to do. As much as he's grateful for everything his family has done for him the last few months, he needs to get his head sorted. There's no way he can do that with an audience watching his every move. At least being here is a little closer to normal. A little closer to getting his life back on track.

Just a pity he fucked things up with Chloe. He should have told her who he was before he laid a finger on her. She's right about that. Fucking stupid selfish dick.

He's also made things so much worse for himself. Now he knows what she feels like, what she tastes like, and he wants more. And for once it's not for selfish reasons. Like everything else in his life until recently, sex had been about what he could get from it. It wasn't like he just laid back and did nothing. There had been no complaints, but everything he did was done so whoever he was with would return the favour. When he was with Chloe, his only thought was making sure he looked after her. He didn't give a damn if she touched him or not.

He walks over to the rack of guitars against the far wall and picks one up. He can either wallow in equal doses of self-pity and self-loathing, or kick his ass back into shape. Tate sits down and runs his thumb over the strings. No time like the present to see if he can still play the damn thing. He closes his eyes and tries to let his mind go blank, just focusing on the chords which come back surprisingly quickly even after five months of being ignored.

Time to stop putting off getting his life back. Delaying things isn't helping anyone. He needs to get back to work and so do the guys. At least if he's locked away in the studio, he'll have a near constant distraction from thoughts of Chloe.

Chloe positions the laptop on her knee and practises her smile in the reflection. There's no way her gran is going to buy that sorry excuse for a smile. As soon as she sees her face she'll know somethings wrong. Most of the last three days had been spent trying not to think about Tate. It was a lost cause. The fight with Tate had replayed over and over in her head as the hours stretched on.

Had she over-reacted? Maybe. Okay, he may not have technically told a bare-faced lie, but he hadn't been entirely honest with her either.

Then again, how would she have expected that introduction to go? He was hardly going to tell her his name and follow it with the fact he's a famous singer. He told her he was a musician. He told her he sings. Was it her fault for not recognising him?

Hence the sleepless nights. This whole mess is far from simple and neither is the solution. If there is one. The way she had left things with him was pretty final.

Chloe rests her head on the table and groans to herself. Has she made a massive mistake? She looks at her phone and the picture of Tate staring back at her. His deep blue eyes bore into her from the screen. He really is absolutely gorgeous... which shouldn't even be a factor.

She turns her phone over. Damn man is everywhere. Her computer signals an incoming video call. Time to put on the performance of her life. She straightens her hair again and smiles as she taps the answer icon.

Her gran's face appears on the screen and she can't hold back the smile. 'Hello, dear. See, I told you I'd be able to figure this technology stuff out.'

'It's good to see you. Are you enjoying your holiday?'

Her gran makes a face. 'It's okay. You know how I hate being fussed over though. I have to say I'm looking forward to getting back to my own house. So, are you going to tell me what's wrong?'

'There's nothing wrong.'

'Try again, dear. What's happened?' Chloe considers lying, but her gran crosses her arms and gives her one of her knowing looks. So Chloe tells her everything. When she's done, she actually feels a little better, not by much, but any improvement is still an improvement.

'What do you plan to do now?'

'What do you mean?'

'Don't try to pull the wool over my eyes. I may be old but I can see you still like Tate. Quite a bit I would imagine.'

'But he lied to me.'

Her gran snorts. 'I wouldn't be so quick to label what he did lying as such. From what I hear, everything else you've told me about him is the real Tate.'

'How long have you known him?'

Her gran makes a face. 'Since he was a kid I suppose. I think he was seven or eight when they adopted him so I suppose I've known him for about twenty-seven years.'

'He's adopted? I didn't know that.'

'Oh yes. I don't know much about that though. I know they wanted more children after Shane but were told they couldn't. It took some time for the adoption to go through but they were finally able to bring Tate home. Then a few years later they fell pregnant with Bria. Strange how life works out.

'Anyway, what I was trying to say is that Tate... he didn't change when he became well known. I don't know how he did it, but he didn't let the fame go to his head. He was still the same Tate. Still dressed the same. Still had the same friends. Still came back to see his family every single chance he got. He even gave me piano lessons when he was back.'

'Hold on. You never said he's the one who's been giving you lessons.'

'I just did. Quite an impressive claim to fame I think - having Tate Archer teach me piano. I think deep down he misses all that.'

'Misses what?'

'He's a teacher, like you.'

'Excuse me?'

'Oh yes. He went to some music college or other after school. He's a highly qualified music teacher of piano and guitar. I think he has some fancy degree or something like that. He's an incredibly talented musician. Very natural teacher too.'

'I didn't know that.'

'I know he wasn't entirely straight with you and if I was there I'd give him a slap for it, but I understand why he did it.'

'You do?

'Of course. I know he loves what he does, but there are few eligible women around here who don't know who Tate is. Then you come along. I'm not surprised he wanted to keep that side to himself, but believe me, you have met the real him. He's an incredibly sweet, thoughtful, caring man.' Her face drops a little. 'He is going through a bad patch. Again, I'd give him a slap for that too. Stupid boy. All I'm saying is that if you like him and it's the fact he was a little reserved about his job that is stopping you, maybe that's a little harsh. He's a good one, Chloe.'

'I do like him, Gran.'

'Of course you do. So, why are you still talking to me? Shouldn't you be contacting him?'

'I don't know how to. We always just sort of bumped into each other. I've already been to the beach and he's not there.'

'Leave it with me.'

'Gran, what are you going to do? Please don't call him yourself.'

'I don't have his number, but I do know how to get him. Stay by your phone. I'll see if I can track him down.'

'Gran.'

'I won't embarrass you, I promise. Trust me. I'm going to hang up now. Stay by your phone.'

Chloe paces the living room, her mobile firmly in her hand. She checks the screen again. Still nothing. How long does it take for her gran to ring whoever she was ringing? Maybe they're busy. Maybe she had to leave a message and they won't get back for hours. It's only been an hour so far. She can't wait hours. She'll drive herself crazy.

She nearly drops the phone when it rings. 'Gran?'

'I'm still working on it. It appears Tate is gone.'

'Gone? What do you mean he's gone?'

'According to my friend who is friends with his mother, he's gone back to his own house and straight back to work. When he's in the studio he's pretty much out of contact. I haven't given up though. There's one more person to try.'

'Maybe this isn't such a good idea. The last thing he's going to want is me chasing him when he's working.'

'Oh hush now. Gran is on the case.'

She cuts the call before Chloe can respond. The fact he's gone back to his old life isn't a great sign. Well, it's great for him, just not for her. She won't be bumping into him on the beach in the mornings. Unless her gran tracks down a contact for him, that'll be it.

Instead of staring at the phone for the day, she showers and gets into a pair of pyjama bottoms, old t-shirt, and fluffy socks. After making herself a cup of tea she turns on the TV and scrolls through the channels until she finds something that looks half watchable.

The doorbell rings and she curses under her breath as she pulls it open. A tall man with messy, dark blond-hair turns to look at her. His hands are in the back pockets of his jeans and black and grey tattoos cover his thick arms.

'Chloe?'

'Yes?'

He holds out his hand and the recognition hits as soon as she sees his lopsided grin. She'd seen that grin quite a few times while she was trying not to look at endless photos of Tate and failing miserably.

'You're Gregg.'

He grins widely at her. 'You recognise me but not Tate? Ha! That's hilarious. Wait till I tell him.' He holds up his hands when her face drops. 'That was a joke. A badly timed one I'll admit. Can I presume you've been doing a bit of online searching?'

'I'm just trying to get my head around things.'

'I get that. I'd imagine there's a fair bit to get your head around. So, your gran summoned me. She thought I'd be able to help you out.'

She checks the screen on her phone then looks up at him again. 'I thought she was getting me his number.'

'Tate's not keen on me handing out his number to random women, not saying you're a random woman of course. Between you and me he can attract a few interesting folk. Not that I'm including you in that either. Wow, I'm on a roll with the foot in mouth comments today, huh. Can I come in?'

'Sorry. Of course.'

He steps inside and sits on the stairs. 'So,' he says as he scratches his beard. 'I'm kind of on borrowed time. We're in the studio for the day. I've got about two hours while Tate does his bit and he notices I've done a runner. I also need to get back before he calls the Garda.'

'What? Why would he do that?'

He grins sheepishly and points to the black pickup parked outside the house. 'I may have borrowed his truck. Can't resist winding him up whenever I can.' Gregg rests his elbows on the step behind him and stretches out.

'My dear buddy wasn't forthcoming with all the details, so let's see if I got this straight. You met Tate. He introduced himself. You didn't recognise him. Not a crime by the way. Tate realised but didn't enlighten you. For the record, I told him that would backfire but so far I've kept away from the I told you so's. He's really not in the mood for that. Anyway, he eventually tells you the truth and you're quite naturally upset. End of Tate and Chloe. Am I right?'

'I guess so.'

'Thought so. Idiot. Him not you. I'll let you in to a little secret. Coming here to get you isn't entirely a selfless act. Myself, Dillon, and Luke are enjoying a fantastic day stuck in the studio with Tate. When I say enjoying I'm being as sarcastic as I can be. The fucker is like a bear with a sore head.'

'In that case I'm not sure me getting in touch would be such a good idea.'

Gregg shakes his head. 'No. That's not what I mean. He's angry at himself. Downright furious actually. He thinks he's messed things up with you for good. Has he?'

'I don't know,' she replies truthfully. 'I do like him, but he... I think

121

I need to talk to him.'

'Please do. For all our sakes. There isn't enough coffee in the world to help us deal with him.'

'Okay. So what's the plan?'

'Your Prince Charming is singing his little heart out so I'm going to take you to him.'

'Are you sure he'll be okay with this? I mean I was just planning on talking to him. I don't want to land on him while he's working.'

'He'll be more than okay with this.' Gregg looks her up and down and makes a face. 'Please don't take this the wrong way, but I'm not so sure the pyjama and fluffy sock combo is the look you want to go for in this particular situation.'

She looks down at her baggy pyjama bottoms and grimaces. 'Oh God. Can you give me a few minutes?'

'Absolutely. Go for it.'

Ten minutes later she locks the door behind her and climbs up into the truck. It smells like leather and sandalwood. Just like Tate. Gregg starts the engine and grimaces as he grinds the gears. 'Fuck. I didn't do that, okay.'

'You're doing me a massive favour. I'm not going to land you in it with him.'

'You're an angel.' He pulls away from the house and heads towards the main road. 'Got to say it's a pleasure to meet you in person. Tate's been bending my ear about you.'

'He has?'

'Of course. Why do you look so surprised? I thought you guys had a thing of sorts.'

'Well, yeah, I guess we do. I mean we did. I just didn't think he'd told anyone about it.'

'As far as I know I'm the only one. He's a fairly private person. Not too keen on everyone knowing his business. Took a bit of ingenious badgering but he eventually spilt the beans. Tate's got oodles of confidence when it comes to getting up on stage and all that other stuff, but when it comes to you for some reason he's second guessing himself.

'I think everything that's transpired lately has knocked him. He genuinely likes you, Chloe and I think that's why he found it so difficult to tell you exactly who he is. He liked how normal it was. No insult intended, I promise.

'He's had one or two... or was it three?' He makes a face then shrugs. 'Whatever. There have been a few people who weren't interested in getting to know him. They were more interested in all the glitz and glamour stuff. I'm sure you've guessed by now that's not how he works. Anyway, because of that, he's usually wary about being himself around certain people. I'm damn impressed he didn't put up his usual wall with you. Says a lot.'

Chloe smiles and looks back out the window. Hearing that from someone who's known Tate for so long means a lot.

'You're absolutely going to make more than his day when he sees you again. He may even forgive me for nicking his truck.'

Gregg parks Tate's truck in the underground parking area and she follows him to the elevator. 'He might still be recording so best not to interrupt his mojo. We'll go to the control room and wait there until he's done. You'll be able to see and hear him, but he won't be able to see or hear you. You can just chill with us and watch him do his thing.'

'I'll follow your lead. I've never been somewhere like this before.'

'It's all fairly relaxed. Dillon and Luke will be there so you can meet them too. You ever seen Tate sing or play live?'

She shakes her head. 'Only on the radio or videos online.'

'Guy is a natural performer. He's at his best with a guitar in his hands. Just do me a favour. Don't go telling him how amazing he is.

Wouldn't want him getting a big head.'

The doors open and he gestures for Chloe to step out of the elevator. He leads her down the corridor and opens the last door. She follows Gregg into the studio and waves at the room full of people who turn to look at her. Gregg introduces the two other members of the band and points to the couch at the back at the room. She squeezes in between Luke and Dillon and thanks Gregg as he passes her a glass of water.

'He can't see you,' Dillon whispers. 'The room is dark so he's not distracted.'

Chloe nods and can't hold back the smile as she watches Tate in the booth opposite them. It's only been three days since their argument, but it feels like a lifetime. As always, he looks incredible. The sleeves of his navy top are pushed up leaving some of his tattoos on display. Some of the buttons on his t-shirt are open teasing her with a glimpse of his inked chest. He pulls off the baseball cap and brushes his hair back before tucking it back under the backwards cap.

The backing track comes on then Tate begins to play. Gregg is right, seeing him in person is so much better than on her computer screen. Then he sings. For someone with such a deep husky voice, he can reach impressive notes. She'd quite happily stay on the couch, listening to him singing all day, but far too soon the song comes to an end and Gregg taps her on the shoulder.

'Told you he was good.'

'That's an understatement.'

'Spare a thought for us poor fuckers who have to try and compete with that.' Dillon laughs as he pushes to his feet and pours coffee into a mug.

'He's due a break now. You're up, Chloe.'

'What? Now?'

'Yep.' Dillon hands her the mug. 'This is for him.'

She takes the mug and Gregg opens the door. 'Next door up. Just knock and he'll let you in.'

Chloe stands outside the door and takes a few breaths. This is absolutely the right thing to do, but now that she knows who he is, it's so much harder. She straightens her shoulders and knocks twice. After a brief wait the door opens and Tate freezes.

'Chloe? What are you doing here?'

Tate instantly regrets his words. That's one way to make it sound like she's not welcome. 'Fuck. Sorry, I didn't mean that to come out that way.'

'No, I shouldn't have come.'

Tate opens his mouth to say something but frowns and looks to the control room. 'Too many ears. Will you come with me for a minute?' He leads Chloe through the building and up to a large roof terrace overlooking the city. 'Yeah, okay I'm going to start again. I'm really glad you're here, I'm just surprised to see you.'

'I needed to see you. I'm sorry for putting you on the spot like this. Gregg said it would be okay.'

'It is. I really didn't think I'd see you again.' He was absolutely sure she was gone for good.

'I know and I'm sorry for how I reacted. It was such a shock when you told me. I'm so embarrassed about what I said. I blew the entire situation completely out of proportion. I just... I mean you're the same person, I know that, but you're also not. I don't mean that in a bad way. It's just going to take a little getting used to.'

Tate leans against the wall and crosses his arms, then drops them to his side when he realises he looks like he's being defensive. 'You don't have anything to apologise for. You had every right to go off on me. I kept telling myself what I was doing technically wasn't lying, but it was. I got so wrapped up in you not knowing about me, I guess I didn't want to give that up. It doesn't excuse it for one minute and I'm not trying to justify it. It was just nice being... uncomplicated for a bit. And to be honest, I didn't have a fucking clue how to even go there with you. I'd ignored every opening and got myself stuck.'

Chloe rests against the wall beside him and doesn't say anything for a few minutes. Tate doesn't push her. The fact she took the time to track him down and come here to see him is more than he could have hoped for. He's not going to tip the scales by saying something stupid.

'I understand that, Tate. I really do. When you told me who you were I assumed you weren't taking me seriously or it was just a fling and that's why you didn't want to tell me the truth.'

'I don't know what this is but it's not a fling. Well, I didn't want it to be. Whatever. You know what I mean.' Tate looks back over the city. He wants to ask her out properly but is afraid he might be pushing his luck. Then again, she had made the effort to track him down. 'Can we, I don't know, maybe grab a coffee sometime? Start over?'

When he turns to look at her, any doubts he had about asking the question disappear. She's smiling at him. 'I'd really like that.'

'How about dinner when I'm done here instead?'

'I'd like that even more.'

Tate gets through the rest of the session in record speed. After saying his goodbyes, he takes Chloe's hand and walks with her down to the basement. His truck may be back where he parked it, but he usually manages to get it between the white lines. Gregg must have borrowed it when he went to get Chloe. Maybe this once he won't give him a hard time about it.

'I could book a table somewhere, or maybe cook you something at my place... unless you'd prefer to go out.' He shuts his mouth in an attempt to stop his foot from getting firmly wedged inside again.

'Your place sounds great. If you're sure it's not too much trouble to cook.'

'No trouble at all. The guys say I make a mean bolognese.'

She climbs into the truck and smirks across at him as he fastens his seatbelt. 'I'll let you know after I've tried it. I'm fairly sure Gran has already awarded herself first place in the best bolognese category. It is pretty amazing.'

He starts the truck and pulls out of the garage. 'No pressure then.'

Chloe looks out the window of Tate's car as he battles his way through Dublin traffic to Blackrock where he lives. Thanks to the rush hour traffic the usual twenty-minute drive has stretched on to well over half an hour.

It's ridiculous to be excited, but she can't wait to see his house. She can't imagine what type of house someone like Tate would pick for himself. Her gran told her his parents live in a spectacular old farmhouse with plenty of outside space. That's somewhere she can picture him. A house in Blackrock, not so much.

'Why Blackrock?'

'We use that studio a fair bit. I didn't want to live in the city but it made sense to be closer to the centre. Easier than getting stuck in traffic every day all the way from Wicklow. It's handy being closer to the airport too. It's not going to be my forever home, but it works for now. I'd prefer to be further down the coast if I can.' He glances sideways at her. 'What? You look confused.'

'It still coming to terms with who you really are. That's not me having a go at you. It's just weird. The funny thing is, I recognised you that first day on the beach. I didn't know who you were but I knew I knew you, if you get what I mean.'

'That's what threw me. Everyone around Newcastle knows who I am. I pretty much grew up there. I go there to see my family every break in my schedule. I'm not used to meeting someone who doesn't know me.'

'I still can't believe I asked if you make a living from your music. I even asked about when you'd be preforming next so I could tag along. I checked online. Tickets to your shows are like hen's teeth.'

'I'm sure I could rustle you up one if you ever want to check us out.'

'How did you keep a straight face that first day?'

'Why the fuck do you think I was frowning so much? I thought you were pulling my leg.'

'I kind of wish I was.' The funny thing is that she's never been one to drool over celebrities or read magazines detailing every minute of their fabulous lives. She never found the attraction to reading about perfect strangers. Of all the people to find themselves with a celebrity, she was at the bottom of the list. If this could be called being with him. It's too soon to label it. All she knows is that she's enjoying spending time with him, no matter how bizarre the whole situation is to her.

From the minute she found out who he really is, he seemed to be everywhere. His picture popped up on the Internet. His music was on the radio. He was probably everywhere before she knew, but something had stopped her from seeing the truth.

He pulls his truck up to a set of metal gates and pushes a remote. When the gates open Chloe realises whatever image of Tate's house she might have had in her head was all wrong. The house isn't modest in any way. With a house like that on a street like this, it would have cost a staggering amount. He parks in front of the impressive white building and looks at her.

'Not what you imagined, right?'

'I'm not sure what I imagined. It's beautiful.'

'It was designed by a wacky architect. That's why this end is curved. Pain in the ass with furniture, but it's got great views of the sea.'

She gets out of the car and strolls around the large garden. The flowerbeds are bursting with colour and well maintained.

'Didn't picture you as an avid gardener.'

Tate leans against the front of his truck and makes a face. 'Not down to me. My mum was getting on my case about letting the garden go, so I have a gardener to look after it. Like I said, this isn't my forever home. I'll sell it at some stage so it's probably a good idea to keep the garden from turning into something from the set of Jumanji.'

He unlocks the front door and turns off the alarm. Chloe instantly falls in love with the house. The wide entranceway leads into an open plan living room with a mezzanine level jutting out above it. The enormous kitchen is wood and chrome with full length windows in the curved seating area overlooking the garden. Expensive looking leather couches are positioned facing a fireplace and TV.

'Want to see the view?'

He takes her hand and leads her up the wooden staircase to the first floor, then brings her along the corridor and up another stairs to the top floor. He opens the only door at the top and steps into an impressive studio that rivals where they just were. He touches a button on the wall and the blackout blinds taking up the entire wall rise, showing an unspoilt view of the sea.

'You must have some amazing parties here. The view is incredible.'

Tate shrugs and his whole demeanour changes. 'Yeah... I wouldn't call them that amazing.' Tate curses and drops onto the couch against the far wall. He scrubs his hand over his face then curses to himself again. 'Okay, can you sit down for a sec, please. I need to tell you something before... well, I probably should have told you before I suggested dinner. Before I brought you back here, but I wasn't thinking.'

She sits down on the couch opposite him and forces a smile on her face. She's got a really bad feeling about this.

Tate leans forward and turns the ring on his thumb, over and over as he stares at the floor in front of her. 'Right. I'm sure you've read stuff about me online. About what happened after Christmas?'

Chloe nods.

He laughs but it's forced. 'Yeah, there's some interesting theories going around. My fault for not setting the record straight yet.' He takes a deep breath and looks away for a moment. Chloe doesn't want to interrupt him. Whatever he's trying to tell her, it's far from easy or comfortable for him.

'What the press is saying about me... about drinking and partying too much. It's true to a certain extent. We got sucked into the lifestyle for a bit. Endless parties, too much drinking, and after a while, drugs too.

'I'm not going to give you blow-by-blow of what I did, but I will say quite a bit has been exaggerated by certain individuals with an axe to grind.'

'You're referring to Astrid?'

He frowns as he looks up at her. 'Yeah. Sorry, forgot my life is an open fucking book. That absolutely wasn't a dig at you, trust me. More a dig at myself for letting her get to me. I'm not saying I didn't have a problem – far from it, but every single time I stepped on stage I was stone cold sober. She knew full well how that comment would get under my skin.

'I take what I do seriously. Bit too much sometimes. Whatever I was doing in my down time was left behind when I was performing. I wouldn't do that to the people who spent their money to come and see us. I've messed up but I can swear to that fact.'

He shrugs and looks at his clasped hands. 'Anyway, the three of us

131

only calmed down when Gregg joined the band. We still drank and used from time to time, but it was nothing like what we were doing.' He smiles and looks down at the floor for a moment. 'He probably saved us when he joined.' He looks back at her again. 'I know it's clichéd and all, but it is what it is. No point denying what I've done.'

Chloe forces what she knows is a pathetic smile on her face. Deep down she knew most of the stories she'd read about him online must have had at least a grain of truth to them, but hearing it from him is a different thing. The entire situation is strange to listen to. She doesn't drink often and has never considered drugs for even a second. The idea of not being in control of her own body terrified her enough to steer her away from anything like that.

Another unsettling thought crosses her mind. If those stories about him are true, does that also mean the stories of his long and varied love life are also true? She shakes her head. She's not so sure she needs or wants to know about that.

'What?' he asks.

'Sorry?'

'You just shook your head.'

'Nothing. Go on.'

He nods but she can tell he's far from convinced by her response. 'Okay, do you know I'm adopted?'

'Yes. My gran told me.'

'Rick and Becca adopted me when I was seven.' He pulls the pendent out from under his t-shirt. 'The griffin was my welcome to the family present. Sort of like a good luck charm. It was the first present I ever got, and I mean ever. I don't remember much about my life before they took me home.' He pauses and looks out the window for a few seconds before he continues again.

'My Dad... well I don't want to say real Dad cause that's what Rick is. The man I share a minuscule amount of DNA with wasn't a nice guy. Far from it. He used to hit me. A lot.'

132

Chloe stares over at him for a minute or two as the words sink in. 'Oh God...'

'I don't remember any of it. Well, didn't remember. I guess I blocked it out over the years. Or I had until Christmas. Then the memories started coming back. I had pretty vivid nightmares. The damn things wouldn't let up.

'Long story short, I fucked up big time. I locked myself away in the house and lived off drinking for a few days. When that didn't work I added drugs to the drink, then stronger drugs when that didn't work. Anything to help block it all out. I opened my house up to complete fucking strangers. The parties would go on for days, but I was past caring. I didn't want to be alone with whatever was going on in my head.'

He stops and scrubs his hand over his face. 'I... I tried heroin when nothing else worked. I honestly can't remember a lot of what happened after that. I don't know how long I was using it for. There was always another fix ready and waiting for me when I came to. It was the only thing I cared about. The only thing I wanted.

'I cut off everyone close to me. Stopped answering the phone. Wouldn't let them in the house. My parents got worried and broke the kitchen window to get inside. They found me unconscious on the couch with a syringe... still in my arm. I was in a coma for six days. I scared myself so much I checked into rehab as soon as I was released from hospital.

'I'm clean, in counselling, and I'm done with drinking too. The whole sorry fucking situation was a beyond stupid mistake and I'll have to live with it for the rest of my life. I'm trying to put the last few crap months behind me, but I'm not always on top of it.'

Tate pushes up the sleeve of his t-shirt and holds his arm out to her. Chloe instantly sees the raw scratch marks covering the inside of his elbow. 'That was where I...' he takes a deep breath and starts again. 'It's where I injected myself. My shrink thinks the scratching is

133

related to it. I don't even know I'm doing it. It's some subconscious thing I do when I think too much or get stressed or I don't know... I still get nightmares too but I'm not going to use again to deal with them.'

Tate smiles briefly and shrugs. 'So, that's everything. All my shit. I know it's not great and that I should have told you sooner, but it's not something I'm proud of. I totally understand if you want to leave and think about it for a while, or leave and never see me again.'

Chloe is struck dumb as some of what he said sinks in. She has no doubts whatsoever that he hasn't told her everything about his early childhood, just enough to explain the reason behind his addiction, but it's enough. He was telling her about the drugs and rehab, not his past. That might come at a later stage. Perhaps not at all and Chloe could accept that. The fact he opened up to her at all means more to her than she can put into words.

It can't have been easy to tell her what he just did. She's knows it's just her imagination, but Tate appears so much smaller than he did a few minutes before. His head is down and his shoulders hunched as he waits for her to respond. Or for her to reject him. Or maybe judge him. But that's the last thing she wants to do.

'What if I want to stay?'

His head shoots up. 'Stay? Really?'

'Yes, really.'

'I'd be okay with that, if that's what you want. Are you sure?'

Chloe smiles at him. 'I appreciate you trusting me enough to tell me all that, but if it's all the same with you, I'd like to stay.'

He frowns across at her, clearly not believing a word she's saying. 'Right. If you're sure. I mean don't worry about hurting my feelings or anything like that. I'll leave the room so you can make your escape in private.'

'Would you shut up? I heard every word you said and I'd like to stay here with you. Now, you mentioned you make a killer bolognese.'

While Tate gets dinner ready, Chloe sits on the incredibly comfortable leather couch sipping a sparkling water. He had offered to go out and get her some wine, but the last thing she wants to do is jeopardise his recovery by bringing alcohol into his house.

She told him that she heard everything he said to her upstairs, but that doesn't mean she understands any of it. Far from it. But she's not going to condemn him for making a mistake... or several mistakes. Big mistakes. Life threatening mistakes. The part she needs to focus on is that he realised he had a problem and he got help.

'Do you like a lot of garlic or a little?'

Hoping for even a kiss later she tells him a little will be fine. Nothing like garlic breath to kill the moment. The spectacular view from the upstairs studio pales in comparison to the well-built, tattooed, beyond gorgeous rock star crushing garlic in the kitchen a few feet from her. Definitely an image for next year's celebrity calendar.

The man has an irritating habit of teasing her without having to do much. Each time she sees him he has a little more skin on show. He'd changed into a short-sleeved t-shirt which gives her another peek at the enormous griffin that covers most of his left arm, chest, and back.

Since that mind-blowing encounter in the summer house, she's wondered what it would be like to have more with him. She's never felt that with anyone before. That raw need she experienced with him is something she wants to feel again. She blushes when she realises he's talking to her.

'Sorry?'

'You sure you're okay about being here? You've got this strange look on your face.'

'Sorry, I was just admiring your house.' More like admiring its owner, but she'll keep that part to herself. 'How long have you lived here for?'

He stirs the garlic in the pan and takes a drink of juice. 'About a year I think. I was living in a flat with Gregg but once he joined the band we decided it was best to go it alone. When you spend months on the road with someone the last thing you want to do is have your down time with them too. We each needed space.'

'I like Gregg. He's... uncomplicated.'

Tate smirks and nods in agreement. 'That's a good way of describing him. He's a good mate. All the guys are.'

'I suppose you'd have to be close for it to work.' She looks at the wall beside the kitchen showing photos of Tate with the band and his family. Right in the centre is a picture of Tate on his motorbike. 'Is your bike here or at your mum's house?'

He looks over at the photos. 'She's in the downstairs bedroom.'

'Say that again?'

He grins and tips the mince into the pan. 'Third door from the left under the stairs.'

'You keep your bike in the spare room?'

'Too right I do.'

Chloe gets up and opens the double doors into the room. Sure enough, there's the impressive bike, sitting at the foot of the double bed. 'You not tuck it in at night?'

'Of course not. That would be ridiculous.' He joins her at the door and shrugs. 'It's safer in here than in the garage. I'm a control freak, remember?'

Tate swings his leg over the saddle and something tightens around Chloe's throat at the sight of him on the machine. He pushes back in the saddle and pats the seat in front of him. Chloe slips in front of him and lets him place her hands on the handlebars. Tate leaves his hands over hers, trapping her between his arms and his chest. Not an unpleasant experience. He leans closer and she can feel his breath on her ear. 'It suits you. I could give you lessons.'

'I think I'll pass.'

'Good. I kind of liked having you behind me. Wouldn't want to kiss that goodbye just yet.'

'So I can look forward to more outings on this?'

His fingers lace with hers on the handlebars as his hair brushes the side of her face. 'Loads more. Like I said, I liked the feel of you pressed against me.'

She more than liked it too, but for some reason she's lost the ability to speak.

'Chloe?'

'What?'

'Do you like salad with your bolognese.'

She laughs and digs him gently in the ribs. 'No, thank you.'

'Thank fuck. I haven't got any.' He kisses her on the neck then climbs off, holding out his hand to help her. 'C'mon. Our table should be about ready.'

Their table turns out to be the couch with their plates balancing on their knees, but Chloe has no complaints. Never in a million years did she think she'd be so relaxed here, but she is. How can he turn her on so much yet make her feel so comfortable at the same time? He's so chilled out it's difficult not to be the same.

His house cost more than she could ever make no matter how hard she worked, but inside it was homely. You could tell it was expensive, but he didn't have any frills or unnecessary gadgets in every corner. There was no airs or graces, just like with Tate himself.

'You were right.'

He wipes his mouth with the back of his hand and frowns. 'About what?'

'That was a killer bolognese.'

Tate laughs and reaches over to take her plate. 'I wouldn't get too excited. It's the only thing I can cook. Well, apart from a bacon butty. We take it in turns to cook when we're touring. That's my contribution.'

'You don't eat out all the time?'

He slips the dishes into the dishwasher and grabs another bottle of water. 'At first sure, but eating out all the time gets old real fast. We usually do self-catering when we're away. Gives us more privacy.'

'I thought you'd be living it up in posh hotels. That's killed that image for me.'

He refills her glass and sits beside her, a little closer than he was before. He drapes his arm across the back of the couch, but unfortunately doesn't actually touch her. 'Sorry about that. I'm sure others do it that way, but we've never been much into that side of things. The crew stay in a hotel but we prefer to rent a house together.'

'But what about all your adoring fans waiting for you in the lobby?'

'We do meet and greets with them, but no ambushes in hotel lobbies. Our bus will be at the hotel, but we'll be squirrelled away somewhere else eating, sleeping, and practising. It's not as glamorous as people think.'

'But you enjoy it.'

His face lights up and she can't help but be jealous. It must be amazing to love your job so much. 'Every second. This is going to sound big-headed, but when you're on stage and there's a crowd of strangers in front of you singing a song you wrote... I can't describe it. Each and every one of those people have paid their hard earned money to come and see us. It makes all the hard work, all the knock backs worth it.' He turns to face her and tucks one leg under the other. 'When I perform, that's all that exists. Jesus, that sounds crap.'

'It's just you, the band and your fans.'

He nods. 'Yes. That sounded a hell of a lot less corny. Have you

138

been to a concert or live performance?'

'Of course.'

'You know what it's like when you're in that moment, watching, dancing, and singing along. It doesn't matter what else is going on in your life. During that hour or two or whatever, there's nothing else.'

She knows exactly what he's talking about. 'Is it like that for you every time you perform?'

'Every single time. It doesn't matter if I've sung the same songs three or four times a week for months, that feeling is new every time I get on stage.'

'You're lucky to have that.'

'I know. What about you? Have you ever thought about doing something more with your art?'

Chloe laughs and shakes her head. 'Eh no. That's purely a hobby for me. It's never going to pay the bills. Besides, I'm really looking forward to teaching. And I will get to do art with them, although it may be more crafting than art, but I can't wait either way. It's about time I finally settled into a job that may actually have a future.'

'I get that.'

'You say that like you think this isn't your forever job.'

Chloe swallows thickly as he twists her hair around his fingers. She doubts he's doing it intentionally, but he's driving her crazy. He couldn't keep his hands off her in the summer house, yet in the privacy of his own house there was barely any contact. Apart from a quick kiss on her neck earlier, this is the first time he's touched her.

'What we do, it's not exactly what you'd call secure. It'll come to an end at some stage. I could wake up one day and my voice is gone, or the songs I write are crap. We can only earn a living if people pay to see us perform or buy our songs.

'And it's not like we're the only ones doing it. The competition is fierce. We have to keep pushing ourselves to make sure we stand out. Everything we do now has to add something to our retirement pot whenever that happens. It could be next year. It might be ten years from now. The rug could be pulled from under our feet at any stage.'

'I never thought of it that way.'

'Don't get me wrong, we're hoping we'll be going for another few years yet. I'm only thirty-six. Wouldn't mind getting to my forties at least before I have to have a rethink my career options.'

'At least you've always got teaching to fall back on. I'm sure Gran would sign up for more piano lessons. Hey, maybe you could teach her the violin too.'

Tate laughs loudly at that. 'Yeah, not so sure I could teach her full time. I'd have no fucking hair left.'

Tate takes the tub of Haagen Dazs out of the freezer and spoons it into two bowls. He still can't quite believe Chloe didn't run for the door after he offloaded on her upstairs. Whatever he's said or done to keep her from leaving, he'll take it. He can't believe how easy it was to open up to her like that.

When he told Gregg or spoke to his therapist, it was like pulling nails. It was far from pleasant and he hated saying every single word. Hated hearing the pathetic recount of his fuck up, even if it had helped. First, it was a relief being able to talk about it with her. Second, she knows most of the details and she stayed. The details of exactly what his father did weren't coming up for discussion, but at least the little he told her helped her understand his pull to drugs. That was the main reason he'd told her.

He really cares about her. The last thing he wanted to do is throw another spanner at what could be a life-changing relationship by ignoring what he did. She deserved to know. He'd already fucked things up once by not making sure she knew exactly who he was.

Everything he's done up to now has only helped to push her away. Time to own his mistakes and show her exactly how important she is to him.

He hands her one of the bowls and sits beside her again. He places his cold bowl on his crotch hoping it kills any ideas his body might have. He's been on his best behaviour with her all night and it's killing him. The last thing she needs is for him to throw himself at her like some fucking caveman. No matter how much he wants her, he's not going to do anything, not after what happened in the summer house. It had been amazing but then he fucked up. This time he's going to take it slow.

He's wanted to kiss her since she walked into the studio. He's never been this worked up about a woman before. He's had girlfriends over the years but no one who held his attention for longer than a few weeks. It was partly down to the fame thing. There are so many interviews with him all over the place, some people assumed they knew him.

The last three women he attempted to date hadn't asked him one question about himself. As far as they were concerned, they knew him already and didn't need to ask him any questions. They didn't want to be with him. They wanted to say they were with him. Big difference and something he nipped in the bud pretty damn fast.

Chloe is different on so many levels. Maybe having those first few meetings without knowing who he was had helped, but something tells him it would have been different with her either way. She's different. He just has to stop letting his fuck up come between them.

Even without looking he knows he's attacking his arm again. He closes his eyes and curses under his breath. But then Chloe takes his hand in hers and holds it as she continues to eat. He looks across at her and watches her thumb move in circles on his hand. Even that small act settles him. She doesn't say anything to him. Doesn't look at him. Doesn't draw attention to what he was doing. And that floors him. Yeah, this girl is so very different. If he's not careful, he could fall for her and that thought terrifies him.

He glances sideways at her and catches her licking the ice-cream from her spoon. There was nothing intentionally seductive about it but his dick thinks differently. He moves the bowl on his lap, hoping to hide what's straining to get out of his jeans.

'You done with your bowl?'

He doesn't get a chance to answer before she stands up and takes it from his lap. Thankfully she heads towards the kitchen giving him time to readjust himself. Not that it does any good. Then she has to go and make things so much worse by leaning down to put the dishes in the machine. Tight jeans hug her incredible ass and long legs. No amount of readjusting is going to help.

What he wants to do is charge over to her, pick her up, lie her on the couch, and bury himself deep inside her. He wants to run his tongue over every curve, to taste the sweat on her skin. He wants to kiss her, lick her, suck her until she screams his name.

Instead, he's going to struggle with a serious hard-on unable to convince himself to make the move he desperately wants to make. Deep down he's terrified she'll reject him. He doubts what's left of his confidence could survive that. Not that sitting on the couch doing fuck all is helping in any way. He just feels like a pathetic eejit. He's not sure what's worse.

'Tate?'

He wipes his face and looks up at her. 'Sorry?'

'Do you want more to drink?'

'Eh, sorry, yeah. Another water would be great.' He grabs a cushion from the chair beside him and hugs it to his lap, hoping it looks casual and not weird. He silently thanks his sister. She had insisted he have some cushions on the couches. Not until this moment did he see the need or the point of them. Maybe he could leave a review for them on Amazon. '5 stars. Perfect for hiding uncomfortable erections. Would *definitely recommend!'*

She passes him the drink and places her glass on the coffee table. 'Where's your bathroom?'

'Door next to the bike's bedroom.'

She smiles at him and his dick jumps in response, pressing painfully against his jeans. He waits until she closes the door behind her before he stands up and rearranges what is downright agonising. His piercings are digging into him, adding pressure to what's already a far from comfortable situation. He needs to calm down. She might not want this with him after everything he offloaded on her tonight. She's still here so clearly she doesn't hate him, so what the fuck is his problem?

He looks down at his arm and grimaces. Since the life changing events after Christmas he hasn't felt like himself. From the second that needle was stuck in his arm he's been messed up. When he woke up in hospital, everything had turned on its head. It was like the world kept turning, everyone went on with their lives but he was on a different level of existence. Until he deals with that and gets his head right he really should keep away from Chloe.

The bathroom door opens and he glances up. 'Fuck, Chloe.'

Instead of the figure-hugging jeans and off the shoulder sweater he's wanted to take off all evening, she's only wearing matching black lace underwear. If he's looking for a hint she may want him, he's pretty sure that's a good sign.

'Is that a good fuck or a bad one?'

He gestures to the bulge desperate to escape his jeans. 'What do you think?'

She smiles but it's more mischievous than the one he's used to seeing. As if reading his mind, she walks over to the rug in front of the fireplace and kneels down. 'I think it's your turn to get a little more naked.'

He absolutely couldn't agree more.

Chloe has no idea where all this confidence is coming from but she's happy to go along with it. When Gregg came to collect her she had taken a long time to decide if she should plan for what might possibly happen. The underwear had gone in and out of her bag a dozen times before she had finally stuffed the set in her purse and zipped the bag so she couldn't take them out again.

Over the evening she thought she caught little signs he wanted more but she kept dismissing them. But when she took his empty bowl from his lap, she knew it was what he wanted. The poor guy had tried to hide it, but it was all the confirmation she needed.

She'd take the lead on this. For the first time in her life, she'd make the first move. It was the most terrifying and exhilarating thing she's ever done. When she locked herself in the bathroom she'd stared at her reflection for a long time before she got the courage to get undressed and slip into the lace set. Knowing he was out there, waiting for her was such a turn on. Seeing him in front of her just upped that to dangerous levels.

As he approaches her, he kicks off his boots and socks. Then he pulls off his t-shirt and Chloe's heart hammers in her chest. When his jeans and boxers drop she realises she may have bitten off more than she can chew. Everything about this man is seriously impressive.

Then she notices the piercings and she loses a little of her nerve. She's never been with a guy who's been pierced down there. Not only does he have the thick black ring piercing the tip, there's also a bar on the underside near the base where his penis meets his balls.

Tate notices her staring at the two piercings. 'I can take them out if you want.'

She shakes her head. 'Don't you dare. Lie down.'

He raises an eyebrow but she doesn't back down. She's on a

confidence high and wants this to play out like she pictured it. This is something she wants to do for him first. He lowers onto the rug and lies on his back, giving her an unobstructed view of every inch of his body. She gets to her hands and knees and slowly crawls towards him.

She doesn't know whether he should have his body on show all the time or whether it's a good thing he covered it. Every single line, every dip and hollow, every ridge and solid muscle is perfect. And naked. So very naked.

She runs her fingers up his chest and he sucks in a breath. 'Put your arms over your head and keep them there. No touching, okay. This is my meet and greet.'

Tate smirks at her. 'Meet and greets don't usually go like this.'

'I sincerely hope not.' Chloe straddles him and shakes her head as his hand moves towards her. 'No touching.'

Tate grips one wrist in his other hand and stretches his arms over his head. 'You expect me not to touch you when you look like that.' He moves his hips and grinds against her. 'You're not playing fair.'

'I haven't even started yet.' She leans down, pressing her breasts against his chest as she kisses him. There's nothing soft and sweet about the kiss from either side. Chloe pulls away and smiles against his neck as he curses. Chloe kisses the side of his neck, tracing the lines of ink with her tongue. She kisses her way down his shoulder to his broad chest, running her tongue across his nipple. He groans as she gently nips it before moving across to the pierced one. She gently flicks her tongue against the black bar running through the centre. All the piercings are completely new to her and the last thing she wants to do is hurt him. 'Fuck.'

'Too much?'

'Not enough.'

Chloe flicks the piercing again, a little harder this time. Tate curses and she feels his arousal twitch under her. There's so much more to explore on his body so she gives his nipple a little more attention before gently pulling the piercing in her teeth then letting go. Tate gasps and his breathing deepens. 'Jesus, Chloe. What the fuck are you doing to me?'

She kisses, licks, and nips her way down his hard chest to his tight stomach and the other piercings that are terrifying and exciting her in equal amounts.

She traces her fingers along his thick length. For some reason, seeing the black piercings turns her on more than she thought they would. Moving slowly, she touches the bar at the base of his penis making it jump in response, tapping against his belly button as he grunts. She moves back to the tip and runs her thumb along the ring, rubbing his pre-cum around the head before she licks it off.

Her tongue plays along the thick ring embedded in the tip and Tate's whole body spasms. She wraps her hand around his cock and holds him upright. As she tastes him, she risks a quick glance up at his face. He's still holding his wrist in his other hand but his knuckles are white as he restrains himself.

He lifts his head to look down at her and another wave of confidence takes hold of her. She's driving this spectacular man crazy just by touching him. She keeps her eyes locked on his as she flicks her tongue against the piercing in the head of his cock while massaging his balls. He breaks eye contact and curses loudly into his arm.

All the windows in the house are soundproofed, but Tate still tries to stifle the loud curse coming from him as Chloe tortures him. He wasn't expecting this. Hell nothing close to this. Not for one second did he think she'd take charge. He wasn't complaining. Fuck the whole macho pride thing. If a stunning woman wearing sexy underwear tells you to lie down and not move, you lie down and don't fucking move. No questions. The thing is, the not moving part is proving harder than he thought. He can't get over how fast she was figuring out his body. If she kept playing with his piercings he was very likely to come in the next few seconds.

Her dark hair tickles his balls as she runs her tongue from the base to the tip of his dick. Chloe smiles up at him as she slowly sucks the ring before letting him go. 'I like these.'

He digs his fingers into his wrist as she pulls the ring into her mouth again. 'Fuck. Is that right?'

Before she answers she licks him, moving her tongue slowly up his length. 'A lot more than I thought I would.'

He glances down as she plays with them again. She's the first one who hasn't shied away from them or asked if he'd take them out. If anything, she doesn't look like she can get enough of them. She slips the ring into her mouth and sucks, pulling it gently and driving him fucking crazy.

'Fuck. You can play with them as much as you want.'

She smiles up at him then slowly slips him into her mouth. Her warm, wet mouth works him hard as her tongue targets the ring every time she moves up his dick. Her other hand grips him tightly as she increases her pace.

He doesn't want her to stop but he's not about to shoot into her mouth. The pressure builds and somehow, although fuck knows how, he convinces his brain to get with the program. 'Chloe. Fuck, I'm close.'

Instead of pulling away, she takes him deeper into her mouth, her lips wrapping tightly around him. When she pulls at his nipple piercing while her tongue slips under the ring in his dick, he loses the little control he had left. His shout is loud and he seriously couldn't give a fuck.

The orgasm rocks through his body in waves as he empties himself into her mouth. Chloe's tongue rubs against the underside of his dick, keeping the pressure on as she grips him tightly in her mouth. When his dick finally stops pulsing, she pulls back while sucking him which does fuck all to calm him down.

Tate peels his fingers out of his wrist and drapes his arm over his face. 'Fuck me.'

Chloe peers at him under his arm, a playful smile on her face. 'Did I not just do that?'

'Too damn right you did. I reckon it's my turn to say wow.'

Chloe's heart hammers in her chest as Tate suddenly flips them over, covering her with his body. He slips his hand around the back of her neck and draws her closer. Chloe's lips part and Tate sinks his tongue in. Unlike at the cliff top, this kiss is torturously slow. He explores her mouth, every stroke hitting her core and sending waves of pleasure through her.

His hand slides from behind her head, his fingers tracing along her jaw and down her neck. She moans as he moves down to her breast, brushing his fingers over her nipple. Goosebumps follow in his finger's wake, down her side and across her stomach.

His fingers find the laced edge of her panties and makes quick work of them, throwing them behind him. His hand caresses her entrance, teasing her by just being there then with a thrust his finger penetrates her. His tongue in her mouth and his finger deep inside her keep perfect timing, making her feel dizzy. She buries her hands in his dark hair and pulls him against her, crushing their mouths together. She wants more but he's holding her back, keeping control. Chloe moans and rocks against his hand, rubbing his palm against her clit as he strokes her inside and out.

Tate adds another finger, stretching and filling her, all the while kissing her deep enough to leave her breathless. She grinds against his hand, desperate for the orgasm growing with every stroke of his fingers.

But then Tate slowly pulls his slick fingers out, drawing her back from the edge. He smiles against her mouth as she whimpers.

He breaks the kiss and slides one finger into his mouth, sucking it clean before doing the same to the second.

'You taste too fucking good, Chloe.'

He keeps his dark eyes locked on hers as he moves down her body, sucking on one nipple then the other before kissing his way further down her body.

Chloe cries out when his tongue drives deep inside her before withdrawing torturously slow.

'Please.' She wants more. She needs more.

As if reading her thoughts, he slides a finger deep inside as his tongue moves up to tease her. When he adds a second finger she groans and moves against his hand. Then his fingers curl up and touch a spot deep inside that has her back arching off the ground.

'Oh, God!' She fists his hair as she grabs his head, holding him tight against her. 'Tate! Don't stop.'

But he has no intention of stopping. Instead, the long firm strokes speed up, his fingers working her inside while his tongue skims over her clit lightly. She cries out in frustration when he denies her the release she needs.

She could swear he actually laughs at her, but maybe that's just her imagination. She can't tell up from down right now and all she wants is for Tate to give her what's promising to be a memorable orgasm.

When his tongue finds her clit again her entire body goes rigid. As his fingers massage her, the pressure of each stroke leaves her writhing against his hand. She's so close. She's perching on the edge and needs him to tip her over. Then he gives her exactly what she wants.

Tate sucks her clit, using his tongue to massage as he works her.

Chloe's breath comes in short gasps as the orgasm builds. She rears back on the rug and screams, her entire body shuddering as it rips through her. Tate doesn't stop what he's doing, drawing the sensations out.

When her vision finally comes back, she gazes down at him. His dark eyes are on her and he looks sexy as hell. He slowly moves his tongue over her, sending another shiver through her body. Tate moves up beside her and holds her jaw as he kisses her. He tastes of her and she loves it.

He fists her hair, moving her head to the side so he can nip along the length of her neck.

'Jesus, Chloe. Do you have any fucking idea how much I want you?' His breath is warm as he nibbles on her ear.

'I'm completely on board with that.'

He smiles as he kisses across her jaw. 'Don't move. I'll be back in a sec.'

Chloe points to her handbag sitting on the couch. 'My bag.'

Tate passes her down her handbag and she rummages inside then passes him a condom. 'Came prepared just in case the underwear worked.'

'And there was me thinking you wore underwear like that all the time.'

She smiles up at him. 'Sorry to disappoint you.'

Tate rubs his hard cock against her hip as he smiles down at her. 'Does that feel like I'm disappointed?'

'No, I don't think so.' She turns her head to the side as he sucks on her ear.

'I can't wait to be inside you, Chloe. I can't wait to watch you bite your bottom lip when my thick cock slides inside and stretches you. I'm going to bury myself so deep in your wet pussy you won't know where I end and you begin. I'm going to look in your eyes as you feel me moving in you. I'm going to make you so fucking desperate to come, you'll be begging me to stop teasing you and fuck you harder. Begging me to let you come.'

Chloe whimpers and licks her dry lips. She could absolutely picture every single word of that and she absolutely wants him to do every single word of it.

'Please, Tate. I want you inside me.'

He opens the condom and slips it on. As she watches him, her nerves creep in a little. Tate is so much bigger than anyone else she's been with.

Chloe's nerves jump up a level as he positions himself between her legs. He slides the tip in then waits as she gets used to him. Chloe looks down and groans as she watches the thick muscles in his stomach roll as he slips his cock in and out of her, teasing her. Every glorious muscle shifts and ripples as he moves.

He pushes deeper into her, filling her. Chloe groans when he pulls out before slowly driving into her again.

'You feel so good.'

'You haven't got all of me yet. Fuck, you're so tight, Chloe.'

Chloe gasps as Tate slowly pushes into her, stretching her until his full length is buried deep inside. She closes her eyes as he rolls his hips, his piercing rubbing against all the right places as he moves.

'Don't you dare close your eyes. Look at me.'

She looks up at him, at his broad chest, at the colourful ink on his skin shifting as he moves. The sight of his thick shaft sliding out then pushing deep inside her again is nearly enough to send her over the edge.

'Oh God, Tate.' He slows his movements, and she moans, 'Don't stop.'

'I'm only getting started.'

Tate kisses her, matching the movements of his tongue with his hips, moving in and out tortuously slow. He's driving her crazy. He's doing everything to keep her on the brink of breaking. She doesn't

152

know how long he keeps it up for. All she knows is that every nerve ending in her body is on fire.

He's too much for her. Whatever he's doing with his hips each time he pushes in and out of her is making thought difficult. But she knows one thing - she absolutely wants him to stop torturing her. She digs her fingers into his ass, trying unsuccessfully to get him to move faster. Each thrust of his hips is slow, deep, and so good.

Tate props himself up on one elbow, and grips her thigh with his other hand, spreading her, filling her impossibly deeper. He pulls out then rams in again, deeper and harder than before.

She opens her eyes to find him staring down at her. His dark hair is tousled and the look in his eyes is one of pure dominance.

'Please, Tate.'

'Please what? Tell me what you want.' His deep voice is gruff and commanding.

'Stop teasing me. Please.'

He withdraws then drives into her again. 'You want to come, Chloe?'

She writhes under him, but he's not letting her have what she wants. Not yet. 'Please, Tate. I want you to go harder.'

Tate thrusts into her, driving the air from her lungs. Her fingernails dig into his forearms as she tries to ground herself, but he's relentless. His body tenses as he gets close to orgasm and the sight does nothing to calm her.

'I want you to hear you scream my name when you come all over my cock.'

Then he slips his hand between them, sliding a finger to either side of her clit. He squeezes gently as he moves them back and forth massaging her clit as he thrusts into her.

'Now, Chloe.' He squeezes his fingers together and pinches her clit. Chloe comes apart, screaming his name. The orgasm hits so hard she claws at the rug as the sensations take over every inch of her body.

Tate holds her in place, keeping her exactly where he wants her. His fingers continue working her, drawing it out, leaving her lost in the intense pleasure.

Tate locks his arms to keep himself from squashing her as the tremors work through his body. He didn't last long after she screamed. When she arched her back off the floor and her pussy squeezed his dick he was a goner. It was without a doubt the most intense orgasm he's ever had.

'You okay?' he gasps.

'No, but in the best possible way.'

He laughs, rolls off her and flops onto his back with his arm over his face. 'Where the hell did that come from?'

'I have no idea but it was nice.'

He props himself up on his elbow and looks down at her. 'I'm sorry, it was nice?'

She opens one eye and smiles up at him. 'Very nice. I'm well and truly fucked.'

Tate laughs and lies back on the rug. 'I'm really hoping you didn't find that black underwear in my bathroom.'

She rolls over and lies on his chest. 'I thought I'd plan for all eventualities. When I took your bowl off your lap I realised we may have been on the same track.'

'I was kind of hoping you didn't notice.'

'A cushion, Tate. Not exactly subtle.' She looks down at his groin and smiles. 'No cushion was going to hide that.'

'That's one-hundred-percent your fault.' Tate wraps his arms around her. 'Thank you.'

'For what?'

'Giving me another chance. I thought I'd fucked things up for good.' He runs his hand over her hair, smoothing the post-sex tangles. 'I've got a problem though.'

She freezes in his arms. 'What?'

He shuffles down so he's looking at her face. 'My problem is that I want you, Chloe. I want you in my life. As messed up and weird as my life is right now, I want you to be part of it.' He wasn't expecting to have this conversation with her so soon. Hell, he's never had this conversation with anyone, but it feels right.

She releases a breath then smiles. 'You mean like see more of each other?'

'A hell of a lot more. And I don't just mean like this, although more of this is part of the deal. I'm talking about dates that involve wearing clothes. Going out in public together as a couple. You on for that?'

'I like you, Tate. I really do, but are you sure it's the right time for you to be seen with someone?'

'I couldn't give a fuck about any of that. I don't want to be without you. Have I mentioned I'm a selfish prick?'

She laughs and kisses him. 'Guess that makes two of us. I don't want to be without you either.'

'I was hoping you'd say that. Would have been a bit awkward otherwise.'

Tate slips on a pair of boxers before he heads back downstairs again. It's got nothing to do with being modest. Maybe with a barrier between them, his damn cock would behave and settle down for a bit. He's always had a healthy appetite when it came to sex, but this is fucking ridiculous. There's just something about Chloe that turns him into a horny teenager. He can't get enough of her.

He stops at the top of the stairs and his chest tightens when he sees her. Chloe is asleep, sprawled on her back on the rug, her deep brown hair splayed out behind her. So much for telling his body to behave. Then again, how could he possibly expect it to when he had her. It's a lost cause.

He quietly crouches down beside her and carefully slips his arms under her. As he stands up Chloe curls against his body. 'Tate?'

'I got you.'

He brings her upstairs and lies her on his bed, then shuffles in beside her, tucking the duvet around them. He carefully slips his arm under her head so he can spoon her to his chest, smiling when she wraps her arms around his to hold him close. It feels so right having her here with him. He could absolutely get used to sharing his bed with her every night.

But there's no way he's going to fall asleep with her here. If he has one of his nightmares he could hurt her and that doesn't bear thinking about. He'll stay with her for a few hours then go upstairs and do some work. He's due in the studio first thing so he'll have to get up early anyway.

Avoiding sleep is bringing its own set of issues to the party. Like right now. There's no way he can lie beside her like this in a warm bed and stay awake. As much as he really doesn't want to leave her or the bed, he slides his arm out from under her and throws on a t-shirt and gym shorts. He grabs a glass of water from the kitchen then goes into the small gym next to the garage.

A few hours working out, a shower, and then to the studio. He curses himself and turns on the light. Probably not the best plan he's ever come up with but it's all he's got.

Chloe resists opening her eyes for a long time after she wakes up. She has never felt so relaxed yet so worn out before. Everything aches but in such a good way. She knows without opening her eyes that she's in his bed. The intoxicating scent of sandalwood and leather is everywhere. She rolls over and eventually opens her eyes. No sign of Tate, but she knows he did join her. She remembers the feel of his body against her. She squints at the bedside table and spots a piece of paper with her name on it.

Had to go to the studio for a few hours. Didn't want to wake you. I'll be back by 12. Make yourself at home. Tate.

She checks the time on her watch. It's just after nine. First things first. Shower. Using more effort than she'd like, she climbs out of the comfortable bed and shakes out the duvet. When Chloe opens the en-suite door her mouth drops open. The bathroom is the size of the ground floor of her gran's house. The shower would easily fit ten in it, as would the deep spa bath.

The polished grey tiles are gleaming and every piece of chrome is mirror clear. She turns on the shower and steps under the huge waterfall. Jets shoot out of the wall and massage her to within an inch of her life. If she had a shower like that at home she'd never leave the house.

She wraps a plush grey towel around her and uses his comb to try and sort out her hair. After dressing she goes downstairs and looks over at the rug by the fire. Her body wakes as the memories come back to her. Her thoughts wander for a minute before she reins herself in. There'll be time for more of that later.

She fills the kettle and turns to the counter finding another note.

Not used to company for breakfast. Only have Coco Pops so I grabbed some pastries from down the road. They're in the fridge.

Under that he scribbled his phone number which she immediately pops into her contacts list, smiling as she hits save. She laughs at the box of cereal on the counter with the clean bowl and spoon beside it. The fact that Tate eats kids' cereal keeps her smiling as she finishes her breakfast then pours herself a cup of tea and demolishes one of the biggest croissants she's ever seen.

After clearing away her breakfast things, she climbs the stairs to the second floor and into the enormous studio. Chloe wanders over to the far wall to examine the awards and plaques on display. Tate's name is engraved into some of the dozen or so plaques with Broken Chords on the rest. She recognises the names of some of their songs but is embarrassed to admit not all of them.

Chloe runs her hand along the stand of guitars under the awards. She doesn't know why she's so nervous about asking him to play for her. It's what he does and does really well if the awards are anything to go by.

She closes the door behind her and goes back downstairs. While she waits for the kettle to boil again she turns on the TV and chooses the music app. She enters Broken Chords in the search bar and plays the first song on the list, turning the volume up high. His deep rich voice fills the room and sends shivers down her spine.

She's slightly relieved she recognises most of their songs, but there are quite a few she's never heard, which isn't great considering she's dating the lead singer now.

Chloe smiles as she listens to him singing. She's dating him. She's dating Tate Archer. Her sister is going to find this entire thing hilarious. She's the one who immerses herself in the glossy magazines and reality shows and the like. No doubt Steph would have recognised him from a mile off.

Chloe is tempted to ring her and tell her the exciting news. The fact she's seeing someone is news enough. The last few years have been more miss than hits when it came to men. Every time she spoke to her sister she would get the usual interrogation about her love life, or lack thereof. When she hears her sister is dating Tate it may actually shut her up for a while. Well, until the questions about the man himself start. And no doubt a surprise visit to meet him.

She lies back on the couch, closes her eyes, and listens to him singing. Maybe she'll hold off on telling anyone and just enjoy having Tate all to herself for a little longer.

Tate closes the front door behind him and smiles to himself when he hears one of his songs playing. Sounds like Chloe is getting to grips with their music. Thousands of people listen to him sing, but for some reason knowing she is sends him into stupid grinning mode.

He slips off his jacket and quietly opens the door from the hallway into the living area - not that you'd be able to hear much over the music. He leans against the bookcase inside the door and watches Chloe dance around his kitchen as she makes herself a cup of tea.

Her long hair is still damp and swings over her shoulders as she moves. Her feet are bare and the jeans and tank top she's wearing hug every stunning curve of her body. It is without a doubt one of the sexiest things he's ever seen. What the fuck did he do to deserve someone like her?

To top off the image, she's singing along with him and getting most of the words right, which isn't easy. He sings the first few lines of each verse pretty fast but she's got the hang of it.

As much as he could happily watch her all day, he wants so much more. His hands need to be all over those curves. Chloe notices him a split second before he grabs her around the waist, spinning her around, and pulling her back against his chest. He brushes her hair out of his way as he kisses along her neck and up to her earlobe. Before he realises what he's doing he sings along with himself on the TV.

He's never been good singing one-on-one, but it feels right with her. As he sings he runs a hand between her breasts and down to her stomach. Chloe groans and presses against him, rubbing against his more than ready cock. All the while he keeps singing to her and Chloe seems to be liking it.

She reaches behind her and fists her hand in his hair as her other hand guides him exactly where she wants him. Tate slips his fingers under the top of her underwear and slides a finger inside. As he sings, Chloe pushes back, grinding her ass against him. Her other hand moves from his hair to rub him through his jeans. He stops singing, spins her around then lifts her onto the edge of the countertop. She wraps her legs around him and pulls his t-shirt off.

'Keep singing.'

Tate does his best but he's struggling to remember the fucking words. She kisses along the side of his neck and uses her legs to hold him close against her. Her tongue flicks against his ear and she gently pulls at his earrings.

Fuck singing. He needs his mouth for other things. He pulls off her t-shirt and bra then lies her back on the counter. Her jeans don't put up much of a fight before he tackles his own clothes. Chloe looks at him as she slides a finger between her legs. Chloe groans as he takes her hand and pushes her fingers further into her pussy.

'I want to watch you fuck yourself.'

His dick throbs as her long fingers disappear deep inside her. She bites her lip and looks at him as she plays with herself. In his kitchen. On his fucking counter. Her breath increases, her breasts rising and falling as she gets closer to coming. Tate takes his cock in his hand as her pace quickens. He's so ready to get inside her, but not yet. If it kills him he's going to wait until she's done.

Her back arches off the counter as she gasps. Her fingers slide out of her pussy and he grabs her wrist guiding it to his mouth, greedily sucking them clean.

He grabs the condom from his wallet and quickly puts it on. There's no taking it gently with her. Not after that. He slips into her, nearly coming as she tightly squeezes him. He pulls her towards him and Chloe rakes her fingernails down his chest, finding his piercing. It didn't take her long to figure out playing with his nipple piercing is guaranteed to drive him fucking crazy.

Tate grips her waist as he thrusts into her. Chloe reaches down and rubs her fingers around her clit, brushing against his cock as he fucks her.

'Fuck, Chloe. Don't stop.'

Tate drives his hips forwards faster and faster, unable to get enough of Chloe and what she does to him. He looks down and grinds out a curse. The sight of his dick sliding in and out of her pussy while she's playing with herself is too much.

'Now, Chloe. Come for me now.'

Tate digs his fingers into her flesh as he holds back, waiting for her to come first. He takes over and runs his thumb over her clit. She's so close. Even after this short time together he's getting to know her body. Getting to know how her breathing changes when she's about to orgasm, the small hitch in her breath like she's doing right now.

She arches off the counter, her pussy tightening around him destroying the last of his restraint. He curses loudly as his orgasm hits, the waves continuing as she milks him until he collapses on the counter, sweaty and gasping for breath. In the background he's still singing away on the TV oblivious to what's just happened.

'Hi.' Chloe brushes his hair back from his face when he finally gets the energy to lift his head. 'How was work?'

He laughs. 'Yeah, not bad, thanks. Hell of a welcome home.'

'I'm pretty sure you instigated it.'

'You swinging your ass in my direction when I came in instigated it.' He slides out and leans over her, taking in the body he can't get enough of. 'You are fucking stunning.'

She blushes which just makes her look completely adorable. 'You mean that, don't you.'

'Of course.' He points to his groin. 'That's a genuine reaction to you, Chloe. Damn thing is permanently standing at attention when you're around. You mind if I shut myself up? I've listened to myself singing enough today.'

Chloe laughs and drapes an arm over her face. 'No problem.'

He throws the condom in the bin then searches for the remote. He picks a random mix instead, turning the sound down a little before he joins her again. 'You need help dismounting the counter?'

'Probably best. I still can't feel my legs.'

Tate picks her up and carries her over to the couch. He tucks in beside her and brushes his hand through her hair.

Chloe traces the wings of the griffin across his chest. 'You know, I've never been like this with anyone before.'

'I fucking hope not,' he replies, surprised at the sudden tightening in his chest at the thought of anyone else laying a finger on her.

'No, I mean all this. I've never felt this comfortable with someone. What happened last night... you know, taking the lead with you. That was a first for me. I don't do things like that. You're a bad influence, Tate Archer.'

'Is that so? That was sexy as hell, Chloe. Both last night and now. I mean it.'

'You're just too damn... shaggable. I can't help myself.'

He pushes back so he can look at her face. 'I'm sorry, I'm what?'

'Every single time I look at you I want you. I was making myself a cup of tea. You walk in and a few seconds later I'm naked on a counter. There are floor to ceiling windows, Tate. Anyone could have seen us.'

'The only person who could see you was me. And if you're complaining about the counter, I've got a very comfortable bed upstairs if you'd prefer.'

'Lunch first.'

He nuzzles into the side of her neck. 'Spoil sport.'

Chloe traces his jaw with her finger. 'We'll need all our energy for your incredibly comfortable bed later.'

'Is that right? And just for the record, this is all new for me too.'

She looks surprised by his admission. 'It is?'

'Yeah. I can be myself with you. I've never felt I could do that before.'

'Maybe me not knowing who you were at the start helped get us to this point.'

He nods. 'You might be right. Whatever the reason, I'm not complaining. Although, I might have to take those songs off our tour setlist.'

'What? Why?'

'Because every single time I hear them I'm going to picture you naked, playing with yourself on my counter. Could wind up being a bit embarrassing for me when my friend springs to life mid song.'

'Ah. I see what you're saying. Sorry about that.'

'Never apologise for that. It's no big deal. It's not like they're popular songs anyway.'

'They are, aren't they?'

'Yep. Always the ones people ask for.'

'So concerts will be fun for you from now on.'

He laughs and pulls her close to him, breathing her in. He has absolutely no interest in moving. Ever. Her fingers play with his hair, the rhythmic stroking nearly sending him to sleep.

He'd only managed two hours sleep last night and they had been purely by accident. Thankfully, he hadn't had a nightmare but was too scared to risk it. Besides, lying awake listening to her breathing wasn't a bad way to spend a few hours. He's paying for it now though. He's exhausted but he doesn't want her to leave. He'll just lie with her for a few minutes then get lunch ready.

Chloe waits a few minutes after he falls asleep before she slowly works her way out from under Tate's arm. She finally manages to extract herself and pulls the blanket from the other couch, carefully laying it over his naked body. She holds her breath as he stirs, but all he does is drape his arm over his face then stills again.

She tiptoes upstairs and showers again, then gets dressed and comes back downstairs. He's still asleep so she leaves the music on to mask any noises she might make. Chloe faces the broad countertop and smiles to herself. She opens a few cupboards before she finds something to clean the top with.

Once every trace of their session is wiped away, she picks up the two brown paper bags Tate left at the door when he came in. She unpacks the food and places it in the fridge for later then makes the cup of tea he had distracted her from making earlier.

She takes her mug back into the sitting room and settles on the armchair facing him. He looks tired. Thinking back he always looks tired. Perhaps the nightmares he spoke about keep him awake. Maybe he doesn't sleep in case he gets dragged into a dream? He must be exhausted. He was barely on the couch for ten minutes before he drifted off.

She smiles as she watches him sleep. He's beautiful. She hasn't used that word to describe many men she's known, but he deserves it. She's not just referring to his looks, although that is a definite plus. The more she gets to know him, the real him, the person he is inside, the more attractive he becomes. The passion he has for his music is hard to miss. His face lit up when he was talking about performing and she found it impossible not to smile along with him. He absolutely loves what he does and rightly so.

What her gran said about him was accurate. He hasn't changed since he found fame. No doubt he's worth quite a bit but didn't flaunt what he has. From what she can make out from her gran, he helped his family and treated himself to a house and some new transport, but that was it. Unless of course he had a few more houses all over the world, but she highly doubts it.

He wasn't doing what he does for the fame and fortune. He was doing it because he loved singing and playing music. All the other stuff was a happy accident.

She has no intention of waking him up. He needs to sleep and she's more than happy to let him get some much needed rest. Problem is, it's half-one and she's hungry. She takes one of the pasta salads he brought home with him and sits at the counter while she eats, looking out the window at the rain.

As she's placing the bowl in the dishwasher, she hears what sounds like a whimper from Tate. The groan that follows is full of pain and stops her in her tracks. He wraps his arms around his head and curls into a ball as he mutters something that sounds like 'please.'

She turns off the music and sits on the arm of the chair next to his head. Tate pulls at his hair and he buries his head further under his arms, like he's trying to protect himself from whatever he's

165

experiencing. Like he had done on the beach a few days ago.

Chloe slowly places her hand on his head and runs her fingers through his hair between his clenched fists. It was something her mother always did for her when she was a child and it soothed her every single time. It seems to be working for him too. She can see the muscles in his arms relaxing and his fingers loosen their painful grip on his hair. After a few minutes his breathing steadies and his whole body relaxes.

She keeps it up until his arm drops from over his face. Chloe gently kisses his cheek then retreats to the other couch and hugs her knees to her chest.

He's not dealing with what happened to him when he was a child. After seeing what she just did she is sure of that much. Rehab helped him overcome his addiction, but the reason for turning to drugs in the first place is still very much there and something he's not talking about.

Chloe rests her chin on her knees and watches as his brow furrows briefly before he relaxes again. Unfortunately she has no idea how to help him. Avoiding sleep is only going to make things so much worse for him. Especially when he begins to tour again.

All she can do is hope that, with time, he'll trust her enough to talk about what really happened to him.

Tate wakes to the smell of something amazing coming from his kitchen. He stretches and rolls over, smiling widely when he spots Chloe in the kitchen getting lunch ready. But then he glances out the window behind her and his stomach drops. Unless the sun is moving all skew ways, it's well past lunchtime.

'How long was I asleep for?'

She checks her watch and smiles at him. 'Six hours or so. How do you feel?'

'Mortified for starters.' Great move to fall asleep and leave her on her own in a strange house for six hours. 'I'm sorry. I didn't mean—'

'Hey. Stop that. You were tired. Did you sleep at all last night?'

'I'm not a great sleeper at the moment. What the hell have you been doing all afternoon?'

She turns down the heat on the hob and picks up a pile of paper from the coffee table. 'Well, I admit I was a little unsure what to do for about half an hour then decided to make myself useful. I planned what I was going to make for dinner. After that I may have stolen some paper from the office. I hope you don't mind.' She hands him the pages and Tate flicks through the landscapes of the view from his house.

'You did all these while I was asleep?'

'It's amazing how much you can get done with no distractions. Well, apart from you snoring away in the background.'

'Oh fuck, please don't tell me I was snoring.'

She kisses him on the forehead before going back to their dinner. 'Not for long.'

He places the drawings back on the table and scrubs a hand over his face. He may be pissed off that he fell asleep, but he hasn't felt this rested in months. Lately, sleep was something he did only when he absolutely had to which was seriously off for him. Before Christmas he'd have happily slept most of the morning away. Now he's scared of it. If he wasn't sleeping deeply, the nightmares wouldn't have a chance to get him. Great in theory but the practice part was falling short. He runs a hand through his hair and winces when he rubs against a cut on his scalp.

'I had a nightmare, didn't I.'

'Yes, but you settled again. You started mumbling so I ran my hand over your hair until you relaxed again. My mother always did it to me when I had nightmares.'

He's at a loss for words. Whatever she'd done, it had bought him a few hours of peace. The nightmare hadn't really registered with him.

She gestures to the stairs. 'Now, why don't you grab a shower and get dressed. I'd prefer you stay naked, but I've gone to a lot of trouble here. I don't want dinner ruined because you're distracting me.'

He does as he's told even though he'd prefer to distract her before dinner. When he comes back downstairs she's dishing up their food. 'Where did you get all this from?'

'I've reheated the leftover pasta dish you brought back for lunch and made a sauce from bits I found in your cupboards and freezer. I hope you don't mind.

'My cupboards? As in the ones in the kitchen?'

'Yes. As in the ones in your kitchen. Why do you look so surprised?'

'That's like my snowed in, absolute desperate for food stash. I didn't actually think there was anything that could make all this.'

'I'm going to be doing most of the cooking, aren't I?'

He sits down beside her and grins. 'Afraid so. Cooking and me - we have a love/hate thing going on.' He tries the food and is really impressed. 'This tastes amazing, Chloe.'

'Glad you like it. So, are you going to tell me how long you've had trouble sleeping?'

He swallows and takes a long drink before he answers. 'A while.'

'That answer firmly sits in the vague category. I'm not trying to be nosey, Tate. I'm just worried about you.'

'I know and I appreciate that, but I'm grand, really. I'm used to getting by on hardly any sleep.' He doesn't bother adding that in the past he'd used artificial means to give himself a boost. He didn't realise until recently how much of a boost he actually got from what he took.

Chloe leans back in the chair and smirks at him. 'It's so obvious you're used to being interviewed. You have a fantastic knack of avoiding giving a straight answer.'

'Sorry. I'm not trying to be evasive.' But she's right. He's avoiding answering her. The last thing he wants is Chloe keeping an eye on everything he does. 'Okay, it was Christmas, but it's getting better. You don't have to worry about me.' He reaches out and squeezes her hand. 'Promise.'

'Just be careful not to push yourself too hard. You need to look after yourself.'

'Yes, ma'am.' His mock salute falls a little short. He's trying to make light of his situation but she's not buying it. Thankfully she changes the subject and the rest of their dinner is eaten while she talks about her eccentric uncle and some of the meals she had to invent while she was living in Alaska with him. Hearing some of the stories, he's not surprised she could make what she did from his cupboard stock.

Tate glares at his phone as it vibrates across the counter towards Chloe. He grimaces when he spots Ellen's name on the screen.

'Are you going to answer that?'

He'd prefer not to, but he'd already gotten an earful from Ellen for taking so long to get in touch after he was released from rehab. He could do without a replay of that conversation so picks up the phone and tries to sound cheery as he answers. 'Hey Ellen.'

'Hey Ellen? Is that it? I've been trying to get a hold of you for days.'

'Sorry. I was in the studio.'

'I know that, Tate. That's why I left numerous messages on your mobile. If you keep ignoring me we're going to fall out. I guarantee you don't want that, Tate. I can't do my job if you go AWOL on me. Do you hear me.'

'Yeah. Sorry.'

'Of course you are. Just like the last time. And the time before. Anyway, I need to know if you're going to the awards?'

'What awards?' he asks.

Ellen sighs loudly on the other end of the phone. 'Have you even read my emails?'

'What emails?'

'Why am I not surprised? The awards dinner in London. I've only sent you about a dozen emails about it. Broken Chords are up for two awards.'

'Ah, right. Forgot about that.'

'Well it's time you refresh your memory. I want the band there but you're kind of integral to that. Dillon, Gregg, and Luke have all got back to me, but I need a yes from you too before I confirm. Read your damn emails and let me know if you're bringing anyone with you.'

'Listen, I—'

'No, Tate. I'm going to stop you right there. How about I make this really easy for you. You are going, okay. No arguments. Do you hear me? This is the perfect opportunity to get back out into the public eye without having to face an interview. It's a dinner. That's it. You go. Smile at the lovely people. Pose for a few photos. Eat a ridiculously priced meal then come home. Simple. Uncomplicated.'

'I just don't think—'

'Again, stopping you right there. You need to get back out there before people forget who you are. Show your face and smile. That's it. Oh, and wear a suit. It's not black-tie but you'll need to look the part.'

He closes his eyes and rubs his forehead. An award ceremony is the last fucking thing he wants to face, but she has a point. He can't keep harping on about finishing this new album if he's just going to hide in the studio for the rest of his life. That's not how it works. He can't do his job and not go to things like this. It's also not fair on the guys. He needs to show his face.

'Hello? Tate? You still there?'

'Yeah. Okay, I'll go.'

Ellen pauses for a few seconds. 'Wow. That was relatively painless for a change. I was all prepped for a battle. So, will you be going alone or bringing a plus one?'

'I'll let you know tomorrow.'

'Great. Talk to you in the morning.' She ends the call and Tate buries his head in his hands.

'Is everything okay?'

'No. Well, yes, it is. I'm just being...' He takes a deep breath and smiles at her. 'Right, so I have a favour to ask, but I don't want you to feel like you have to say yes. Believe me, I want to refuse but I'm kind of stuck.'

'Okay, you're going to have to back up a little. What do you want to ask?'

171

'We've been nominated for an award. Actually I think it's two. I need to check.'

'Oh my God! That's amazing, Tate. Congratulations!'

'I wouldn't get too excited. We were nominated a few weeks before I went off the rails. I seriously doubt we'll get it now. But Ellen, she's our manager, she really wants me to go. As in I'm going and that's it. I just thought you might fancy a night out. Well, it'll be two nights. The dinner is in London so it would mean flying out on the Friday and back on Sunday. Like I said, you don't have to come.'

'Are you finished?'

Tate grins. 'Sorry. I'll shut up.'

'Are you sure you want me to come? It'll be the first time we're... you know, out together.'

'Why the hell do you think I'm all iffy about it? I don't want you to feel pressured to be seen with me.'

'I was thinking about you being seen with me,' Chloe replies with a smile.

'You can knock that off for starters. It's you I'm worried about.'

'I'd love to come with you.'

'You sure?'

'Of course. When exactly is it? Do you have any details?'

He pulls up his email on his phone, grimacing when he sees quite a few from Ellen about the event. 'Fuck, bit short notice. It's in two weeks. Probably should have read the emails before. The band are up for Best Rock Album and I'm nominated in the Song of the Year group for a song I wrote.'

Until Ellen's phone call he had completely forgotten about the two nominations. Being nominated is such a big deal for the band. Having the lead singer all over the media alongside the words heroin, addict, and rehab, probably would have ruined any chance they had at winning. Years of hard work gone to waste all thanks to him. He's managed to destroy not only his career but that of his three closest

172

friends.

Chloe takes his hand in hers and he looks down. He was scratching his arm again.

'Are you okay?'

He smiles and nods although okay is far from how he feels. 'Yeah. All good.' He focuses on the email again, trying to sound at least a little excited about the event for her sake. 'Ellen suggests flying to London on Friday evening. The dinner is on Saturday night, so we'll have the day to ourselves. The car will pick us up from the hotel at six. There'll be some photos, then a dinner. After that they'll announce the awards. Might go on till the early hours. Ellen will get us back home sometime on Sunday afternoon.'

'Will there be loads of famous people there?'

Tate looks up from his phone and laughs. 'Yeah. There usually are a few at these things.'

She slaps his arm. 'Stop laughing at me. This is all new to me. I've never met anyone famous before.'

Tate smirks and crosses his arms. 'Is that right?'

Chloe takes a few seconds to realise what she said, then the blush comes out in full force. 'I can't believe I just said that. Oh God. Now I feel like an idiot. I didn't mean... I just don't think of you that way. I'll shut up now.' She buries her face in her hands and groans to herself.

He gets up and wraps his arms around her as she curses to herself. 'Hey. That's the best thing you could have said to me.'

One eye peers out from behind her fingers. 'How is that a good thing? I just offended you.'

'It would take a lot more than that to offend me. If anything, the fact you don't think about all the celebrity stuff is a definite plus.' He kisses her forehead then clears the plates away, leaving her to curse herself under her breath.

She sits up straight and sweeps her hair back from her shoulders. 'Right, so naturally we're both going to forget I said all that. So, have you been to this before?'

He sits down again and restrains the smirk that wants to break out. She's still blushing slightly at her slip-up, and he fucking loves it. 'Last year. We won our category but there's a strong change we won't be making it two in a row.'

'Don't count yourself out just yet.'

'Yeah well I'm only going because Ellen is on my case about it. She thinks I need to get my face back out there again before people forget who I am.' It's getting them to forget about his overdose that's his priority. He's tired of seeing the words addict or troubled in front of his name. Seems the press have a longer memory than he would have liked.

'I was thinking you might like to go shopping. I'm not saying you need something new to wear. Just that you might want something new. I'll cover the cost.'

'I don't need you to do that, but I will definitely get something new. Do you think your sister would come with me?'

Tate frowns as he looks up at her. 'Bria? Why?'

'I just thought it would be a good chance to get to know her. This is her area of expertise isn't it?'

'Yeah, but you've never met. It'd be like going shopping with a stranger.'

'She's your sister, Tate. I wouldn't call her a stranger. I honestly can't think of anyone better to go with. I presume she knows all about these events?'

'Well, yeah.'

'Perfect! You've probably guessed this is all new to me. I could do with another woman's advice. It's easy for you - you just throw on a suit and you're done. I need to put a little more thought into it. Bria is the perfect choice. Only if it's okay with you.'

'Me? Hell yes. I want you two to get along. It's just... well, she's not a fan of mine right now. She's been off with me since I got out of rehab.'

'Off how?'

'Well she barely acknowledged me when I got out then took off a few minutes later and I haven't seen her since. She's busy with work apparently.' He laughs harshly. 'I let her down and she's not ready to forgive and forget. The odds are in favour of a definite no from her.'

Chloe shrugs. 'All you can do is try.'

Tate takes a long breath then sends a text to his sister and places the phone on the counter. The phone buzzes and he stares at it. 'Fuck. She responded.' He checks the message. 'Huh. Weird.'

'What? Is there a problem?'

'Oh no. Sorry. I just wasn't expecting her to reply. She's on for it. She wants me to give you her number. Should have known she wouldn't say no to a shopping trip.'

'Are you sure you're okay with me doing this?'

He nods but doesn't smile.

'Tate?'

'I guess it just hit me how much I miss her.'

Chloe squeezes his hand and he smiles at her. 'Just give her some time. I'm sure things will work out.'

'Yeah. I hope so. I'll send you her number and let Ellen know you're on for this. I haven't given you much time so make sure you get in touch with Bria ASAP. Probably best you get together in the next few days.'

The intercom on the gate buzzes and he glares over at the door. 'Who the fuck is that?' He hits the button on the speaker. 'Yeah?'

'Wehey! It's your loyal band, oh-esteemed-leader. Open the gate!'

Tate curses as he turns to look at Chloe again. 'Okay, so it appears I completely forgot the rest of the band were coming over tonight.'

'It's fine. I probably should head back to Gran's anyway.'

'I'm not saying you should go. I'd like you to stay and maybe get to know them a little better.' He pulls her into his arms and runs his thumb over her lips. 'Besides, you promised we'd try out my bed after lunch. I'm holding you to that.'

'Well, if you insist.'

He kisses her, groaning as he stops before he gets carried away. 'Okay, you get that sexy ass of yours over the far side of the room. Any closer and I'm going to have to take you upstairs.'

Chloe laughs and nods to the window. 'Too late for that. Would you let them in already? Gregg is going to do himself serious damage if you don't.'

Tate follows where she's pointing and curses. Gregg is half way over his wall but looks like he's stuck. 'Idiot. He's got a fucking remote for the gate. Are you really sure you want me to let them in? He's not over yet - there's still time to change your mind. Or I could set the dogs on him.'

'You don't have dogs.'

He leans on the sink and shakes his head as Gregg drops into the garden, landing in a thick hedge under the wall. Tate silently watches his friend as he tries to right himself but Gregg is well and truly embedded in the hedge and seems to be struggling to extract himself. 'I really should get myself some dogs.'

Chloe stretches out on the couch and listens to the laughter coming from upstairs. After a brief hello the guys had bundled Tate up to the studio to work on the intro to one of the songs they couldn't get right at the recording this morning.

She's looking forward to spending more time with them. She'd read a little about them online, but as with the information about Tate, it's difficult to tell fact from fiction.

From what she can make out, Luke also has a girlfriend, but Dillon and Gregg are single. She's seen a few pictures of Luke and Pippa at various events. Luke's girlfriend is stunning. In every single photo she's beautifully dressed and her hair and make-up perfect. She hasn't found an unflattering picture of her. Clearly she's got the hang of dating someone in the public eye.

'Chloe?'

She turns and sees Tate at the top of the stairs. 'Hey. Are you done?'

'Nearly. Can I borrow you for a minute?'

'Sure.'

She follows him up to the studio and frowns when she steps through the door. Dillon, Gregg, and Luke are in the inner room. If she didn't know any better, she'd swear they were ready to perform. Tate leads her over to the vast leather couch against the wall and crouches down in front of her. 'Do you fancy a private concert?'

Her heart beats rapidly in her chest as she looks around at the other guys. 'Really?'

Tate shrugs. 'Thought you might like to see us in action.'

'I'd love that, but you were in the studio all morning. If you don't fancy—'

Dillon holds up his hand. 'Stop right there. We don't do this for the fame and fortune.'

'Speak for yourself,' Luke interrupts. 'I'm all about the fame and fortune.'

'Yeah well you have to be. That woman of yours isn't cheap.'

Luke flicks him the bird. 'At least I have her. You still sleeping alone, Dillon?'

'Hell yes. Footloose and fancy free, mate. Getting off point a bit,' Dillon continues. 'While the fame and fortune works as whopping great incentives, if we hadn't got signed, we'd still be doing this.' He looks around the room and smirks. 'Although we wouldn't be in a custom-built studio. We'd be back in one of the barns on Tate's parents' farm. Fucking hay always made me sneeze.'

177

Tate gets to his feet and picks up a guitar from the rack by the wall. 'Yeah. That was more than a bit distracting.' He smirks over at Chloe. 'So, we were thinking about a few songs you might know and a couple from the new album. I'll finish up on the piano. Give you a chance to see what a kickass teacher your gran has.'

Chloe tries to keep the ridiculous grin from her face but absolutely knows she's failing miserably. Seeing him playing the piano with the rest of the guys is exciting her more than it probably should. 'Sounds amazing. Thank you.'

Tate slips the guitar strap over his head. 'It's all part of the deal I'm afraid. Whether you like it or not you're going to hear us play a lot. It'll get boring real quick.'

'I doubt that.'

Tate grabs another round of soft drinks from the fridge and walks back into the living room. Chloe is curled up in the armchair while the guys take up the two couches.

The wide grin refused to leave Chloe's face for the entire mini concert. It may even have grown in size when Tate took his guitar off and played the piano instead for the last two songs. He doesn't play the piano often in their songs, but thought he'd mix it up a little more on the new album. From her reaction the change seems to have been a hit. Then again, she's probably a little biased.

He drops onto the couch beside her chair and stretches his legs out in front of him. 'So, have we earned ourselves a new fan?'

'Absolutely. That was incredible. Thank you all so much.'

Dillon takes a bottle of juice from Tate and leans back on the couch. 'Never a problem. It was kinda nice to play to small crowd... well, a very small crowd. Miss that intimacy.'

Tate nods. 'Yeah. Made a nice change.'

Gregg nods and stretches out on the other chair. 'Maybe Ellen could arrange some smaller venues for us. Let a select number of fans get up close and personal for an evening. Hey, Tate could answer questions from the audience, takes requests and things like that.'

Chloe laughs as Tate sneers at them. 'Yeah to everything except the questions. They pay to hear music, not me talking.'

Gregg makes a face. 'Still think it sounds like a winner. And you'd hate the question bit so that just makes it all the more enticing.'

'You're an asshole, Gregg.'

Gregg lifts his drink and winks at him.

Instead of taking the hint and shutting up, Gregg, Dillon, and Luke spend the next hour sharing too many embarrassing stories from long weeks on the road, much to Chloe's amusement. He'd given up trying to glare the others into silence. They were on a roll and there was no stopping them.

He didn't mind, really. They were making an effort with her and vice versa. He couldn't ask for more than that. Although, he would have preferred both sides were getting a little less enjoyment out of the stories but fuck it.

'I have a question,' she says after taking a sip of sparking water. 'What's the story with the dares? Tate mentioned someone dared him to learn the violin.'

Gregg grins widely. 'That ingenious plan was all me. Fucker had to go and actually learn the damn thing though. He's scarily good at it too.'

'So is it on ongoing thing? The dares I mean.'

Gregg wiggles his eyebrows and smiles widely at Chloe. 'Of course. I think the London dare is the most interesting one?'

'No way,' Tate says, pushing upright in the seat. 'Not going there. Gregg, shut it.'

'Oh button it, Tate. Chloe asked a reasonable question. It's only polite we answer it.'

Dillon nudges Tate in the ribs. 'Quit glaring. So, we were in London two years ago. It was the last day of our European tour so we went out afterwards. Ellen recommended this authentic Chinese restaurant in town. Top class joint. Bit different from our usual haunts, but we thought we'd push the boat out. In all fairness, the food was the best we'd had for a while, especially after being on the road for so long. We had an amazing meal.' Dillon grins at Tate. 'Well most of us did.'

'What happened?' Chloe asks, leaning forward in her seat.

'During dinner Gregg mentioned he'd dared Tate to learn a new instrument in a week a few years ago and Tate did it. So we decided, thanks in part to a little too much beer, that we'd dare him to eat something he really didn't fancy. A century egg.'

Chloe covers her mouth. 'Oh God. Those are the black eggs, right?'

'Fucking rotten things,' Luke continues. 'It had to be done. So we dared him to eat two or face a forfeit.'

'Did you eat them?'

Tate makes a face. 'Of course not. The look of the damn things was enough. There was no way I was going to stick one in my mouth let alone two.'

'Understatement. He bolted for the bathroom after looking at them.' Dillon snorts and shakes his head. 'Waste of an expensive meal.'

'I'm fairly fucking sure you were quick to follow me in there,' Tate fires back at Dillon.

'Of course! I was watching out for you. It's what mates do.'

Tate snorts as he looks over at Dillon. 'Is that what you were doing? Cause it sounded like you were throwing up.'

'This is about you, buddy. Not me,' Dillon replies as he grins at Tate.

'So what was the forfeit?' Chloe asks.

As one, Dillon, Luke, and Gregg point to Tate's groin and he grins.

Chloe looks at the four men sitting opposite her and then down at

Tate's groin. 'Hang on one second. Are you saying you wouldn't eat rotten eggs so you had to get yourself pierced? Is that seriously what you're telling me?'

They grin and Tate nods. 'Believe me. It was better than eating the eggs.'

'But why the two piercings?'

'Two eggs,' Tate explains.

'He cried like a baby when he was getting them done.'

'I did not cry, Gregg.'

'There was a tear in your eye.'

'There were two needles in my dick. It wasn't entirely comfortable.'

Luke snorts and waves his hand at Tate's arms. 'Like all those tats were comfortable. You had no problem with getting the piercings. You were just pissed you lost the dare.'

'Of course I was.'

Chloe shakes her head as she looks at the four of them. 'I can't believe they actually let you four out unsupervised. You need a babysitter. So are you done with these dares now?' Chloe asks.

Gregg makes a face. 'I'd love to say yes, but you see Tate here isn't one for backing away from something. He was the same in school.'

'Half of the trouble I got into was down to you.'

'Right back at you mate.'

Luke snorts and reaches out to take his glass from the table. 'From what I heard, you were both as bad as each other. Still are. You can't help winding each other up. Best thing all around is for both of you to avoid all contact. Stay the hell away from each other. Actually scrap that, one of you needs to move to another country.'

Chloe stands up and puts her glass in the kitchen. 'Well as informative as this has been, I'm tired so I'll leave you all to it.'

Tate follows her into the kitchen and moves her out of earshot. 'Are you okay?'

'Of course I am. You need time with them alone. I'm going to get some sleep.' She winks and walks up the stairs, waving over at the guys as she goes upstairs. Tate goes back to the couch, wincing when Dillon kicks him in the shin.

'What?'

'You,' Dillon answers. 'Gazing after her with a goofy smile on your face. She's got you mate.'

'Absolutely,' Luke says with a smirk.

'I have to wholeheartedly agree.' Gregg raises his glass to Tate. 'It's about time you found someone half decent.'

'Hey, watch it.'

Dillon stretches out his legs, resting them on the coffee table. 'No, I know what he means. The last few you've been with weren't good for you. Take Astrid for example. Pampered spoilt princess. Of course she was going to go for someone like you.'

'Hold up. What exactly do you mean by someone like me?'

'Someone Daddy wouldn't approve of. She was with you to prove a point and get a few steps up the social ladder. You used her for—'

'Stop right there.' Tate interrupts. 'I'm begging you not to finish that sentence.'

Dillon grins over at him. 'Reckon she liked the idea of being with you more than actually being with you.'

Gregg nods enthusiastically. 'To be fair, Dillon, I'd imagine most people would prefer the idea of being with Tate more than the reality. Grumpy fucker.'

Tate rests his arm along the back of the couch and glowers at them. 'Grumpy fucker? Cheers. Luke, you fancy chipping in?'

Luke smirks and shakes his head. 'Nah, I'm good just watching the show.'

'Chloe's leagues apart from her,' Dillon says, his face turning serious. 'She likes you. The real you. She's good for you, Tate. We can all see it.'

Tate crosses his arms and looks at them, waiting for the imminent joke or dig, but there's nothing. He can't remember the last time they approved of anyone he dated.

'She's coming to London with me.'

Gregg smiles widely. 'Hang on one second. We may have just entered a parallel universe. Are you telling me you're bringing a date?'

'I've brought dates before.'

Gregg shakes his head. 'Once, and it was Bria. Your sister doesn't count. You have never ever brought an actual date to any of these things. Ever.'

He frowns as he thinks back to the numerous events he's attended in the past. He'd brought dates to parties, but Gregg is right. He's always gone to these things alone. 'You think it's too fast?'

'You're thirty-six and you've finally asked someone to go with you to a work do. I don't think too fast is the term I'd use to describe it.'

'You know what I mean. Am I rushing things with Chloe?'

'You know what I think?' Dillon says as he gets up and opens a few kitchen cupboards.

Tate glares across at Dillon. 'No, that's why I'm asking.'

Dillon grabs a few bags of crisps and hands them out. 'I think the fact you asked her is all the answer you need. Go with it, Tate. What did Ellen say about it?'

'I haven't told her yet. I have to ring her in the morning.'

'She'll be fine with it. Think she's given up worrying about who we're seeing. First public event though. Is Chloe prepared for what that means?'

Tate opens the crisps and stares into the bag. 'Don't think it's sunk in yet. Not properly. We haven't been out in public together. Just hope it doesn't freak her out and scare her off.'

'Hey. It'll be grand, okay. We'll keep an eye on her on Saturday. There's no way she'll be overwhelmed with all the celebrity bullshit with us four louts hanging around her.'

Tate has to laugh at that. Dillon has a point. 'I just wanted to bring her. Let her experience one event like this in case we're not nominated again.'

Dillon, Gregg, and Luke look at each other then over to him. Gregg holds up his glass. 'We started this band in your parents' barn. A few years later we're headlining venues that hold thousands. No award is going to change that.'

Dillon taps his glass against Greggs, followed by Luke. They look over at him again and Tate slowly clinks his glass against the others. 'Thanks.'

Gregg waves the comment away. 'Don't go getting all mushy on us. Besides, there's nothing to say we won't clean up this year. Chloe could be our good luck charm for the evening.'

'Could be. So no more talking about dares or anything I may or may not have done in my past. The last thing I want to do is send her running for the hills... again. I'm already on my last life with her. I don't need any more help messing things up.'

'We've got your back, Tate,' Dillon says. 'She'll never know about the karaoke bar incident. I promise.'

'Don't even joke about that.'

Gregg shakes his head and looks over at Tate. 'Now I wouldn't just go agreeing to that so fast, Dillon. I reckon we should see how much it's worth for us to keep that particular embarrassing incident from Chloe?'

Chloe tucks the duvet around herself and breathes in Tate's seriously intoxicating scent. He's still downstairs with the others but it sounds like they're wrapping things up. She smiles as they burst into laughter. Tate's deep rumble is clearly audible among all the others.

The last two days have been incredible, but she knows it has to come to an end. She's starting work in a few weeks and he'll be doing whatever he normally does when she's not around to distract him. The new album will be released soon and from the conversations tonight, the second leg of the tour he had to cancel will be rescheduled for the upcoming months. That's something she doesn't want to think about at the moment.

She has no idea how touring works. She doesn't know if he'll be leaving for months and won't be back until he's finished or if he'll be back every few weeks. She presumes he'll stay in contact but will he give her his schedule or timetable or plan so she'll know what city he's in? Or what country. It's all so alien to her.

And that's before she gets to the whole famous singer part of the equation. Screaming fans. Meet and greets. Autographs. The dreaded groupies.

If she allowed herself to think about all that, she'd head down a rabbit hole she wants to avoid. She still hasn't quite got her head around the fame part. It hit her again when he asked her to go to the awards evening with him. She doesn't think of him as famous. It would have been a great idea not to actually ask if she would meet any famous people. Another comment to go down on the 'Did you really say that, Chloe?' list.

She hears footsteps on the stairs. Tate told her the guys always stayed the night when they came over. Probably because, in the past, they would have had a few drinks. The fact that all of them had stuck to soft drinks is a testament to their friendship. She seriously doubts Tate would have stopped them if they'd wanted a drink, but they hadn't even suggested it.

As much as she doesn't want to, she should probably go home tomorrow too. If she doesn't get some clean clothes, he's going to kick her out himself. Either that or insist she ditches her clothes altogether.

The door opens and she smiles as he locks it behind him. Tate undresses, his impressive body silhouetted in the dim light from the bedside table. He climbs in beside her and she wraps her arms around him.

'I thought you were asleep. We didn't keep you up with all the racket did we?'

'No, you didn't. I think I dozed off for a bit. Has everyone gone to bed?'

'Yeah. They'll be off early enough in the morning.'

'I don't think there's anything for breakfast for them.'

'Coco Pops. Always plenty of Coco Pops.'

'Of course. How stupid of me. I was thinking I probably should go back to Gran's tomorrow.'

He sighs and rolls onto his back, pulling her close to his chest. 'I was kind of expecting you to say that. Guess I can't keep you locked away in here forever no matter how much I want to. I can bring you back in the morning after the guys leave. I probably should sort things out with my folks too before they change the locks and completely disown me. I'm really not looking forward to that conversation.'

He kisses her on the forehead and tucks the duvet around them.

'Tate? Can I ask you something?'

'Go for it.'

'Why was Pippa not here tonight?'

He looks down at her. 'Pippa? Why would she come?'

'I know me being here wasn't planned, but I was just wondering why Luke didn't bring her with him.'

Tate doesn't answer her immediately. Instead he plays with the ring on his thumb as he frowns at the ceiling.

'Okay. Spit it out. What's wrong.'

He licks his lips then frowns again. 'Okay. Pippa may not be overly... she doesn't... There was this thing and I'm fairly sure she hates me because of it. Not that I'm losing any sleep over it.'

Chloe pushes on to her elbow and looks down at him. 'What thing?'

'I may have said something she didn't appreciate hearing.'

'Oh Tate. What did you do?'

'Okay, there's something you need to understand about Pippa. She's a heartless, soul destroying, money grabbing leech.'

Chloe stares down at him and gets a really bad feeling. 'Please tell me you didn't say that to Luke?'

'What? No of course not. What do you take me for? I said it to her.'

Chloe laughs and shakes her head. 'Well, that could explain why she's not fond of you. What possessed you to say that to her?'

'I was drunk at the time. Probably more than just drunk thinking back, but that's not the reason I said it. I would have said it to her even if I was sober.'

'Helpful.'

'She was giving Luke serious attitude about spending time with us. What we do... it's more than standing on stage and singing a few songs. We have to practice a hell of a lot. Then there's all the other stuff like interviews, photoshoots, touring. It's part of the job. We can't just pick and choose which bits we want to do. Pippa's happy to spend his money but gets her nose out of joint when he leaves her for five fucking minutes.

'We were due to fly to London for an interview and performance, and she kicked off. She wanted him to go to some work do and, strangely enough, we needed him on stage with us, so I said no using a few choice words. She argued back, called me a few interesting names. I countered by telling her what I thought of her. She went red, slapped me, and we haven't spoken since.'

'She slapped you?'

Tate shrugs. 'More like a tap but Ellen decided it would be best if we steered clear of each other. There's the odd time she has to go to things I'm attending too, but I just smile politely, curse her under my breath, and leave her to it.'

Chloe lies on his chest and traces the tattoo with her finger. Luke seems so... normal. She can't imagine what Tate just described. She's also no desire whatsoever to meet the delightful Pippa. She pauses as a thought hits her.

'Is she going to the awards?'

'Unfortunately. Don't worry though. I've already asked Dillon and Gregg to keep me the hell away from her. Ellen's apparently had a chat with her too. Luke said it didn't go down well. Big surprise there. The delightful Pippa has been told to give me a wide berth for the evening. The last thing Broken needs is more bad publicity. We've all to be on our best behaviour.'

'So do Dillon and Gregg have scary girlfriends too?'

'Nope. Dillon isn't a one girl kind of guy. He'll be one of those old rockers with a twenty-year-old on his arm. Gregg...' He shrugs. 'I'd like to see him find someone. To be honest, I thought he'd settle down before me. Funny how things work out.'

He rolls onto his side and hugs her to his chest.

'Well, I'm beat. Night.'

Chloe smirks against his chest as a certain part of his body presses against her leg. 'Is that so? You might want to tell your friend to go to sleep.'

'He never listens to a word I say,' he mutters into the pillow.

'Tate?'

'Yeah?'

'I'm not tired.' She laughs as he scrambles to tear off his boxers and pulls her on top of him.

Tate slips on his sunglasses then starts the engine. He's knackered. Chloe had kept him up until well after four. The stunning woman was impossible to sleep next to without wanting to do a hell of a lot more than sleep. He's definitely paying for it now. No complaints though. If anything, it's the thought of bringing her back to her gran's that's getting to him, which was strange.

He's always preferred his own company to others, especially at home. He loved having the guys over but it was maybe once or twice a week at most. The rest of the time he was alone. And he loved it. Or did.

Coming back home tonight without Chloe doesn't feel right. It's throwing him how much he wants her around. That's probably the best reason to have a few nights away from her. It's too soon to be living in each other's pockets.

All he can do is keep busy, work out for a bit and hopefully grab some sleep. He's got a call scheduled with his counsellor tonight anyway so he'd prefer she wasn't around for that.

She climbs in beside him and he turns the truck around and heads out the gate.

'So, I sent Bria a text while you were seeing the guys off. We're going to go shopping in a few days. She's going to make an appointment at a boutique in town.'

He's slightly taken aback by the willingness of his sister to help Chloe. It's not a bad thing at all. Maybe he's a little jealous she's so eager to meet Chloe but can't answer the phone when he calls.

'That's great. She'll be able to sort you out. You got the photo I sent you?'

Chloe nods. 'I know it makes no sense, but she looks like you.'

'You're not the first one to say that. Just one of those freaky coincidences I guess.' He opens the window as the traffic comes to a stop. The stunning weather has brought everyone out early, turning the N11 into a slow-moving line of cars. At this rate they'll be lucky to get to Newcastle in time for lunch.

Tate rests his arm on the door and taps the roof with his fingers as he edges the car forward at a snail's pace. He frowns when he hears something familiar. Chloe looks over at him, a huge smile on her face.

'That wouldn't happen to be one of your songs?'

'Yep.' He grins across at her. 'It would appear I may have been spotted.'

'It could just be a coincidence. Or not,' she adds quickly when the volume increases and the occupants of the car alongside them shout his name. Thankfully, the traffic eases, giving him an escape route. He waves at them as he pulls away and they respond by beeping their horn a few times. Tate manages to put a fair bit of distance between them before the traffic stops again.

'Okay. That was a first.'

Chloe looks in the rear-view mirror. 'I think you've lost them. You certainly keep things interesting, don't you? Maybe you should get a less conspicuous car?'

Tate slowly looks over at her and raises his eyebrows. 'Eh, no. We'll just have to use the bike a lot more. A helmet is a great disguise.'

Chloe may laugh at that suggestion but he's being serious. Having her body tight against his is another great selling point for the bike.

'So, what do you have planned for today?'

He was kind of hoping not to think about that until he had to.

'Well, I'll drop you home then head over to my folks for a few hours. I've got to be back at my place for a call at five so at least I have an out if things get awkward.'

'I'm sure it will be fine. Just grovel and mean it.'

'Oh I'll mean it all right.' He looks down as Chloe takes his hand. It's only then he realises he's been scratching his arm again. 'Shit. Sorry.'

'It's not me you have to apologise to, it's your skin. It would be a shame if you damaged that tattoo. I like it.'

That surprises him. He didn't think she was overly fond of his tattoos. 'You do?'

'Of course. You look surprised to hear that.'

He shrugs as he pulls up at a red light. 'I didn't think you liked them.'

'Okay, if someone asked if I liked that many or for them to be as visible as some of yours are, I probably would have said no.'

'I'm hoping there's a 'but' coming.'

'But,' she adds with a smile, 'they really suit you and your body.'

'Don't you mean my shaggable body? That is what you called it, or am I imagining that part?'

She blushes and looks out the window. 'Yes, Tate. They suit your shaggable body. I absolutely love every single one of them.'

He pulls away from the light and turns on to the road that leads back to her gran's. 'So, you wouldn't have a problem with more?'

'You're getting another tattoo?'

Her face drops a little. Yeah, she's not thrilled about that prospect. 'Plural and yeah, that's the plan. Next up is a Celtic dragon up my side. It won't be for a few months yet but I've had it designed.'

'How many more are you planning?'

'Quite a few. I'm kind of hooked. You're giving me the same look my mum does when I mention getting more done.'

'What about piercings? Any more plans?'

'No plans.' He glances over at her and frowns when he catches something in her expression. 'Why do you look a little disappointed by that?'

'I was just wondering why you only got one nipple done. It's clearly a turn on for you.'

'You noticed that, huh?' he replies with a grin. 'You've seen what I'm like with one done. Getting the other pierced would be seriously dangerous for both of us.'

'Right.'

'Okay, I'm getting a definite vibe here. Do you want me to get the other one pierced?'

Chloe shrugs and looks out the side window. 'I don't know. I really like it. Ignore me.'

'Sorry? I didn't quite catch that middle part.'

'I like it,' she repeats a little louder even though she knows full well he heard her the first time.

'So that's a yes.'

'I don't know. Well, no. It's your body. I'm not going to tell you what to do with it.'

'So you don't want me to.'

'All I'm trying to say is that if you ever decided to get the other one done I wouldn't be overly upset about it.'

Tate smirks. 'Clear as mud, thanks.'

'But can you promise me something?'

'I'll give it a shot.'

'Whatever tattoo you get can you please promise me you won't let Gregg anywhere near you when it's being done. Actually, make sure he's in another country altogether. I dread to think what he could dare you to get done.'

After saving goodbye to Chloe, Tate pulls into his parents' driveway and stares over at the front door. For some reason facing them after getting out of rehab was easier than this is going to be. He had a meltdown and beat his friend. It was stupid and childish. If he was looking for a way to prove to his mum that he was coping grand with everything, that wasn't the way to do it.

He jumps when someone knocks on his window. His dad smiles at him as he opens the door and gets out. 'You sitting in there all day or do you fancy actually coming into the house?'

'Am I welcome?'

Rick looks away and makes a face. 'You eaten yet?'

'No.'

'Right. C'mon then. You can do your grovelling while we eat.'

Two hours later, Tate wanders outside and over to the stables. His grovelling comprised of an I'm sorry and a hug. They were cutting him way too much slack and he knows why. They were afraid to push him too hard in case he did something stupid again. The infuriating itching builds again but he ignores it. After saddling Jove, he brings him to the beach and heads away from the house.

Lunch had been one of the single most awkward experiences he's had for a while. Putting on a show for his parents so they'd think everything was hunky-fucking-dory wasn't easy.

He's keeping so much shit to himself to protect the people he loves. To protect the band, his parents, and Chloe. An invisible hand twists in his gut at the thought of losing her. Even after this short time, she is quickly becoming an important part of his life. He'd do anything to keep her away from all the mental shit he's dealing with.

She's taking a chance attaching herself to someone like him. A heroin addict just out of rehab with too many public ex-girlfriends. Not exactly what people look for in a partner.

But she had said yes. She's his girlfriend.

He says it over and over in his head but it's still not sinking in.

He never thought calling someone his girlfriend would sound so good. Thirty-six years-old and he's finally in a real relationship. Sex and parties. That was as deep and meaningful as it got for him in the past. And that's probably down to him. Thinking back he's disgusted at some of the things he'd done over the last few years. He'd been a right selfish asshole at times.

Tate snaps out of his thoughts as a wave hits his leg, soaking him. He hadn't realised he was in the fucking sea. He can't keep zoning out like this. Things improved while she was with him. She distracted him, calmed him. She was able to keep his head from wandering to stuff he didn't want to remember. Without her, there's nothing to stop the darkness from taking him.

He turns Jove around and guides him back to the beach. Being with her made him feel more like himself. Like the old, pre-fuck up version. Then again, it's not like that version of himself was anything to write home about.

Tate looks up the beach as he rubs the side of Jove's neck. No sign of Chloe. Less than a few hours have gone by since he dropped her home. Getting through the day without her is going to be fun at this rate.

He readjusts his grip on the reins as Jove paws at the sand. He's desperate to be set free. It takes barely a nudge from Tate to spur Jove on, his hooves crashing through the shallows as he gallops down the beach. As the wind whistles past him, Tate realises he may be heading down another unfamiliar path with Chloe.

If he's not careful he could easily fall for her.

Chloe looks out the window of Tate's truck. 'Why won't you tell me where we're going?'

Tate pulls away as the light turns green. 'Because it wouldn't be a surprise if I told you. Do you not get the concept of a surprise?'

'Fine. I'll stop asking.'

Tate smirks and concentrates on driving again. The last three days were spent writing, recording, and doing a few painfully long photo-shoots for the new album.

He hadn't seen Chloe since he dropped her back to her gran's place and he'd missed being with her. The days were busy enough but it was when he was at home alone that the problems surfaced.

The house seemed strangely empty without Chloe there. His bed smelt like her which just made the irrational loneliness worse. Instead of sleeping he'd tried doing some writing, played guitar, worked out, watched endless episodes of CSI then crashed on the couch when he couldn't keep his eyes open any longer.

They'd be heading off to London for the awards in just over a week and he's a nervous wreck about it. If that wasn't bad enough, Ellen scheduled a quick slot on a talk show in the UK the day after tomorrow. No amount of excuses or arguing had convinced her to let him off the hook. He was going and that was that.

He knows she's right. Just like she's right about going to the award ceremony, but that didn't mean he was ready. He had toyed with the idea of asking Chloe to tag along, but he needs to grow a fucking backbone and do it without her support. It's not like it's his first show and the guys will be with him. They were closing the show so were all heading over together. Strength in numbers and all that.

'Are you thinking about the interview?'

Tate looks across at her. 'How the fuck did you know that?'

'You're doing one of your seriously deep frowns. And you've moved to scratch your arm a few times. You didn't which is great, but you've thought about it.'

'Remind me never to take up poker. Those are some serious tells.'

'Ellen isn't going to put you into a situation she doesn't think you're ready for.'

'I know. I think it's just the build up to it. Once I'm there and I get going I'll be grand. I need to get this one done and out of the way.'

'Do you have any idea when it will be aired?'

'Saturday night. They want to get it out before the awards are announced next week. I won't be back until Sunday afternoon though.'

'So I'll be watching it without you.'

'Thank fuck. I hate watching myself on TV. I always notice too any things I'm not happy with.'

'Control freak, huh?'

He smiles at her as he pulls into the car park. 'You got it. Anyway, enough about that. I'd prefer not to think about it until I'm on the flight.' He turns off the engine and smirks across at her. 'Today is about you. Ready for your surprise?'

He takes her hand as they leave the carpark and step onto the busy Dublin street. As they make their way through the crowd, Chloe catches someone staring at them more than once. Well, more specifically staring at him. A woman about her age stops and asks for an autograph and a photo with him, which he agrees to. After gushing over him for a minute, Tate finally manages to break away, taking Chloe's hand again.

'Sorry about that.'

'Does that happen often?'

'It's hit and miss. One day I could walk through Grafton Street at lunchtime and no one would bat an eyelid. Then something like this happens on a side street.'

'And you always agree?'

'Of course. Well, unless they're being a dick about it. I had one girl ask me for five autographs once. She wanted to sell them. She got fuck all. The way I see it, I can only be successful at what I do if they support me and the guys. If no one buys our music, I'll be back to singing in the shower to myself. A few autographs and photos is nothing.'

He opens the door to a shop and gestures for her to go in. Chloe smiles as she looks around. There are art supplies crammed into every corner of the small shop. A woman steps out from behind the counter and comes up to shake his hand. 'Mr. Archer. I'm Rachel. So nice to meet you.'

'You too. And it's Tate.'

'Of course. We're at your disposal.'

Tate drapes his arm around Chloe's shoulder. 'This is Chloe. With your help she's going to go a little nuts in here, if that's okay?'

Rachel grins widely. 'I have no problem with that in the slightest.' She locks the door, turns the sign from open to closed then faces Chloe. 'Shall we get started?'

'Get started on what? What's going on?'

'Tate rang us yesterday and asked if we would be able to sort you out with some supplies.'

'What supplies?'

'Whatever you want,' Tate says. 'You had to use a pen and some copier paper before. I'm not having that. Rachel is going to make sure you have anything and everything you need.' He leans closer to whisper in her ear, 'I fully intend for you to stay over a lot. This will give you something to do while I'm snoring my ass off.'

'No way, Tate. I can't accept this.'

'Tough. You either cooperate and let Rachel sort you out or I'm going to have to do it myself and fuck knows what you'll get. I want to do this for you. Let me.'

Chloe is quiet for a few minutes then the smile breaks. 'You're an irritating man. Do you know that?'

'It's been mentioned a few times. Go on. Have fun.'

Two hours later, Chloe thanks Rachel for her help and Tate gently pushes her towards the door and away from the till. He arranges to have everything delivered to her gran's house the following day so she can sort through it all and see what she wants to bring to his house. Rachel writes down the total and shows it to Tate who simply nods and hands his credit card over.

Chloe had tried to keep a tally of the total in her head as they walked around the shop but gave up after the first few minutes. She had made a valiant effort to keep the total as low as possible, but as items were added to the list, she realised Rachel had been prepped in advance. She knew exactly what Tate's budget was and from the length of the receipt, it was a healthy one. She dreads to think how much of his money Rachel helped her spend. Not that the shop owner would be complaining about that.

Tate finishes with Rachel and shakes her hand. 'Chloe, could you take a picture. Bit of publicity for the shop.'

Rachel holds out her phone and Tate wraps his arm around her shoulder as Chloe takes a few pictures. Rachel thanks them again then Tate leads Chloe back outside and towards the car park.

'That's now officially Tate Archer's favourite art supply shop.'

He laughs and squeezes her hand. 'Independent places like that are a dying breed. If a photo of me brings more people through the door that's a good thing. Now, I don't know about you but I am starving.'

'You're always starving. I dread to think how much exercise you have to do to work it all off.'

'There's only one kind of exercise I'm interested in.' He lifts his sunglasses up and wiggles his eyebrows.

'Oh my God. Do you ever stop?'

He opens the passenger door for her then climbs into the driver's seat. 'Nope. Back to the food issue. I know somewhere that does amazing seafood.'

Tate drives them back down the coast to Bray, stopping on the way to sort out the seafood he promised. He pulls up at the side of the road and a man hurries out of a doorway with a bag which he carefully places on the floor in the back of the truck. Tate thanks him and drives them to down to the seafront. He pulls into the carpark at the promenade overlooking the sea.

Chloe takes a deep breath and laughs. 'That smells a lot like fish and chips.'

'Amazing fish and chips thanks very much.'

He reverses into a spot far away from the other cars then grabs his jacket and hoody from the backseat. 'C'mon, our table is ready.'

He drops the back and helps her onto the load bed. After laying out his sweatshirt and handing her his leather jacket to put on, they sit back against the cab facing the sea. Tate passes her a portion of fish and chips and a bottle of water. Chloe opens the container and takes a deep breath. 'Smells fantastic, but wasn't quite what I had in mind when you said amazing seafood.'

He chews on a chip before he answers. 'I promise I will take you to a fancy restaurant at some stage. I just want to be alone with you right now.'

'This is perfect, Tate. Really.' After one chip, Chloe has to agree with his choice of dinner. Who needs fancy restaurants when they have this? Eating fresh fish and chips by the sea in the back of Tate's truck is so much better. At least like this they're still relatively inconspicuous. They're just like a half dozen other couples doing the same thing. No one is giving them a second look. Well, apart from the two women parked a few spaces down from them. Chloe smiles as she eats a chip. 'I think you've been spotted.'

Tate looks over at the other car and snorts. 'Yep. Jeez, their we're-not-really-staring look needs a little work.'

Chloe laughs and picks up another chip. 'Do you think they want a chip?'

'They can fuck off.'

'I don't think that's going to happen. It looks like they're arguing over who's going to come over.'

Tate glances over at the car again and groans. 'Damn it. You're right. Okay. You stay here. I'm going to sort them out before they well and truly ruin my dinner.' He wipes his hands on his jeans and smiles at Chloe. 'No ketchup on my face?'

She laughs and shakes her head. 'You're good.'

He vaults over the side of the truck and walks over to the car. She can't hear what he says to them, but she can see them both blush when he crouches down beside the open window. He talks to them for a minute then they burst out of the car and he poses for a photo. When they get what they wanted the girls climb back into their car and

202

huddle over the phone.

Tate joins Chloe and smiles apologetically at her. 'Sorry about that.'

'You made their day. Nothing to apologise for.'

Tate eats another chip and waves at the girls as they pull out of the car park. 'Yeah. Weird.'

'What is?'

'The whole fame thing. If you think about it, it really doesn't make sense. I'm just a normal guy. I grew up on a farm a few miles down the road. I went to school around here. All that time under their noses and no interest at all. Add a bit of celebrity to that and suddenly I'm fucking irresistible.' He picks another chip out of the tray and grins at her. 'Could have done with that in school.'

Chloe turns and frowns at him. 'Are you saying no one was interested in you in school?'

He shakes his head as he chews. 'I was always the weird, scrawny, quiet kid. More interested in music than making friends. Gregg went to the same school and we'd meet up with Dillon and Luke after school, but apart from that I kept to myself. I was either in trouble for dicking around with Gregg during class or hiding behind an instrument. Not the sort of guy the girls went for.'

She leans back and looks at the well-built man sitting beside her. 'Hold on a second. You? Scrawny?'

'Like a rake with limbs.'

'I can wholeheartedly vouch for that.'

They look around and she can feel Tate's body tense against hers. 'Dara? Hi.'

The blond-haired man steps out from beside the car and leans over the side. 'Fish and chips? Splashing out, eh, Tate.'

'Yeah. Chloe this is my cousin Dara. Dara, this is Chloe.'

He smiles as he shakes Chloe's hand. 'Nice to meet you. And as he was saying, he was a slow bloomer. The Tate you see before you broke out while he was in college. I remember I hadn't seen him for… it must have been about six months after we left school and there was a family thing at my parents' house.' Dara laughs and points over at Tate. 'This one walks in and I swear you could have heard a pin drop. Floppy hair shaved off, ears pierced and a tattoo on his neck. I honestly will never forget the look on everyone's faces.'

Tate smiles but it doesn't reach his eyes. He's got his performer facade on for some reason. 'Yeah. At least they were predictable. Got the reaction I knew I would. Wasn't expecting to see you here. Bit far from your place isn't it?'

Dara pats his stomach. 'Loads of space here for a good run. Trying to get in shape.' He looks at Tate and grins. 'Think I've got a fair bit of running to do before I get to where you are. So, you look well. How are you?'

'Good, thanks.'

'I'm sorry to hear about rehab. Fair play to you for sorting yourself out. Can't have been easy.'

Tate glances over at her then nods at Dara. 'No, it wasn't. So Dad said you helped out with Jove while I was away. He behave for you?'

Dara laughs. 'He's a handful. I'm not sure who was in control of who, but I managed to stay on him so I'm happy. If you need anyone to take him out when you're busy just give me a shout.'

'Thanks. I'll keep that in mind.'

'Has the patch-up job on the hay shed roof held?'

Chloe glances over at Tate when he doesn't immediately respond. He's turning the ring on his thumb – something he seems to do when he's not entirely at ease.

'You fixed that?'

Dara helps himself to one of Tate's chips. 'I hope so. You might need to put another layer of sealant over the hole. I also replaced the pump to the troughs in the back field.'

'Great. Thanks.'

'It's no problem at all. I can't imagine you have a lot of free time to help out as much as you'd probably like.'

'No. I guess not.'

Chloe tries not to attract any attention to herself as the two cousins sit in a slightly awkward silence. Tate is clearly on edge having Dara here. It probably didn't help that his cousin mentioned rehab, especially in front of her.

Dara bangs the side of the truck and smiles at Chloe. 'Well, I'll leave you to your dinner. Nice to meet you, Chloe.'

She returns the smile. 'You too, Dara.'

Tate nods but doesn't bid his cousin a fond farewell. He silently watches as Dara gets into his car. His cousin waves and sounds his horn as he drives by. Chloe discretely looks over at Tate. His jaw is clenched and he's playing with the ring on his thumb as he stares after the car.

'Tate?'

He doesn't respond, still focused on the road from the car park even though Dara is long gone.

'Tate?'

He turns and frowns at her. 'What?'

'Are you okay?'

Tate seems to come out of his daze and smiles at her, but it's a little forced. He sits back against the cab and picks up a chip before dropping it back in the tray. 'Cold. Do you want me to grab you some fresh chips?'

'No. I'm stuffed.' Chloe gathers the leftover food and slides off the load bed. She throws it in the bin and leans on the side of the truck facing Tate. 'I really need a walk after all that food. You coming?'

'Yeah.' He hops down from the back, closes the tailgate and locks the car. A group of girls sitting on the rocks at the top of the beach stop talking as he walks past them. Chloe hopes they don't ask him for a photo. She seriously doubts they'd get the answer they were hoping for. He takes Chloe's hand and that action alone seems to halt any ideas they might have had.

Tate keeps the silence going for a good ten minutes as they walk along the water's edge. He's deep in his head and she doesn't know how to get him back. Any attempts at conversation resulted in either a grunt, a yes, or a no.

'You're wrong you know.'

He turns to look at her. Success. 'What?'

'I said you're wrong.'

'About what?'

'The fish and chips. There's a place at the harbour in Greystones that does really amazing fish and chips. I'd argue theirs are marginally better than what we just had.'

He stops walking and stares at her for a moment before he smiles and continues walking. 'Is that so.'

'Absolutely. I'll treat you next time and we'll see who's right.' She stops and turns him to face her. 'Are you going to talk to me about what's going on in there?' She taps her finger on the side of his head and smiles at him. 'I haven't seen you not finish food so there must be something up.'

He sits on the shingles and pulls her onto his lap. 'I'm sorry. I got... I don't know. Guess I was overthinking.'

'Overthinking what?'

He looks out at the sea. 'It's fucking ridiculous really. Dara's the same age as me. I was behind when I started school. I guess I missed out on the first few years. I eventually worked my ass off to catch up, but I could never get close to him. It didn't matter how hard I tried I was always a little behind him.

'My parents never made any comments about it and neither did his as far as I know, but every time the rest of the family got together, we were compared. I don't mean like there was a list and they went through it. It was more that I... I guess I never quite made the grade.

206

He has degrees coming out of his arse, then a wife and now a kid on the way. He's some hotshot lawyer in a firm in town.

'I've done pretty well for myself, I know, but I don't have a normal job. I didn't do myself any favours by going down the drink and drugs route either.' He laughs once and shrugs. 'This is going to sound unbelievable childish. I know he was helping my parents and I know I wasn't there, but hearing he picked up the slack...' He shakes his head angrily. 'It's petty but that got my back up. A lot. It's not his fault and I know he did me a favour helping out with Jove and the farm.'

'But it still feels like he was stepping into your place.'

'I should be thanking him not getting all narky with him. Or you. I'm sorry.'

'You don't have anything to apologise for. It's understandable to feel the way you do, but you're back now. Besides, I can't see Dara being able to handle Jove. I get the impression he's a one-man horse.'

Tate finally smiles. 'Too fucking right.'

Chloe wraps her arm around his neck. 'You've got to forgive yourself for what happened, Tate. It was a mistake. People make mistakes all the time. I'm even sure the amazing Dara has made a fair few in his day. You can't go back and change what you did. You really have to stop giving yourself such a hard time. You need to forgive yourself or else you'll never get over this.'

Tate hugs her close as he watches the waves break on the sand. She's right. He doesn't forgive himself for what he did. He was stupid and weak and nearly killed himself as a result. He worked so hard to get through his addiction. Why the hell did he put himself through all that if he's not going to get on with his life? If his parents hadn't broken into his house when they did, he wouldn't be sitting here with Chloe. Waking up in that hospital had been his second chance.

He closes his eyes and buries his face in Chloe's hair. The woman from his nightmares wasn't so lucky. Where's her second chance? How the hell does he even begin to forgive himself for that?

Chloe gets off the DART at Connolly Station and walks to the newspaper stand. She looks down at the family photo Tate sent her then scans the faces of the commuters milling around the station. It doesn't take long to pick Bria out from the crowd. Her strawberry blonde hair is tied in a high ponytail which swishes from side to side as she hurries over to Chloe. Bria holds out her hand and smiles warmly.

'Chloe?'

'Nice to meet you, Bria. Thank you so much for agreeing to help me out. I'm not ashamed to admit I haven't got a clue what I'm doing.'

When she smiles again, Chloe can't help but like her.

'I'm so touched you asked me to help you out. I was really surprised if I'm honest.'

'It made perfect sense. This is your world after all.'

'How do you know that?'

'Tate talks about you a lot.'

Bria smiles tightly and nods. 'Right. Well, I've made an appointment at an amazing boutique. You'll absolutely find something there that will be perfect.' She checks her watch. 'Time for coffee first though. We can't go shopping unless I get to know you a little better.'

They walk to a coffee shop down the street and Bria orders two mochas and a scone which they split. 'So, you're his girlfriend. How long has he been keeping you secret for?'

'It's only been a few weeks.'

'How exactly did you meet him? You appear normal, and I mean that in a good way. Believe me.'

'I bumped into him on the beach. I was trying to draw the wildlife and got Tate on Jove instead. My car broke down and he came to my rescue. We ran into each other again the following day. It grew from there.'

'I presume this is your first public event with him.'

Chloe doesn't miss the fact Bria doesn't say Tate's name. 'Yes, it is. Between you and me, I'm terrified. Don't get me wrong, I'm over the moon he asked me, I just don't want to mess up. It's a lot of pressure.'

'It's not that bad. I don't know if he told you but I went with him to his first event.'

'You did? No, he didn't say.'

'When he was signed he promised he'd take me to his first award ceremony. If Broken Chords ever made it big of course. Which they did less than a year later. I didn't think he'd remember.' She looks into her coffee and smiles. 'Come to think about it, I'm the only person he's ever brought with him. Can't say why but he always goes alone. Maybe taking me turned him off bringing a date.'

Bria laughs briefly, but there's little humour in it. Whatever the problem between them, Bria is clearly as upset about it as Tate is.

'It was an amazing night, Chloe. Trust me, you have nothing to worry about. He'll look after you every second. Now, we'll get you sorted dress-wise and I've got someone ready to do your hair and makeup at the hotel. I hope that's okay.'

'I never even thought of hair and makeup.'

'That's what you have me for. So how long are you staying in London for? Has he arranged anything else for you two? Will you need any other outfits?'

'We're staying for two nights but I don't know what else is planned. He mentioned flying out on Friday and back on Sunday. I'm not sure what flight he's booking or any other details.'

Bria laughs and takes a sip of her coffee.

'What?'

'You won't be flying like that.'

'What do you mean?'

'You'll be going by helicopter.'

'Excuse me?'

'If he's going to the UK he always goes by helicopter. It'll take you straight to the hotel then a car will pick you up from there and take you to the ceremony. It will be booked to take you back again on Sunday. Believe me it's so much easier than fighting your way through an airport. Long haul is different but for a quick hop like this, the door to door thing is quicker.'

Chloe smiles but it's entirely forced. It just hit her that this isn't going away for a weekend with her boyfriend. This is something so far removed from anything else she's been to. She'll be going to a very public event with a very public man and other very public people.

Bria reaches across and squeezes her hand. 'Just registered, huh?'

'Oh my god! Am I that transparent?'

'Not quite. You did go a smidge pale though.'

'I knew he was... I mean I know Tate's known, but this is the first public thing I've been to with him. I thought there might be a limo. But a helicopter? I'm so completely out of my depth.'

'No, you're not. Now, I know you haven't known my brother for

211

long but can you honestly tell me dressing up in a suit, being ferried around in a limo, and going to a fancy dinner matches with the Tate you know?'

Chloe can't help but laugh at that. 'Not in the slightest.'

'Exactly. If he had the option, he'd arrive on his bike wearing jeans and a t-shirt. This event is just part of the craziness that comes with what he does. Think of the night as an over-the-top work do. That's exactly how he thinks of it, I can promise you.'

'Thanks Bria. I know I'm being silly. I guess I need to rein in my imagination. I'm going to get myself into a state.'

Bria looks away for a moment then turns back to Chloe. 'Okay, I know myself and... Tate, have a problem. I'm upset with him, but I can honestly say you're in good hands. When we went together, he didn't leave my side for a second. He's incredibly protective, Chloe. I absolutely guarantee he will be there for you. Now, how about we finish these coffees and get to spending some of this.' She holds up a credit card and smiles.

'I'm paying for my dress.'

'Oh no you're not. He gave me strict instructions to use his credit card. I'm on this account in case there are any problems with his house while he's away. He's picking up the bill.'

Bria talks non-stop as they walk to the boutique about five minutes from the coffee shop. She pushes the buzzer on the door and is admitted after giving her name to the attendant on the other end.

Chloe stares in wonder at all the dresses, shoes, and bags as they are taken downstairs to a private dressing room with plush couches, fresh flowers, and soothing music playing.

Clearly Tate's name, and his credit card, carried a bit of weight. The assistant hurries off to get some champagne and to collect suitable dresses in her size for the occasion.

'So you do things like this often?'

Bria laughs as she helps herself to a drink. 'It's a difficult job but someone has to do it.'

'Are there any rules for these events? Do I have to match him or anything like that? Sorry, I've never been to something like this before.'

Bria thanks the assistant as she hangs some dresses on the rail then disappears to find some more. 'Oooh, these are promising. Sorry, about matching him. You don't have to. You're more than free to go as mad as you want. I checked with Ellen though just in case he's planning to wear something completely random, but he's sticking to conventional attire. Well, conventional for Tate. He'll be wearing a dark navy three-piece suit so it'll be difficult to clash with that. He'll add some Tate to the look with slightly edgier embellishments no doubt. Might even ditch the tie. You'll have to wait and see, but don't worry, it won't be anything extreme.'

'Three-piece suit? I can't imagine him in formal wear. I've only seen him in jeans and t-shirts.'

Bria laughs. 'Yeah. Don't even get me started on that. What I wouldn't give to completely overhaul all their wardrobes. Believe it or not, my brother scrubs up pretty well. He's one of those irritating people who can roll out of bed, throw on the first thing they see, and still manage to look good. It's infuriating.' She holds out her phone and shows Chloe a photo. 'This is last year.'

Scrubs up well is an understatement. Tate looks incredible in a suit. Trying to hide the heat touching her cheeks she clears her throat and takes a sip of champagne.

Bria tucks the phone into her pocket and smirks at Chloe. 'You've got it so bad.'

'Got what?'

'Don't play all innocent with me. You fancy my brother.'

'This is so wrong on so many levels.'

'What is discussed in the changing room stays in the changing room. Seriously, I'm happy for you both. It's about time he found someone who'll treat him right. He's had a few near misses in the past.'

'It's early days.'

'Very true.' Bria pulls out a stunning emerald green dress with a full skirt. 'But after he sees you in this, he won't be able to let you go.'

Chloe lies back in bed and flicks through the photos of her in the incredible green dress. She'd tried on too many dresses to count, but both Bria and herself had agreed the first green one was the best. She can't believe how different she looks in it. She's never worn anything so beautiful.

Bria hadn't let her see the total once they'd added shoes and a bag to the bill, but she had no doubt it was quite a bit. Certainly more than she could have afforded. Nothing in the shop had a price label on it which was a dead giveaway that she absolutely couldn't have afforded anything in there.

She tried to call Tate to say thank you, but he hadn't picked up. He must still be busy with the band. They hadn't made any plans to see each other for the next few days. He was going to be working and she had to get the house ready for her gran. Spending time with Tate had meant the housework her gran was always on top of had been seriously neglected.

Her phone rings and she smiles when she sees Tate's name on the screen.

'Hi.'

'Hey. Sorry I missed your call. I've been locked in a room all day.'

'Don't worry. I just wanted to say thank you for today.'

'How'd it go? Bria max out my credit card?'

'Don't even joke about that. I have no idea how much it all cost. Thank you, Tate. Between the art supplies and the dress I dread to think how much you've spent.'

'The art stuff was a present and you wouldn't need the dress unless you were saving my ass by tagging along. You get something you like?'

'Like? Tate, I love it. They have to make a few adjustments. They said they'll send it to the hotel in time for the awards.'

'One less thing to lose on the way. So you're all set?'

'I think so. Bria arranged hair and makeup too. She just needs me to send her the details of where we're staying.'

'I'll put Ellen in touch with her. Listen, I'm going to be tied up here for the next few days. I don't think I'll be able to get back. As much as I'd love to see you, I'll be in the studio most of the time.'

'Seriously, it's fine Tate. Gran is back in a few weeks, and I've got a lot to do to get this place up to her standards by then.'

'Don't forget to take the dishes out of the cupboard over the fridge.'

Chloe pauses then remembers about stuffing things into random cupboards that first time he came up for coffee. 'You saw me?'

'Yeah. Please tell me you've dealt with them. They're not still there, are they?'

'I'm going to say no.'

'Yeah, sounds like you need some time to sort it out. Hang on.' He moves away from the phone but Chloe still hears him shouting, 'For fuck's sake, I'm coming!'

'Got to go?'

'Sorry. Gregg is threatening to beat Dillon with a keyboard. Can I call you tonight?'

'Of course.'

'Bye.' He ends the call before Chloe gets a chance to say goodbye. As she stares at the end of the bed, she hates the empty feeling that follows. It doesn't make any sense. She's only known him a few weeks, but he's got to her on so many levels. Sitting here thinking about him isn't going to help with the dishes she had completely forgotten about until he mentioned it.

Chloe sits in the back of the car and pulls down the sleeve of her jacket again. She feels sick. Nerves had taken hold last night and no matter what she tried, she couldn't distract herself.

Bria reaches across and squeezes her arm. 'Relax. Just think of it as going on a date with him. It's no big deal.'

Chloe tries to smile but she knows it comes across as a grimace. She's just grateful Bria offered to come to the pick up point with her. Tate couldn't get away from work in time to come back to collect her, so he was going to meet her there. Chloe hasn't seen him for four days and can't wait, but the whole date, as Bria called it, is terrifying her. The fact they're meeting the helicopter in a field is just another bizarre detail in this already bizarre date.

As the Land Rover pulls off the main road and heads down a dirt track between two high hedges, Bria hands her a business card decorated in gold and purple. 'This is Dani. She's the hair and make-up expert I was telling you about. She'll give you a ring when she's on the way. She'll also be able to help you get dressed. Ellen booked a suite so there'll be plenty of room for you to get ready without Tate pacing while looking at his watch. Relax, Chloe. You'll have a blast. Trust me. You'll be pampered and spoilt rotten.'

Chloe smiles feeling a little more at ease. Bria is right. This is the experience of a lifetime. She should be excited. It's the celebrity thing that keeps rearing its head.

Since she first found out who he was, it was never that part of Tate that gave her hesitation. When she made that stupid statement about famous people, she honestly hadn't thought of him that way. But that's exactly what he is. As soon as she steps out of the car with him, the cameras will be going.

The car slows and turns through a double gate into a field. The helicopter is sitting in the middle of the field and her nervousness jumps to excitement when she spots Tate leaning against the bonnet of another Land Rover.

As soon as Chloe steps out of the car, he wraps his arms around her and pulls her close. He pushes his sunglasses up his head and kisses her like he hadn't seen her for weeks. When he finally breaks contact he smiles down at her.

'Hey.'

'Hey yourself. What was that for?'

'I might have missed you. Did you sort out the dishes in the cupboard?'

She makes a face. 'Eventually. Cornflakes are surprisingly resilient.'

'I'm not even going to ask,' Bria says as she gets out of the car.

Tate and Bria look at each other, neither one saying anything for a few minutes.

Tate eventually breaks the awkward silence. 'Thanks for everything, Bria. I really appreciate it.'

'I did it for Chloe.'

His face drops and he nods once. 'Got it. I'll leave you to it. We're scheduled to leave in the next ten minutes.'

'Sure.'

He lowers his glasses and walks back to the other car. Bria watches him leave and wraps her arms around herself. 'Yeah, that was bitchy.'

'I'm sure he understands. It's not easy for any of you.'

'I'm hate that I'm hurting him, but every time I look at him I just think about what he did to himself. It won't go away.'

Bria looks across the field to Tate, propped up against the bonnet of the car again with his arms crossed. 'I always looked up to him. He's my big brother. Shane is amazing, but Tate was the one I grew up with. He was the one who threatened anyone who looked at me sideways. Typical over protective big brother stuff. But I kind of liked it. I knew I could always depend on him. No matter what.'

'He made a mistake, Bria. A really serious one and I'm not taking away from that, but he's still your big brother. He really misses you.'

'I miss him too. Do you think I'm being too hard on him?'

'It's absolutely none of my business, Bria. You've known him a lot longer than I have. There's no right or wrong way to deal with it.'

Bria nods and signals to one of the men standing by the helicopter. He comes over and takes Chloe's bag from the boot and loads it inside. 'You better go. Have fun. I can't wait to hear all about it.'

Chloe hugs Bria then walks over to the other car where Tate is waiting. It doesn't take a genius to figure out the curt brush-off from Bria had hit him badly. Even from this distance she can see him playing with the ring on his thumb as he stares down at the grass in front of him. He's so deep in his thoughts he doesn't realise she's come to a stop in front of him.

'Tate? You okay?'

He pushes off the bonnet of the car and takes her hand. 'All good. You ready?'

'Tate!'

He freezes as Bria runs over and throws her arms around him. Tate doesn't move for a few seconds then hugs her back.

'Good luck tomorrow. You've got this.' Bria smiles at him then hurries back to the car.

Tate turns back to Chloe. 'What the hell did you say to her?'

'Me? Nothing.'

The look he gives her says he doesn't believe her for one second. 'Yeah well whatever it was, thank you.'

Tate slowly gets out of bed and closes the double doors behind him. He's too worked up to sleep.

He drops onto the couch, then gets up again and paces the living room. Coming here was a big mistake. He's not ready to get in front of the cameras again. What if they ask him about where he's been? What if he zones out and the whole fucking world witnesses it?

'For fuck's sake, Tate. Get a grip.'

He opens the doors onto the balcony and leans on the railing, looking down to the street below. There's hardly anyone around at this hour of the morning. Most people are asleep. Like he should be. He sits on one of the chairs and buries his head in his hands.

'Are you okay?'

He looks up as Chloe joins him on the balcony.

'Yeah. I just couldn't sleep and didn't want to wake you.'

'Did you have a dream?'

'No. Can't switch off though. You should go back to bed.'

She holds out her hand. 'C'mon. You're coming with me.'

'Seriously, I'm done for the night.'

'Get your ass back in the bed, Tate.'

He follows her back to the bedroom and climbs in beside her. This is a waste of time, but if it gets her back to bed he'll play along. Chloe piles the pillows up behind her and lies back against them. 'Lie down.'

He rests his head on her chest and she wraps her arms around him. 'Chloe, this is—'

'Will you stop arguing with me? Please humour me for a few minutes, okay? You think you can do that?'

'Yes, boss.'

'Thank you. Now shut up.'

Tate does as he's told and tries to focus on the sound of her heartbeat. Chloe runs her fingers through his hair as her other hand strokes his arm, slowly tracing the lines of his tattoo.

His last thought is how she's wasting her time before he drifts off to sleep.

Chloe smiles as Tate comes up behind her on the balcony and wraps his arms around her shoulders. In spite of all his objections, the stubborn man had slept the rest of the night. She had stayed awake for a little while after he fell asleep in case he had a dream, but exhaustion had him firmly in its grasp. When he'd finally woken, he seemed more relaxed than she'd seen him for a while.

'What do you fancy doing today?'

'Do you not have to meet with Dillon, Luke, and Gregg?'

'Nope. We're heading to the dinner separately, so you've got me all to yourself today. Dani is coming at four and the car is booked for six so we've got a few hours to kill. I was thinking we could grab some food then do some touristy stuff. You been in London before?'

'Once or twice visiting my sister, but that usually involved being dragged out to a few clubs.'

'Yeah, we won't be doing that. Anything else take your fancy?'

'Are you okay to just walk around in London?'

He sits on one of the chairs and rests his feet on the railing. 'I'm not fucking royalty or anything. Of course I can. Besides, I've got my trusty disguise with me.' He holds up a baseball cap and his sunglasses. 'I'll be in stealth mode.'

She raises her eyebrows and waves her hand at him. 'It's not just your face that will get you recognised. Your arms aren't exactly inconspicuous.'

He pulls her onto his knee and Chloe straddles him. 'I guess I'll just have to rely on my girlfriend to protect me.'

Chloe beams when he calls her his girlfriend. It doesn't matter how many times he says it, she doubts she'll ever tire of hearing it. The fact she's in a relationship after too many years alone is taking time to get used to. When you add in the small detail of the boyfriend in question being a famous rock star, it makes the entire situation so much more incredible.

Tate looks up at her and smiles. There are so many photos of him online, but in most of them he's serious. He absolutely should be photographed more often smiling.

'I'm sorry but there's no way I'm getting in between you and your fans. I value my life, thank you.'

'I'm sure you can more than handle them. So where do you want to go?'

'You mean like Madam Tussaud's and things like that?'

He makes a face. 'Yeah, no. Not that place. Waxwork figures are creepy as hell.'

'Seriously?'

'Too right. My parents took me to the museum in Dublin when I was a kid. Memorable day out for all the wrong reasons.'

'Anything else a big guy like you is afraid of?'

He slips his baseball cap on backwards as he thinks. 'I wouldn't go calling it afraid. More like I have a healthy distrust of them.'

'Healthy distrust, huh. Okay, so what else do you have a healthy distrust of?'

'Puppets. China dolls. Regular dolls. People dressed up as characters at theme parks. Clowns too. I really fucking hate clowns.'

'Okay. Your parents must have loved taking you out when you were a kid.'

'You could say that.' Tate smirks at her as he pulls his phone out of his pocket. 'There's bound to be somewhere you want to go in London that doesn't have scary ass clowns.' He checks the screen and laughs loudly. 'Now that's just spooky.' He tuns the phone around to show Chloe the picture of Dillon and Gregg standing outside Madam Tussaud's with cheesy grins on their faces.

'That is spooky. Are you sure you don't want to go meet them?'

Chloe laughs loudly at the look of horror on his face at the suggestion. 'Absolutely not.'

'Well, there is somewhere I've always wanted to go and I'm certain it doesn't have any rampaging clowns in it.'

'Sounds promising already.'

'You're going to laugh, but I've always wanted to go to the Tate Modern.'

He grins as he lifts her off his knee and grabs his coat. 'Absolutely can't argue with that. C'mon then. Lunch first, then Tate will take you to the Tate.'

They decide on a small cafe for lunch and eat monstrous rolls filled to bursting with chicken salad, then watch the world go by for a bit while they have their tea and coffee. Chloe is pleasantly surprised that no one has launched themselves at Tate so far, but he's blending in remarkably well.

After lunch she spends the next few hours absorbed in the art in the Tate. She rabbits on continuously to him as she moves from piece to piece and he listens to every word. She doesn't even mind when she loses him for a moment as a group of art students swarm around him, temporarily trapping him in one of the rooms.

As she orders a couple of drinks in the cafe, he disappears in the gift shop, returning with two bags. He hands one to Chloe. 'That's for you.'

She peers inside and pulls out a snow globe with a model of the museum inside. 'Very cute. Thank you.'

'Got to get a memento when you visit places like this.'

'You get one for yourself?'

'I got a few bits and bobs for my nieces. I always try to get them something small when I go away. I make up a box and send it to them when I've got enough things.'

'That's so nice. I didn't know you had nieces.'

'Molly and Tilly. They're my brother's kids.'

'How old are they?'

'Molly is eight and Tilly's four. I don't get to see them often so I tend to spoil them. I used to get them Lego sets when I was away but I've been banned by my sister-in-law, Annabelle. Apparently it's taking over their house.'

'You can never have enough Lego.'

He grins at her. 'Thank you. That's exactly what I said. I won't repeat what she said. Let's just say she is adamant they have enough. Just keep me out of any toy shops. Better safe than sorry.'

'I used to get a set every birthday and Christmas. It would keep me entertained for hours. Grown up presents aren't nearly as much fun.'

'I'll let you explain all that to Annabelle. So, I've changed tactics and now I just pick up small things I think they'll like. I'm also under orders from them to send merchandise every time new stuff is released. They're my biggest fans.'

'You miss them?'

He nods and finishes his coffee. 'Yeah. I try to visit when I can but my schedule has been full on the last few years. They come here every Christmas from mid-December to the end of January.' He goes quiet for a minute. 'I missed the end of their visit this year. Shane didn't want them to see me like that. He sent them home once he knew I was going to be okay. I didn't get to say goodbye to them though.'

'I'm sorry, Tate.'

He shrugs. 'I wouldn't have wanted them to see me in hospital. I still don't know what he told them. Annabelle isn't keen on my talking to them right now. I email them every week or so and sent them a video apologising for not saying goodbye because I had to go away with work. I get she's protecting them. I'd probably do the exact same thing if I was her.'

Chloe doesn't have a response to that. She didn't realise how deeply his actions had affected both Tate and his family. He's slowly scratching his arm, something she hasn't seen him do for a while. 'So,' she says, trying to distract him, 'what's your schedule like for the next few weeks?'

He frowns as he looks up at her. He seems to snap out of his daze and drops his hand. 'What?'

'Are you recording or do you have other musician stuff to do?'

That seems to do the trick. The frown disappears and he appears to relax a little. 'Recording I think. So, when do you start at school?'

'Oh nice one Mr. Archer. Great way to get the subject off you.'

He grins and winks.

'Last Wednesday in August. Two and a half days initially to ease us in.'

'You looking forward to it?'

'Absolutely terrified and excited at the same time. I don't know if dealing with a class of eight-year-olds is better or worse than a class of teenagers.'

'Definitely eight-year-olds. They're still like sponges at that stage. They'll be hanging on your every word.'

'You miss teaching, don't you?'

Tate takes a long breath before he answers. 'I absolutely love what I'm doing, but yes, sometimes I miss the one-on-one. Singing is great, but it's playing guitar or piano that's the main bit of it for me.'

'And violin.'

He laughs. 'That too. Believe it or not I'm working on a few ideas to incorporate that into some of our music. I just think it's incredible that a few keys or strings can make millions of different melodies. Teaching people the basic notes and watching them move on to playing full songs and then composing their own music was so rewarding.'

'You're just a big softy under all that muscle.'

'Don't tell anyone. I've got an image to uphold.'

'There's no way you could take on a few students again?'

'Nah. Don't think it would work. My schedule is all over the place. I couldn't commit to anything right now. Besides, teaching your gran whenever I can is work enough. She really doesn't like to be told what to do. I need the patience of a fucking saint to deal with her.'

Chloe manages to stop herself from spraying Tate with her tea as she laughs. 'Sorry. I just got a picture of the two of you facing up to each other. I can't see either of you backing down.'

'That's where my super teacher skills come in to their own, and a few cups of her posh coffee of course. Her stubbornness actually helps her. She doesn't stop until she gets it right.' He looks at his watch and makes a face. 'Damn. I guess we better head back to the hotel. Wouldn't want to be late.'

He takes her hand as they walk back on to the busy street and head back towards the hotel. With every step, the nerves increase, sending the butterflies in Chloe's stomach into a frenzy.

In a few hours she'll be stepping out of a limo in front of reporters, cameras, and fans as the new woman in Tate Archer's life. He may have tried to play it down, but she knows tonight is so important for both Tate and the rest of the band.

She's just going to have to ignore the nerves and do her best not to let him down.

Tate sits on the edge of the enormous bed and stares at his reflection in the mirror opposite him. He feels like he's going to throw up. He's never liked these award ceremonies, even at the best of times. He's not a natural people person, preferring his own company to crowds of people making small talk with each other.

He never took to the attention fame brings with it, but if he didn't get it tonight or got it for the wrong reason, his career will be on the rocks. Not only his career, but Dillon, Gregg, and Luke's career too. They depended on him. This will be the first real test and he desperately doesn't want to fail, especially with Chloe there to witness it.

He slips on his waistcoat and fastens the buttons as he paces the thick carpet. The vice of pressure across his chest refuses to let go. It's been with him all day, getting worse as the dinner drew closer.

The countless cups of black coffee probably hadn't helped. If he's not careful he'll be adding caffeine to his list of things to avoid. Since getting out of rehab he's been drinking the stuff like it's going out of fashion.

He knows he's scratching his arm, but he couldn't care less. It's offering a little distraction from the fact he can't breathe. The damn tie is like a noose around his neck, so he tears it off and throws it on the bed.

He's going to ditch the tie tonight. Ellen will just have to be happy he's wearing a suit. It's not like he'll have to get up on stage and give any speeches. There isn't a hope in hell he'll be coming away with any of the awards tonight. It's not going to matter what he's wearing.

He opens the top two buttons of his shirt and rubs his neck. It still feels like there's something around it. He leans on the dressing table and glares at his reflection.

Tonight isn't about the awards or getting him back in the limelight again. It's about seeing if he can survive a very public walk of shame.

'Get yourself together. This is for Chloe.'

He knows she's nervous about tonight, but he wants her to see this side of him. It's a part of his job and he would love for her to join him at every single event. Assuming there will be more of them of course, which he very much doubts. She might as well go to one while she still can.

He looks over his shoulder at the fridge sitting under the enormous TV on the far wall. There's no alcohol in it. He already checked and he hates himself for that. He doesn't doubt Ellen had a hand in making sure all temptation had been removed before he arrived. For some reason that irritates him more than it should. Then again, he opened the damn fridge in the first place. Not a great start.

He doubles over as a wave of nausea hits. Would he have shut the fridge door again without taking anything out? Or would he have had a glass to steady his nerves?

The way he feels right now he's not sure which way it would have gone.

He groans as his phone rings on the table beside him.

'Hey Gregg.'

'Hey buddy. We're heading in about fifteen minutes. You going to be on time or fashionably late?'

'On time.'

Gregg pauses for a second. 'Put the video on.'

'Gregg, I—'

'Video, Tate.' He taps the button and Gregg's face appears on the screen. 'Hey. Nice suit, buddy. Oh dear. Is the colour off or are you a tad grey?'

'I'm trying not to throw up so make it quick.'

'Sit down, close your eyes, and take a few deep breaths. Quit glaring at me and just do it.'

He does as he's told and little by little the queasiness eases.

'Gregg?'

'Yeah.'

'I checked out the mini bar. I mean opened it to see... you know...'

Gregg's face drops a little. 'Yeah, thought you might.'

'You asked them to clear it? I thought it was Ellen.'

'Nope. All down to me. Better safe than sorry, buddy. It's not that I don't trust you. I just know every other time you've been to one of these things you've had a little help.'

Tate drops his head into his hand, hating, but also unbelievably grateful that Gregg knows him so well. 'Fucking predictable, right.'

'Just watching out for you. You feeling any better?'

'Think so.'

'Look at the screen again. I can only see your arm.'

Tate lifts his head and looks down at the screen. 'Happy now?'

'Ecstatic. Seriously though, you've got this, Tate. Stop second guessing yourself and walk down that red carpet like you've done who knows how many times before. You became a fucking superstar without any help from drink or drugs. That was all you. Get your shit together and show Chloe how monstrously boring these events are, then take her back to the hotel room and make it up to her.'

Tate smiles down at the screen at Gregg's wide grin. 'Will do. Thank you, Gregg. I mean that.'

'Any time. You good now?'

'Guess so.' He looks over at the door when someone knocks. 'I got to go now.'

'Okay. Well I guess I'll see you in a bit. I'll save you a seat next to Pippa.' Gregg winks and ends the call before Tate can comment.

He gets up and, after taking a deep breath, opens the door.

'Hey Dani.'

'I'm done with Chloe. You ready for me?'

He nods and lowers into the chair so Dani can sort out his hair. 'How's Chloe?'

Dani smiles widely. 'She's stunning, Tate. Bria picked one hell of a dress for her. Oh and the front desk just sent a message up. There's a bit of a crowd outside so they've decided to take you and Chloe down in the service elevator and out the back door. The car will meet you there. You'll be getting extra security too.'

What a way to introduce Chloe to his public life. Sneaking her down in a service elevator. Better than having her face whatever crowd is outside.

'How long until they're ready?'

'They'll collect you in ten minutes or so.'

Ten minutes to get his shit together. No problem.

Chloe stares at her reflection not quite believing she's looking at herself. The dress fits her like a glove thanks to the alterations the boutique made. Dani had left her long hair down, the thick curls swept over one shoulder with a sparkling comb. She feels amazing.

She checks her reflection again then steps out into the living room.

Dani is finishing packing her things away. She gives Chloe a quick check then squeezes her shoulders.

'Perfect. Tate's just on the phone to Ellen.'

Tate walks out of the other room and comes to a stop when he looks at Chloe.

'You look absolutely... Fuck.'

Dani slaps him on the chest. 'Beautifully put.'

Chloe feels the heat rising in her body as he walks towards her. His suit is the same dark blue as his eyes and fits him perfectly, highlighting his tall, broad body.

Bria was right, he's left his tie off, but Chloe has no complaints. The crisp white shirt is open at the neck, leaving part of his chest and neck tattoo on show. Dani had tamed his hair, giving a little order to his naturally dishevelled look.

He wraps his arm around her waist and kisses her neck. 'I am absolutely going to enjoy taking that off you later.'

'And I will absolutely let you.'

He grins and holds out his hand. 'Better get this show on the road. Ready?'

'The sooner we go, the sooner we can get back here.'

'I like your thinking.' He squeezes her hand and leads her out the door and into his other life. As soon as they cross the threshold of the room Chloe enters a foreign world. Two rather large security guards lead them down the corridor to the service elevator. The door closes behind them and one of the men speaks into his radio, telling someone on the other end that they're on the way.

Chloe squeezes Tate's hand as they walk between the two guards into the large underground service garage. The butterflies come back with a bang as a shiny black limo pulls up beside them and the driver steps out to open the door for her.

Chloe smiles at him and slips inside the car, taking care not to damage her dress. Tate speaks to the security guards then joins her in the back. One of the guards gets into the front with the driver while the other follows in a separate car.

Tate pulls a jewellery box from his pocket and hands it to her as the car moves away from the hotel and joins the busy London traffic.

'What's this?'

'Open it.'

Chloe's breath catches in her throat when she sees what's inside. 'Tate, it's beautiful.' She stares down at the stunning emerald teardrop necklace. 'I don't know what to say.'

'Bria told me the colour of your dress. Just relieved it matches. I didn't realise there were so many shades of green.'

'You bought it yourself?'

'Of course. Why?'

She shrugs. 'I don't know. I guess I thought you'd have people to do that for you.'

'Believe it or not I actually went into a real brick-and-mortar shop and picked it out all on my lonesome. If I buy something for you it means I have actually picked it out myself - well apart from the dress. That was way out of my league.'

'Well thank you. It really is beautiful, Tate. I love it.'

He takes it from her and reaches over to fasten it around her neck. 'You look incredible, Chloe. I mean that.'

She doesn't know how he does it, but every single time he compliments her, a lump forms in her throat. She's been complimented before, but the way he looks at her is so intense, she doesn't doubt he means every word.

Instead of replying, she leans over and kisses him. It's going to be a long night. The combination of the suit and Tate's body is more than a little distracting.

'Thanks for coming with me tonight.'

'What are you thanking me for? You've spent an absolute fortune on me. I should be thanking you.'

'You being here with me is worth it. You're worth it. You know that, right?'

'You're going to make me cry and mess up my make-up.'

'Well, you better get a hold of that. We're here.'

The car slowly comes to a stop and Chloe stares out the window at the crowd waiting at either side of the wide walkway.

Tate leans across and kisses her then slips on his sunglasses as the door opens for him. He steps out to a constant flash from cameras and people shouting his name. He leans down into the car and smirks at her. 'You're up, gorgeous.'

She takes his hand and steps into the most surreal situation she's ever been in. Everywhere she looks are cameras and reporters. Tate leans down to speak in her ear. 'Just go with the flow and keep breathing. You look stunning.'

Tate closes the door to their suite and locks it, then turns around to face Chloe. The last six hours have been the longest six hours of his life. Every damn time he looked at her he wanted her. Tate drapes his jacket over the back of the couch and pulls her into his arms.

'I'm kind of torn.'

'About what?'

'I'm torn between not being able to get enough of you in that dress and wanting to get you out of it.'

'That's strange because I'm equally as torn as you are.' She runs her hand down his chest. 'Should you leave the suit on or take it off? How about you give me five minutes then join me in the bedroom.'

'You honestly expect me to wait five minutes?'

'It'll be worth it. Oh and leave the suit on.'

She smiles at him as she closes the double doors into the bedroom. Tate lowers onto the arm of the couch and massages the back of his neck, trying to relieve some of the tension. The night had gone so much better than he ever could have imagined. Not only had he not made a complete eejit of himself, but both the band and Tate himself had won awards.

Winning Best Rock Album had been a fucking miracle. When they called out his name for Song of the Year, Chloe actually had to give him a nudge to get up. He'd heard the words, but they didn't fully register. He went tonight to show his face. Coming home with two awards hadn't even crossed his mind.

It took him a good hour or so to allow himself to relax after he stepped out of the car. Every time a reporter approached him, he prepared for the worst, but rehab hadn't been mentioned once. After a while, his forced smile turned into a real one, but it was a very different experience to every other ceremony he'd been to.

Being stone cold sober for the entire thing probably had a lot to do with that. He'd never been drunk at any event, not once, but he'd always had something to drink over dinner. Usually something stronger beforehand too to help with nerves.

Thinking back, it's scary how often he resorted to drink and drugs to help him through nights like tonight. He'd always told himself he was in control, but the truth was he hadn't been in control for a long time. That old family photo may have thrown his life on its head, but if he hadn't already been using and drinking too much, he wouldn't have fallen as disastrously as he had.

Bad shit happens to people every day and they don't turn to heroin to deal with it. By that stage, drugs were deeply embedded in his life whether he knew it or wanted to accept it. His first go-to option had been Eddie and whatever cocktail he'd given him over those few weeks. In his mind there was no other way to deal with what was happening. Whether the letter arrived or not, he would have fallen sooner or later. He'd been on borrowed time. Just one push away from ending up exactly where he did... or worse.

He honestly doesn't know what he would have done without Chloe by his side this evening. While he'd struggled to get into conversation,

234

she'd come into her own. He couldn't be more proud of her. She was incredible. You'd swear she'd been to dozens of events like this and he was the out-of-his-depth newbie.

His impressively brief acceptance speech had been made to her and her alone. His eyes locked onto hers from the stage and he didn't look away until he was finished talking. He can't even remember who he thanked. His main concern was getting off the stage as fast as he could.

It was ridiculous how off balance the entire evening made him feel. Even with Chloe and the band by his side, he felt completely out of place. Like he was an imposter. His job involved him getting on stage in front of thousands of people. Tonight's performance doesn't bode well for his future.

He takes off his watch and checks the time. Four minutes. Fuck it. That's long enough rehashing what he could have done better tonight. Time to put it behind him and enjoy what's left of the night.

He opens the double doors to the bedroom and stops when he sees what's waiting for him. Chloe has taken off her stunning dress and is sitting on the end of the bed in equally stunning underwear and a pair of killer heels. If he'd known she had that on under her dress he would have ditched the dinner a few hours earlier.

She shakes her head when she notices him. 'You couldn't wait five measly minutes?'

'Not when I know you're in here.'

He walks towards her, but she holds up a hand. 'You stop right there.'

Tate stops in the middle of the room and watches as Chloe slowly crosses her legs. He licks his lips as his eyes travel over every inch of her body. The underwear is fucking hot but he wants to tear it off her as soon as possible.

'Now Mr. Archer, I want you to get undressed. Slowly.'

Yeah, this is a new one for him. He's all about getting clothes off as fast as he can in whatever order they happen to come off. He's done stuff like this for photo shoots, but this is different. This is in front of Chloe.

'How exactly do you envision my shoes and socks in this display? Ditch them first or maybe you'd prefer I leave them on? You like that naked with socks on look?' He laughs when she makes a face and shakes her head.

'Okay, you're going to have to work so much harder to get that image out of my head. Take them off first. I beg you.'

He removes the offending items and straightens again.

'Now, take off your waistcoat.'

Tate open his mouth, but she shakes her head.

'No more talking. I said, take off your waistcoat.'

Tate takes a deep breath and clenches his jaw. He can either laugh off what she just said or do as he's told and see how it plays out. Nothing to lose by doing as he's told for a bit.

He keeps his eyes locked on hers as he unbuttons his waistcoat and drops it to the ground.

'Your shirt next.'

Starting at his chest, he undoes each button on his shirt, then unfastens one cufflink followed by the other, dropping them on to his waistcoat. He slowly slides his shirt off his shoulders and down his arms. Chloe intently watches his every move as she traces her fingers down her body, cupping each breast. When she pinches her nipples between her thumb and forefinger and moans softly, Tate's cock twitches in response.

Chloe's eyes slowly travel up his body then settle back on his crotch.

'Belt, trousers, and boxers now.'

His belt ends up on the floor then he opens the button on his trousers and unzips his fly. He pushes his trousers over his hips and down his legs, followed by his boxers then stands naked in front of her.

He nearly launches himself at her when she slowly uncrosses her legs. Chloe's fingers skim over the lace thong as she moves her legs to the side. His dick hits against his stomach as she moans again.

She's driving him fucking crazy and she knows it. If she has any sense she'll let him touch her. Instead she leaves him where he is, frustrated, horny, and desperate to be released.

Chloe rubs her fingers against her pussy, covering the thin lace in her delicious juices. He clenches his fists at his sides. He's wound like a fucking spring, every single muscle locked to keep himself in place.

He needs to get his mouth, tongue, and fingers all over her pussy. He can picture exactly what he's going to do to her in detail. He can taste her on his tongue and he hasn't laid a finger on her yet.

He's not used to being held back like this. Not used to being told what to do and he fucking loves it. The longer she holds him back the harder he's going to fuck her when he eventually gets his hands on her.

'Now, I want to see you make yourself come.'

Chloe peers up at Tate and waits for him to react to what she just said. Every single time he's been naked with her, she's been mesmerised by his body. Watching the way he moves, the way the muscles flex and contract when he was with her drove her nearly as crazy as what he was doing to her. The thought of watching him towering above her, every inch of his body on show while he touched himself has been something she'd imagined a lot since their first time together.

Even just watching him undress had been intense. His dark eyes hadn't left hers the entire time. She is under no doubt he's going to make her pay for drawing things out for him. And she can't wait. But first she desperately wants to see him do this in front of her.

With his gaze still locked on her, Tate's arm lifts from his side. Chloe's heart beats faster as his tattooed hand begins to slowly and steadily work over his shaft, back and forth. She can feel him looking at her but there's no way she can tear her eyes away from what he's doing to himself. His hand clenches and slides, gliding up, covering the head and the thick piercing in his fist then twisting back down in a steady rhythm.

She knew seeing him like this would be incredible, but not for one second did she think it would be so downright hot. He's not exactly being gentle with himself. Just like everything else he does, he's not holding back. Chloe had been cautious with his piercings, but he can take a lot more than she's been giving him.

Chloe slides her fingers under the thin lace of her thong and slips a finger inside. She has no idea whether she's doing it to frustrate him or to pleasure herself. Maybe a little of both.

Tate's breath comes out in short pants as he works himself harder and faster. She can see he's getting close. See the tremors working through his body, see the muscles in his arms tensing, his stomach tightening as his hips flex.

Then he reaches up and pulls on his nipple piercing, twisting it in his fingers.

With a shout, he comes all over his hand. He braces his legs as he keeps stroking himself, his body trembling and his breathing rapid. Tate shudders and meets her eyes as he lets go of himself and drops his arms to his side again. The fact he hasn't said a word to her since she told him to get undressed only adds to the all-consuming look in his eyes. Time to let him go. She licks her juices from her fingers, and she swears she hears him growl.

'Would you like a taste?'

'Yes.'

Yeah, that was as close to a growl as he could do without actually growling at her. 'Yes, what?'

She can see the muscles in his jaw move as he clenches his jaw. 'Yes, please.'

'I really think you should get on the bed now.'

Chloe barely has time to scramble out of the way before Tate launches himself onto the bed. He pushes her onto her back and slides her thong down her legs. Tate pulls her hips back and Chloe gasps as he buries his tongue in her as deep as he can go.

Tate's rough hands grip her hips, holding her firmly in place so he can suck and lick her with a desperation that has her gasping for breath. Her body jolts as his tongue circles her clit, massaging her as his fingers plunge into her. Chloe's body jolts and she screams into the sheet as her orgasm slams through her.

'Get onto your hands and knees then don't fucking move.' Tate grabs a condom from the bathroom and slips it on. Without hesitating, he thrusts into her hard and deep, wrapping his hands around her waist to hold her in place as he drives into her.

Chloe's arms give in under the strain of his attack, so Tate wraps an arm around her, pulling her back against his chest as he keeps up the pace. When he slides his other hand down her body to rub her clit, Chloe moans loudly and reaches back to grab his hair.

His sole purpose at the moment is satisfying the raw need that's taken over as the pressure builds in his balls. He tilts Chloe's head back against his shoulder, holding her tightly in place so he can kiss her neck.

'You better fucking come now, Chloe. Jesus Chloe, now!'

When she tightens around him he covers her mouth with his hand, stifling her scream. Her pussy squeezes him firmly, and two thrusts later the spasm works through his body.

'Fuck me!' The shout tears out of him before he can stop it. He holds on to Chloe as the intense grip on his dick keeps his own orgasm coming.

He loses track of time as their bodies slowly come down. When she eventually relaxes in his arms, he pulls out of her then lowers them both on to the covers as they try to catch their breath.

Chloe sighs and runs her hand along his arm. 'Please say the room is soundproofed?'

'I hope so otherwise I might be on the banned list after that.'

Chloe turns around to face him. Her face is flushed and the sly smile she gives him is sexy as hell. 'Was it worth it?'

'What do you think?' He brushes her hair back from her face and traces his thumb across her bottom lip. He leans closer and kisses her. Unlike the frantic raw need of a few minutes ago, the kiss is slow but no less intense.

Tate rests his forehead against her and sighs. 'I really don't want to move but I better get cleaned up. You hungry?'

'Excuse me? You've just had a five-course meal. How can you possibly be hungry already?'

'I'm talking about real food not whatever they served tonight.'

She gets up and slips on one of the plush hotel robes as he sorts himself out in the bathroom. 'Let me guess. You want chips.'

She throws him the other robe when he joins her in the bedroom. 'That predictable, huh?'

She traces her finger over his chest and abs. 'Where exactly do you put it all?'

'Don't worry. I plan on working it all off.'

'Is that so.' She takes his hand and leads him into the living room. 'Let's get you some chips then.'

When room service arrives, they sprawl out on the couch, watching The Mummy while they demolish two plates of chips with plenty of sauce.

Tate gets caught up watching Chloe for a minute. He's in a posh hotel after spending the evening at a star packed awards event but eating chips on the couch with Chloe far exceeds all of that.

She licks her fingers and turns to look at him. 'What?'

'You're a dark horse, Chloe Quinn. You know that?'

'In what way?'

'What you did in the bedroom.' He taps the side of his head. 'You've gotten in here. I don't know how the fuck you did it but you know exactly how to push my buttons. And I mean that in a good way.'

'You're not that difficult to figure out.'

He moves back from her so he can look down at her face. 'I'm an enigma thank you very much.'

'You're a control freak, Tate. You like to be in charge. Like things to go your way. I would imagine you're not a fan of being told what to do.'

'And?'

'So I wanted to see how you'd react if I took that away from you. Like I said, it wasn't difficult. It was going to go one of two ways. You'd either get a bit irritated about it and nothing would happen, or you'd get worked up so much at being told you couldn't do what you wanted that you'd go a little... well, alpha male on me. You have no idea how relived I was when you leapt onto the bed like the floor was on fire.'

Tate stares down at her. He's been with his share of partners, but not one of them had taken the time to figure him out. Then again, it's not like he tried to figure them out either. The fact she'd even thought about how he'd react in that situation is surprising.

It also helps that she figured him out before he did himself. He never thought he'd like or get so fucking turned on by being held back like that. 'Watching you look at me playing with myself... Yeah we can do that again. But next time I'm finishing in your mouth.'

'You are such a sweet talker, you know that. I'd never guess you were a songwriter.'

'That's award-winning songwriter thank you very much.'

Chloe smirks at him. 'Sincerest apologies.'

'I should hope so.' He leans over her and kisses her. 'And if you're naked in front of me there will be absolutely no sweet talking. Just a hell of a lot of me fucking you.'

'Like I said, such a sweet talker.'

She snuggles into his side and traces the tattoo on the back of his hand. His eyes drift close as the exhaustion, great sex, good food, and Chloe's touch work their magic on him.

'Tate?'

'Yeah?'

'I'm proud of you.'

He pulls her closer and tucks her head under his chin. 'For what?'

'Tonight. And I don't mean the awards. I mean obviously I'm proud of you about those. I really am. But I mean for facing everyone. I know it wasn't easy for you.'

His stomach does a bizarre flip at her words.

She peers up at him and runs her finger down his jaw. 'I know you didn't want to go, and I know you were far from comfortable, but you did it and I'm proud of you.'

'I really thought I'd done a better job hiding it from you.'

'You tried. I'm getting to know you though. I can tell the difference between your real smile and fake smile. You were performing for most of the evening.'

'Am I that fucking transparent?'

She laughs and reaches up to kiss him on the cheek. 'Like I said, I'm getting to know you.'

'So much for thinking I'm an enigma. You've well and truly destroyed that.'

'Sorry about that. You must be losing your touch.'

He gathers her in his arms and rests his chin on her head. Either that or he's dropping his wall for the first time ever.

Chloe yawns and opens her eyes, smiling when she sees Tate beside her. He's still asleep, lying on his front with his arm over his face. The imposing and highly detailed griffin peers across at her from his bicep.

Moving slowly so she doesn't wake him, she props herself up on one elbow and examines the tattoo that stretches the full width of his broad back. She dreads to think how long it took to complete. Whoever the artist was, they did an incredible job. Each and every feather is drawn to perfection and remarkably realistic giving it a three-dimensional feel.

It's the same with all his tattoos. From the Celtic knots on the back of each hand to the swirling Celtic designs circling both arms and surrounding the griffin. Each design blended seamlessly into the next turning Tate into an impressive canvas of Celtic artwork.

'You want a picture?'

Tate peeks out from under his arm and smiles at her.

'Sorry. I was just admiring the detail. They really are stunning.'

'They'd want to be. We had a love/hate thing going on while they were being done.'

She traces her finger over the wing on his back, following the lines down his side. Chloe looks up at his face. He's staring at her, his head resting on his arms, his dark blue eyes focused on her.

'You're absolutely gorgeous, Tate.' She winces as the words come out. He's probably heard that from countless people over the years. Surely she could have come up with a more inventive way of telling him.

'I am?'

'You know you are. I'm sure enough people have told you.'

'People blow smoke up my ass all the time. Doesn't mean I take any of it seriously. No one I give a damn about has said that to me.'

'Really?'

'Yeah, really.' He wraps his arm around her waist, pressing his chest to her back as he kisses the side of her neck. Chloe moans as his hand moves down her body.

'Tate?'

'Yeah.'

'I want you inside me.'

'Since you asked so nicely.'

When she finally manages to extract herself from him, it's an hour later and her stomach is seriously complaining about the lack of food.

While he's checking in with the rest of the band, Chloe brushes her wet hair then turns to face the enormous bed. There's no way she's leaving it like that for housekeeping to find. The pillows are on the floor and the sheet a tangled mess hanging over the side. As she does her best to make the bed, she looks over at her dress draped across the chair at the side of the room.

Last night had been incredible. She will never forget the feeling of taking Tate's hand and stepping out of the car in front of all those cameras. The initial fear of the unknown had quickly disappeared with him by her side. Even when she was led away for a few minutes so he could get photos taken, she didn't feel scared or intimidated. Everywhere she looked she saw familiar famous faces. And in the middle of it all was her Tate.

Watching him interact with the press, with the other celebrities, and having countless photos taken was surreal. It was like there was two sides to him. Seeing him in that environment last night, dressed the way he was... she couldn't have been more proud of him. Or more attracted to him.

She knows he wasn't looking forward to the evening. It was his first time in front of the world since he finished rehab. The fact he agreed to go in the first place was an achievement. Wining two awards was the affirmation he desperately needed. Hopefully, after last night, he won't be so quick to second guess himself. He's an incredible singer, songwriter, and performer. Nothing that's happened since Christmas changed that. His confidence just needs to be built up again.

Tate steps out of the living room in his usual jeans and t-shirt. How the man can look equally good in a three-piece suit or jeans she'll never know.

'How are the guys?'

'Yeah. Good. Pippa has a sore head. Not surprised with the amount she was putting away. Think she was making up for the rest of us not drinking.'

Chloe doesn't comment. She doesn't know Pippa and it's not her place to pass judgement. As much as she wants to.

Tate has a problem with alcohol. Pippa knew that. While the rest of the table had shied away from the copious amounts of free drink being offered, Pippa happily drank glass after glass of champagne. Tate hadn't been exaggerating the issue between Luke's girlfriend and him. Pippa didn't hold back on the dirty looks being thrown across the table.

It was actually a relief that she hadn't acknowledged Chloe's existence. Apart from glaring at Tate while she drank her expensive champagne, there was nothing from the woman.

As the night went on, Chloe couldn't help but feel sorry for Luke. Pippa and her mood completely overshadowed the poor guy all night.

'You hungry?'

Chloe nods enthusiastically. 'Absolutely.'

'We're out of time to go anywhere. Our ride will be here in an hour or so. Pick what you want from room service.' He pulls out his phone and grimaces. 'I better take this. It's my mum.'

Chloe peruses the menu as Tate has what sounds like a conversation with his mother he's not winning. He ends the call and looks across at Chloe.

'Is everything okay?'

'Depends on your definition of okay. She was just quizzing me about you.'

'Me? You hadn't told her we're going out?'

He shakes his head. 'Nope. I'm sorry about this, but she's insisting we meet up tonight for a quick dinner thing. She doesn't take no for an answer. Ever. Could you spare a few hours?'

'Of course. I'd love to meet your family.'

'I've got to have a quick meeting with Ellen tonight. I'm being interviewed first thing tomorrow so she wants to make sure I say what I'm supposed to. I've told Mum we can only make it for an hour or so. She's eager to meet you.' He holds out his phone and Chloe stares at a picture.

'Oh my God, that's us! Where did you get that?'

'Internet. There's quite a few on there.'

Chloe takes his phone and scrolls through the photos. 'I guess we're out.'

'Yep. I guess we are. Any regrets?'

'Absolutely not. You look amazing in these.'

'You look pretty fucking hot yourself, Ms Quinn.'

Chloe reads the headline aloud. 'Is heartthrob Tate Archer off the market?'

He makes a face. 'Yeah, I really fucking hate that word. The rest of the caption is right though. I'm off the market.'

'Does that mean I'm going to have hordes of fans coming after me looking for blood?'

He gathers her in his arms and reads the menu over her shoulder. 'Don't worry, I'll protect you.' He points to the chicken burger and sweet potato fries. 'That's the one for me.'

Tate unlocks his front door and dumps his bag in the hall. He's exhausted but happier than he remembers being for a hell of a long time. The weekend went better than he could have imagined. Winning the awards was great but spending that time with Chloe is what made the weekend so good. He's going to miss her tonight, but he's meeting Ellen then getting an early night.

The intercom on his gate sounds. Ellen mentioned she had a few congratulations presents for him and would be sending a driver around so he opens the gates, a little surprised when two men come in. They deposit the flowers and baskets of other goodies on the counter in his kitchen.

He never got the point of being sent flowers as a congrats present. He couldn't keep the ones planted outside alive without paying someone to do it. Cut flowers didn't have a hope in hell. He'll rehome them to his mum, Bria, and Chloe tomorrow. At least that way they may have a chance at surviving longer than a day.

After sticking the flowers in a sink full of water, he makes himself a coffee then pulls the cards off the plastic holders.

He'd been so worried about stepping back into public after what he did. Downright terrified in fact. He was sure no one would want to have anything to do with him. The support he received on Saturday night shocked him. Reading some of these cards has that feeling coming back tenfold. Some of the biggest names in the industry have congratulated him. That means as much as the awards themselves.

He slides a glossy black gift box nearer and peels the card from the front before lifting the lid. He sweeps aside the brightly coloured shredded paper, and his hand drops to the counter as he stares at the gift.

Tate tears open the envelope that came with the box, the dread already taking hold. He's not surprised to find the card is blank. Instead there are two neatly folded pieces of paper inside. His heart hammers in his chest as he unfolds the first one and frowns at the picture on the page. He reads the words underneath, then looks back at the carefully packaged gift.

Chloe turns on the bedside light as her phone vibrates across the wooden surface. She squints at the display on the clock. It's a little after midnight. Tate wouldn't be ringing her so late.

'Hello.'

'Hey, Chloe. It's Gregg. Don't suppose Tate is with you, is he?'

'Tate? No. He went home a few hours ago. Why?'

'It's probably nothing but he had arranged to meet Ellen after he got back from London and he didn't show which isn't like him. Did he mention meeting her? I mean he might have forgotten with all the excitement.'

'He left the dinner with his parents early so he could meet her. He dropped me home first then went back to his.' Chloe sits up and brushes her hair out of her face. 'Gregg, should I be worried?'

The line goes quiet for a moment. 'I don't know. I'm at my parents' place so I'll pop by and pick you up. How about you try ringing him. He might just be ghosting me.'

Gregg cuts the call and Chloe quickly taps Tate's contact. No answer. She tries again and again, but the call goes to voicemail both times. When Gregg arrives at her door she has her bag and coat in her hands.

'We need to go.'

Gregg makes a face. 'Fuck. I was hoping he was pissed with me about something and that's why he wasn't answering.' He doesn't wait for her to fasten her seatbelt before he drives off. 'Did anything weird happen today?'

She shakes her head. 'Nothing. We got back from London, went to the dinner then home. He was in great form. We had a brilliant weekend and he was happy. Genuinely happy. It was busy though. Maybe he just fell asleep and has his phone on silent?'

'Yeah. Maybe. Listen, don't freak out but I gave Eddie a shout. He was Tate's go-to guy for drugs.'

Chloe swallows before speaking. 'And?'

'It's all good. He swears he hasn't heard a peep from Tate since he went into rehab.'

'And you believe him?'

Gregg nods. 'He's a fucking asshole, but he's got no reason to lie.'

Chloe nods but doesn't feel comforted. There's nothing to say Tate hasn't found someone else to supply him.

They eventually pull up to his gate and Gregg takes out the spare remote. The relief at finding his truck parked in the drive is quashed when they unlock the door and step into the living room. Tate is sprawled face down on the couch, one arm draped over the edge.

Chloe's feet refuse to move past the kitchen. Frozen to the spot, her heart hammers in her chest as Gregg hurries over to Tate and checks for a pulse.

'He's still with us. Tate? Hey, wake up. C'mon Sleeping Beauty.' Gregg slaps him on the cheek and Chloe's feet unlock from the floor when he lifts his hand and covers his head.

When Gregg gets no further reaction from Tate, he shakes him roughly, trying to wake him. Tate groans and swats Gregg's hand away while muttering a curt. 'Fuck off.'

Chloe holds up an empty rum bottle and Gregg blows out a long breath. 'That explains it. The stuff always knocks him out. You're a fucking idiot, Tate.'

Chloe slowly lowers onto the coffee table and looks at Tate. So much for being happy after London. Why would he come back here and drink like this? Gregg checks both of Tate's arms, narrowly avoiding a fist to his face when Tate objects.

'Calm down, Tate.' He feels in Tate's pockets and around the cushions.

'What are you doing?'

'Just making sure he hasn't taken anything. Looks like he's just smashed but...' He doesn't finish the sentence, instead gets down on his hands and knees and peers under the couch.

Chloe watches Gregg in a bit of a daze. Tate had been honest with her about what he'd done but seeing even a small part of it for herself is terrifying.

Gregg eventually gives up the search and drops onto the armchair facing the couch. He scrubs a hand over his jaw then rests his head in his hands as he glowers over at Tate. 'I'm sorry, Chloe. If I'd known he was like this I would never have brought you here.'

'Why not?'

'Because like I said, he's a fucking idiot that's why. You hear that, Tate!'

Tate buries his head further under his arm and ignores Gregg.

'Are you really sure that's all it is. I mean, has he done this before?'

Gregg gets up and fills the kettle. 'Yeah, he's done it before. Not for a while, mind you, but it's not a first. My dear friend can put it away when he wants to. Always could do. There's a reason he's been told to steer clear of alcohol too. Infuriating git doesn't know when to call it quits.'

She pulls the blanket off the back of the couch and drapes it over Tate then joins Gregg in the kitchen. 'Are you okay, Gregg?'

He crosses his arms and shrugs. 'Not really. He was getting over it, Chloe. Why the fuck would he do this? He's going to have one hell of a hangover in the morning. Serves him right.'

Chloe doesn't respond. Gregg is angry but she knows it's only because he cares about Tate. That's why he's as upset as he is. 'Have you told Dillon and Luke?'

He shakes his head. 'Doubt he'd appreciate me spreading this around. Best to keep it to ourselves.'

'Tate said you were the one who helped sort them all out when you joined the band.'

Gregg looks surprised to hear her say that. 'Really?'

'Yes. He speaks very highly of you.'

'Did he tell you why they toned it down?'

'Well, no. He just said they did when you joined.'

'I used to be a Garda.' Gregg laughs at the look of shock on her face. 'Yeah I know. I can be serious when I have to be, believe me. I joined after school and stepped away about a year and a half ago to work with Tate. Having an ex-cop hanging around put a bit of a dampener on their partying. Don't get me wrong, I'm no saint. I didn't sit back and not partake, but Tate, Dillon and Luke... well, there was no keeping up with them. Fuck, Chloe. I shouldn't be saying this to you of all people.'

'No, it's fine. He told me about that side of things and how much what happened terrified him. That's what I don't understand? Why

251

would he do this? Why now? I thought he was okay.'

Gregg takes a deep breath then looks over at her. 'He'll kill me for this but fuck him. Tate's been getting fan mail and I'm not talking the nice kind. They know about his pre Tate Archer past and keep waving it in his face.'

'You mean about his father?'

'So he told you about that? That's something I guess. They're fucking with him and clearly it's working.'

'Has he gone to the Garda about it?'

'He told me about it when he got out of rehab. Well, he did after a lot of kicking. He's not a fan of talking about what's going on in his head. He wouldn't let me get some old mates to investigate it. He said there's nothing on the letters that would give them anything to go on.'

'He's probably right. It's not the first time he's been sent not so warm-and-fuzzy letters. One guy even thought Tate was sending his girlfriend secret messages through his songs. There are some interesting people out there. All they can do is keep a file and leave it at that. I'm guessing this slip-up has something to do with that. We'll have to wait until his lordship comes to properly and is clear-headed enough to spill the beans. Unless...'

He pulls open the cupboard under the sink and peers into the bin. He takes out a scrunched-up piece of paper and smiles. 'That was easier than I thought.' Gregg unfolds the page and they both stare at what drove Tate over the edge.

It's a picture of Tate sitting on the beach with her on his lap. Typed under the photo in thick bold print is a single line of text.

What did she do to deserve a fuck-up like you?

Gregg leans on the counter and chews the inside of his cheek as he stares at the page. 'Well, that's not particularly friendly. You know where this was taken?'

'Bray seafront. He took me shopping for art supplies then we had a takeaway in the back of his truck. We went for a walk on the beach after. Someone was watching us?'

'You're dating Tate, Chloe. Someone's always going to be watching. This takes it to a new level though.' He leans down and digs in the bin again. 'There's something else.' He smooths the second piece of paper and Chloe instantly knows something is seriously wrong. She's never seen Gregg look so angry.

'Do I want to know?'

Gregg wipes a hand over his jaw. 'I don't want to know. I shouldn't be reading this.' He folds the page and slips it into his pocket. 'It's a page from the report his social worker did when he was put in foster care. It's got bits from an evaluation they did on him. About his suitability for permanent placement with a family and how being used as a punching bag would affect him long term. How the hell did whoever this is get their hands on it?'

Chloe peers into a fancy black gift box sitting on the counter and gently brushes the padding to the side. 'Gregg. They sent him the drink.'

He curses when he sees the perfect imprint of the bottle in the base of the box. 'Bastards handed him a loaded gun.'

Chloe slumps onto one of the bar stools and clasps her hands together. 'This is more than a few unpleasant letters, Gregg.' She looks over her shoulder at Tate. 'He could just as easily have called Eddie.'

'But he didn't. I know him getting stupidly drunk isn't going to help him, but it's done. He's just got to get sober so we can have a nice little chat about what the fuck is going on. He should have called his sponsor, or me, or you, or anyone before he opened the bottle. He knows full well what he's supposed to do when he feels like he's struggling. Looks like he ignored all that and went for the easy option.'

Gregg sits beside her and turns the stool around so she's facing him.

'Hey, he'll be grand.' He makes a face. 'Well, he'll be sick as a dog for a bit, but he'll be grand eventually.'

'What about whoever is doing this to him? They're following us, Gregg. We were having a private conversation, and someone was taking a picture of us. It feels...'

'Creepy. I know. Take some advice from a relatively new entry to the crazy celebrity world – assume there are no private conversations or private moments when you're in public. And by public, I mean anywhere that isn't behind closed doors.' He squeezes her arm and nods towards the stairs. 'He's going to be out of it for a good few hours. How about you grab some sleep. I'll sit with him for a bit. Make sure he's okay.'

'I don't think I'll be able to sleep. I'll stay with him too if that's okay.'

'Of course. I'll get some blankets. Now, do you fancy spending an uncomfortable night in the left or the right armchair?'

Tate groans as he rolls onto his back. It takes less than a second to seriously regret moving at all. He hangs on to the back of the couch as the room tilts and sways around him.

'Good morning, gorgeous.'

He winces as Gregg's voice booms loudly in his head. 'Too loud.'

'Oh sorry buddy. Does your head hurt?'

Tate winces as Gregg pretty much shouts in his ear. 'Yeah, it hurts.'

'Good!' Gregg shouts in his ear again. 'Serves you right!'

Tate slowly pushes himself up and sits back as his head catches up with the rest of his body. 'Why are you here?'

'Ellen rang me when you missed the meeting with her yesterday. Then I called Chloe. Do you have any idea what you put her through, you selfish dick?'

He leans forward, resting his head in his hands as a wave of nausea hits him. 'You were the one who called her. Not me. You had no fucking right to call her.'

'Yeah well that's not how things work. You're with her, so when you do things like this it affects her too.'

Gregg sits beside him and hands him a glass of water. Tate takes it and manages one mouthful before his stomach objects.

'Where's Chloe?'

'At the cafe down the road. If you're going to pull fucking stupid stunts like this at least make sure you have some food for breakfast. You've got a hell of a lot of making up to do with her, Tate.'

'Is she okay?'

'She found her boyfriend passed out on the couch after drinking himself unconscious. Of course she's not okay. I told her about the letters too.'

'You did what?' He moves his head faster than his headache is happy with. 'Oh shit that hurts.'

'What the hell did you expect me to say? You won two awards then came home and got smashed after being clean and sober for months. You not think the timing would have confused her just a smidge? I presume this little episode is thanks to the love letter?'

'Yeah. Was in a congratulations card.'

'Nice touch.' Gregg takes the page out of his pocket and slaps it down onto the coffee table in front of Tate. 'Time to talk, buddy.'

Tate stares down at the creased page in front of him. 'Where the hell did you find that?'

'In the bin. Bit of an obvious place to ditch it.'

Tate grabs for the page but Gregg pulls it out of his reach. 'I don't want her to see that.'

'She already did.' Gregg takes the second page out and leaves in on the table still folded. 'She didn't see what's on this one though.'

Tate slumps back on the couch and closes his eyes as the room spins again. 'Did you tell her?'

'No. I gave her the outline – no details. Did you know about this?'

'No and I'm not going there so please shut up. Destroy that and forget about it.'

Gregg doesn't say anything for a few minutes so he convinces himself to face the spinning room again. He peers over at Gregg, slightly relieved when he's not moving around.

'I'm your friend, Tate. How can you honestly expect me to forget what I read and just move on? You need to talk to someone about this.'

'Why? Knowing he kicked the shit out of me is bad enough. If he did that to me too... I don't want to remember! I can't deal with that on top of everything else.' He groans as a wave of nausea hits. It could be the drink. It could be thinking about what he read in the report. 'He was my dad. It was his job to keep me safe not do that. Sick fuck. I was just a kid, Gregg.'

'I know, Tate. And I don't blame you for wanting a drink. I really don't. But I'm worried about you, buddy. This isn't something you should be processing alone.'

'Please, Gregg. Leave it.'

'I can't just leave it. Your therapist needs to know about this. She can help you deal with this. You drank because of it. What's to stop you taking it up a level next time. I know the dickhead helped you out by putting that bottle in your hand, but you were the one who opened it. Why didn't you call me? I'm not blaming you for wanting something after reading that, but you know the drill, Tate.'

'I fucked up, okay. I get it.'

'This isn't about fucking up. It's about helping you deal with this. Your father—'

'Don't say it. Please. And you read the report. They don't know for sure. They just think he did.'

'Tate—' He stops talking when Chloe opens the door from the hall and places the bags of groceries on the counter.

Tate throws his best warning look at Gregg and his friend slips the page back into his pocket.

Chloe smiles as she sits in the other armchair facing Tate. 'Morning. How do you feel?'

'Fucking awful.'

'Can I get you anything?'

He shakes his head and winces. 'A new brain would be good.'

She reaches across and holds his hand. 'All out of those I'm afraid. So, you two looked deep in conversation when I came in. What's going on?'

Gregg nods towards the page still sitting in the table with the photo of Chloe on it. 'Just trying to convince this stubborn git to do something about these letters.'

'It's just some out of control—'

'Stop right there,' Gregg interrupts. 'Don't go mentioning out of control fans. Someone has got access to your life, Tate. The photo of you and Chloe is wrong, but having that assessment is a few dozen steps too far.'

Tate rubs his forehead as the pressure builds behind his eyes. He feels like death warmed up. The last thing he needs or wants right now is to head down that fucked up road.

'Leave it.' Tate closes his eyes as a wave of nausea hits. When it passes, he pushes to his feet and wobbles as he tries to get his balance. 'You can both relax. It won't happen again. I'm grand.' He realises the stupidity of that statement before he sees the look on their faces. 'Well, I will be. It was a slip up, but I'll deal with it.'

'No offence buddy, but the last time you tried to deal with something yourself you ended up sticking a needle in your arm.'

He buries his head in his hands, wincing as the throbbing kicks up a level. 'Jesus, Gregg.'

'Sorry, but you don't have a great track record.'

'I had a fucking drink. It's not a big deal.'

'It is when you've not touched a drop since February. And you didn't have a drink. You had a whole bottle.'

'Back off, Gregg. I don't need a fucking lecture from you.'

'What about from me then?'

Tate sighs and looks over at Chloe. 'You know what? How about you both talk about me behind my back while I go and throw up.' He has no idea how he convinces his body to move but it does.

Tate drags his sorry ass into the downstairs bathroom and frowns when he catches his reflection in the mirror. He didn't think it was possible but he looks worse than he feels, which is an achievement in itself.

He lunges for the toilet and spends a few minutes seriously regretting opening that fucking bottle.

Once his stomach gives him a break, he slumps back against the shower stall and closes his eyes as the room spins. How the hell has he ended up here again? It was like the small part of his brain reserved for making sensible decisions took leave of his body for a few hours. Seeing Chloe's face on the page above those words had knocked him off course. Then he read the report attached to the back and he knew he was in trouble.

Whoever is messing with him successfully upped the ante with that last message. They really wanted to get to him and it worked. The photo of Chloe would have been enough, but to add the drink and the report... that was the final straw.

Just because the doctor who examined him suspected sexual abuse doesn't mean it actually happened. He laughs harshly to himself. Who's he trying to convince? Gregg didn't buy it and he doesn't either. His dad hit him and his mother, then killed her. Is it really so difficult to believe he was capable of other unspeakable acts?

'Stop thinking about it!'

He grabs the edge of the sink and pulls himself to his feet. Chloe doesn't deserve to be dragged into his past. It's got nothing to do with her.

Gregg pounds on the door. 'Hey! You okay?'

'Can I not get five fucking minutes alone?'

'You've been in there for half an hour.'

There's no answer to that so he turns on the shower and dumps his clothes on the floor. The hot water helps him feel a little more human but uses up the last of his energy reserves. He wraps a towel around his waist and slowly picks up his clothes. When he walks back to the living room, Chloe and Gregg are cooking something that pushes his stomach to its limits. He dumps his clothes and disappears back into the bathroom until he comes to an uneasy truce with his body.

'I take it from your reaction you don't fancy a bacon butty?' Gregg says as he reappears.

'I'll pass.'

Chloe leaves her breakfast and takes his clothes from him. 'Do you want me to get you clean clothes?'

'I can manage.' Desperate to get away from the look of pity on her face, Tate turns away from her and drags himself upstairs relying heavily on the banisters to stop himself falling on his ass. He pulls on a pair of boxers then collapses on the bed to recover from that immense task. He'll need a few minutes before he attempts jeans or a top.

Chloe finishes tidying Tate's house and brings the rubbish bag to the bin outside. She takes the empty rum bottle from the top of the bag and glares at it before throwing it into the recycling. Less than twenty-four hours had gone by since Gregg called her, but it feels like a lot longer. She barely got any sleep last night. While Gregg snored away in one armchair, she kept getting up to check Tate was okay. He'd slept for the most part, only waking to complain when she tried to check him.

Instead of coming back downstairs after his shower this morning,

Tate had fallen asleep on his bed and hadn't stirred since. He was exhausted from weeks of not sleeping properly and too drunk to force himself to stay awake any longer.

Gregg went to meet with Ellen a few hours ago to try to smooth things over with her. He'd told her Tate had picked up a stomach bug while he was away so he couldn't do the interviews. Apparently she was less than happy but there wasn't anything she could do about it. If Chloe needed him to come back later he would, but with Tate asleep, there was no point dragging him back.

She wanders into the spare room and looks at the expensive collection of art supplies Tate bought her, but she honestly couldn't feel less like drawing if she tried. Chloe goes back upstairs and slowly lowers onto the bed bedside him. She rolls onto her side and tucks her hand under her head. As usual, Tate is asleep with his arm over his head, hiding his face from her.

With nothing else to do, she tucks the duvet around her body and closes her eyes. A few minutes later she hears his breathing change. His chest is rising and falling rapidly and his fingers dig into his hair. She places her hand on his hair like she'd done before but instead of soothing him, it's like she's struck him. He jolts away from her and mutters to himself, 'Please stop.'

Chloe backs away from him and gets out of bed. As much as she wants to help him, she's not keen on getting too close. If he lashed out he could seriously hurt her. His whole body is rigid, the muscles in his arms tremble as he covers his head.

'Tate. It's okay.'

A lump forms in her throat when she hears him moan. 'I'm sorry. Don't.'

She doesn't know how much more she can listen to. 'Tate. Wake up.' Still not keen on getting close to his arms, she stands at the bottom of the bed and touches his leg. It does the trick. Tate lurches away and scrambles up the bed. She flicks on the bedside light and lowers onto the edge of the bed.

'Are you okay?'

He pulls his legs up to his chest and rests his head against the wall as he takes a few shaky breaths. 'Yeah.' He looks over at her. 'Where's Gregg?'

'He left a few hours ago. Do you want me to get you anything? Are you hungry?'

Tate shakes his head then winces. 'Fuck. No, thanks. I'm not brave enough to try food yet.' He slowly turns his head to look at her. 'I'm sorry you've been dragged into this.'

'I'm not worried about myself, Tate. I'm worried about you. Maybe you should let Gregg take this latest letter in to his old colleagues.'

'No.'

'Tate—'

'I said no.' He takes a deep breath and closes his eyes. He doesn't say or do anything for so long Chloe wonders if he's actually fallen asleep again. 'I've gotten... I guess you'd call it hate mail before. We all have. Kind of comes with the territory. But this is private shit, Chloe. That's what's throwing me. Someone found out private things about me and instead of doing what most normal people would do and ignore it or destroy it, they're using it to fuck with me. And I'm letting them.

'I can deal with this. I was just caught off guard. Seeing the photo of us got my back up and I reacted badly. That's all it was. They'll get bored and move on sooner or later. If I go to the Guards about it, I'll just bring more people into this mess. I need to stop letting it get to me and move on.'

'Okay, I understand that, but they're trying to hurt you, Tate. They sent you drink knowing what could happen. What's next?'

'Anyone with internet access would know how to get to me. It was a messed up thing to do. I'm not taking away from that. But I was the one who opened the fucking bottle. Seriously, it's nothing to worry about, Chloe. They just hit me in a sensitive spot and I caved. Won't happen again.'

'I know you said you don't know who it is, but do you have any ideas at all?'

He shakes his head and opens his eyes again. 'Not a fucking clue. Believe me, if I had even the slightest inkling who it is, I'd be having a one-on-one with them, and it wouldn't go in their favour.'

Tate lies back against the pillow and squeezes his eyes shut.

'Headache bad?'

'Oh yeah.'

'Can you take anything? I mean are you allowed to?' The question sounds unbelievably naïve when she hears it out loud, but she honestly doesn't know the answer.

'Nothing I can take is going to touch this.' He sits up again and winces. 'Fuck this. I need some fresh air. Do you want to go for a walk?'

Chloe glances at the clock on the bedside table. 'It's nearly ten pm.'

'I've been festering in here for too long. I'm not talking about driving anywhere, just walking from here. I really couldn't care where the fuck we go.'

'I'd like that if you're sure.'

'I'll just grab a quick shower first then we can head.'

While Tate showers, Chloe bundles her hair into a ponytail, trying to make herself look half decent, then goes downstairs and makes sure everything is locked. Tate is showered and dressed five minutes later. He grabs a baseball cap and his jacket then takes her hand as they leave the house.

Even on a weekday at this hour there are still a lot of people around. They head towards the seafront and sit on the sand listening to the sea. He wraps his arms around her, holding her close to him.

'Do you feel any better?'

Tate nods and kisses the top of her head. 'Bit of sea air is the best hangover cure.' He takes a deep breath. 'Chloe, I'm sorry you saw me like that. I don't know how to make it right with you.'

She turns around to face him. 'This isn't about making it right with me. It's about figuring out why you did that after not drinking for so long.'

'I messed up, okay? I get that. You're allowed to be angry with me, Chloe. Shout and scream at me if you want. I deserve it.'

'I'm not going to shout at you, Tate. I am scared though.'

He tilts her chin up so she's looking in his eyes. 'Hey, I'm not planning on doing that again.'

'Were you planning on doing it yesterday? Did you plan to spend three months in rehab? I'm not an expert, Tate, but I'm fairly sure no one plans to take things too far.' She pauses, not sure if she should continue. She needs to tell him how she feels but the last thing she wants to do is make him feel worse than he already does.

'Talk to me.'

'Okay. When we found you like that on the couch, I thought you were dead.' She takes a deep breath as the image of him sprawled out like that comes back to her. 'I was scared.'

His hand drops from her face. 'Chloe—'

'No. Let me finish. I was scared because I didn't have a clue what to do for you. Gregg was brilliant and I just stood there. I realised I don't have any idea about your addictions.'

She instantly notices his reaction to that last word. He looks away and his shoulders drop a little.

'I care about you, Tate. I really do.'

'But?'

She shakes her head and squeezes his hand. 'There's no but. I was going to ask if there's someone at the centre where you were that I could talk to. I don't mean talk about you personally. I should have known what to do yesterday. But I just stood there and looked at you. Gregg and your family had a few sessions with someone from the centre, right?'

He nods. 'Yeah. My sponsor talked to them all. You really want that?'

'Yes – for me as much as for you.'

'Okay.' He looks over at her again and nods. 'I'll arrange it. I probably should have suggested it first, but I guess I was trying not to bring my problems into our relationship. Messed that up big time, didn't I.'

He shrugs and stares out to sea for a long few minutes then curses loudly. 'Sorry. I'm not pissed off with you. I'm well and truly fucked off with myself. I thought I had a handle on it, you know? It kind of snuck up on me. Months of hard work down the drain – literally. For what? A raging headache, and a shedload of disappointment. Fucking waste.'

He squeezes his eyes shut and hits his fist against his forehead. Chloe gathers him into her arms and holds him as they listen to the sea. There's nothing she can say to him to make it better.

As she holds him, she can't help looking around the beach. Is the person who's tormenting Tate here right now? Is he or she watching them? Are they giving themselves a pat on the back for breaking him?

Chloe holds him close as she examines every person walking along the beach. What if the bastard isn't done yet? They had no issue sending him a bottle of alcohol. Would they take things a step further next time and send him drugs?

The thought is ridiculous, but after what she's learned the last two days, it's not something they can rule out.

Tate parks his truck in a spot away from the other cars and shuts off the engine. He checks his watch. Ten minutes early. Ten minutes for the coffee to kick in.

It's been two days since he destroyed months of hard work and drank himself into a stupor. He's still got the fucking headache as a constant reminder of his screw-up. Hopefully Bria won't notice he's a mess. Wouldn't be the best start to their meeting.

He had been shocked to get the text from her this morning asking if he was free to meet her today. It's not the best timing, but there was no way he was going to refuse after she kept her distance for the last few months. If she wanted to meet him, he was going to be there. After this he was going to put things right with Gregg. Again. He's going to run out of lives with his friend if he keeps this up.

He smiles when he sees Bria's VW Golf. The beat up car is on its last legs. He'd tried so many times to convince her to let him buy her a new car but she flat out refused. She was independent. Always had been. So instead he'd put some money aside for her. She had a healthy fund for when she needed it and there was no way he was going to take no for an answer.

Time to face the music. He adjusts the baseball cap and pulls the arms of his hoodie down. He has no regrets about a single one of his tattoos, but they're not exactly subtle. This was about getting his relationship with Bria back on track, not attracting attention.

They stand and face either other, neither one sure how to act.

'Do you want to go for a walk on the beach?'

He nods. 'Sure.'

The slightly awkward silence stretches on until they get near the sea and head away from the car park. He slips his glasses on as the sun hits the sand, making him squint. He's sure she didn't bring him down here for a leisurely stroll along the beach, but he's not ready to peel the scab off this particular wound. If it's coming off, it should be on her terms.

About half a mile down the beach she sits down on the sand above the high tide mark and hugs her knees to her chest. He joins her and watches some kids playing in the water.

'Thanks for meeting me.'

'Kind of surprised you wanted to see me.' Perfect start, Tate. Remind her she had an issue with him.

'Congratulations on the awards. Chloe seems to have enjoyed herself.'

'Yeah. Think she enjoyed it more than I did.'

'I like her.'

'So do I.'

Bria looks across at him. 'Don't treat her like all the others. She doesn't deserve that.'

'I'm not planning on—'

'When it comes to you and relationships, you don't plan. You find someone, spend a few weeks with them then get bored.'

'You seriously brought me here to lecture me about my love life? I'm not going there with you.'

'You don't have to. Every time you decide you've had enough it's all over the net again. When it comes to your love life, it's out there, Tate. After going public with Chloe, she's out there now too. Just remember that.'

Tate doesn't respond. Not a great start that she assumes he's going to throw Chloe aside when he gets bored. Just because he's done that with every single relationship he's been in before. He looks out to the sea and grimaces. She might have a point.

'I need to ask you something.'

He knew it. There was no way she could move on without knowing why he did it. 'You want to know what drove me to drugs?'

'Yeah. I need to understand. I need to know why the person I've known my whole life became an addict in the space of a few weeks. We saw each other at Christmas. You were fine. The tour was going really well and you'd gotten number one for the second year in a row. Everything was great. What the fuck happened?'

'Don't curse.'

'Stop treating me like I'm a kid. I'll curse if I fucking want to. If I added to a swear jar every time you cursed, I'd be worth more than you are at this stage.'

'Seriously? You're having a go at me about cursing now?'

'No, I'm having a go at you because you won't talk to me. You can't expect me to be okay with you if you're being dishonest with me.'

'Hey, don't go there. What the fu—' he pauses and swallows the curse. 'What have I been dishonest about?'

'There's no way you fell into taking something like heroin out of nowhere. Do you think I'm stupid?' She sniffs and wipes her face on her arm.

Tate looks over at his sister. She's crying. He did that.

'Do you have any idea what it was like to get that call from Mum?

Tate's in hospital. He's unconscious. It looks like a drug overdose.' She looks at him and wipes more tears away. 'How would you feel if you got that call, huh? You'd want answers, wouldn't you? You'd be desperate to know why it happened so you could do everything in your power to make sure the person you love would never get into that situation again.

'You'd second guess every single thing they said and did in the weeks leading up to it. You'd wonder if it had been going on for longer and you just didn't notice. Or if something terrible happened to them and they couldn't deal with it. All these thoughts would be racing around your head, over and over again. Then when they eventually wake up after six terrifying days unconscious, they won't tell you a thing. No reason. No explanation. Nothing to help you to help them.'

'Bria—'

'You were my damn hero, Tate. You protected me from the monsters under the bed, from the goblins I swore were hiding in my wardrobe. You remember how the left-hand door would never close properly? I swore there were things hiding in here, looking out the open door. You propped a chair against it to keep it closed.'

'Yeah. Didn't help though. You thought I was doing it to keep the goblins inside and if you moved the chair they'd fall out and come after you. You didn't go near the thing for going on a year.'

She laughs and wipes her face again. 'I hated that wardrobe.' She falls into silence and looks at the waves crashing further down the beach. He feels like she's just reached into his chest and beaten the shit out of his heart.

He gets it. It shouldn't have taken her saying all that for the truth to sink in, but he absolutely understands why she wanted nothing to do with him when he woke up. He never thought about her getting that phone call. He had focused on the fact his parents found him, but never thought about her hearing what he did.

'I've been using for years, Bria.'

269

'What?'

'Nothing as serious as heroin, but using full stop was fucking stupid. Doesn't matter what it was.'

'Do Mum and Dad know? Do the guys know?'

'I don't think Mum knows, but Dad does. I didn't use alone. Dillon and Luke did too. Gregg a little, but he was the one who eventually kicked us all into shape. We took a step back, but never fully stopped.'

'Right. You managed to keep that well hidden.'

'It wasn't all the time. Anyway things escalated after Christmas. I started remembering stuff about my past... from before I was adopted.'

Bria looks over at him but doesn't say anything.

'My father, at least I think he's my father, hit me. I think I blocked it all out and forgot about it until Christmas. I got really intense nightmares. Every single night. Then the memories would hit when I was awake. I couldn't escape them. I couldn't sleep. I was knackered from the tour anyway and this just made it worse. I tried blocking it out with drink, but it didn't work so I stepped it up.'

He shrugs and picks at some seaweed beside him. 'I didn't think about what I was doing. It didn't register that I was taking heroin. I just kept focusing on the fact that when I took it, I didn't care about the dreams and my memories. They went away.'

'Were the nightmares that bad?'

He nods. 'It's a shite excuse and I can't tell you how much I wish I could go back and do things differently, but I can't.'

She reaches out and takes his hand. 'Are you still getting nightmares?'

'Sometimes. I don't want Mum and Dad to know about this, okay?'

'Why not?'

'Because I'm saying I don't want them to know.'

'Fine. I won't tell them. Have you been tempted to...'

'Use again?' She nods. 'I don't want to, but I can't promise it won't happen. All I can do is keep up with my appointments and take it day by day. Not a great answer, I know.'

Bria leans against him and strokes his arm. 'It's an honest answer. Do you remember anything else from when you were a child?'

'Nothing definitive.' He's disgusted how easily the lie comes to him. 'It's just images. Kind of like watching snippets from a badly filmed show with no sound. All I know is that I'm being hurt. To be honest, I'm not sure I want to remember. I've been doing okay so far not knowing what the fuck happened.'

'I know, but maybe you need to—'

'No, Bria. I don't. I'll be grand so please leave it.'

She gives him one of her disapproving looks but doesn't push him. They're both too stubborn for their own good. She knows they could easily spend the next hour going over this with neither side backing down.

'Does Chloe know about all this?'

'I had to tell her. It wouldn't have been fair to see her and not be honest with her. She deserved to know what she was getting in to.'

'You really like her, don't you?'

'Probably shouldn't until I get myself sorted, but yeah. I really do.'

'So what do you have planned this weekend?'

'I was going to do some writing, but I don't have to. You want to do something?'

Bria pushes away from him and looks at him like he's speaking another language. 'You're joking, right?'

'You could just have said no. If it's too early to—' He grunts as she punches him in the shoulder. 'What the fuck was that for?'

'Chloe's birthday is on Sunday.'

Tate stares at his sister as the words take their sweet time to register with him. 'Her what? This Sunday? As in the Sunday at the end of this week?'

'Yes, this Sunday. She didn't tell you?'

'No, she didn't. Why didn't she tell me?'

Bria shrugs. 'Maybe she thought you had too much on your plate already? Whatever the reason, you know now, so what's the plan?'

He doesn't have a plan. Where does he even start sorting out a plan? He's never done anything like this before. When one of the guys had a birthday, they'd go out and get wasted. Not a good idea or anything Chloe would appreciate.

'I haven't got a clue. We've only been with each other for a few weeks. What the hell should I do? It's not a big birthday, is it?'

'You're off the hook there. She's turning thirty-one. Okay, no need to panic. There's plenty of time. What are you up to today?'

'Sounds like I need to crack on and get her a birthday present.'

She gets to her feet and brushes off her jeans. 'And organise a dinner or a party or something special. C'mon, you don't have time to be sitting on the beach staring at the sea. It's the first birthday with you as a couple. It has to be special.'

'Great. Thanks. No pressure then.'

Chloe straightens the hem of her top and makes a face at her reflection. Her sister is due to pick her up in half an hour and take her for a birthday dinner with the family. She hasn't seen Steph for a few months and is looking forward to a proper catch up. Someone will be missing from the evening and that's the part that's making her a little less enthusiastic.

It's her fault for not telling Tate it's her birthday. The event had completely slipped her mind until a few days ago then he'd gotten drunk and any thoughts of her birthday were pushed to the back of her mind.

She wants to see her family again, but she wants Tate there too. By the time she plucked up the courage to tell him earlier today, he had already arranged to spend the evening in the studio. He'll be less than happy when she does tell him, but she didn't know what else to do.

An hour later, she's still kicking herself for not coming clean with Tate. Although after being asked the millionth question about him by Steph it's probably a good idea he's not coming tonight. It didn't help that she was a fairly big fan of his and knew more about his music than Chloe herself did.

Chloe manages to dodge yet another probing question about Tate as Steph drives up the gravel driveway and parks her car in a vacant spot beside all the other patrons. The country house is spectacular. Dozens of trees lining the driveway are covered in white fairy lights. The place is beautiful.

'Wow. I'm impressed.'

'I found it on the net. It gets brilliant reviews.'

'I'll give it five stars for the outside alone.'

'Good start. Come on. Mum and Dad are probably waiting.'

Steph leads the way through the stone archway into a medieval style entranceway. A well-dressed attendant smiles as they approach.

'We have a table booked under the name Quinn.'

He disappears down the corridor and around the corner. Chloe's stomach rumbles as the enticing aroma of dinner hits her. It's a shame Tate can't be here to see this place, but she is still going to enjoy her evening.

He comes back and gestures for them to follow. He opens a set of heavy, wooden double doors into a breath-taking dining room. The ceiling stretches high above them, supported by exposed beams. Wrought iron chandeliers hang from the beams, each one filled with dozens of candles. Chloe sits on the chair he pulls out and smiles at her parents.

'Oh my God. This place is gorgeous.'

Her mother looks around the room and smiles. 'It is, isn't it? So, how has your day been so far?'

'Not too bad. This is certainly the highlight.'

Her parents laugh and Steph joins in. They sit back in their chairs and look at her, each one with a ridiculous smile on their faces.

'Okay, what's with the cheesy grins?'

'Have you looked around you?' Steph asks.

'Of course I have.' Chloe is seriously confused. Her family is acting like she's missing something glaringly obvious. The room suddenly falls silent. She glances to her left and sees a familiar face at the table next to her. And the one next to that. And the one next to that. She knows everyone in the room. They're all her friends, family or work colleagues. 'Oh God. What's going on?'

Steph points to the doorframe behind her. Chloe looks over her shoulder and sees an enormous banner. Happy Birthday, Chloe.

The applause starts and builds as everyone stands and claps. 'You did this?' she asks her family. Her mother shakes her head and points to her right. Chloe follows her direction and spots Bria sitting at a table on the far side of the room. Right behind her is Tate. She gets up and walks over to him, hugging him tightly as he stands.

'You did this for me?'

'Happy birthday.' He kisses her and the room erupts in clapping and caterwauling. 'This okay?'

'Are you freaking kidding me? I can't believe you organised this.'

'Well I had a fair bit of help from Bria and your folks.' He takes a step back and looks her up and down. 'You are fucking gorgeous.'

Chloe smiles at him. She's never had someone say that to her the way he does. People throw that compliment around quite a bit but every single time he tells her she knows it's the truth. He thinks she's gorgeous. Then again, in his navy suit, white shirt, and navy tie, he's rather impressive himself.

'A suit twice in the space of a few weeks - and a tie this time. I could get used to this.'

'Yeah, well don't. It won't be a regular occurrence. First time meeting your parents. I have to make a good impression. How about some grub? I hear it's pretty amazing.'

Tate can't keep his eyes off Chloe as dinner is served. He thought organising a surprise dinner might not have gone down well but after having a chat with her gran who then put him in touch with her parents, they assured him she would love it. Seems he was right to trust them.

It looks like the venue is a hit too. She mentioned she likes these old-style buildings with beams and monstrous fireplaces, and he can't argue with her. Give him something like this any day over the sterile hotels he's spent quite a few nights in. That's part of the reason the band decided to do self-catering. They couldn't relax, couldn't switch off being cooped up in a featureless white room.

He smiles as she runs her hand over his leg under the table moving dangerously close to something she'll be getting a whole lot of later. He's a little ticked off that she felt she couldn't tell him about her birthday, but he has a fair idea why she didn't.

He had been pretty absorbed in his own issues lately. Getting into a drunken stupor hadn't helped and that's not sitting well with him. She's his girlfriend. She shouldn't be keeping things to herself because she's scared about overloading him.

She pulls her hand away as the main course is served and Tate spends the next hour answering numerous questions from her parents. He'd spoken to them briefly on the phone and they'd seemed happy enough about him being with their daughter, but he was still nervous as hell meeting them earlier this evening.

After a thorough visual drilling, they warmed to him. Well, he hopes they did and aren't just being polite. He's just glad he made the effort and wore the suit. He catches her mother looking at his hands a few times during the meal but he doesn't mind. If his tattoos are their main issue that's more than fine with him.

Chloe's father wipes his mouth with his napkin as he looks across the table at him. 'So, Tate. Do you mind me asking how you started in this career?'

'I guess I sort of fell into it. I was teaching and the uncle of one of my students heard me singing during the lesson. He knew someone who was in the industry and put him in touch with me. It grew from there.'

Her mother looks from Chloe to Tate. 'Teaching? You're a teacher too?'

He nods. 'Music. I taught guitar and piano mainly.'

'And you're qualified?'

'Dad!' hisses Chloe. 'Please.'

'It's fine,' Tate says, smiling at her. If they want to quiz him he can't really complain. 'Yeah. I'm a classically trained piano and guitar player and I've got a master degree in music education.' That shuts them up for a minute. It's not something he mentions often but whenever he does it surprises people. He still hasn't quite worked out if he should be offended by that reaction or not.

Chloe lowers her glass onto the table with a thump. 'You have? You never told me that.'

Tate shrugs. 'It never really came up in conversation.'

'And you've no regrets about not using your qualifications?'

Chloe glares at her father again.

'Well believe it or not, I still use everything I studied to this day. It's like riding a horse or learning how to drive a car. When you get the foundation right from the start everything else falls into place a lot easier. I write everything we perform so it's absolutely not going to waste. Well, I guess that could be a matter of opinion depending on whether people like what I write or not.'

'From what I hear, quite a few people do.' Chloe's father raises his glass. 'Congratulations, Tate. Very impressive indeed.'

Tate taps his glass against her father's and glances over at Chloe. She raises her eyebrows and shrugs. He may just have moved from his daughter's potential problem boyfriend to one with a little bit of sense.

As the dessert is being cleared away, Bria walks over to their table and leans on Tate's shoulders. 'Sorry to interrupt but I need to steal my brother for a few minutes.'

Tate apologises and walks away with Bria. Chloe waits until they've gone before she faces her family again. 'Well? What do you think?'

Steph nods and raises her champagne glass. 'Well done, Sis. He's hot.'

'Right, well no thinking of him like that if you don't mind.'

'Just saying I acknowledge what attracted you to him. He's a lot more impressive in the flesh.'

'Okay, moving on from you. Mum and Dad? Do you like him?'

'He seems like a nice man...'

Chloe knows a but is coming so decides to get it over with. 'But?'

'We know about what happened to him earlier this year. We're just worried about you getting involved in this lifestyle. It's nothing against him. Clearly he cares about you to have gone to so much trouble, but we're not entirely at ease with his situation.'

'I understand what you're saying, but he got himself help. He's genuinely an amazing person. He's kind and protective and—'

'Hot.'

Chloe laughs. 'Yes, thanks Steph. He is hot.'

'I'm glad to hear that,' her father says. 'And I'm not talking about the 'hot' part. How do you feel about the whole celebrity thing?'

'I'm still getting used to that part, but it's not something he's overly immersed in himself. He's a private person so he tries to keep out of the limelight unless necessary.'

'Well, he certainly has done all the right things tonight. I just love this building. It has so much character.'

'Food's good too,' her dad says around a mouthful of cheesecake.

The wall at the side of the room is pushed back like a concertina and Chloe's mouth drops open. Tate is on a low stage at the far end of the room with Gregg, Luke, and Dillon. He's changed out of his suit into jeans and a navy shirt with the sleeves rolled up. Tate picks up his guitar and smirks at her.

'Oh my God. They're all here? Is Tate going to sing?'

Bria sits down on Tate's seat and hugs Chloe. 'Of course he is. He has another band lined up for later, but he mentioned you hadn't seen him and the band perform properly. He thought you'd like it.'

'Are you kidding me? I can't believe this is happening. In a good way,' she adds when Bria glances at her. 'I've always wanted to hear him sing like this. I just didn't want to ask.'

Bria waves her comment away. 'Never be afraid to ask him to play. Sometimes getting him to shut up is the problem.'

The guests follow her into the far room as the band begins to play. Tate winks at her as he moves closer to the mic and sings.

Tate flops back in the bed and wipes his hair off his forehead. After taking a few minutes to get himself together he looks over at Chloe. Her arm is draped over her face. 'You okay?' She waves her hand at him and he laughs. 'I'll take that as a sort of.'

'Happy birthday to me.' She rolls over and drapes her leg over his. 'I think that might have worked off the cake.'

'Both slices?'

She frowns up at him. 'Hey. It was a very nice cake. I had to grab the second slice before you and your horde demolished the lot.'

'My horde had just played for an hour and that always makes us hungry.'

'You're always hungry, it had nothing to do with performing.' She leans on his chest and rubs the side of his face. 'Did I tell you how amazing that was?'

'The sex or the performance at your party?'

'Both.'

'Glad to hear it.'

'I just realised something. I have no idea when your birthday is.'

'Fourth of April.' She looks away and he knows what she's thinking. 'Yeah, my thirty-sixth birthday was a bit of a non-event. Being in rehab kind of took the fun out of it. Takes the pressure off you next year though. A takeaway and a movie would top that any day.' He brushes hair away from her face and decides to ask the question he needs an answer to but is kind of dreading hearing. He's also not keen on putting a downer on her birthday.

'Okay, so I need to ask you something. Actually, it's more that I've got a bone to pick with you.'

'You want to know why I didn't tell you about my birthday?'

'Yeah.'

Chloe pulls the duvet up over her shoulder and looks away from him for a minute. 'I just... I didn't want to... there's a lot on your plate right now and I didn't want to add to it. And then you... Seriously, it's not a big deal. I don't usually do anything crazy for my birthday anyway.'

Tate props himself up on an elbow and looks down at her. She may have stopped herself from saying it but he knows full well what she was going to say. He got drunk and that overshadowed all thoughts of her birthday.

Chloe rests her hand on the side of his face and smiles up at him. 'Hey, I wasn't having a go at you. I really wasn't.'

He squeezes her hand. 'I know, but let's get one thing straight, Chloe. I'm your boyfriend. Forget everything else. that part comes first. You hear me? We're a couple. I want to — scrap that, I need to know stuff like this. It's my job to know stuff like this. It doesn't matter what other crazy shit is going on in my life, you come first. It's my right to spoil you rotten on your birthday.'

'This is all new to me, Tate. I'm still trying to figure out... you, I guess. Your life. Your job. It's all so different to me.'

'Talk to me about it. I can't help you understand if you don't ask.'

'I'd probably be firing questions at you all the time.'

'That's grand. I'd prefer you to do that than have any worries about things.' He pats the pillow beside him, and she lies down facing him. Tate pulls the duvet up and drapes his arm over her waist. 'Fire away. Ask whatever you want.'

Chloe traces along the tattoo on his chest for a few minutes before she looks up at him again.

'Okay, so the studio. When you're there for the day can I call you if I need you for something or are you off limits? I have no idea what Ellen does for you and how much control she has over what you're doing. I've heard you talking about touring again but you could be talking about going to the moon for all I know. Are you going for a week? Or a month? Longer? Will you be gone the whole time or be able to come home? I think that'll do for starters.'

Tate blows out a long breath. 'Wow. Okay. Studio first. If I'm recording, my phone will be on silent but I check it regularly. I'll give you Dillon, Gregg, and Luke's numbers and the one for the main studio reception. If you need to get a hold of me urgently when I'm there ring the reception first. They'll pass a message on. Never be afraid to ring me whenever you want. If I can't answer I'll have it turned off or on silent.'

'That's good to hear. I was afraid I'd ring you mid interview or whatever and get you in trouble.'

'No risk of that. I promise. Ellen's job is looking after everything, bar the music side of things. I write everything. Music and the lyrics. Ellen makes sure our music gets in front of the right people at the right time. She arranges our publicity, any interviews we do, appearances, signings, tour dates. You name it, Ellen and her team look after it.'

'Do you have a say at all?'

'Ideally I should give her free rein and go with it, but that interferes with my control freak side. We bump heads a lot, but she doesn't take any shit from me. Under normal circumstances, if she tells me or the guys she wants us to do something or go somewhere, we'll do it.'

'And touring?'

She looks as thrilled about the thought of touring as he is. He needs to get back to live performances again but leaving her is the part he's not so keen about. 'I should have talked to you about this before now. Nothing's set in stone yet so I didn't think to bring it up. No excuse though. Okay, well the plan is to head off at the beginning of September until Christmas. It's the second leg of the tour we had to cancel when I went to rehab.'

'So will you be away for all of that?'

'Well, what I hope to do, if you're up for it, would be to go for maybe a month or so then fly you over for a weekend to meet me wherever I am. I still haven't got the finalised schedule yet. Then I'd try to get back or if I couldn't maybe you could meet me again. I'd be back in time for Christmas. I know it's bad timing with you starting work, but I'll be here for your first day. As soon as everything is finalised you'll get a copy of where I'm going to be. I'll be on the other end of the phone and I'll talk to you every single day I'm gone.'

'Okay. I'm sorry if I sound silly.'

'Hey. Stop. I should have told you what's going to happen. I guess I've been trying to avoid thinking about it.'

'Why?'

He lies down beside her and brushes his fingers through her hair. 'Because I don't want to think about leaving you for a week let alone a few months, that's why. It's not great timing, but if I'm going to salvage my career I need to go. And just for the record - all the fame stuff, it's nothing for you to worry about.' He moves closer to her and makes sure she's looking him in the eyes. 'I mean that, Chloe. I know how I'd feel if guys were giving you attention. I'd be... well I'll just leave it at not happy. It doesn't matter how many photos are taken or how many people recognise me. I only see you. I only want you.'

The smile she gives him tells him he's said the right thing. Better late than never. He should have cleared all that up ages ago. He keeps forgetting she's new to his life and his job.

'Sorry, I really should have brought it up sooner. I just didn't know how to.'

'Don't be afraid to give me a nudge when I need it. I'm not used to sharing my life with someone. It's a learning curve for both of us.'

'Thanks, Tate.'

'For what?'

'For what you said. You know, about the fame part. I'm not a jealous person. Really. I've just never had to share my boyfriend with... well, a lot of people. It'll take some getting used to.'

'You're not sharing me with anyone. They get the lead singer of Broken Chords. You get me.'

'All to myself?'

'Too right. Damn it!' He rolls out of bed and pulls on his boxers.

'What's wrong.'

'I forgot to give you your present. Stay put.' He grabs the box from the garage and places it on the bed beside her. 'Happy birthday.'

She tears off the wrapping and stares at box with a picture of a Lego Millennium Falcon from Star Wars on the outside. She suddenly jumps off the bed and throws her arms around him. 'This is absolutely the best present I got. I can't believe you got this!'

'You said you liked Lego kits and it's the biggest one you can get. Should keep you busy for a bit.'

'Do you think? I might tackle it when you go away, or was that the idea?'

'Might have been.' He tucks back into bed beside her and wraps his arms around her. 'I've got to go to the studio in the morning for the day. I might not be able to see you tomorrow.'

'Seriously, it's fine. I really should get some prep work done.' She gets out of bed and searches in her bag.

'What are you doing?'

'Looking for something to sleep in.'

'Ah come on, that's not fair.'

She pulls on a t-shirt and some underwear. 'You need to sleep. No arguments,' she adds quickly when he opens his mouth to do just that. 'You look tired. When was the last time you slept? And I mean all night?'

She's got him there. It's been a few days at least and it is getting to him. 'Fine. Get your ass back in the bed. I promise I'll behave.' He pulls her to his chest and runs his hand over her hair as he stares at the ceiling.

As soon as he hears her breathing slow, he slides his arm out from under her and quietly closes the bedroom door behind himself. He wanders downstairs and pulls open the fridge, sighing to himself when he sees what's on offer. With little enthusiasm, he grabs a bottle of juice and turns off the kitchen light.

He stops at the door to the gym when something catches his attention. He looks over his shoulder to the kitchen window. He could have sworn he saw his car lights flash in the reflection in the picture on the wall.

Tate leaves his drink on the bookcase and makes his way back over to the kitchen window, leaving the light off this time. He peers into the darkness outside but can't see anything out of place. Just to be on the safe side he takes his keys from the drawer and presses the button to lock the truck. The lights turn on for a few seconds before shutting down again.

He throws the keys back in the drawer and goes back to the gym. Nice to know he can add seeing things to his list of issues. He steps onto the treadmill and turns it on. What he wouldn't give for a few miles of empty beach in front of him right now. He'd love to saddle up Jove and take him out for a few hours.

Maybe it's time to find himself somewhere a little more permanent. Blackrock is great and all, but it's a little claustrophobic. He needs space. He can certainly afford a house with some land on the coast. Enough room for Jove and maybe an art studio for Chloe too.

He shakes his head and turns up the speed. He's been with her two months and is already thinking about living with her. A month is a record for him. Not once had he ever considered staying with someone for a few months. Living with someone is a whole new thing for him and something he didn't think he'd ever want. Not until meeting her.

It's not the right time to even go there with her though. He needs to put some more sober months behind him first. Hell, a week staying sober would be a great start. Prove to her he can be the man she deserves – not just a recovering addict one fuck up away from throwing it all away again.

He keeps to the shadows behind the truck for another few minutes just to be safe. He peers around the truck but can't see any life inside the house.

That was too close.

It's three in the morning. The bastard should have been in bed, not wandering around the house. With Tate out of sight, he pushes the button on the remote and the truck lights flash again. He holds his position and his breath, but Tate doesn't come back to the window.

Moving painfully slow, he gets to his feet and opens passenger door. The interior of the cab lights up and he quickly looks at the house again. Still nothing.

He pulls the package from his pocket and stuffs it into the bottom of the glove box, covering it with the papers and other bits and pieces.

He closes the truck door as quietly as he can then locks it again.

The temptation to leave an impressive dent in the door or to scratch the pristine paintwork is difficult to ignore but being reckless and emotional at this stage would undo all his hard work. Besides, if he damaged the truck Tate would know someone had been here.

So instead, he turns away and keys in the code to the gate, making sure to close them again after him. He pulls off his gloves and smiles to himself as he walks back to his car.

He's so looking forward to making a phone call in the morning.

Chloe stretches her legs out on the sand and takes a long breath. Life is pretty great at the moment. She woke up this morning with Tate beside her and she honestly can't think of a better way to start the day. After saying good morning to her in his own special way, he'd treated her to breakfast in bed before dropping her home.

Until she meets her sister for lunch, it's just her, a sketch pad, and a stretch of beach. At least this time she has permission from the owners to be here. It took longer than it should have to realise that Tate bought the surrounding farmland for his parents which meant in a roundabout way, it's his beach.

She pulls her phone out and checks the screen. As soon as she sees Gregg's name the dread settles like a weight on her shoulders.

'What's wrong?'

'Where are you?' he asks.

'On the beach.'

'Can you walk back up to the road. I need to ask you something?'

'I'll be there in a few minutes.' She packs up her things and hurries up the path back towards the road. Gregg's car pulls up beside her when she steps out from the path. He reaches over and opens the passenger door.

'Hop in.'

She climbs in and Gregg takes off before she's fastened her seatbelt. 'What's happened?'

'Tate's been taken into custody.'

Chloe turns to look at Gregg, fully expecting him to break out into one of his stupid grins and laugh at her. But he doesn't.

'I'm being fucking serious, Chloe. They took him from the studio. Apparently, they received a tip-off that Tate was seen in possession of drugs. They found heroin in his truck, Chloe.'

'But they can't have. That doesn't make sense. He's clean.'

'Don't know what to say to you. You know as much as I do now. Ellen went to the station but they won't let her talk to him until they're done questioning him. None of my old mates are talking to me about it. Fair enough I guess. Anyway, we're all regrouping in Tate's parents' place until we know what's happening. His folks are in Canada for a few weeks visiting their grandkids so we'll have the place to ourselves.'

The rest of the drive to Tate's parents' house takes place in complete in silence. She heard every word of what Gregg said to her, but the meaning is taking time to sink in.

When she woke up beside Tate this morning everything had been perfect. She'd had an incredible party last night. She'd watched in proud awe as Tate and the guys performed for her family and friends. He'd dropped her home this morning then left to go to work. It was as close to normal as it could be when you're with someone like Tate. So where did it all go so very wrong? How, in the space of a few hours, had that happy picture turned to Tate being arrested? It made no sense.

And where had this anonymous tip come from? He may have had a drink recently but surely they would have known if he was taking drugs again? She may miss it but she has no doubts Gregg would see the signs a mile off. After his reaction to Tate drinking again she knows he would have made his feelings clear if he suspected anything else.

She comes out of her thoughts as Gregg turns off the road and drives down a narrow gravel track. It opens into a vast parking area in front of a stunning farmhouse. This is absolutely a house she can see Tate living in.

A grey Audi is parked outside and the driver steps out when Gregg stops the car. The woman hugs Gregg then holds out her hand to Chloe.

'I'm Ellen, Tate's manager. I presume you're Chloe?'

Ellen is very different to what she imagined. She must be in her early forties with short brown hair tied back in a ponytail. Her jeans and shirt show off her lean figure. When Chloe shakes her hand she has to hold back a wince. The woman has a powerful grip.

'Nice to meet you, Ellen. Any news?'

'How about we go inside?'

Gregg unlocks the door and they sit on the couch facing Ellen. 'Did you call Dillon and Luke?

'Yeah. They're on the way. Should be here in a bit,' Gregg says. 'So, what's happening?'

'I know as much as you do. There wasn't a lot I could do for him and he has his lawyer with him. All we can do is wait.'

Tate pulls into one of the empty sheds around the back of his parents' house and turns off the engine. All he wants to do is have a shower. He feels grimy and so does his truck. Who knows how many people have been crawling around in it for the last few hours—starting with the fucker who put the drugs there in the first place.

Tate glares over at the glove box. Whoever put the heroin in there wasn't the most inventive. Leaving the package on the fucking seat would have been just as obvious. At least he knows he wasn't losing his mind last night. Someone had been messing with his truck outside his own house. Bastard has balls.

He slumps forward and rests his head on the steering wheel. The last hour had been spent with his sponsor. Tate had called him as soon as he was released, and it was the best decision he's made for a while. Better than calling Eddie which came a too close second. He doesn't doubt that if Eddie appeared like his Fairy Godmother in the car park he would have happily taken anything and everything he was offered.

The urge to use had died down but he's calling on everything he has left to keep it under control. Just a shame he's running on empty. He barely has enough energy to get out of the damn truck. At least if he's here he's got a house full of people who will be watching him like a hawk.

He catches movement behind his truck and looks in the rear view mirror. Chloe is standing outside the shed with her arms wrapped around herself. She looks just as shattered as he feels. No point putting this off. Tate climbs out and locks the truck. Not that locking it means a damn thing. Someone had still managed to get into it and fuck him over.

She pulls him into a hug, the feel of her arms wrapping tightly around him is just what he needs right now. When she lets him go he rests his forehead against hers. 'Are you okay?'

She laughs and rubs the side of his face. 'I was just about to ask you that.'

'Can we go inside? I need to talk to you.' She takes his hand and he follows her into the house to face Ellen, Bria, Gregg, Dillon, and Luke.

'Having a party without me?'

'I thought it was prudent to keep the four of you under the one roof until we know what's going on,' Ellen explains.

He pushes past his sister and Gregg and collapses on the couch with Chloe beside him.

'What happened?' Ellen asks before anyone else can get the question out.

'I've been charged with possession. They found drugs in the glove box of my truck apparently. I'm in court in a few days. It wasn't a lot, not enough to get me for intent to supply so my lawyer reckons I'll get a fine.'

'Could it be worse than a fine?' Chloe asks.

'Yeah, it could.' Tate looks up at his friends. 'I'm innocent by the way or does that even matter?'

Gregg stands up and paces in front of the fireplace. 'They found drugs, Tate. In your truck. They didn't just magically appear.'

'Are you using again?' Dillon asks.

He glares over at Dillon. 'No fucking way. They did a test on me. I'm clean. I'll get you a copy of the results if you want.' He looks around at the people in the room. Each one of them is like family to him – Chloe included. Of all the people in his life these are the ones he can depend on. The fact that not one of them is looking him in the eye hits like a punch in the gut. 'You think the heroin was mine.'

Gregg stops pacing and crosses his arms. 'The Garda aren't in the habit of planting drugs in cars for a laugh. If you didn't put them there who did?'

'If I knew do you not think I'd have said something? Having a fucking criminal record wasn't on my to-do-list. I could be facing time for this so I guarantee I would have told them if I knew. I'm telling the truth. I'm not using again.'

Gregg glances up at him and raises his eyebrows.

'Oh I get it. You think because I got drunk the next step is using again.'

Dillon, Luke, and Ellen all target Tate. Ellen pushes to her feet and stands in front of him. 'You've been drinking?'

'Once, okay.'

She narrows her gaze then laughs harshly. 'Stomach bug. I knew there was something off about that. You never get sick. So, you stood me up because you were drunk. That's great, Tate. How much? Stop glaring at me. You've come this far. Might as well spill the beans.'

'A bottle of rum.'

Ellen rubs her forehead and turns away from him. Dillon stands beside Gregg and mirrors his pissed off stance. 'Why the fuck didn't you say anything?'

'Because I'm on top of it again, Dillon.'

'Yeah, it looks that way. You're a fucking mess.'

'Please just fuck off. I'm tired.'

Dillon grabs him by the arm and pushes him back a step. 'No mate. I'm not going to fuck off. This is my life you're messing up too. Jesus, Tate. We've been working our arses off trying to get this album done. Why did we bother? What the fuck have we been putting in all the hours for? We could have ditched it and got smashed with you.'

'Dillon, back off a little.'

'No, Gregg. He needs to hear this. When he fucks up he drags us down with him. Are you using again?'

'I already said I'm not.'

'But you've been tempted.'

'Of course I have. I just spent an hour with my sponsor before coming back here. I'm dealing with-'

Dillon snorts loudly. 'Yeah, yeah, yeah. We know. You're dealing with it. That's all you keep saying. How was getting pissed dealing, huh?'

Ellen steps up and tries to get between them. 'Okay, you both need to calm down. This isn't helping.'

Tate ignores her attempt to break them up. Right now the holier-than-thou expression on Dillon's face is hitting a raw nerve. 'Don't you dare fucking judge me, Dillon. You were just as deep into it as I was so don't look at me that way.'

'The difference is I didn't end up in hospital being resuscitated.' Dillon wipes a hand over his face as he glowers across at Tate. 'We lost you, Tate, so that judging look is actually me giving a fuck about you. None of us are keen to go through that again with you. You promised you'd talk. You promised you'd follow the rules. Before you opened that bottle you should have called any one of us. So why didn't you?'

Tate's gone head-to-head with Dillon too many times over the years, but there's something about this time that feels different. Dillon takes a step closer to him and Tate instinctively backs away, bumping against the mantlepiece. Usually he'd push back. That's what they do. Dillon pushes. He pushes. They're broken up by the others and it's out of their system. But Tate suddenly can't get his mouth to work, let alone his limbs to push back.

He looks at Dillon and the image distorts. Instead of his parents' living room with his friends, he's in the sparsely furnished room with the man looming over him again. When the shouting starts he hears Dillon's voice, but then it's his father. He closes his eyes as the memory and reality merge to well and truly fuck with his head.

'Tate? Are you even listening?'

He opens his eyes and Dillon is back.

'Am I boring you?'

Tate doesn't answer. He can't answer. He barely breathes as he presses himself against the wall beside the fireplace, trying to make himself as small as possible. His racing heartbeat pounds in his ears, drowning out everything else.

A small part of his brain knows he's safe and in his parents' house, but right now that's not the part the rest of him believes... or trusts.

More people come closer, crowding him, making breathing nearly impossible. Nausea and dizziness threaten to bring him to the ground, but he forces himself to remain motionless.

'Tate?'

He slowly raises his eyes to look at the person in front of him and his stomach drops. His father is looming over him, a cold look in his eyes and blood on his fists. He takes a step closer, and Tate buries his head under his arms.

'Please don't. I'm sorry.'

His father's voice dies away, leaving him listening to his racing heart again. When the expected blow doesn't come, Tate slowly drops his arms.

His eyes dart from Chloe to Dillon and then to Gregg, Ellen, Bria, and Luke, now standing beside the couch staring over at him.

He focuses on Chloe again, hating the look of pity on her face. 'Are you okay?'

Tate licks his lips and forces his head to tip in a half convincing nod.

He looks over at Dillon but can't meet his eyes. Dillon's face has lost all trace of colour. 'I'm sorry, Tate. I wasn't going to hit you.'

Tate shakes his head at Dillon. 'Ignore me. I'm just tired.'

Nothing like a beyond stupid statement to kill whatever dignity he has left after that display.

'I'm going to grab a shower.' Without waiting for an acknowledgment he steps into the annex off the living room and comes to a stop in the middle of the room.

He can't believe he just zoned out like that in front of everyone. He made his friend think he was scared of him. If Dillon thought he wasn't dealing with everything, that display would have done nothing to prove him wrong. Fuck knows what he must be thinking.

The door opens and closes behind him.

'Is Dillon okay?'

'He's fine,' Chloe replies as she steps around to face him. 'Are you okay?'

He opens his mouth then frowns and closes it again. 'I... Dillon... I thought he was my father.' He presses the heels of his hands against his eyes. 'Fuck! I have to apologise.'

She pulls his hands away from his face. 'Dillon is fine. Lie down on the bed with me for a minute. Please.' Tate doesn't have the energy to argue so does as he's told. He shuffles closer so she can gather him in her arms.

'I'm just really fucking tired, Chloe.'

She places her hand on the side of his face and he closes his eyes. He's not talking about needing a few hours of sleep. This goes much deeper. Every single time life goes right for him lately, something rears its ugly head and pulls him back down again.

He's winning. Whoever is doing this to him is slowly breaking him down. Tate can't keep doing this. He's already teetering on the edge. If this dickhead pushes him once more, he seriously doubts he'll be able to get up again.

He lies against Chloe's chest, listening to her heartbeat as she runs her fingers through his hair, holding him tight until he finally drifts off to sleep.

When Chloe wakes she's alone and, from the feel of the bed beside her, she's been alone for a few hours. She showers quickly and gets dressed. There's no sign of Tate in the living room or the kitchen so she goes outside and walks around the back of the house. She finds him leaning on a stable door talking to Jove.

'Does he have any words of wisdom?'

Tate turns around to face her and makes a face. 'If he does he's keeping quiet.' Jove lifts his head over the door and rests it against Tate's chest. 'Thought about taking him out for a bit but I'd be sorely tempted to keep heading down the beach and not come back. That was a joke by the way. I'm not planning on doing a runner. I don't think it would help.'

She rubs Jove's head. 'No. It's not like you can hide. You sort of stand out.'

'Guess I'm screwed then.' He smiles to take the sting out of his words, but he's right. There's no escaping or running from this.

'Have you seen Dillon?'

'Yeah. I apologised to him before I came out here.'

'What did you say to him?'

Tate makes a face and looks out towards the sea. 'Just that I'm remembering shit from my past and I freaked out. He's fine with me, but it shouldn't have happened.'

They both look around as Ellen walks over to them. 'That's not a happy face.'

'No, Tate. I'm afraid it's not. I need to speak to you both inside.' She turns and walks briskly back towards the house.

Chloe holds out her hand and he looks at it for a minute before he reaches out and takes it. 'Knew I should have rode off into the distance.'

When they get back to the house Ellen is sitting at the kitchen table, her hands clasped in front of her. Tate sits opposite her and Chloe next to him. The feeling of dread is weighing heavily on her. Something has happened and it's far from good. 'I've asked the others to give us a minute so I can talk to you in private.'

'What is it?'

'As you know the press are all over this story. You've made the front pages today - which isn't a surprise. Unfortunately there's also a video of your arrest on the net.'

'What? Who the fuck recorded that?'

'We don't know. It shows them taking you out of the studio and putting you in the back of a Garda car. The video is decent quality. There's no denying who it is I'm afraid. It's not looking good, Tate. We'll do what we can to diffuse the situation, but social media is already running rife with comments about you relapsing.

'Now, my team are working on a few possible statements we can make about it, whether you like it or not. It's not just your career on the rocks, Tate. Dillon, Gregg, and Luke deserve for you to take this seriously.'

'You think this is some joke to me?'

'I need you to take a few deep breaths, Tate. I'm on your side, but we need to own this before the press blows it out of all proportion. Anyway, before we even get to that I'm afraid there's another problem.'

Tate laughs harshly as he pushes to his feet. 'Of course there is. Go for it.' He grabs a bottle of water from the fridge and leans against the counter. Ellen opens a file and passes him a piece of paper. Tate reads it and his expression darkens.

'What is it?' Chloe asks, even though she's not so sure she wants to know.

Tate ignores her and addresses Ellen instead. 'Is this legit?'

'I'm afraid so. It'll be out tomorrow.'

'Fuck!' Tate scrubs his hand through his hair and looks like he'd happily kill something.

Chloe takes the page from his hand and reads what she now sees is a mock-up of a newspaper article. "Rehab Love." I don't understand?'

'Read the rest,' Ellen says as Tate continues to glare at a tile on the floor.

'Tate Archer appears to have finally found love with school teacher Chloe Quinn. The couple met while they attended a drug rehabilitation facility at the same time a few months ago.'

She reads the words again and again, but they don't change.

'Oh my God. They actually say I'm a recovering heroin addict.' Chloe looks up at Tate but he's still glaring at the floor, so she turns to Ellen. 'You can stop this, right?'

'I'm afraid not.'

'But you have to. I'm a teacher. If they think for one second this is true, my career is over. It's a lie. They can't print it if it's a lie.'

'There's no way of stopping it, Chloe. They may be willing to print a retraction the following day, but this is going out. Tate... well, he's big news, especially after yesterday. There's so much speculation about what happened anything that gives the reporters the slightest hint of a story, they'll grab it. I'm so sorry, Chloe.'

'No. You have to do something. Tate? Please say you can stop this.'

Tate finally looks up from the floor but doesn't say anything. He won't even look her in the eye and that pisses her off.

'Look at me!' Still nothing so she gets up and stands in front of him. 'So you're not even going to look at me now?'

Instead of replying he scratches his arm. It's the first time she's seen him do that for weeks. She grabs his hand. 'Stop that and look at me.' He lifts his head but she can't read anything in his expression. 'Help me. What can I do? There has to be some way of stopping this. What can I do?'

He shakes his head. 'Nothing.'

Chloe drops his hand and takes a step back. 'Nothing? You mean to tell me my boss, all the parents of my students, all my friends, my family are going to read an article saying I'm an addict?'

'Chloe—'

'But hey! What am I worried about?' she says, feeling a little hysterical. 'I got to meet superstar Tate Archer while I was there. That'll make up for having no job and no future!'

That gets a reaction, but not the one she wanted. His dark eyes target her. 'You're not the only one who's just had their career pulled out from under them. I'm facing seven years, Chloe!'

'The big difference is you did it to yourself. You made the choice to fuck up your career. I didn't! My only mistake was—' Chloe hates herself the second the words come out of her mouth, but she's furious. At him. At the situation. At everything. She knows she's rammed her fist into his chest by the look on his face, but at that moment, her career is the one she's worried about.

'Your only mistake was what?'

Chloe doesn't know where they came from but the guys appear and put themselves between Tate and Chloe.

'Calm down, mate.' Gregg tries to get Tate's attention, but he's refusing to break eye contact with Chloe.

'Your only mistake was what?'

Ellen takes Chloe's arm and leads her into the living room. Chloe looks back at Tate but she can barely see him behind Luke and Gregg who are trying to talk him down.

Ellen closes the door and takes a long breath. 'Sorry about dragging you away, but I need to talk to you without all that drama.'

'I can't believe I just said that to him.'

'He'll be fine. I'm worried about you right now. You're collateral damage and I'm going to do whatever I can to help you. You can trust me, okay? I've been dealing with Tate since he was signed. I know what I'm doing.'

Chloe nods, but doesn't feel reassured in any way. She's worried about Tate, but right now he comes second to this story being released.

Tate pulls open the door and storms out to his truck. Chloe went for a walk about ten minutes ago. Can't blame her for wanting to get away from him. At least Bria and Luke had tagged along too in case she ran into any unwanted media attention. As much as he'd like to chase after her and sort things out, he's not in the right frame of mind. He's fucking furious and until he gets that under control he's best to keep away from everyone.

They're all going to lose it with him, but he needs to get away for half an hour. Tate reverses out of the shed and his tyres spin on the gravel as he accelerates away. Chloe's words are on constant fucking replay in his head and he can't shut them off. It didn't help that she was right. He had made the choice to risk his career and his life months ago. She didn't. All she had done was spend time with him. And how had he repaid her? By tearing a huge fucking hole in her life. Great way to show someone you love them.

He slams his head against the headrest.

He loves her.

He was going to tell her how he felt about her. Had this whole romantic evening planned. Instead he got arrested. Great timing as usual. Whoever has it out for him deserves a fucking medal for perfect timing. Every time he thinks he's getting things on track, he's punched in the gut again. This last blow had been a knock-out. He won't be getting back up again.

He heads away from Newcastle, driving nowhere in particular. All he knows is that he needs to get away from everyone. Fifteen minutes later, he weaves his truck through the traffic in Wicklow town and drives down to the harbour. He parks well away from everyone else, opens the window, and watches the trawlers and pleasure boats in the water.

He can't forget the look on Chloe's face when she begged him to help. There is only one thing he can do. Ellen is probably going to quit when she finds out, but he can't let Chloe's life be destroyed because of him. Fuck his own career, hers was far more important.

So he does the only thing he can think of. He fires a message to a contact at the paper running Chloe's story and, in exchange for sitting on the story about Chloe, tells him he'll give them an exclusive statement detailing his dramatic fall into drugs and rehab and his recent arrest.

He had to give them something juicy enough to leave Chloe out of it. So what if everyone knows he was weak and let the lifestyle draw him in. So what if they knew he partied too much and took things too far. Either way, his career would take a hit. Probably a terminal one. He'd prefer he took that hit alone instead of bringing her into it.

He glances over at his phone as it rings again. It's Gregg. He knows he should answer it. He knows they're probably freaking out. Instead of answering, he sends a quick text to Gregg.

I'm grand.

Not exactly deep and meaningful but it'll do. Gregg responds immediately.

Where the fuck are you? Get your ass back here now!

He ignores the message and jumps when someone knocks on the passenger window. He stares at the face on the other side but takes a minute to get his body to move. He opens the window and stares at his cousin.

'Dara? What are you doing here?'

He lifts his cup of coffee. 'I'm on my way to a meeting. Thought one of these would help me stay awake during it. The food van does amazing coffee. How about you? I don't usually see you here.'

'I just drove and ended up here.'

'You look like you haven't slept for days.'

'What? Yeah, sorry. Just got a lot going on.'

'I've got a few minutes. Do you want a coffee yourself? You seriously look like you could do with one.'

Tate nods absently. He wants to be alone, but a coffee might help clear his head. 'Just black would be great.'

Dara reappears a few minutes later and climbs into the passenger seat. He hands the coffee over and Tate takes a drink. Hopefully the caffeine will give him a kick. He can feel Dara staring over at him as the silence drags on.

'Excuse the lack of tact, Tate, but you really look shit.'

'Rough day yesterday.'

'Yeah, I heard. Sorry about that.'

Tate closes his eyes and rests his head against the headrest. Perfect. That means his parents will know soon enough. 'You know me, have to be the talk of the family.'

'Is it going to blow over?'

Tate takes another mouthful of coffee as he considers what to tell Dara. He'll probably just go straight back to the family and fill them in. But with everything in the papers and all over the net anyway did it really matter at this stage?

'Don't know. I'll find out in a few days.'

'Well I know a good lawyer if you need one.' He nudges Tate in the arm. 'I'll even give you mates rates.'

'Thanks but I'm sorted.'

'Any idea what you're facing yet? I'm not asking so I can run back and tell everyone. I'm asking as a lawyer who's used to keeping his mouth shut.'

Tate looks out the window at the boats wishing he could jump on one of the trawlers and head off to sea. 'She reckons it'll just be a fine but there's a chance it could be time. It shouldn't be as it's my first offence, but who knows.' He smiles at Dara. 'I might be needing you to take Jove out for me. Can't having him waiting seven years for me to exercise him.'

'Positive thinking, Tate. Like you said, it's your first offence. I'm sure you'll get a slap on the wrist and that'll be it. You're the lead singer of one of the hottest bands in Ireland. They're not going to give someone like you a custodial sentence on a minor drug possession charge. I hope it works out for you, Tate. I mean that.'

Tate puts on what he hopes looks like a genuine smile. 'Yeah. Thanks.' He drinks more coffee and rubs his eyes. Instead of helping, the coffee is making him feel worse.

Dara leans over and frowns at him. 'Are you sure you're okay? You've gone a bit grey. Tate? Tate!'

He stares over at Dara, taking a few seconds to focus on his face. 'Sorry. What?'

'Okay, I think I should take you home. You shouldn't drive when you're like this. Swap seats and I'll drive.' Dara gets out and walks around the front of the truck. He opens the driver's door and gestures

303

for Tate to get out.

'You need some help?'

'I'm grand. I can drive myself.'

'Fair enough. If you can take five paces without falling, I'll be on my way.'

Tate steps out and his legs instantly buckle under him. It feels like the damn things aren't attached to his body. Dara catches him before he lands on a stack of lobster pots.

'It's okay, Tate. I got you.' He gets under Tate's arm and helps him stand up. 'God, you weigh a ton.'

'Sorry. I feel strange.'

'Don't worry. We'll get you home in no time.'

With one arm around Dara's shoulders and the other braced against the bonnet of his truck, he somehow manages to stumble around to the passenger side and pull himself into the leather seat. Exhaustion goes over him in waves. He can barely keep his eyes open. So much for extra strong coffee. Dara climbs in and adjusts the driver's seat.

'I don't... feel...'

Dara reaches over and fastens the seatbelt across Tate's chest then starts the engine. 'Don't try to talk. It's okay, Tate. Just sleep.'

Tate wants to talk but his mouth won't form the words. His body has turned to lead. Dara puts Tate's truck in gear then pulls out of the parking spot, but Tate is already asleep.

Chloe looks out the window at the driveway but there's still no sign of his truck. Tate disappeared about two hours ago and hasn't turned up again. Dillon, Luke, and Gregg had left a few minutes ago to see if they could track him down. She'd tried calling him but he wasn't picking up. She can't blame him. She was angry and shouldn't have said what she did.

Ellen comes back into the room muttering to herself. She sits down and glares at her phone in her hand before slamming it onto the table.

'What's wrong?'

'Fucking Tate, that's what! I could just—' she stops talking and wrings her hands together. 'You know what he's gone and done? He's thrown himself on his damn sword to save you. Don't get me wrong,' she adds quickly, 'he's sorted your issue, but left me with an even bigger one.'

'What did he do?'

'He contacted someone at the paper and agreed to an exclusive on what happened to him if they drop the story about you.'

'What? Why did he do that?'

'Because he cares about you, of course.'

'What did he say?'

'To me? Nothing. I just got word from the paper. Apparently he told them he'd been battling drugs for a while. He mentions excessive partying and drinking and whatever else you can think of. Idiot gave them enough juicy titbits to make them forget all about you. Which they're going to do by the way. He's even mentioned the overdose and his arrest. He's well and truly screwed himself.'

'Where is he?'

'Tate? Haven't got a clue. He's conveniently ignoring my calls. I can't believe he did this! Why couldn't he just wait? I was trying to sort it. I don't suppose he's picking up the phone for you?'

Chloe shakes her head. 'Gregg just sent me a message. He got an 'I'm grand' message from him but nothing since. Gregg's on his way back. You don't think Tate would...' Chloe can't finish the sentence.

Clearly she doesn't need to. Ellen's face turns sombre and she shrugs. 'I hope not, but he hasn't been himself for I don't know how long. Dillon and Luke should be at his house by now. I'll give then a ring. See if they've heard anything.'

305

She walks into the living room leaving Chloe staring at the driveway. Since he stormed off, she can't shake the sinking feeling in her gut.

'Please be okay.'

Tate tries to wake up, but his brain is seriously struggling. He moves his head a little but instantly regrets it when the headache bounces around his skull like a spiked metal ball. Fuck he feels shite. He convinces one eye to do its job, but it doesn't help him figure out what the hell is wrong with him. His other eye joins the party, and his vision clears a little, not that it helps at all.

He's lying on a bed in a small bedroom. Something is familiar about it, but his brain is too foggy to give it much thought.

How the fuck did he get here? He's sure he was in his truck. Wasn't he? He shuts his eyes and tries to remember, but his brain won't get with the program. Whether his brain or body wants to, it's time to get up. But he can't. Neither hand will move.

Using far too much energy he looks up to the head of the bed where his hands are and knows he's in a whole world of trouble. He's chained to the metal bed frame. He pulls at the restraints, but the thick chain is painfully wrapped around his wrists and padlocked in place. Someone wants him to stay put.

With his brain still playing catch-up, Tate looks down at his feet and sees similar restraints securing his ankles. It takes him a few seconds longer to realise where he is. This is one of the small downstairs bedrooms in his grandparent's old farmhouse. The windows have been boarded up from the outside, but everything else is still the same as he remembers it. It was the room he stayed in when he spent the night as a child.

Something pinches the crook of his left arm. He twists his arm around and his stomach takes a dive. There's an IV line disappearing into his arm under a thick layer of tape. The tube has been secured with more tape all the way down his arm to make sure it doesn't come out. The other end of the tube isn't attached to anything but that doesn't make him feel any better. The fact it's there in the first place is a serious worry.

He hasn't got a fucking clue what's going on, but he knows he really needs to get out of here. He yanks his arms towards him, but the damn chain won't shift. He grabs onto the bed frame and pulls his legs up hard. Nothing happens. The bed is one of those old-fashioned ones with a heavy metal frame. He hasn't got a chance of breaking it.

He gives up and lies still, trying to give his stomach and head a few minutes to get back to where they should be. He swallows deeply a few times. His stomach is having serious objections to something. Tate quickly leans over the side of the bed as he loses the battle with his stomach.

Each time he throws up the spiked ball in his skull rattles around his head sending more waves of nausea through him. When there's nothing left in his stomach, he flops onto his back and stares up at the ceiling.

He's having another nightmare. There's no other explanation. He's asleep in his parents' house and he'll wake up any second.

But when the door leading from the hallway opens, Tate's memory comes back with a wallop.

'Dara?'

'How are you feeling?' His cousin grimaces when he spots the mess on the floor. 'Seriously, Tate?' He grabs a dustsheet from the pile in the corner and drops it on the floor beside the bed, covering the vomit. 'I suppose that's my fault. I think I might have given you a little too much. You're a big guy. I wanted to make sure you were well and truly knocked out.'

'Dara? What the fuck?' It's not a question that is going to give him any definite answers but it's all he can come out with.

'Don't worry. The sedative I put in your coffee will make you feel a little disoriented for a bit, but it should ease.' He pulls up a weathered green plastic deckchair and sits down in front of him. 'You really do look like shit. Have you been pushing yourself too hard?'

'What the fuck are you doing?'

'That was a whole sentence that time. Good for you. What am I doing? To be honest, I haven't got an end game in mind just yet. When I followed you from your parents' house, I wasn't expecting to do this. I thought I'd get a few more weeks of fun out of you, but when I saw your face, I knew I'd probably pushed you enough.'

The words take a ridiculously long time to register. 'You? This has been you? You've been fucking with me?'

Dara nods, looking extremely pleased with himself. 'I thought you would have figured it out by now, but I guess that's down to the excessive drug use. I've heard long-term use can mess with your head.' He leans forward and clasps his hands together. 'You know, when I gave you that old family photo at Christmas, I never thought you'd react so spectacularly. I mean, I couldn't have planned it better myself. I just wanted to throw you off your guard a little. Mess with your head. But then Dad rings me at work and tells me you're in a coma after a heroin overdose.' Dara claps his hand together as he laughs. 'I mean, wow. Never saw that coming. Then again, I should have guessed you'd have gone down the clichéd drink and drugs route, but you kept that side of yourself secret. Couldn't have you tarnishing your image. That was one impressive fall from grace, Tate. Well done.'

'Did you put drugs in my car?'

'Guilty as charged. Sorry, that was a little cruel considering what you're facing. But yes. That was me. I tried to get my hands on enough so you'd be done for intent to supply, but I couldn't risk being caught myself.'

'What the fuck is wrong with you?'

The smile disappears as Dara pulls his chair closer to the bed. Tate barely recognises the person in front of him. There's so much hatred, so much rage. And that makes Tate seriously worried.

'I'll tell you what's wrong with me. You, Tate. You're my problem. You know, I remember being introduced to you for the first time. I remember being excited. Having a new cousin who was the same age as me. Someone I could play with. Be friends with. Shame it didn't work out that way.'

'But we were friends.'

'Give me a fucking break. We were never friends. We were rivals. It was always 'be kind to Tate. Don't upset Tate. Make sure you let him play with whatever he wants.' I had to walk on eggshells around you. Everyone did. If you kicked a fucking ball and it went in a straight line there was praise all round. Nan and Pops were the worst. You'd swear you were the only grandchild they had. You practically lived here. Pops even gave you a fucking horse. It was non-stop with the attention.'

'They were trying to make me feel welcome.'

'Oh I know that. The problem is it didn't stop. The sun shone out of your arse. That door was always open to you,' he says, pointing at the back door.

Dara closes his eyes and takes a long breath. He's known Dara for nearly three decades. He's never seen him like this before. Never seen him this manic.

Dara opens his eyes and smiles at him as he gets to his feet. He runs his hand over the worn wallpaper and sighs loudly.

'So, what do you think of the old place? Dad is trying to renovate it, but it's taking time and too much money. Think he's losing interest in it. I've tried to tell him just to call it quits. Sell it as it is, but he won't give it up. He's got this emotional attachment to it, I guess. You probably feel the same. You spent so long here I wouldn't be surprised. Were you tempted to buy it yourself?'

Of course he was but he's not going there with Dara. He knew Eric wanted the house so he didn't get in his way. Up until he woke up chained to the bed, Tate had nothing but great memories of the house. Now... well, Dara's just fucked that up for him too.

'That was a fucking question, Tate. This will go a lot easier for you if you answer me.'

'No.'

'Strange. But I suppose you had just done some major spending around the same time. I hear you paid off the mortgage on your parents' farm and bought them a sizable chunk of additional farmland next to it. You paid a hefty price from what I can see online. But you did owe them. They had to put up with a serious amount of shit from you over the years. You were hardly the model son now, were you.

'Then you get yourself that swanky pad in town. Again, impressive price you paid for that. Add the over-the-top truck and the bike to the mix and I doubt you would have had much left to get this place too. Bet you could afford it now though. Having a few more number one songs under your belt can't have hurt your bank balance. All in all, I'd say you've done pretty well for yourself considering what you came from.'

'What do you want, Dara? Or is your plan to get back at me by droning on, because it's working. You're boring the fuck out of me.'

Tate knows the blow is coming, but it still hurts when Dara's fist ploughs into his gut. He coughs and tries to ease some of the pressure from this stomach but the chains won't give.

'This is nothing but a joke to you.'

'Of course it's a fucking joke. You've kidnapped me, you crazy motherfucker. How exactly do you see this playing out, huh? How about you let me go and I promise I won't knock out too many of your expensive teeth.'

'God I hate you.'

'Right now the feeling's mutual. What do you want!'

Dara leans over and wraps his hand around Tate's neck.

'I want you to suffer, Tate. That's all. Think you can do that?'

He tries to swallow past Dara's grip. 'Does it look like I'm having fun?'

Dara squeezes a little harder. 'I mean really suffer, Tate. What I want is for everything and everyone you know and love to disappear.' He clicks his fingers in Tate's face. 'Just like that. I want you alone. I want people to say the name Tate Archer and remember a failed musician who threw it all away for his next drink or his next fix. And I'm going to make sure that happens.'

Tate wants to come back with something, but he's all out of replies. Dara's seriously crazy and that makes him dangerous.

'That's shut you up, hasn't it. Now you're wondering exactly how far I'm willing to go with this. Would I keep you here so you miss your court appearance? I'd imagine the authorities would be less than happy about that. Maybe so much so they'd move past the fine and take you in. That would be fatal for your career, wouldn't it?'

Tate tries to take a deep breath but Dara's weight on his neck isn't helping.

'Here's another scenario for you. You're found in your car at some deserted beach somewhere. Maybe you've had a little too much to drink. Maybe you've relapsed. Maybe you've taken things too far again. It's a strong possibility, isn't it? I mean you've been under so much stress lately and it's not like you don't have a history.'

Tate glances up at the tube strapped to his arm and Dara smiles.

'You're catching on.' He gets up and disappears from the room for a few minutes. When he comes back, he's holding something that scares Tate more than being stuck in a room with his crazy-ass cousin.

'Don't, Dara. Please don't do this.'

Dara smiles and looks down at the syringe. 'Full of manners now aren't you. I had hoped you'd take this step yourself, but I don't think you will, not without a little nudge.'

Tate thrashes in the bed, pulling at the chains.

'I swear to God, I will fucking kill you, Dara!'

'Do you know what I think? I think you'll thank me.' He picks up the end of the tube and slides the needle in. The bed groans and creaks under Tate's attack but like Dara, the damn thing just ignores his protests. He watches in horror as Dara empties the syringe into his arm. He pats Tate on the cheek and laughs when Tate jerks his head to the side.

'Fuck you.'

'I know. Have fun.' He turns off the light, plunging him into darkness then shuts and locks the door behind him.

Frustration firmly takes hold of Tate. He shouts and pulls against the restraints until he runs out of energy and lies still. All he's managed to do is tear his wrists and send his headache into a stomach-churning somersault.

Tate closes his eyes and tries to calm down. He can already feel the welcoming pull of the drug and he realises he missed it. His body missed it. And that terrifies him. He'd struggled to break free of it the first time. Each painful minute of his withdrawal had felt like a week. It was excruciating, humiliating, and fucking miserable, but he'd got through it. For what? Just to be forced back into that hell again by someone he's known for decades.

Dara.

He's been kidnapped by his cousin. His cousin is keeping him chained to a bed in his grandparent's house. Whatever way he says it to himself, it sounds fucking ridiculous, but nothing about this makes any sense. The scary part is if he's found in his car like Dara described, no one would be surprised. It's not like anyone would believe him if he told them Dara kidnapped him. He barely believes it himself so why would anyone else?

He closes his eyes and tries desperately to think about Chloe. At least he contacted the paper before Dara got to him. That's one consolation. Whatever happens he won't be dragging her along with him for the ride.

He tries to open his eyes again, but it's a lost cause. So instead he gives in lets the drug take him away from the nightmare.

'He's a big fucking guy. He can't just vanish.' Gregg smiles apologetically at Chloe. 'Sorry about cursing.'

'I'm going out with Tate. Curse all you fucking want.'

Gregg grins at her and nods his head. Chloe takes out her phone but there's no new message from Tate. No missed call. Nothing. Dillon and Luke had gone back to Tate's house just in case he decided to go there instead. Tidying the place after the Garda search would take a few hours anyway so they were going to get started on that while they waited for news.

'Where would he go if he wanted to be alone?'

Gregg slumps onto the couch and sighs loudly. 'The beach, but he's not there. Up the mountains on his bike but that's still at his house. Lock himself in his studio but that's a no too. Realistically he could be fucking anywhere. If he absolutely doesn't want us to find him all he has to do is keep driving. He's got the whole of Ireland to hide in.'

'Does he own any other properties?'

Gregg shakes his head. 'Nope. Just the house in Blackrock. I checked and the bus we use for touring is still locked up and empty. He's vanished.'

'What time is his court case tomorrow?'

'Ten.'

Chloe knows the answer but asks the question anyway. 'What happens if he misses it?'

'They'll either issue a warrant for his arrest or go ahead without him. Both would probably result in us not seeing him for a while. Best all round we find him before it comes to that.' He gets up and drags a hand through his blond hair as he paces again. He seems to be doing that quite a bit the last few days.

Bria joins them and flops down beside Chloe. 'Well that was fun. An hour-long chat with Mum and Dad. They're freaking out. I think I've managed to convince them to stay put until we hear from Tate, but I'm not sure how effective I was.'

'I presume they haven't heard from him?'

'No, they haven't. Shane tried to call him while they were talking to me, but it went straight to voicemail. I'm really worried, guys. They last time he disappeared he...'

Gregg crouches down in front of her and takes her hands. 'Hey, he's not going to do anything stupid, okay. Not after everything he's done to get better. He's probably broken down somewhere and his phone is dead. It'll be something or nothing.'

Bria smiles and nods, but Chloe sees the look on Gregg's face as he stands up. He doesn't believe a word of what he just said. 'I think I need to call in a favour.'

'What are you going to do?' Chloe asks.

'The only thing we know for sure is that he left here in his car. I'll call one of my old colleagues. He owes me a favour so fingers crossed he can discretely look for his truck. The last thing we want to do is broadcast the fact he's missing.'

Tate wakes up with a start when he's slapped on the face. He opens his eyes and groans when he sees Dara crouching down beside the bed. He sits down on the chair and puts the bag of chips on his knee.

'How are you doing?'

Tate doesn't bother replying. He's done participating in whatever the fuck is going on with Dara.

'So, you with me yet?'

Tate doesn't know where the fuck he is. His body won't do anything he wants it to do and he swears his head is bouncing off the beams in the roof. The unpleasant aftereffects are bad enough without the accompanying exhaustion. He can barely keep his eyes open and Dara's droning in the background is just adding to his frustration.

He grabs Tate by the jaw and turns his head around. 'Are you listening to me?'

Tate's eyes close again. Fuck Dara. All he wants to do is sleep and wake up when this nightmare is over.

Dara jostles his head. 'C'mon. Look at me.'

Tate glares over at him which just makes Dara laugh.

'You know what? I much prefer you this way. You're far less annoying when you're off your head. I may not have been driven to these lengths if I knew this side of you.'

'What...' Tate struggles to get his thoughts in order. 'What was you? Did you do it all?'

He chews on a chip before he answers. 'Yes. All me. The photo in the post I handed you at Christmas. All the reports. Leaking your dirty overdose secret to the press. The bottle of rum to celebrate your exciting win. That little story about meeting Chloe in rehab. All me.'

'She didn't deserve that.'

Dara laughs loudly. 'I completely agree. She didn't. From what I

317

could tell she was a good one. Not like the dozens of others you've no doubt used and abused over the years. Personally, I reckon she owes me a big thank you. I just showed her what being with you will do to her. Better she gets away from you now before you get bored and turf her aside.'

It's a complete waste of energy but Tate savagely jerks against his bonds. It does fuck all to get his fists any closer to Dara, but it does make him jump and drop his chips on the floor. Better than nothing. At least it wiped the smug smile off the bastard's face. In spite of the absolute shit situation he's in he can't help but laugh.

Dara retaliates by punching Tate in the jaw. He kicks the bedframe then sits back on the chair and looks down at his ruined dinner.

'Why do you always have to steal the limelight, huh? Why can't you ever just blend into the background? I mean it was a continual thing when we were kids. It didn't matter what I did or how hard I worked I couldn't get out from your shadow.

'And you want to know the worst part? I was falling short of someone who wasn't even related to any of us. I seriously don't get it. I played by the rules. I worked hard. Didn't get in trouble. Top of my class all the way through school. All the way through college.'

Tate tries to pay attention to what Dara's saying, but he's seriously struggling. He's exhausted, his head is fucking killing him, and he's craving something he thought he had broken free from.

He grunts as Dara grabs a handful of his hair and turns his head around.

'And then there's you, Tate. A re-homed stray. Always in trouble. Detention every week for fighting or talking back, or whatever else you did to draw attention to yourself. Okay, so you've got a masters in music, but seriously how hard is that to get? It's just part of the whole look at me thing you do. You did everything you possibly could to stand out, to show off. I mean look at you. All those ridiculous tattoos. We couldn't be more different if we tried, yet I always fell short. Do you remember the party your parents held for you when you won those awards?'

Tate looks at him but doesn't reply.

'I'll take that as a yes. Do you know what my father said to me that night about you? He said that you've had a tough year and I should show you some compassion. Can you believe that? You do everything wrong. You drink, you take drugs, you hurt your family and everyone who stupidly gives a damn about you. And that deserves compassion. That there sums up everything I hate about you. Everything I detest about you and what you've done to me. You must know what that feels like now though.'

Tate frowns at him. 'What?'

'Oh don't go all coy with me. I know you were less than happy about me riding Jove while you were... indisposed. Like I know you were less than happy about me helping out around the farm. I could see it clear as day on your face. You were sitting beside your lady friend trying to be all gracious thanking me for my help, but I could see how much it pissed you off.

'You probably wouldn't be happy to know I also helped them clean up your bachelor pad after you let your junkie friends destroy it.'

Dara laughs when he sees the shock on Tate's face.

'Oh yes. I got to see your work first-hand. You see, I've been sticking close to your parents for months. How do you think I got a set of keys to your truck? I made a copy of their set. Same goes for the code to your gate. I couldn't get my hands on your house keys unfortunately but getting the drugs into your car worked just fine.'

'You used them to get to me?'

'Of course. Obviously they thought I was being all helpful and friendly. Same with Dad. He'd happily tell me anything he heard about you from his dear sister.'

Tate feels sick and it's got nothing to do with the drugs. Dara got into his life through his parents. That explains why the letters came when things were finally going his way. His mum had told Dara's dad and then he sent a letter.

His cousin is seriously fucked in the head. Tate snorts which doesn't go down well with Dara. He grabs a handful of Tate's hair and pulls his head up.

'Sorry. I missed that.'

Tate licks his dry lips and smiles at him. 'I'm flattered I occupy so much of your time. I feel kind of bad though. I can honestly say I don't think about you from one painful family gathering to the next. Are you even listening to the crap you're spouting? You're whining on about favourites, about who was better at what. It's fucking ridiculous. I don't know how the fuck you go from jealous kid to psycho dick. You've got some serious fucking issues.'

'I have issues? Wow. You've got some brass neck. You forget I know where you came from. I know you killed your mother.'

'I didn't kill her.'

'Yes you did. I'm sure you read the report. You were found next to her body. She was dead and there was blood on your hands. She's dead because of you.'

Tate closes his eyes again. 'It was thirty fucking years ago. Who cares?'

'You do or else you wouldn't have reacted the way you did when I gave you the photo. Only you know what really happened that night. I'd say given the way you're dealing with everything since you got that touching photo you have a fair amount of guilt eating you up. That must be painful to live with.' Dara takes a long breath and squeezes Tate's arm. 'Your father wasn't a nice man, was he? What he did to you... I have to admit I got a little choked up when I read the doctor's report.'

'Fuck you, Dara.'

'After reading that... I'm not surprised you needed to resort to drugs to deal with it.'

320

Dara pushes to his feet and stretches. 'Well, I think it's time to put more manners on you. I've got another fix in the kitchen with your name on it. Do you want it?'

He desperately wants it. 'No.'

'I don't know why you're fighting it, Tate. You're an addict. Just accept what you are.' He pats him on the shoulder and smiles down at him. 'Hang tight. I'll be back in a minute.'

As disgusted as he is with himself for admitting it, he desperately wants more of what Dara is offering. He throws his head back against the bed, hitting it off the headboard. The metal frame rattles under the abuse. Tate twists his head around and smiles to himself.

With the light off he had completely forgotten about the one flaw in the bed. The decorative metal rods in the bed-frame screw in and out. He continuously played with them when he stayed over. So much so, the threads had become worn over time. It was something he got in trouble about too many times to count when he was a kid.

Tate quickly unscrews one of the rods and slips the chain off the end before fixing it back onto the frame. He gets the other one done as he hears Dara outside the door. His ankles are still locked in place but it's a start.

Tate keeps his eyes locked on Dara as he slowly wraps the lengths of chain around his hands. As Dara reaches over to give him another fix, Tate hits him.

After being chained up the blow doesn't pack its usual punch but the addition of the chain around his hand does the trick. He connects with the side of Dara's face, sending him spinning into the wall. Not waiting for him to recover, Tate grabs him by the neck and hauls him onto the bed, using his weight to keep him pinned to the mattress. Tate slams his fist into Dara's jaw spraying blood across the wall. He hits him again breaking his nose.

Dara gropes blindly at Tate, trying to push him off but Tate isn't budging. Dara's fingers tear at Tate's face and arms, but he really couldn't give a fuck. Dara bucks under him and gets in a lucky jab to his ribs. He scrambles out from under Tate, but Tate pulls him back onto the bed and elbows him in the ribs. Dara curses and lashes out trying to make contact wherever he can.

Dara rams his elbow into Tate's side. The blow hits soft tissue, sending the pain through his body. As he's trying to clear his head, Dara punches him in the face and scrambles over to the syringe of heroin on the floor a few feet from them. Tate tries to stop him but the chains fixing his ankles to the bed keep him just out of reach.

Tate sprawls back in the bed and breaths heavily as he watches Dara pick up the syringe and collapse back against the far wall. Dara's laugh is a little crazed as he gingerly touches his broken nose.

'Valiant effort.' He takes a few deep breaths then pushes his hair back from his face. 'You broke my nose, Tate. That wasn't a clever move.'

Tate laughs. 'Felt pretty fucking good. You're not exactly a worthy rival, Dara. Drugged and chained up and I still kicked your ass. You're fucking pathetic. But you always have been. You're a spoilt fucking brat, Dara. I detest people like you. Entitled pricks who have everything handed to them on a silver platter and still find something to bitch about. You're not worth bothering with.' Tate closes his eyes and turns his head from Dara. He needs the fucker to come closer and Dara may be many things but he's not stupid. He won't budge if he thinks Tate is still a threat.

'Tate?'

He doesn't get a response and after a few minutes, Tate feels him pull on the tube in his arm. Tate lunges and rams his fist into the side of Dara's face, destroying any cartilage he hasn't already smashed up. He drags himself on top of Dara and grabs the end of the chain attached to his wrist. He drapes it over Dara's neck and leans on it. Dara's hands scramble to push Tate off, but he's too heavy to push away.

'Get the fuck off me!'

Tate pushes down harder. 'I told you I'd fucking kill you.' At this stage he really couldn't care if he kills Dara. His cousin's face turns a strange colour and Dara's protests die away as he loses consciousness. Common sense breaks through and he eases up on the pressure.

Tate roughly turns Dara over and searches his pockets. Keys to the padlocks would be perfect but he'd settle for a phone.

No keys. He must have left them in the kitchen. 'C'mon fucker. Where's your phone?' He shoves Dara against the wall and tries the other pocket. 'Bingo.' As well as Dara's phone he also finds his. He powers up his phone, silently praying there's some battery left. The screen lights up and he's in luck. Fifty-percent charge left.

His first instinct is to call Chloe but he talks himself out of it. The least she knows about any of this the better, so he calls Gregg.

'Tate! What the fuck? You've got an hour before you're due in court. What the fuck are you playing at?'

'Long story, but I was taken by my cousin, Dara. He's got me chained up. He's been the one fucking with me, Gregg. I knocked him out but I can't find his keys and if I'm here with him much longer I'm going to kill the bastard.'

'Back up. He's got you what?'

'I'm chained to a fucking bed in my nan's old place.'

'Fuck. Okay, Sit tight. I'm already on the way. Your truck was last spotted on a camera a few miles from there yesterday, so I was heading that way to check it out. Just don't kill him until I get there. Are you okay?'

'No. Gregg, he gave me...' Tate looks over at the syringe lying within reach. 'I've had a fix, Gregg. He gave it to me. And there's more of it. It's on the floor. I can reach it so I need you to distract me cause I really fucking want it.'

Gregg stays quiet for a minute then Chloe comes on the phone. 'Hey.'

He turns on his side to face the window and Dara. Even though he was hoping to keep her away from this, hearing her voice is just what he needs right now. 'Hey. I'm sorry. I shouldn't have—'

'So I was thinking about what we could do the next nice weekend. I thought we could have another picnic at Grace's summer house.'

He nods to the empty room. He knows what she's doing. 'Yeah. That would be nice.'

'We could go for an evening picnic instead. Maybe build a campfire and lie back watching the stars. Do you like toasted marshmallows?'

Tate rocks himself on the bed and tries to imagine himself there with Chloe. 'Yeah. I do.'

'Okay, so we'll go all out with the marshmallows. Then we can curl up together under a blanket.'

'For the love of God do not expand on that,' Greggs shouts from somewhere in the background. 'I'm trying not to crash.'

'I'm not talking to you so shush,' Chloe says. 'Anyway, like I was saying, we could finish what we started last time we were there.'

'Without the fight.'

She laughs and he smiles to himself. 'Yes, without the fight. I might even let you give me a lesson on your bike.'

He buries his head under his arm and nods, forgetting that she can't she see him.

'Tate? Tate. Are you still there?'

'Yeah. Where are you?'

'Where are we, Gregg?'

'Five minutes, buddy,' Gregg shouts into the phone.

Tate groans to himself. The way he feels right now that's a fucking lifetime. He's vaguely aware of Chloe and Gregg arguing then hears one of Broken's songs being played.

'Tate? You remember this song.'

He smiles. 'Yeah.'

'I want you to close your eyes and put yourself in your kitchen. You walked in from work and caught me dancing badly and singing even more terribly to this song. This is the first song you ever sang to me. You remember what you were doing while you were singing?'

'Can't forget that.'

'Just keep thinking about that, Tate. We'll be with you before the song is over, okay.'

He squeezes his eyes shut and tries to do what she's asking, but he's struggling to keep the images straight in his head. He drops the phone onto the bed beside him, the tiny sound of his song still playing though the phone's speakers. One more verse then the chorus again.

He just needs to hang on a little longer.

'What the fuck is going on here?'

Chloe walks around Tate and joins the others in his living room. If first impressions are anything to go by, Tate is less than happy about the ambush, but he doesn't have a choice. They had found him barely conscious chained to a bed a mere six hours ago. No amount of arguing or pleading had convinced him to stay in hospital for observation.

Apart from a few cuts and bruises, he wasn't too badly injured so there was no reason to keep him there as much as Chloe would have liked. He looks absolutely terrible. He's far too pale and can barely hold himself upright.

Then again, it was probably a good idea to get him as far from Dara as possible. His cousin was currently secured to a hospital bed waiting to have his nose reset. Tate had done an impressive job demolishing it. It's less than he deserved.

Chloe takes a deep breath and faces him. 'Okay, so we've all been talking.'

'Is that right? I'm guessing about me.'

Dillon crosses his arms and stares over at him from the couch. 'Hey, shut up and listen to her.'

'We're all moving in with you. Just until you've over this.'

'What? You mean like fucking babysitters?'

Gregg snorts loudly. 'No, you dick. Not like babysitters. We're going to get you through this as a family. Cause despite your monumental efforts to keep us out of your problems, we are your family and there isn't a hope in hell you can push us away. So, like Chloe said, we're all moving into your place. We'll eat and watch embarrassing 80's action films. You're going to rest when you can, then we'll work out together, go for a walk, go for a drive, take the bikes out, whatever we have to do to keep you distracted. Then, when you're up for it, we're going to finish the damn album and get it out there.'

Chloe holds her breath as she watches Tate's face. There's no doubt he's tempted to tell them all where to go, but the fact he hasn't said it in as many words is a definite plus. For the last few hours he's been in a foul mood. If he wasn't biting someone's head off he was glowering, and both were equally effective. She knows it's all part of the aftereffects of what Dara gave him and the fact he was craving more, but that didn't make him any easier to deal with.

Tate eventually sighs and nods. 'I'm not going to be fun to live with.'

'When are you ever?' Luke asks, smiling to soften his words. 'We want to do this. So, you going to let us?'

'Do I have a choice?'

Gregg shakes his head. 'Nope.'

'Guess there's no point arguing then.'

Tate wakes suddenly and takes a few seconds to realise he's in his room in his house. He slowly looks to his left and relaxes when he sees Chloe asleep beside him. It's hard to believe he started this day chained to a bed in a derelict house and now he's back in his own house with Chloe. Strangest fucking few days of his life.

He slowly rolls out of bed and creeps into the bathroom, closing the door quietly so he doesn't wake her. Physically he's going to be fine which is a relief considering how crap he feels. The two impressive bruises colouring his stomach and his side hurt, the lesions surrounding each wrist are itchy, and the bruise on his cheek complains when he moves his jaw. The worst of the lot is the angry red trail of irritation the length of his arm thanks to the tape Dara used to secure the IV. Removing that had been worse than all the punches combined.

He sits on the edge of the bath and clasps his hands together. He's restless and it's doing his head in. Just part of the other issue Dara left him with.

Chloe crouches down in front of him, scaring the hell out of him.

'Sorry. I didn't mean to startle you.'

'I was miles away. Didn't hear you come in. Did I wake you?'

'No. You can't sit on the bath all night. Come back to bed.' She stands up and holds out her hand. Tate takes it and allows her to lead him back to the bedroom.

He turns on the bedside light and looks over at her as she lies down beside him. 'Are you okay?'

She smiles at him and squeezes his hand. 'Me? I'm fine.'

'You don't look fine.' He tries to wrap his arms around her but she sits up and swings her legs out of the bed.

'Do you want something to eat?'

'Why haven't you asked me about it?'

Tate can see her shoulders tensing at his question. He knew she was avoiding the whole Dara and drugs situation.

'Asked you about what?'

'Oh come on. You seriously expect me to buy that? Everyone wants me to be honest and talk and open up and bare my soul to the world. Is it too much to ask for a little honesty in return?'

She turns to face him and leans back against the headboard. 'I'm scared, okay. I have no idea how bad this is going to get.'

'You mean me?'

She nods and looks down at the end of the bed. 'Gregg and the guys... they saw a part of what you went through the first time. I'm going into this blind.'

'This isn't anything like the last time. If it was, I wouldn't be able to deal with it at home.'

She finally meets his eyes. 'Do you want more? I mean do you want to use again?'

'Yes, but that'll ease. That's why the guys have all this stuff planned. It's not a constant feeling but when it hits it's the only thing I can think about. The last time doing things like working out helped keep my mind off it.'

'On a scale of one to ten, how bad is the craving when it hits?'

'It's a strong nine.'

Her face drops and, not for the first time, he feels shite for bringing her into this nightmare.

'Oh. Do you really think you can get through this without rehab?'

'Yes. With the support I have, I'll be over the worst of it in a week or so, fingers crossed. I will absolutely understand if you want to keep away for the moment.' He laughs to himself as another thought hits. 'Or keep away for good. Fuck knows I wouldn't blame you.'

'I want to be here for you.'

'You really sure? I've been told I'm a moody, awkward, difficult patient.'

Chloe laughs and some of the weight lifts from his shoulders. It seems like a lifetime since he's heard her laugh. He hadn't given her much to laugh about lately.

'Yes, your mum did mention something along those lines. Actually, I'm fairly sure she used those exact words.'

'Cheers, Mum. I think I'd prefer if you two didn't talk.'

'Too late for that I'm afraid. I'm having lunch with your mum and Bria next week.'

As much as the thought of them meeting to have a chat fills him with dread, having the three women in his life getting on can't be a bad thing. The fact his mum wants to socialise with Chloe is a big deal.

'That sounds like something I should be worried about.'

She smirks at him which does nothing to put him at ease.

He runs his hand up her arm as he tries to get the next bit out without fumbling. 'I'm going to sit down with everyone tomorrow. I need to be honest about... everything I guess.'

Chloe pushes back to look up at him. 'You are? Are you sure you're ready?'

'Probably not but putting it off isn't going to help. The press are going to be all over this. Without meaning to sound like a prize dick – you can't kidnap someone like me without someone hearing about it. Even if it's somehow downplayed to... I don't know, a family squabble or something like that, it's still going to come back on all of us. Then there's the whole possession charge to deal with. It's only fair everyone close to me knows what really happened.'

'Mum, Dad, and Bria are coming over first thing. I need to get things straight in my head. About Dara and the paperwork he sent me. Can you be there too?'

Chloe squeezes his hand. 'Of course. Whatever you need.'

'Thanks.' He kisses her on the forehead and pulls her against him again. 'Go back to sleep.'

Tate stares at the ceiling as Chloe snuggles in beside him and falls back asleep. More fun and games tomorrow, but it's the right thing to do. The problem is he'd prefer to go another few rounds with Dara than talk to any of them about his past.

Tate waits until everyone is sitting down before he joins them in the living room. He'd prefer to do pretty much anything than what he's got planned but it has to happen. After everything he's put them through the least he can do is tell them the truth face to face.

He sits on the armchair next to the fireplace and leans forward, resting his arms on his legs. He turns the ring on his thumb as he gets his thoughts in order.

The last hour had been spent with his family and Chloe talking about what he was going to say but his thoughts are still all over the place. After a few minutes he finally convinces himself to look up.

Chloe, Gregg, Dillon, and Luke are on the couch and the other armchair facing him. It's unusual for them to be so quiet. It's probably the longest Gregg has gone without making a smart comment.

Fuck it. Better get this over with before he changes his mind. 'My biological father used to hit me and my mother. Scrap that. He used to beat the shit out of us. I don't remember a lot of it thank fuck. What I do remember is pushing him too far one day. I don't know what I did, but I know I did something I shouldn't have. I tried to apologise, but he wasn't having any of it. My mother got in between the two of us, but he just turned on her instead.

'When I came to, she was beside me on the floor.' He frowns and twists the ring on his thumb again. 'I tried to get her to wake up, but she wouldn't. He'd killed her.

He keeps his eyes on his hands and ploughs on, ignoring the quiet curse from one of the guys. If he stops talking, he doubts he'll be able to convince himself to keep going.

'That's all I remember about either of them. Mum and Dad were able to find out other bits for me from my assessments and Gregg's mates were able to help out with some other information. Apparently, my father is serving life for murdering her. He was caught a few days after he killed her. Some neighbours called the Garda when he ran out of the house covered in blood and I was taken to hospital. I had a few broken bones and a concussion.'

He glances over at Gregg and his friend flashes him a small smile. 'From what the doctors could tell I had a fair few old injuries. They also reported that he...' he falters again. He just can't get himself to say it. 'He hadn't just stuck to hitting me. They think he might have... I don't remember if he did do that...'

'It's okay, buddy,' Luke says. Tate looks up at him, a little surprised at the anger on his friend's face. Better than pity. Luke shakes his head. 'You don't have to say it.'

Tate nods and goes back to concentrating on his ring. 'I went into foster care when I was better. According to the assessments we could find, I didn't say a lot for a few weeks. When I did start talking again, I didn't say anything about what happened. Never did. A year later I was adopted and that was the end of it. I didn't remember anything, so it wasn't brought up again.

'Then last year Dara's dad bought my grandparent's old place. Mum had stored some stuff there when they were renovating the farm a few years back. She must have forgotten to get all the boxes back. Dara found one of them and unfortunately for me, it had all my adoption paperwork in it, including some of the assessments.

'He's a damn good lawyer. It didn't take him long to do a bit of digging and join the dots. When I got that first photo from him it triggered my memories, I guess. I got bad nightmares and couldn't deal with them. I drank and then I called Eddie and... well, you know the rest.

'I don't know if more memories are going to come back to me or if this is it. I'm hoping this is the end of it, but after everything that's happened who the fuck knows. I'm going to talk to Ellen in a bit and fill her in too. There's no way to keep this under wraps as much as I'd like to. Dara is being charged with kidnapping among other things.

'Kidnapping me will keep him in the headlines for a bit. Me too unfortunately. Unless Ellen can work some impressive magic, it's only a matter of time before what my father did comes out. Bar my family, the four of you are the most important people in my life. I wanted you to know before the shit hits the fan.'

He smiles awkwardly to himself, still unable to look away from his ring which he's still twisting around his thumb.

Dillon crouches down in front of him, pulling him out of his thoughts. 'I think we should take the bikes out for a spin.'

Tate wishes he could put into words how fucking grateful he is. He needed to tell them what happened, but that didn't mean he wanted to have a discussion about it afterwards. If they had looked at him differently it would have killed him. 'Sounds great.'

Dillon gets up and goes into the spare room. He wheels Tate's bike out as Luke grabs their helmets off the counter. 'Get your gear and meet us outside when you're ready.'

Gregg drapes his arm around Tate's shoulder as they watch Dillon push his bike out the patio doors. 'You good?'

'Yeah. Glad to get it all out.'

'Things can only get better from here buddy. You'll see.' He playfully punches Tate in the stomach before he walks into the kitchen. 'Chloe, I'll bring you to the deli when this lot have fucked off. We can get lunch ready. I'm bloody starving.'

Tate drops down onto the couch beside Chloe and blows out a long breath. It feels like an immense weight had been lifted from his shoulders. The last few days have taken it out of him, but he feels a hell of a lot better than he has for a long time.

Chloe leans against his arm and hugs him close. 'I'm unbelievably proud of you.'

'I should have said something a long time ago. I just didn't... I

333

didn't know what I was remembering, and I was terrified I'd scare you all off.'

'I'm not going anywhere. None of us are.' She kisses him then smiles as she looks up at him. 'Go. Have fun. You deserve it.'

'I feel bad leaving you here.'

'Don't. I could do with a break from you lot. Living under the same roof as four rock stars has been a little... trying at times. Go. Blow off some steam. I'll have lunch ready when you get back.'

Tate kisses her then slips on his jacket and takes his helmet from the cupboard. Dillon and Luke are already on their bikes with the engines running when he goes outside. Tate swings his leg over the saddle and puts on his helmet. He starts the engine and smiles when the Kawasaki roars to life.

As Tate follows Dillon and Luke out the gate he glances over his shoulder. Chloe is standing in his doorway smiling at him. She blows him a kiss and he's glad she can't see his stupid grin under the helmet.

Chloe walks into the playground with her class. The last three days had gone better than she could have imagined. The children were amazing, and she quickly settled into her new job. As the parents come forward to collect their children she spots someone on the far side of the road. He's sitting on the bonnet of his truck wearing a cap and sunglasses to hide his face. She smiles when she notices some of the mums glancing over at him. He really needs to work on his disguise.

As the last child heads home, he slides off the bonnet and crosses the road. He leans on the stone wall surrounding the playground and takes off his glasses. 'Ms Quinn. How was your day?'

'It was so good, Tate. I think I've finally found a job I like doing. Better late than never, I guess. And the other teachers are so nice.'

He smirks and waves over Chloe's shoulder. 'I can see that.'

She looks around to see four of her colleagues waving at them. 'Oh my God. Do you have to do that wherever you go?'

'Do what?'

She gestures over her shoulder. 'That. I could really do without my colleagues looking at you that way.'

'You want me to go and say hi?'

'No I don't. You didn't have to collect me. I was planning on getting the bus.'

'Fuck that. I'm taking you to lunch then we are going back to my house to work off lunch until we have to go to dinner with my parents.'

'Oh and let me guess. Then back to yours to work off dinner.'

'Absolutely. So are you ready to go yet?'

'Stop distracting everyone and go back to your truck. I'll just grab my bag.'

When she comes back out and climbs into the truck he's frowning at his phone. 'Is everything all right?'

'So, I just got a call from my lawyer.'

Her stomach drops a little. 'And...'

'And it's all done and dusted. I'm free as a bird.'

'Really? They're not going to do anything to you?'

He shakes his head. 'My delightful cousin fessed up to everything – including planting the drugs in my truck. They've dropped the charges against me and, as he's admitted to everything, I won't be needed again.'

'I can't believe it's all done.'

'Tell me about it. Just glad he had the balls to admit to what he was doing. Nice to get it sorted before I head off.' He pulls out of the car park and drives around the seafront.

'How are the ticket sales going?'

He glances around and smirks. 'Sold out.'

'That's amazing, Tate.'

'I know. We lost a hell of a lot when we had to reschedule. It always happens though. People can't make the new date or they get pissed off that the dates changed in the first place. Wasn't expecting those shortfalls to be made up again so fast.'

'So Ellen was right. Making a statement about everything was the right thing to do.'

He nods. 'Guess so. Might have to stop arguing with her when she comes up with plans like that.'

Arguing is a bit of an understatement. Tate had been less than enthusiastic about making a statement. He knew the truth was going to come out but didn't want to talk about it publicly. After a heated discussion, he begrudgingly agreed to the management company making a statement on his behalf. It was brief but confirmed all the facts about Dara, about his childhood, and about his addiction. Ellen had kept a lot of details back about what his father did, but he wasn't keen on any of the details getting out.

It hadn't taken long for Ellen's decision to pay off. Support had poured in and helped bring back a little of his confidence. She'd seen the change in him over the last week. As the days passed, his mood had improved, but there had been more than a few tense moments while he got over what Dara did.

Difficult patient had been a monstrous understatement. He was irritable and would bite the head off anyone who looked at him the wrong way. Over the last few days things had slowly taken a turn in the right direction.

He was sleeping a little better. The nightmares still came. The guilt over what happened to his mother was still there, but she hopes in time that will ease.

Sending him on tour for a few months is the part she's not convinced about. It had taken a long and heartfelt conversation with Dillon, Gregg, and Luke to convince her otherwise. Tate doesn't know they spoke to her and he never will. They made her promise on pain of death not to tell him. The talk had helped her understand why he had to go.

Tate came alive when he was on stage. He adored performing and getting back to what he loves doing could only help him. He needed to see that he hadn't messed things up for all of them. What better way to do it that on a stage with his fans in front of him?

They assured her they'd keep a close eye on him and, now they know all the facts, also know what to look out for when he's getting lost in his thoughts.

All she can do is trust they have his back and try not to worry. She just wishes it wasn't going to be six weeks before she saw him again. But this is the way it's going to be from now on. She'd been spoilt since she'd met him. With neither of them working they'd had plenty of time to spend together. That was all changing. She'd had Tate to herself for months and now she was going to have to share her boyfriend with a lot of other people.

'Stop.'

She looks across at him. 'Sorry?'

'You're thinking. We promised no thinking until tomorrow.'

'I know. I'm sorry. You're right.'

Tate reaches across and holds her hand. 'Hey. I'm going to miss you like crazy. You know that, right?'

Chloe nods and squeezes his hand. 'I know.' She takes a deep breath and pushes thoughts about him leaving to the back of her mind. There'll be enough time to miss him when he's actually gone. 'So the plan for today is lunch, sex, dinner, sex. Did I get that right?'

'Sounds like the perfect way to spend the afternoon.'

Tate keeps to just below the speed limit as he drives through the empty Dublin streets. He can't wait to get Chloe home and naked. Dinner with his parents was nice but there were other things... well, one other thing on his mind.

Chloe.

He finally pulls up at his gates and taps his fingers on the steering wheel as he waits for them to open.

'Are they always this slow?'

She runs her hand up his leg and rubs his dick through his jeans. 'They're doing it on purpose.'

'Keep that up and we won't make it into the house.'

Once the gates finally open he parks and grabs Chloe as soon as she steps around the bonnet.

Tate struggles to unlock the front door while kissing Chloe at the same time. She untucks his shirt and her hands travel up his chest. He curses as she traces a nail over his nipple, pulling against the piercing. The key and the lock finally line up and he holds her against him as the door swings open. After kicking it closed behind them, he locks it then picks her up and throws her over his shoulder. Chloe squeals as he hurries up the stairs and lowers her to her feet when he gets her into the bedroom.

Then Chloe puts her hand against his chest and pushes him back. 'Get naked.'

He tears off his clothes as she slips out of her dress, leaving on her underwear.

Tate stares at his stunning girlfriend and, not for the first time, wonders what the hell he did to have someone like her in his life. The red corset and thong hug her curves, lifting her breasts and torturing him with glimpses of her smooth skin through the lace. 'Jesus, Chloe. You trying to kill me or what? That new?'

'Going away present. Now, sit on the armchair.'

He lowers into the chair at the bottom of the bed and Chloe pulls his hips forward. She takes him in her hand and runs her thumb over the heavy piercing. Tate sucks in a breath when she pulls against it a little.

'Hands on the arms of the chair.'

'Yes, ma'am.' He digs his fingers into the arms as she kneels and takes him in her mouth. She cups his balls and runs her thumb over the bar at the base. Chloe looks up at him as she draws her tongue over the tip. The way she looks at him when she's taking the lead is such a fucking turn on.

Chloe takes him deep into her mouth and applies a little pressure behind his balls as her tongue plays with the two piercings. She picks up the pace until Tate's whole body trembles as the pressure builds. He's so close but instead of letting him come, she slows down and slides him out of her mouth. She smiles up at him.

'You look a little frustrated.'

He hisses as she draws her tongue along him again, pulling the tip into her mouth, teasing him. 'Too fucking right I am.'

She slowly takes him into her mouth then pulls back again, running her tongue along his dick before flicking the metal ring. Chloe gently massages his balls and runs her tongue back up his shaft.

'Jesus, Chloe. What the fuck are you doing to me?'

She kisses the base and down to his balls. 'What do you want me to do?'

A spasm works through him as she rapidly flicks her tongue over his balls. 'I want you to suck me until I come in your fucking mouth.'

'Whatever you say.' She keeps the pressure on behind his balls as she massages him, using her tongue to play with the piercings. It doesn't take long for her to give him exactly what he asked for.

The curse tears out of him as she keeps working him until he's well and truly fucked. When she gets to her feet, the smile on her face has his dick springing to life again. Without saying a word, he picks her up, then lies on his back on the bed, pulling her down with him. He gropes blindly in the bedside table drawer only breaking their kiss long enough to slip the condom on.

Both hands grip her waist, holding her in place as he pulls her down his length. She falls forward, resting her hands on his chest over the griffin's wing. His hips thrust upward as he pulls her down, driving any remaining air from his lungs. She matches his thrusts, forcing him deeper into her. Her hand rests on his nipple piercing and she gives him a seriously sexy look as she twists it in her fingers. Tate throws his head back against the pillow and ups the pace, a feral need taking over. When she tugs on it again, he growls and she gives up trying to match him.

'Don't stop, Tate.'

No risk of that. He slips one hand down to circle her clit and she bucks against him. He gasps as she digs her fingernails into his chest, but it feels so fucking amazing. He holds her steady as he rams into her again and again until his back arches on the bed and he lets out a roar. Chloe shudders and wipes sweat soaked hair from her face.

'Fuck.'

His laugh comes out as a snort but that's her fault. He can't catch his breath. 'Yeah. Fuck.'

She slowly rises off him then collapses onto the bed. 'That was nice.'

'Excuse me?'

'Fine, it was fucking amazing.'

He pulls her into his arms so he can kiss her. 'Fuck I love when you say 'fuck' like that.'

She grins at him and his chest tightens.

'I love you, Chloe.'

Chloe's eyes go wide as she stares over at him.

His stomach drops a little. He hadn't planned on saying that. The words just popped out. It's the truth though. He loves her. Has for a few weeks, but with the whole kidnapping and relapse mess, he couldn't bring himself to tell her. Seems his mouth decided to override his brain and all the second guessing. 'Too soon?'

Then the smile comes back and she rests her hand on the side of his face. 'I love you too, Tate.'

'Really?'

She nods. 'Hell yeah.'

Tate laughs and runs his thumb across her lips. 'Hell yeah. I like that.' His smile drops a little at the thought of having to say goodbye to her tomorrow. He's looking forward to getting back to work again, but he's going to miss her like crazy.

'Now it's my turn to tell you to stop thinking.'

'Easier said than done, Chloe.'

Chloe smiles thinly as she looks at him. 'I know. But we've got...' she pauses talking to look over at the clock and scrunches her face up, 'eight hours or so. Now I don't know about you, but I can think of one or two things we can do to pass the time. Unless you'd prefer to sleep or course?'

He sucks in a breath as she takes his dick in her hand. 'Not a chance. I can sleep on the road.'

Tate quietly places his bag on the ground at the foot of the bed and watches Chloe sleep. He's never been so torn up about going on tour before. On one hand he can't wait to get back on stage. On the other, he'd love to crawl back into bed beside her and not go anywhere. It's six weeks until he sees her again in Barcelona. Might as well be six months.

His phone vibrates in his pocket. He pulls it out and frowns at the screen. The car just arrived to bring him to the airport. He sits on the bed beside her and runs his fingers through her hair.

'Chloe.'

She groans and opens her eyes. It takes her a few seconds to realise he's dressed. 'Did I sleep through the alarm?'

'I'm heading a bit earlier than planned.'

She sits up and brushes her hair back from her face. 'What? When?'

'The car's outside.'

'You're going now? But I can't get dressed that fast.'

'Relax. You don't have to get dressed.' He holds out a keyring with a few keys on it. 'The big key is the front door and the small one is the back.' He checks her phone screen to make sure the message went through okay. 'I've sent you a text with the gate and alarm code on it. Best to memorise them and delete the message just in case.'

'What are you saying?'

'I'm saying stay here. Use the house like it's your own while I'm gone.'

'But I can't do that.'

'Why not?'

'Well... because I can't.'

He smiles and holds up a key fob. 'Yeah – great argument. This is the key for the truck. I sorted out the insurance so you're good to go.'

'Hold on. I can't drive that.'

'Of course you can. Just don't go under any low barriers. It's too high for most of them.'

'Tate—'

'You'd prefer the bike?'

He laughs at the horrified look on her face. 'I can't— You can't—'

'You can and I am so quit arguing. I'm leaving the keys in the house so you might as well take them. Please.'

Chloe slowly reaches out and takes the keys from his hand. 'You really trust me that much?'

'Yes. Besides, I kind of like the idea of you being here and driving my truck.' He holds out a small box. 'Going away present.'

She opens the box and smiles widely. He pulls the griffin pendent from under his shirt and holds it out. 'It's the exact same. This means a lot to me and I just thought... well it might keep you safe or something. I don't know. You don't have to wear it. You can stick it on your keyring.'

'Aww. You've gone all cute again.'

'I've gone what?'

'Like you did when you were asking me out. You're adorable.'

'Yeah, well you can knock that off right now.'

She wraps her arms around his neck and kisses him. 'I love it.' Chloe fastens the pendent around her neck and holds the griffin in her hand. 'Thank you, Tate.'

'I suppose I better go. Don't want them leaving without me.'

He kisses her, holding her tight until he feels his phone vibrating again.

'Damn it. I really have to go. I'll call you when I get there.'

Before he makes a complete eejit of himself, he stands up, grabs his jacket from the chair and picks up his bag. 'I love you, Chloe.'

'I love you too.'

Tate turns and pulls out his phone as he walks down the stairs. He sends a quick message to Bria then locks the front door behind him. The driver opens the back door of the Land Rover and he climbs inside. As the car pulls out of the driveway, Bria replies to his message.

She's on her way to his place to spend some time with Chloe.

Tate stares out the window as the car takes him to the airport. It's going to be a long six weeks.

Three months later...

Chloe checks her watch again. Less than a minute has passed since the last time she checked. She gets up and paces the dressing room then sits down again.

It's been a little over six weeks since she saw Tate in Barcelona and it's been the longest six weeks she can remember. Each day had dragged by painfully slow.

She looks at her watch again and curses herself. This is the last night of the tour. They arrived back in Dublin earlier in the day but Ellen had scheduled an interview shortly after he landed so he couldn't see her until he gets to the venue. He's due on stage in two hours, after which he's all hers for the whole of January and she cannot wait.

She is so looking forward to spending their first Christmas together. She'd already decided to have the Christmas party at Tate's house and Becca was in total agreement - unlike Tate. He wasn't overly keen about the party full stop, let alone in his house, but he eventually gave in. In a break from their usual tradition, Tate's family would be landing at his doorstop tomorrow evening.

In truth, Chloe can't wait. The Archer's had welcomed her as part of the family. Not a day went by while he was gone without either Becca or Bria getting in touch with her. Her fortnightly shopping trips with Bria were something she looked forward to greatly.

She hears voices outside and smiles as the door opens. Tate steps inside and shuts the door, locking it behind him. It doesn't matter how many times she sees him, she'll never be able to get enough of the six-foot-three, well-built, tattooed, stunning rock star who right now is looking at her in a way that means trouble.

'Hi.'

Instead of responding, he grabs her around the waist, pressing her back against the wall as his mouth finds hers. His kiss is desperate as his hands seem to touch everywhere at once. She pulls at his t-shirt and he tears it off, throwing it across the room. Chloe looks at his chest and her smile grows. There's a matching black bar through his left nipple.

'I'm going to have to watch what I say around you.'

'No touching until it heals. You go pulling on that and there's a strong chance you'll see a grown man cry. It won't be pretty.'

She slowly runs her hands down his chest, taking care not to touch the new piercing. He looked sexy as hell with one, having the second one pierced elevates him to a whole new level of sex appeal.

Chloe kisses the original piercing, flicking her tongue across the metal bar as he reaches down to open her jeans. She gasps as he slips a finger inside, followed by another. Chloe writhes against his hand as she fumbles with his belt, desperate to touch him. Once the belt has been dealt with, she unfastens his jeans and takes him in her hand through his boxers. She slips her hand under the waistband and runs her thumb over the tip.

He hisses as she pulls against the piercing. 'Jesus, Chloe. Keep that up and I'll be ripping your fucking jeans off, bending you over, and burying my cock in you so hard and deep you won't be able to walk straight for a week.'

She smiles and flicks her tongue across the bar in his nipple. 'Go on then. I dare you.'

That's all it takes to convince him to do just that. Then again, it wouldn't take more than seeing Chloe for him to want to get his hands all over her.

Tate glances at the door, making sure he locked it properly then carries her over to the counter that serves as a dressing table. He pulls off her shirt and unfastens her bra, throwing them behind him somewhere, then rips her jeans down her legs and bends her over the dressing table. He kicks her legs apart then slips a finger inside. She feels better than he remembers. Warm and wet and begging for attention.

He's been thinking about this moment every spare second for the last few weeks. Knowing she was waiting for him made the interview the longest of his fucking life. He's played this entire scene out in his mind too many times to count.

He looks at her reflection in the mirror in front of them and has to take a few breaths to calm down before he ends this too fast. Her dark hair is hanging over her shoulders, spilling over her breasts onto the dressing table. He runs his thumb over her lips and meets her eyes in the reflection.

'Look at me and don't make a fucking sound.' He rams his hips towards her, burying himself as far as he can go. Chloe drops her head to the table to stifle her scream but he reaches around and lifts her head up. He locks eyes with her in the reflection as he pulls out then rams in again, harder this time.

He slips his hand around her hips and covers his thumb in her juices. 'Open your mouth.' He watches as she sucks him clean and the small semblance of control he had disappears. The dressing table groans with each thrust of his hips but he couldn't give a fuck if he destroys the whole room. They've got six weeks to make up for. If he wasn't on stage tonight his dick wouldn't be leaving her pussy for the next few hours.

Her eyes don't move from his as his thrusts turn more desperate, more frantic as the need builds.

'Fuck me, Tate. Please.'

Her words hit him like a shock to his dick, and the familiar tingle builds at the base of his spine. He drops his hand to circle her clit with his thumb then does exactly as she demanded. He fucks her until they both collapse onto the dressing table, sweating, exhausted, and breathless.

Tate keeps hold of her as they try to catch their breath. He rests his head between her shoulder blades with one thick arm braced on either side of her.

'Fuck me, Tate?' he mumbles into her shoulder.

She smiles lazily up at his reflection as he lifts his head. 'And you absolutely did. Thank you. Can you get off me now?'

'Not sure I can move. I'm kind of fucked myself.' He pushes off the dressing table and wraps his arms around her, holding her against his chest. He wipes sweat soaked hair back from her forehead. 'And for the record, you can demand I fuck you whenever you want.'

'Not quite sure where that come from.'

'Yeah well, you can let it out again. It was such a turn on.'

'I'll keep that in mind.'

He looks up as someone bangs loudly on the door. 'Tate! You finished yet?'

'Fuck off, Gregg!'

'We need you for a sound check in ten minutes.'

'All right!'

'As in on stage. Ideally dressed.'

'I heard you. Now fuck off!'

'Will do. Hi, Chloe.'

She laughs into Tate's shoulder. 'Hi, Gregg.'

Tate shakes his head as Gregg laughs and bangs once more on the door before walking away. 'Sorry about him. He's completely un-trainable. I suppose I better grab a shower.'

'I suppose you better.' He doesn't make a move to let her go. 'I thought you were going to have a shower.'

'I kind of want to go again.'

She squirms to get out of his arms, but it's like trying to move a tank. 'Get off me you oaf. If you're late Gregg will burst in and I'm not keen on that, thanks all the same.'

'Fine. But as soon as the show is finished, we're picking this up again.'

'No arguments there. I really like the piercing by the way.'

He smiles widely at her. 'Thought you would. Don't say I didn't warn you though. Fucking thing is driving me crazy already. I'll show you exactly how much later.'

'You just did show me.'

'That? No, that was just the warm-up act. I'm only getting started with you.'

'Well if you don't get on stage you're going to run out of time. Now go. You need to get ready.'

She watches as he goes into the bathroom and turns on the shower. 'Do you fancy—'

'No, Tate. You've got eight minutes.'

'Believe me, after not seeing you for six weeks, eight minutes is more than enough time.'

She gets up and pushes him into the bathroom, closing the door in his face. Once he's done, she has a quick shower herself. When she goes back into the dressing room, he's dressed and pulling on his boots.

'I've got one minute. You sure?'

'You are unbelievable.'

'Thanks.'

Right on schedule, Gregg pounds on the door. 'C'mon Prince Charming. Move your arse.'

'Okay!' He pulls her into a tight hug again. 'How long you need to get ready?'

'I was ready until you went all caveman on me.'

'Not going to apologise for that. Ten minutes be okay?'

'Should be more than enough time. Why?'

'I'll ask someone to come and get you. Bring you up to the stage. They've got somewhere set up at the front where you can watch from. Gregg was going to bring Bria there while I was saying hello to you.'

'That's how you say hello?'

'To you? Fuck yes.' She stands back and looks at him. 'What?'

'Is this you ready to go on stage?'

He looks down at his dark blue jeans and black t-shirt. 'What? You expecting platform boots and glitter?'

'No, it's just nice I guess.'

'I'm not following?'

'You don't change who you are. It's just you and your mates playing music.'

'That's what I've been trying to tell you all along. Glad it's finally gotten through to you.'

Gregg kicks the door this time so Tate yanks it open. 'Would you calm the fuck down? I'm coming.' He gives Chloe a quick kiss. 'Sorry.

I better go.'

Gregg sticks his head around the corner and wiggles his eyebrows. 'Looking good, Chloe. I like this dishevelled, out of bed thing you've got going on.' He grunts as Tate thumps him in the stomach.

'You say another word and I'll flatten you. Walk.'

Chloe thanks the waitress as she places their lunch on the table in front of them. The fact she is completely engrossed in her lunch companion instead of listening to a word Chloe herself says is no surprise. If anything, Chloe is getting used to the attention Tate sometimes brings to their trips out. He wasn't recognised every time, but it was definitely more often than not.

Although initially irked by the attention he was getting from people who could clearly see he was out with her, she had become strangely accustomed to it. Tate was polite and allowed photos and gave autographs, but as soon as he was done, his attention immediately swung back to her.

She stifles a yawn and looks out at the boats in the harbour as the waitress gushes over Tate. Her magnificent boyfriend had kept her up until the early hours and, after a long lie in, had continued to show her how much he missed her when they woke up. By the time they had finally left the bedroom, it was well past noon. Instead of his usual request for chips, he'd surprised her by suggesting they go to a restaurant for lunch.

The waitress finally finishes rearranging pretty much everything on the table. When Tate smiles and thanks her she blushes then backs away with a huge grin on her face.

'I think you have a fan.'

He glances over his shoulder at the girl as she waves and blushes again. Tate nods to her and turns back to Chloe, his eyebrows raised. 'Yeah. You might be right. She'll get bored in a minute. So, you okay while I was gone? Was work good?'

She nods as she chews her sandwich. 'Work is great. The kids are wonderful and so are the other teachers. It was nice to have something to occupy myself while I was eagerly waiting for you to grace me with your presence.'

'Sincerest apologies for leaving you waiting. Did being at my place help or was it too far from work?'

'It was fine. I have to admit, having use of your truck had its advantages.' She frowns slightly at him. 'Okay, out with it. I know that look. What's wrong?'

He wipes his mouth with the back of his hand and takes a deep breath. 'Busted. Right, so I was thinking a lot while I was away. Not much else to do some days. Anyway, I... do you want to move in?'

'To your house? With you?'

'Well I'm not planning on moving out, so yeah, with me. I just thought it could work. I know it's a bit of a longer commute to work for you, but you could take one of the spare rooms as your office. Take another for your art stuff. I don't know. It was just an idea.'

She examines him over the rim of her cup as she sips her tea. 'Are you really sure you want to share your personal space with someone?'

'No. I want to share it with you. I want to come home from work and find you in my, I mean our, kitchen. I want to wake up beside you. I want to laze on the couch watching crap TV with you. I want you to offload on me if you have a bad day at work. I want to do online grocery shopping with you.'

She laughs at that one. 'How romantic.'

'I'm all about the romance.' He reaches across the table and holds her hand. 'Seriously though. I love you, Chloe. I've never been more sure of anything in my life. So, what do you reckon? You want to give it a shot?'

'I'd love to give it a shot.' She leans across the table and kisses him, much to the waitress's obvious annoyance.

Tate reaches into this pocket and pulls out a set of keys and a control for the gate. 'Better take these then.'

'I already have a set of keys.'

'No, you have the spare set. This is your set. Cut just for you.'

After lunch he takes her hand and walks back over to the bike. He looks down at his phone and curses. 'What is it?'

'Salad.'

'Excuse me?'

'My mum wants me to get some salad for tonight. Who the fuck eats salad at these things?'

'People who want to eat healthy food.'

'That better not be a dig at me and don't go thinking it'll be all salad and fucking goat cheese tarts when you move in.'

She taps him on the cheek. 'Don't worry. I know you're a simple kind of guy.'

'Fucking charming. Anyway, you better go and pack. Might as well move in today.'

'You don't have time to drop me back and get salad and help your mum.'

'I've no intention of dropping you anywhere. You're perfectly capable of driving yourself.' He points over her shoulder and Chloe turns to see a bright red Mini at the far side of the car park. 'Happy Christmas.'

'Tate. What the hell have you done?'

'It's 1984 and fully restored so it should last you for a bit.'

Chloe can't get any words out. It's better than she could have ever afforded herself. The paint is immaculate. It looks like it's just rolled off the production line. It either cost him a small fortune or he had it restored - which would have cost him a small fortune. Either way, she's speechless.

'How did you know?'

'About the make? You can thank your sister for that.'

'Hold on. When did you talk to Steph?'

'At your party. She was kind of drunk and started rambling on about you. I think she gave me a breakdown of your entire life in half an hour.'

'Oh dear God. I'm going to kill her.'

'I've no fucking idea how she got onto cars but she mentioned your mum and how she'd bundle you both into the back of one of these and head off on beach holidays while your dad was stuck at work. Steph said you have a thing for Mini's and apparently have been saving for one for a few years.'

'Are you serious? She said all that to you?'

He grins. 'That and so much more. I've got enough info to dip into for years. Please tell me she wasn't making it all up?'

'No. It's true, but I'm still going to kill her for telling you.' She gazes over at the car and smiles. 'This is too much. It's beautiful, but far too much. You can't spend his much on me, Tate.'

'I'm a control freak, remember. If I want to buy you a car, I'll buy you a car. Best to go with it and not argue.'

'Are you sure?'

'Yes. It's yours so get used to it. The damn thing was a pain in the arse to restore too so it's absolutely not going back. I bought it just before I went on tour and a mate of mine did all the work. The keys are on the ring with your house keys.'

'Tate. I don't know what to say. Thank you. I really do love it.'

'Glad to hear it. How about you take it for a spin back to your gran's, load it up with some of your stuff and bring it back to mine?'

'Do you not want to come too?'

Tate laughs and shakes his head. 'Eh, no. You'd need a can opener to get me in and out of that. Besides, it appears I have a date with some salad. God help me if I arrive back without it. Mum will kick my ass.'

She runs her hand over the pristine paintwork and smiles as she takes the keys out of her pocket. She finds the correct one and unlocks the door. Even the inside is immaculate. Chloe starts the engine and claps much to Tate's amusement.

'You okay?'

'This is fucking amazing! Enjoy the party - I'm off for a spin.' She closes the door, ignoring his threats that she better fucking be at the party as it was her fucking idea or something along those lines. She waves at him and pulls out of the parking spot, laughing as he flicks her the bird as she drives away.

Tate leans against the counter and watches his family and friends eat and drink him out of house and home. Chloe and his mum weave through the guests, each holding a plate of food, stopping to talk to anyone they pass.

He'll never know how he managed to find and hang on to someone like Chloe. Since that first day on the beach when she burst into his life, she's been changing it and him for the better. He has no doubts this year would have ended very differently if not for Chloe.

He looks down at the inside of his left arm. For the first time in months, the skin is clear. He also managed to get on top of the scratching before he permanently damaged the tattoo. Again, thanks to Chloe.

She looks over at him and smiles widely. He points to his watch then gestures towards his crotch. She laughs and walks away, swinging her gorgeous ass.

He curses when he gets an elbow in his ribs. Shane leans against the counter beside him and looks over the room.

'Not a bad party. Is this going to be a regular thing now?'

'That depends on Chloe. No way I'm volunteering to do this on a regular basis. They're like a bunch of savages.'

'Ah quit complaining. It's going well. Look.' He points to the far side of the room. 'Gary is having a one-on-one with the tree.'

Tate laughs when he sees Gary raise his glass and toast the ten-foot tree. 'Worrying that's how we decide if it's a good party or not.'

Shane nods towards Chloe. 'I really like her. She's a good one, Tate.'

'I know she is.'

'You love her?'

'Yeah, I do.'

'Well, well, well. My baby brother is finally growing up.'

'Oh shut up.'

Shane gestures across the room to Gregg, Dillon, and Luke laughing with some of his cousins. 'What's the deal with Gregg?'

'Generally or tonight?'

'Tonight you idiot. He's wearing a shirt. I can't remember the last time I saw him in anything other than a t-shirt. He's made an effort.'

Tate shrugs. 'Christmas. Who knows?'

'Or maybe he's got his eye on someone.'

Tate looks around the room, quickly dismissing that idea. 'In this lot? Can't see it.'

'Whatever the reason he's made more of an effort than you have. And it's your party.'

'I've let this lot into my house. That's the full extent of my effort for the evening.'

Shane opens the fridge and takes out two bottles of juice, passing one to Tate.

'You can drink if you want.'

Shane shakes his head. 'My beautiful wife needs a little of my attention when we're done here. This will make sure I'm on my game.'

'Yeah, thanks for that image.'

Shane grins and clinks bottles with Tate. 'So, the girls want to see you tomorrow. You up for taking them for a few hours?'

Tate turns to look at his brother. 'Seriously? How does Annabelle feel about that?'

Shane looks at the ground and takes a breath before he answers. 'Listen, we shouldn't have kept you from them like we did. We were trying to protect them and you.'

'Me?'

'You know what they're like, Tate. It would have been non-stop questions. I didn't want you to feel overwhelmed and... well, they love you to bits. There's no way they would have been able to give you space. We never had an issue with you spending time with them. I'm sorry if you thought that.'

'I wasn't blaming you. Can't say I was much of a role model for them.'

Shane nudges him in the side. 'I wouldn't be so quick to say that. A year ago you were in a very different place. Now look at you. You beat it, Tate. That's something to be damn proud of. And you demolished Dara's nose. Also something to be proud of. Fucker deserved a hell of a lot more.' Shane laughs harshly then takes another drink. 'Can't quite believe what he did, what he's been doing to you. Not surprised Eric and Sandy didn't show their faces.'

'Doubt they knew what he was doing.'

Shane grunts but doesn't say anything else. Tate had a few long talks with his brother while he was on tour. Shane hadn't taken the news about Dara well. Their father had to talk him down more than once. He'd wanted to get on a plane and personally make sure Dara paid for what he did. His reaction hadn't surprised anyone. Shane had always been protective of Tate. From the first moment Tate met Shane, his new big brother had taken him under his wing.

'It's done. Doubt we'll be seeing Dara again. I just want to forget about the whole fucking thing and concentrate on getting myself back on track.'

'Are you okay though?'

Tate nods at his brother. 'Getting there. I'm remembering more stuff but it's just snippets. I have to write down whatever I can remember after the dreams. Not exactly a barrel of laughs but I guess it's helping. I've got weekly appointments and yes, I'm talking.'

'Good. I'm always on the other end of the phone, Tate. You know that right?'

'I know. Thanks.'

'We want you and Chloe to come over for a few weeks after Christmas, if you fancy it. I know the girls would love to show their favourite uncle around.'

'Their only uncle.'

'Technicality. Have a think about it. Might do you both good to get away from here for a bit. Give yourselves a break.'

'You sure Annabelle is on board with that?'

'Of course. As long as you don't bring any more fucking Lego into the house she'll be grand.'

'Sounds amazing. A change of scenery might not be a bad thing. The last eight months with her have been a fucking car crash. Not the bits with her, just everything else. What I really want is a few months with no hospital visits and no crazy relatives kidnapping either of us.'

'Doesn't sound like too much to ask.' Shane slaps him on the shoulder. 'Talk to Chloe and let me know.' He places the empty bottle on the counter behind him and rubs his hands together. 'Well, I think it's time for the yearly sing-along with Tate Archer. Bria wants to show off her violin skills to Robbie.'

'He the one we intimidated last year?'

'Clearly we're losing our touch. I don't like the look of the guy so I'm on for trying again if you're up to it.'

'I need something to get me through the night.'

'Let the games begin. I'll grab a few instruments. You want your guitar?'

'Yeah. The black one on the left of the stand.'

Tate weaves through his relatives and grabs Chloe's hand. He holds her against his chest and runs his thumb over her lips.

'Have I told you that you look stunning tonight?'

'A few times. Now are you going to let me go? Your family is watching.'

'I really couldn't give a fuck who's watching. I only see you.'

He picks her up, ignoring the cheering and hollering from his family and friends. Chloe squeals but doesn't fight to get out of his arms. He rests his forehead against hers. 'I love you.'

'I love you too.'

When they kiss the cheering increases in volume until Shane shouts above the noise. 'If my brother can tear himself away from the lovely Chloe, he may do his party piece for us.'

As people clear some space on the couches, Tate carries Chloe to the edge of the room and sets her back on her feet. 'Okay, so this is the plan. I do a few songs. We give everyone a couple of cases of drink and call the minibus to take them home. You get naked and I show you exactly how much I missed you. Twice. Maybe three times. Probably best not to over promise, it's been a long day. I'll go for twice.'

She leans back against him, slipping her hand between them and discreetly rubs him through his jeans. 'Interesting proposition, Mr. Archer.'

'If you keep that up I might only manage once. Also, don't move for a few minutes. I'm kind of indecent.'

'You feel kind of indecent.'

'Hey lover boy! We're waiting!'

'I'm coming!' He turns back to her and rests his head against her forehead. 'Next time we're hiring a DJ.'

She reaches up and kisses him. 'You know you love performing so don't even go there.'

'I know I love you.' When she blushes and smiles at him he can't help but grin like a lovestruck teenager. He runs his thumb along her lips. 'I'm yours, Chloe. Always will be. You know that, right?'

'And I'm yours, Tate.' She looks around him into the living room and sighs. 'Unfortunately, I have to share you right now. There's going to be a riot if you don't get that incredible ass of yours in there. Your adoring public is waiting.'

'Fine. You coming too?'

'I'll just grab us a couple of drinks. Oh and Tate?' He stops in the middle of the living room and looks at her. 'I fully expect three.'

He frowns, not having a clue what she's talking about. She points to the stairs and he understands.

'Whatever you want.' He winks and takes a seat on the armchair. He picks up his guitar as Chloe settles on the arm beside him, one hand on his shoulder as he begins to play.

Epilogue

Gregg is in pain. Not a physical pain... although it feels like he's gone a few rounds with someone. This pain is deeper, like it's a part of him. It's been with him for so long he can't remember what it's like to live without it.

The party is still in full swing behind him. He has to hand it to Chloe. She certainly knows how to put on a party. If someone had told him a few months ago that he'd be attending a Christmas bash at Tate's house he quite possibly would have pissed himself laughing. But that's what she did to Tate. Helped to bring him out from all the darkness. And he's so fucking grateful for that.

He's genuinely happy for Tate and Chloe. A year ago he thought he'd be saying goodbye to his friend for good. Now he's got himself a solid career and a beautiful woman to share his life with.

He leans back against the fence and watches Dillon talking to two of Tate's cousins. No doubt he'll be making a move on both of them before the night is out. Luke is beside him talking to Tate's brother.

His girlfriend may be a complete nightmare, but he's happy with her.

So that's Tate sorted, Dillon chasing anything that moves, and Luke not leaving Pippa any time soon.

And here he is, hiding in the garden, lusting after his best mate's sister. Hence the pain.

He's not quite sure when she transformed from Tate's little sister into a gorgeous woman, but she had and he hasn't got the first clue what to do about it. Every single time he sees her he gets this ache in his chest.

Gregg smiles when Bria comes out of the kitchen and drapes her arm around Tate's shoulder as she laughs with him. She gestures to Tate's clothes and he swats her away like he'd done so many times before. Bria was determined Tate let her loose on their wardrobes.

He sighs and looks down at his shirt and jeans. God he's pathetic. Did he seriously think she'd notice him if he ditched his scruffy jeans and t-shirt? He's her big brother's eejit of a friend. The joker of the group. The one no one took too seriously. The newbie who still feels so far out of his depth every time he steps on stage with Tate.

He takes a swig of his non-alcoholic beer and grimaces. Yeah, that's not good. He'll give the party another hour then go home and grab some real beer. He's got no issue not drinking around Tate, but he's going to need something stronger than this zero percent alcohol shit to get him through the night.

Bria grabs Chloe's hand and they start dancing, Bria's long strawberry-blonde hair swirling around her as she spins. Then Robbie interrupts the dancing and kisses her.

'Fuck.'

Gregg turns back to look at the hedge surrounding the garden. He lifts his bottle up in front of him. 'Merry fucking Christmas.' Not able to face another mouthful, Gregg tips the rest onto the grass. He closes his eyes and takes a few long breaths then straightens his shoulders and turns back to the house. As much as he'd like to, he can't hide out here all night.

He comes to a stop when he sees Tate standing at the door looking at him. 'There you are. You okay?'

Gregg nods and returns the smile 'Never better.'

Coming next...

Broken Chords #2

K.A. FINN

Printed in Great Britain
by Amazon

85564249R00222